THE ACTIVATOR

ELEMENTS SERIES
BOOK 2

SEREN GOODE

The Activator

Written and published by Seren Goode

Cover by We Got You Covered (Molly Phipps)

Grace's Image by RMGraphX (Rhiannon Gilmore) tunnel image by grandfailure (Tithi Luadthong) via deposit photo

Formatting by Goode Star

Print ISBN: 978-1-7365387-3-9

Ebook ISBN: 978-1-7365387-4-6

D2d ISBN: 9798223185741

This is a work of fiction. Any resemblance to actual events or persons, living or dead, is entirely coincidental.

SerenGoode.com

Dedicated to my father. Happy Birthday!
Thank you for sharing your love of sci-fi and for your unwavering belief that I can do anything.

EARTH

WHEN THE WALL of water raced towards me, time stopped. My head cleared. My heartbeat slowed to a steady pulse. Paddling faster, my longboard found the glassy blue-green section of the wave, and I popped up. Wind sprayed me with briny water, and the crisp, salty air filled my lungs and poured over into my soul. Exhilarated, I rode the face up to the lip, kicking out the tail of my board, the fins released, and I found my balance.

Finally.

Nothing in my life flowed except the wave I was riding, so I took on its rhythm, letting it move through me, shape me, bring me closer to the *Source*. In the ocean, life made sense. I felt human again, which was ironic because I wasn't—fully human, that is.

The bottom of the yellow sun melted into the horizon as the sky turned a soft red. We had been at Natural Bridges Beach for over an hour and twilight was coming.

The Federal Agents who kept us imprisoned in protective custody hadn't let us communicate with our friends for months. We didn't even know if we would get to spend Christmas with them in two weeks. We were only allowed to leave our apartment once a day. Anyone else would have done real-life things like grocery shop or laundry—we hit the beach and tried to pretend we weren't being watched.

While I headed for the water like it had a tether on my heart, my dad went straight to the tidal pools. In no time, he had a group of kids surrounding him on his marine biology expedition.

My dad, Noah, was human, one hundred percent. My mom, Amé, wasn't from around here—not Santa Cruz, not California, not even Earth. I didn't know this when she was with us.

This summer I found her diary where she had confessed everything, including how she felt responsible for trapping the others on Earth.

Cause she was an alien.

I was still coming to terms with the idea. Of course, my dad had known. My parents had lied to me my whole life. My stomach clenched.

It was hard to remember a time when I could trust them.

I sat up on my board, my feet dangling over the sides. I reached up and patted the lump of the necklace secured around my neck under my hooded wetsuit. Besides the diary, this piece of jewelry was the only thing I had left from my mom. That, and her green-streaked hair, which usually made me look like I was being swallowed by seaweed. Genetics, go figure.

The necklace was a torc, a sturdy strip of solid metal that curved around my neck. It was made of some alien bronze, but the real valuable part was the cabochon that dangled from slim chains in the center. It was a sliver, one-sixth of a rock called the Keystone.

Wait—

The stone should be snug in the hollow of my throat; instead, it was over by my collarbone.

Had the chain broken?

With one hand holding the necklace against my neck, I crouched low on my board and headed for the shore.

Once my toes hit dry sand, I dipped my fingers into my wetsuit, feeling for the chain and the stone. All I found was my ocean-chilled skin and the sharp hoop of a broken link. My heart was in my throat, and I shivered against the wind even as sweat beaded on my forehead. My knees trembled and I did a full body shiver when I located the lump of the stone.

It could have disappeared into the ocean, never to be seen again. I blew out a strangled breath and waited for my heart to stop racing.

The waves tugged at the needy place in my soul. They were still clean, and there were at least another fifteen minutes before it got dark. I had time to make another run.

I couldn't leave the necklace out on the beach—this was by far the most valuable thing I owned. The Keystone had somehow brought them to Earth... no one knew how it worked, just that it had. Everyone wanted this stone, so I never let it out of my sight.

What if I put it up on a ledge on the cliff?

The cliff face was full of nooks and crannies, but if I tried to climb up to one of them, people from the beach and the parking lot above would see. However, the wall of rock stretched out into the ocean and the other side wouldn't be visible.

With one hand on the stone at my neck, I waded through the water and around the formation. On the other side was a small sandy beach cut off from the world. I looked up to the fence around the parking area above. No one was there.

I dropped my board and scaled the wall, being careful to avoid stepping on the sea anemone and the row of mussels hanging out in the small tidal pool at the base. The six-foot leash on my board was stretched taut when I found a ledge with a deep lip and a hole slightly angled down. That was as good as I was going to get.

I had a solid foothold, so I used one hand to push back my hood, unzip my suit, and unwrap the torque from my neck. One of the chains had broken, and the stone dangled loosely from the other.

I hesitated; this was crazy. I rarely did dumb things. I didn't have the luxury. But it would only be for a few minutes. I glanced around, then up. No one could see me.

It would be fine. I tried to convince myself and pushed the necklace to the very back of the gap. There was a moss growth on the rock above, and I peeled it off and used it to plug the hole. There. That would work.

I carefully noted features around the location and then climbed back down the cliff and splashed back into the water.

It took a while to find a wave I liked, and I tipped my nose down, diving under the first couple until the right one came along.

Here it was. This wave was what I had been dreaming of. I paddled hard. The water glowed copper, and dark shadows moved beneath the surface, but I kept my eye on the building swell. I gave a couple extra strokes, then braced my hands on the rails and popped onto my feet. Shifting my weight, I extended a leg, turning into the shape of the wave, carving back and forth, rail to rail, the gentle pumping helping me pick up speed.

Someone shouted. I risked a glance at the shore. My father was sprinting away from the tidal pools—and he was being chased.

The Helios had found us!

Three people dressed in navy blue suits had disembarked from a boat and were following my father.

I pointed my board to the shore. Even as fast as I was moving, I was too far away. I watched my dad slip. I gasped and got a mouthful of saltwater. My muscles tensed up, and the board rocked. I willed myself to relax. Wiping out now would only slow me down.

Dad recovered, but the shadowy figures chasing him had made up a lot of the distance.

I reached back and pulled the pin on my leash. As the tip of my board slid up on the beach, I jumped off and hit the ground at a run, splashing through the shallows. In seconds, I was beside my father.

A gunshot sounded behind us. The sound was deafening, and an involuntary flinch almost folded my body in half.

"Grace!" Dad stumbled again. I grabbed for his arm. There was a scramble as we grasped at each other. I was moving too fast, my surf booties sinking into the sand, but he caught himself and stayed on his feet. There was a pedestrian path that led to the parking area. If we could make it up the hill—

Lights flared. An engine roared.

A large, black SUV barreled down the access road toward us. More shots were fired, this time directed at the vehicle. Unfortunately, we were between it and the Helios. The vehicle barely slowed as it left the pavement and ate its way through the dunes. We kept running. The SUV shot past us and did a fancy U-turn that sent a spray of sand on our pursuers. Barely slowing, it changed directions. A side door flew open, and we dived inside.

Our Federal watchdogs were in the front seat, returning fire. For once, I was relieved to see them.

"It's the Helios—go!" My father slammed his hand against the seat back and before he had completed the sentence, we were in motion again.

I lay on my stomach in the backseat, my knees on the floor, panting. My father pushed down my shoulder. I guess he thought he was shielding me. As the minutes passed and the loud booms of the agents' guns stopped echoing through the interior, I became aware that something sticky from the seat was now stuck on my cheek. I tried to pull myself free.

"Let me up."

"No! They are shooting!"

So, I stayed there, crushed into the leather seats, breathing in a foul combo of stale coffee and body odor. Time did this funny thing when mixed with adrenaline. Seconds felt like a lifetime. I could tell by the squeals and the rhythm of the tires that we were back on the pavement and had made several sharp turns. We were probably out of the park. And the shooting had stopped.

"They aren't shooting anymore. Let me up!"

I was only sixteen, but I'd already been in enough of these situations, especially this last summer, that I'd learned to recover quickly. React, rebound, re-access, as Waters, my badass defense teacher, taught us this summer.

Re-access. *Oh no! I left the necklace behind.*

"We have to go back!" I called into the front of the vehicle. My father seized my shoulders and pulled me up.

"Are you crazy? We have to go home!" His eyes were wide with terror.

"You are both wrong." The agent in the front passenger seat who had been doing most of the shooting, turned briefly away from the window and looked back at us. Her gun was still out, and her finger was on the earbud in her right ear. "We expected something like this. It has been happening in the other locations all week."

Other locations—my first thought was of my boyfriend, Shim. Was he safe? I hadn't heard from him or his brother in months. Nor the twins. We were all aliens, or half-half, or Alien Americans—or whatever term wouldn't get us shot.

"We are falling back to a safe house." The agent said. She

was already back to scanning the street for threats and continuing her low-voiced update with whoever was on the phone.

Frustrated, I peeled the thing stuck to my cheek off and looked at it. Raisinet? *Stars, I hoped so.* I shuddered and tossed it to the floorboard, then pulled the zipper on my wetsuit to my waist and yanked my neoprene hood back. I extracted my arms like peeling a banana. Better. After a whiff of the Feds' leather seats, I was unconcerned that I was shedding water and sand all over them. I reached up and pushed my hair back. Much better.

Dad snorted at my sigh of relief. He looked down at me; his face grew alarmed as he looked at my throat. He'd noticed the necklace was missing.

Don't say anything. I thought. He opened his mouth, and I shook my head at him.

"Shhhh." I glanced at the agents in the front seats.

Dad smacked his hand over his face and collapsed back in his seat with a groan. He looked like he had aged ten years in thirty seconds.

Exposed and shivering, sitting in my damp swimsuit and cold itchy wetsuit. I felt like I'd wiped out in the emotional equivalent of an impact zone.

My father looked like he was going through an existential crisis next to me. The Helios were chasing us. We were moving, again. I didn't know where Shim and the others were or when I would see them. And I'd managed to leave the Keystone, the catalyst for all this and something I never let out of my sight before, hidden on a beach with a rising tide.

At least, I hoped it was still hidden.

2

THE OTHERS

"GRACE!"

I looked up and had only seconds to appreciate the view approaching before being swept into a warm, muscled hug. A whispered sigh swept over my ear. I recognized the minty scent. The clenched knot in my gut, the one that guarded me so I could handle all this on my own, unfurled.

I was safe. I wasn't stuck figuring this all out on my own anymore.

"What are you doing here? Are you okay? I've missed you."

I didn't know which to address first, so I let myself sink further into Shim's chest. Turning my head, my lips brushed against the warm brown skin of his neck. He chuckled and rubbed his cheek against mine, springy curls tickling me. I took my first deep breath in months.

Since we learned our parents were aliens and the government put us in protective custody, my head had been a mess. Talk about redefining who you are! I'd always been an outsider and a loner, but being hunted was new, and knowing it was the Helios after us, a homegrown terrorist cell with plans to take over the world, scared the crap out of me.

I tilted my head and asked, "Shim, why did you stop talking through the stones?" Of all the questions running through my brain, this one bothered me the most.

We learned the secret this summer that we could communicate through the keystones we all wore. When the Feds split us up, we kept talking through them. But a couple of weeks after the confinement started, the twins had stopped responding. Then a week after, so had Jaxon and Shim.

Shim raised his head and looked at me, one side of his mouth tilted up as his eyebrows pinched together. "They took our stones when they took yours." He glanced around and lowered his voice. "I don't think the government knows we can talk through them, but they know they're tied to how our parents arrived on Earth. They took them all—the twin's cuff, the ancient amulet that Jaxon found, even the slice of the stone Kindle was using. I'm assuming they also took Micah's brooch, but he works so closely with them that he might have just given it to them." His voice was bitter. Then it softened as he rubbed a thumb along my collarbone. "And I see they got your necklace."

My breath caught. "Shim—" He didn't know I still had my necklace, well, sort of.

Without warning, we were body-slammed on both sides by mini-tornadoes of energy and cheer.

"Grace!" The twins Breeze and Skylar screamed in stereo, then squeezed us like they were afraid we would escape. I loved it.

"I can't believe you are here!" Breeze flipped her long blond bangs back, revealing twinkling blue eyes that exactly matched her twin's.

Skylar shook his head, barely letting Breeze finish before he asked, "How are you here?" Then added, "How are any of us here?"

"We've missed you so much!" Breeze's tanned arms reached around both Shim and me and gave another squeeze.

I interrupted the questions they were lobbing at me before they turned this into an opportunity for a sing-along. "Why are we here?"

Under my ear, I felt Shim's voice rumble in his chest as he responded, "Same as you, we got attacked by the Helios. They hit Micah and his family first." He let that sink in. Micah was the oldest of the five teens that had arrived on Earth twenty-some years ago; his wife, Trystal, the second oldest. If they were here, so was their son, Jada. I knew he was a little older, sixteen, almost seventeen. I'd never met him. "Then, three days ago they went after Arie and the twins in San Francisco."

With a gasp, I turned in Shim's arms and studied the twins for injuries. "Are you okay?"

Skylar shrugged, "Yeh. But Dad was furious. Said the government had left us with a target on our backs. That they were using us as bait. After the attack, they moved us here."

Here appeared to be a large compound in the Santa Cruz mountains.

Shim gave me a squeeze and continued with the bad news. "Then, yesterday, the Helios went after us in Las Vegas. Tried to take us when Kindle, Jaxon, and I went out to the store." I turned back to look at Shim. He shook his head, face solemn. "There was a firefight in a parking lot. One of the agents got hit—we don't know what happened to him." I held Shim as he breathed heavily through the memory. A shudder racked through me; it could have been Shim hurt, dead. His arms tightened around me and pulled me back into a tight hug.

"Why does your hair always look like crap?" Arms dropped, we spun around. Jaxon strolled out of the house with a smug smile. A tall boy I'd never seen before trailed behind him.

"I was surfing," I defended myself. Raising my arms, I tried to finger comb the matted ash-brown and green strands.

"Is that why you're wearing that?" Breeze had her nose turned up as if she just realized a wet suit wasn't my fashion statement.

I grunted an affirmative, still preoccupied with my hair.

"Always dressing to impress," Jaxon mocked, but his smirk was friendly.

"Shut up, you little shit." Shim must have missed the humor in Jaxon's tone, and as always, things escalated from zero, to one hundred, in seconds.

The two brothers could not be more opposite. Shim was all lean muscle and about my height, I might be slightly taller, but I'd never tell him. With warm brown skin and the delicate facial features of his mother, except his nose was wider, he was perfect. Even though Jaxon was a year younger, he was almost as tall as Shim. Jaxon had the hard muscles of a sports enthusiast and seemed to have picked up more since this summer. He was pale skinned, like me, but his was coated with freckles that fought for attention with his copper hair.

I looked around at everyone; we all looked a little tougher.

I'd been practicing every day the fighting skills Waters had taught us this summer. I hesitated to call Waters a defense teacher, he subscribed to the kill or be killed book of life, but with his help, we were as ready as we could be for whoever came after us next.

Jaxon approached and shouldered his way past the twins to give me an unexpected hug and a gruff pat on the back that ended up more like a shove, pushing me back into Shim, who reached around and shoved Jaxon back.

Things might have escalated if the boy who came in with Jaxon hadn't stepped forward. He didn't look shy, just hesitant to intrude.

"I'm Jada." When we didn't respond, Jada made a motion toward the house. "Do you want to know why we are here?" There was something off about the pattern of his words. But before he even spoke, he commandeered our attention in his khakis, jacket, and tie, and I suddenly felt even more awkward in my briny wetsuit. Straight, jet black hair, short on the sides and swept back on top, added at least an inch to his height and towered over the rest of us. His deep brown eyes probed our group, issuing a challenge.

"You know?" I stepped towards him.

Jada's ridiculously handsome smile didn't reach his eyes. "The agents are briefing our parents now."

We started to shuffle to the front door, and Jaxon said, "Why bother? They won't let us in."

"I've got a better idea." As Shim led us around the side of the large farmhouse, he whispered to me, "There is a window they always keep open in the bathroom off the main room. We should be able to hear something from there." I crouched low as I followed him under a series of windows until he reached a large oak tree in front of a small, open, shoulder-height window. A few yards away, large French doors opened onto a patio that stretched around the back of the two-story house. Through the window, I saw my father sitting in a chair, facing away from us. Occasionally, someone would pace by the French doors, but unless they pressed their face against the glass, they were unlikely to see us.

Agents started leaving the back of the house and heading to the parking area. We must have missed the briefing. But our parents were still inside talking. I recognized Arie's raised voice, the twin's father—also Shim's father—speaking. Kindle, Jaxon and Shim's mother, yelled a response we easily heard. Worried for Shim, I reached for his hand. He squeezed my fingers. Then Kindle started yelling at someone else.

"No," Kindle shouted to whatever the person had said. "No, it's just how you Teran's work. Protecting each other and never letting anyone from the other colonies have a chance, especially someone from Nadun."

I caught my breath. Pins of excitement raced up my spine. Ever since we learned from my mother's diary that our parents weren't from Earth, we had tried to talk to them about their home worlds. They wouldn't tell us anything, claimed it wasn't safe to talk about. Shim had taken photos of the diary before we lost it—before I traded it to get our parents back. But a lot of it was the ramblings of a homesick fifteen-year-old girl.

Before we lost communication with each other, we had been pressuring our parents to tell us more. We knew Teran was the main planet, and its three moons each held a colony. Jada's parents, Micah and Trystal, were from Teran. But since we hadn't been able to talk to him, we didn't know any more than that. My mother was from LaDer, a water-covered moon. I wish I had learned about her home directly from her, but my father would do no more than confirm the name.

The twin's father, Arie, was from a colony on the moon called Mirah. He was furious when he found out we knew that much.

Brothers Shim and Jaxon had a little more luck with Kindle. She had been furious at Micah for forcing her to keep the secret so long, so it hadn't taken much for her to tell them all about her family on the moon Nadun. The privileged life she led growing up the "Daughter of the Mayor" of one of the largest underground mining cities on the moon, and how much she hated her life since they had landed in a field in Santa Cruz decades before. She cataloged in detail Micah's failings in getting the group home.

"Now, Kindle, that's not true. Micah has been working closely with the government to try and keep us safe. He is the one that negotiated our protection." I strained to hear my father's voice as he tentatively broke into the argument. That wasn't exactly true. I had negotiated their release but didn't want him to know I had given up my mom's diary for their freedom.

"Protection? Prison you mean. We have been hunted ever since we arrived at Prather's Spot. Now we aren't free to come and go. They take our stones without asking; they tell us where to live, who to see, what to do...."

Prather's Spot, what was that?

Shim grabbed my arm and pointed to the end of the drive. An agent doing his rounds was headed our way.

"So what?" I said, my voice low. "We aren't doing anything wrong."

Breeze's eyes bugged out. Skylar wrapped an arm around his sister's shoulder. "Come on Breeze, let's get inside." They headed back to the front of the house.

Jaxon gave his brother a shove and muttered "later" before boldly crossing in front of the French doors and disappearing around the back. Jada quirked a brow at us and followed Jaxon.

Recovering his balance, Shim squeezed my hand and, leaning back against the tree, pulled me closer to him. He gave a relaxed wave to the agent that passed by.

I waited until the man in the navy windbreaker disappeared around the back of the house. Speaking softly so my voice didn't carry, I asked, "Does that name sound familiar to you?"

"What?"

"Prather's Spot?"

Shim pursed his lips and tilted his head. "Sort of. I feel like I've heard it before."

I nodded. Kindle's words tickled a memory like an itch I couldn't reach. Something about Santa Cruz...Prather's Spot... spot...something, mystery. That was it!

"Mystery spot!" I grabbed Shim's hand and squeezed.

Shim's eyes widened. "Yes, you're right! I think I know something you should see." He straightened and pulled me towards the house.

Did we finally have the answer to one of our biggest questions?

But if we were right. What should we do with the information?

Shim pulled me behind him over the threshold into the dark house. We passed several rooms, each decorated with a blizzard of paper snowflakes, until he stopped at a library. A small pine tree still wrapped in netting was leaning against the wall, waiting to be set up and decorated. A knee-high pile of paper chains was a next to it made of newspaper, tin foil, paper towels, old boxes, and a couple of other types of paper I didn't recognize.

"The twins?"

"Yeah, and Jaxon. Can you believe it?" Shim chuckled.

"Is there any paper left in the house?"

"Doubt it. I'd double-check you have toilet paper before you use the bathroom."

"Oh, yeah, I see the rolls." I pointed to a series of small cardboard rings next to a chain of FBI lanyards that had been hooked together.

"Look here." Shim called my attention away from the post-apocalyptic tree decorations. "I was searching for something to read last night, and I saw it..."

His voice trailed off as he started pulling books off the shelves and flipping through the pages. "No, not the historical section." Shim muttered

I pushed a plush leather chair under the desk and looked at the computer. Should I do an online search?

Shim yanked several heavy, hardback books off the shelf. He pushed a few into my hands. "Help me look."

"Look for what. What are these?" I flipped open the gold foil-stamped cover of the book, "*Stars*, it's an encyclopedia! I've not seen one of these outside of a library; why would anyone buy one for their home?"

"Some people like to read real books," he said, blushing.

I agreed, but anyone that moved around as much as I did would understand the value of an e-book collection. Shim flipped quickly through another. And I started doing the same. Something stuck out of the next book, and it caught his eye.

"There it is!" I leaned over his shoulder as Shim flipped to the page. A canary yellow card beckoned to us, and all my synopsis fired in recognition.

"Yes!" Shim pulled the book into his lap and collapsed cross-legged on the floor. Latching onto my arm, he pulled me down, almost on top of him. I laughed and wrapped an arm around him. My internal happy dance kicked up a notch as I snuggled in and reached across him. Thumbing the big book in his lap open, I pulled out the bookmark. It wasn't a card; it was a bright yellow bumper sticker. I handed it to Shim and started to read aloud the section on Vortexes. A couple of minutes in, Shim stopped me. He slapped the bumper sticker reading "MYS-TERY SPOT" on the opposite page.

"Here it is. George Prather discovered the Mystery Spot, also called Prather's Spot, in Santa Cruz."

"But that is a hoax," I said and then shivered. Shim let me go to shrug out of his jacket and then dropped it over my shoulders before wrapping his arms around me again.

"That's where Kindle said they got stuck. This is where they arrived on Earth. We have to check it out." Shim's voice was firm.

I didn't agree with him, which was an unsettling feeling.

"They went back again and again, and nothing ever happened. Thousands of tourists have been there over the years, and nothing has happened."

"But don't you feel it?" Shim's face scrunched up. "This incompleteness, like we only know half of who we are, like, if we figured out how they got here we would understand who they are, who we are. And I swear it's not just about my father—"

"I know," I interrupted him. "I'm just not sure now, with the Helios chasing us and the Feds monitoring everything we do, is the time to try and find the passage. But I do know why you want to. I feel the hole, this big unknown about our past. And it's not just about my mother." Shim nodded. He got me. He always had.

"*Oh, Stars,* maybe it's not even worth it without one of the Keystones." He thumped his fist into the floor and closed the book with a snap.

I plucked at the neoprene covering my knee. "Well, Shim, I think I can help with that." He tilted his head and studied me with narrow eyes. "I just happened to know where a Keystone is, and I need your help to get it back."

3

VAN EKMAN

SHIVERING, I blew into the cup of my hands and rubbed them together, trying to ward off the pre-dawn chill.

Last night it had taken forever to clean up. By the time I was finally warm and showered, my father was watching too closely for us to sneak out. Retrieving the necklace before the parents woke up had seemed like a good idea. But, now standing, freezing, in the dark with no coffee, no sleep, and no Shim, I was starting to rethink the plan.

I had spent most of the night staring at the ceiling with my muscles tensed for action as frightening scenarios replayed like waves in my head. *What if my mom's necklace was gone? What if someone found it? What if a sleeper wave carried it out to sea?*

When I did fall asleep, I dreamed the Helios were torturing me to show them how I communicated through the stone in the necklace.

When my alarm went off at five, I woke up with a kink in my neck and that queasy feeling that said I hadn't gotten enough sleep.

And I felt guilty. I slumped back into the open door of Van Ekman, my dad's old VW van. Going through my father's pockets, looking for the keys while he slept, was a new low for me. But, if I hadn't done it, I wouldn't have discovered what a tight leash they had on us here.

Dad always kept VanEkman's key in his right pocket on a fob with a photo of my mom in it and, when nervous, he would rub his thumb across the portrait.

The key was missing.

I checked his left pocket and found his wallet: it was empty. His driver's license and all his credit cards were gone. Those bastards must have taken them from him as soon as we arrived. Fortunately, they hadn't thought his library card was threatening. And tucked behind the card was the small piece of plastic I was looking for. My dad had locked his keys in the van so many times he had made a backup key from an old plastic container. A little brittle from age. Hopefully, it wouldn't break.

A shiver ran through me, and I considered returning for a jacket. *Where was Shim?* As worried as I was, my heart was thrilled at getting to spend a couple of hours alone with him. He was the only person who really understood me. Not hearing from him for months had left me feeling more isolated and alone than I had before I met him. Which was weird, because since I'd known him, I spent more time without him than with him.

"Grace."

At my whispered name, I jumped up from the front seat and searched for the source, recoiling at the ghostly figure. It was Breeze. She had the light from her phone pointed at her pale face, the glare harsh on her protruding features and throwing the rest in shadow. As the glow spread, I could see she was standing at the head of the path that led to this pole barn where the extra cars were kept, through the woods, back to the house. She shivered in her thin jacket and were those pajama pants? At least she had put on shoes.

"What are you doing here?" I hissed.

"W-w-what are *you* doing here?" she countered, stepping closer to the van, her shrill voice loud in the silence. "T-this is dangerous. If you told the parents you were going, they might send people to protect you." Breeze's body shook as she made her accusation, nervous fingers twisting her long blond bangs.

"Shhh—" I whispered, "If we told the parents, they would probably tell the agents to stop us, and we have to go *now*."

A twig snapped and we both whirled to look down the path.

Jaxon sauntered out of the woods into the moonlight. He was chewing on something that looked like a protein bar and had the robot dog Duchess tucked under one arm. Ever since Jaxon had borrowed—stolen— Duchess this summer, he had carted her around like his own metal teddy bear. It was the only soft thing about him.

"Whatcha doing waiting out here?" Jaxon asked. He was fully dressed but his hair still looked like he'd just escaped a sandstorm.

Breeze pointed her finger at me. "Shim and Grace think they can just leave—" Her voice was indignant even as she leaned into Jaxon like a magnet.

"Yeah, yeah, I know. Shim told me. Said I couldn't come along, which is why I let everyone know and we are coming with you. But why are you waiting out here instead of in the van where it's warm?" Jaxon pushed past me to climb into the driver's seat. "I'm driving," he declared, setting Duchess on the floorboards. He examined the plastic key in his hand.

My jaw dropped. He pinched the key from me when he pushed past. This summer we had all taken old-man-Waters' street-smarts bootcamp where lifts, B&E, and fighting dirty were all part of the class.

It looked like Jaxon has been practicing.

"Does this really work?" When he moved to put it in the

ignition, I stopped him. "Wait, the key'll break, it's just for unlocking the door and turning on the power. We're going to push start it."

"Huh?" Jaxon looked at me like I had grown antenna.

"Just—just—give it here. Where is Shim?" This was crazy. Was everyone coming with us? This was supposed to be a *secret* mission, just Shim and I running to Natural Bridges Beach to get the necklace. There and back in an hour or two. Now we are taking on passengers like the S.S. Minnow.

"Yeah, about that. He and Kindle are having it out at the house. I'd be surprised if they didn't wake everyone up by the time they are done. I'm here to get us started."

"She found out we were leaving?" I asked my heart in my throat.

"Actually, no. So, that is the only thing she isn't mad about."

I waited.

Jaxon gave a frustrated sigh. "Grace, she's still scream'n 'bout all the hoopla this summer but, you know, it's just like transference or deflection or whatever they call that shit. Cause she knows—she knows she did wrong not telling Shim that Arie was his father. Hell, and not telling Arie either. She's mad at herself. Mad at Shim. Mad at you—" He cut off at my look of surprise. Jaxon swore and pulled a hand through his hair, the red strands standing at attention for him. "Grace, you and Shim really need to talk."

What did Jaxon mean? Shim and I talked last night. We talked every chance we got, which, admittedly, hadn't been often since the government had gotten involved in our lives.

Kicking the dash, Jaxon pushed off and slithered over the seat into the back, calling out to Breeze as he went. "Blue Eyes, you come'n or not?"

Breeze shifted her weight from side to side, the rocking

motion pushing her closer and farther from the van. "Well, I don't know if I should."

"You should stay," I responded automatically to Breeze as my gaze followed Jaxon. "Why is Kindle upset with me?"

"Not really with you. About you. Talk to Shim." Jaxon said, with a mulish look. He made a motion of sealing his lips shut.

"Wham."

I jumped. In the moonlight, I could see Jada standing with his fists planted on the hood. He looked furious and cute. I hadn't seen him since our introductions yesterday. Today, there was no school uniform, just a sweater vest over a button-up shirt and jeans. He scowled. "You're going." It was more of an accusation than a question.

"Jada..." I broke off as he swung around the side of the van and climbed in the back. I guess he was coming, too. As he settled next to Jaxon, I noticed that he had hearing aids in his ears. I wonder why I didn't notice that yesterday.

When Jada looked up, Jaxon gave him a chin lift.

Twilight was lifting the darkness and the moonglow was losing its strength when I heard someone else coming down the path. There was a collective sigh of relief from the van when Shim emerged from the woods, zipping up his backpack. He stalked the few yards from the path to the van, bypassing the other vehicles in the lot.

All the tension in my body disappeared and my brain went fuzzy for a second as he seemed to move in slow-mo, muscles bunching, the dark curls of his hair bouncing with each step, the strange pre-dawn light kissing his features.

Jaxon snickered behind me, and I snapped out of it, shaking my head. Shim looked serious and I missed his crooked grin. I reached out and wrapped an arm around his strong bicep and smiled as just touching him made something click into place inside me, settling my nerves.

Until he stiffened.

Jaxon made a gagging sound and some comment.

"Grace, I need to tell you something—" Shim started with the opening line no girl ever wants to hear. My breath caught as my chest tightened. Bracing myself, I pulled back and looked into his grim eyes. He looked away.

"We have to go!" Skylar shouted as he exploded from the woods at a run. "Agents right behind me." Skylar grabbed Breeze's hand as he raced past, pulling her along in his wake. Breeze looked relieved to have the decision made for her. The twins started to climb in, and I stopped them.

"Wait, everyone needs to push." I got into the front seat and put the fragile key in the ignition, turning it halfway to turn on the power. The key bent but held. I thrust in the clutch and jammed the gear into second. There was a mad scramble as everyone latched onto a portion of the van. Huffing and cursing was drowned out by the metal groan the van's frame gave as it rolled through the silent lot and onto the main street. I waited a little longer than needed to get us further from the house before I released the clutch and popped the gear. The engine sputtered and caught with a loud belch.

As soon as they heard the sound, everyone jumped in. The side door slammed, and Jaxon called, "Let's hit it!"

Over the engine's roar, Skylar filled us in. His voice faded in and out of my hearing. "I don't know if the agents saw me, but they were right behind me, headed down the path in a hurry and they were arguing. There was something going on," he paused, gasping for breath, then continued. "They said there were new orders that no one liked and that they were prepping to leave today."

There was some cursing in the back of the van and a scrambling sound. I glanced in the rearview mirror as Skylar and Breeze slid into the back row of seats.

"Leave...them or us?" Someone asked. I shifted gears and the engine quieted as the ride smoothed out.

My hand searched under the wheel until I found the switch and flipped on the headlights in time to take a sharp bend in the road. Fighting the force of gravity, Jaxon leaned forward between the front seats. He patted Duchess's head and out of the corner of my eye I could see her wag her little spring tail, mechanical head pushing up into his palm.

"The chances of them leaving us alone—zero. The chances of them splitting us up—high. If we are leaving today, this is our only chance to check out the landing zone," Jaxon said.

"It's not a landing zone. They came here through some type of Einstein–Rosen bridge. And Grace and I agreed we were not going to Prather's Spot. We are just going to get the necklace and then go back. This isn't a field trip." Shim's tone was just short of explosive, but still, his geek-side burst through his dark mood.

I agreed with him. The necklace was most important. And last night we had both expressed how much we were looking forward to spending time alone. So, why had he invited everyone else to go with us? It was like he was trying to avoid me.

My heart clenched along with my hands on the steering wheel. "Shim, are you okay?" When he didn't respond, I added, "Jaxon said you were arguing with Kindle."

The road straightened, and I was able to glance over at Shim, who shot a warning glare at his brother. Jaxon raised his hands and eased back into his seat. I waited for Shim to say something. The distance caused physical pain as he pulled away and stared out the window. I left it for a couple of minutes as we entered a dark curvy patch where the accommodating road wove around immovable ancient Coastal redwoods. The van whined and groaned through the turns. We emerged from the deep darkness of their branches and several minutes later, when we finally reached the freeway, I could relax a little.

I drove in silence, contemplating what had changed with Shim. Yesterday was wonderful except for someone trying to kill us. But seeing Shim again, being back with the others, made me feel like I was part of the group again, not stumbling around in the dark on my own. I had been so reluctant to let them in, but they had become my family. Now, I was scared of losing them and every bump in the road felt like a fore-warning of disaster.

Shim had been happy to see me. It was just like the summer, the way we knew each other, trusted each other. We immediately reconnected and started solving problems together. What we had, it just worked. But this morning, something had changed.

I thought about it. I could sit here festering in doubt or I could ask Shim.

There was a quick dip in the road and my stomach clenched. I pushed the words out. "Shim, what did you want to tell me?"

He was silent as I exited the freeway and headed toward the coast. I chanced to glance over at him. I thought it was the fading twilight that gave Shim a haunted look, but then I saw his eyes. The misery in them took my breath away. Without saying a word, I pulled off the road into a wide gravel shoulder.

Before the van's wheels had stopped rolling, Shim hopped out of the van and walked back in the direction we had come.

"Hey, where's he going?" Someone in the back shouted.

"Are we there?"

I stood on the brakes and we coasted several yards before the van stopped.

"Keep the engine running," I told no one in particular. Steeling myself, I got out.

Jada slid open the side door of the van and looked out. He turned towards Shim, then looked at me and with a sigh. He moved into the driver's seat.

I hesitated at the back of the van. A hard shiver shook me as I watched Shim pace up the narrow strip of gravel that separated stop from go. My initial instinct to go to him was stalled when I realized I wasn't sure I wanted to hear what he had to say.

Jada revved the sputtering engine and the resulting cloud of diesel fumes propelled me forward, coughing and sputtering, down the gravel shoulder. I'd almost caught my breath by the time I reached Shim, who was now standing and waiting for me. His eyes were somber, and his shoulders slumped. Even his hair had lost its bounce.

"Are you sick?" I asked, a little ashamed of sounding hopeful. Shim rubbed his chest as he shook his head. When he finally spoke, I wished that he hadn't.

"Grace, I have a girlfriend."

My eyes widened, and I felt the words like numbing blows. Stumbling back, I tripped over a broken, rejected tire tread. Shim reached out to catch me and I pushed his arm away as I landed on my backside, pointy pieces of gravel inflicting dull wounds that don't kill you but leave painful bruises. It took a minute for me to find my tongue.

"Are you kidding?" He wasn't. It was something in the slump of his shoulders and the miserable look on his face. This wasn't something he would joke about. I knew him, or at least, I thought I had.

When he shook his head, my hope that this was all a misunderstanding evaporated.

"For how long?" I asked as I wiped off the gravel stuck in my hand on my jeans and scrambled to my feet. He reached to help me and shrunk back at my glare.

When I stood again, he wouldn't meet my eyes, studying his clenched fists instead. "Two years."

The words knifed through me. "Two...so...before we even got together?" I gasped.

Shim's head sunk another inch.

At that instant, I knew what a magnet felt like when it was flipped around. Everything in me that had always been attracted to Shim and drawn to him was suddenly repelled.

"Grace, I want to explain—" Without looking at him, I headed back to the van.

Jada was still in the driver's seat, keeping the engine going. I slid into the passenger seat but felt like I was on display. Had they known? Did everyone know but me?

"Skylar, switch with me." I crawled over the seats, too tall, too gangly, my knees and elbows knocking into the others. They were probably laughing at what a mess I was. I squeezed between Breeze and Skylar, forcing him to move to the middle seat.

As I stared out the window of the van I was acutely aware of everyone's gaze like grains of sand stuck in a swimsuit. I hunkered deeper into the seat, turning my head almost all the way to the back. Why didn't Shim tell me? Why hadn't anyone told me?

It seemed like just yesterday I was learning that everything I knew about myself was a lie. And here I was again. I sniffed and quickly swiped the palm of my hand over my face, wiping away the wetness. If Shim lied about this—what else isn't he telling me?

4

MYSTERY SPOT

WE RETRIEVED the stone without fuss. Well, a little fuss. Shim wanted to help, wanted to explain. I took Jada instead and he held my ankles as I went from the top of the rock outcropping head-first down the face to find the hole where I'd stashed the necklace.

I cried when I found it. Hanging upside down, the ocean waves crashing greedily below, licking up the saltwater dripping from my face.

Jada pulled me up and then wrapped an arm around my shoulders. We both pretended it was a relief that the necklace was safe. When I got back to the van, Shim was in the driver's seat, keeping the engine running.

Skylar hung on the frame of the sliding door, blocking our entrance, and announced, "We are going to Prather's Spot."

No one questioned the declaration, so they must have been discussing it while Jada and I were busy and had decided without us. I wonder how much Shim had instigated that.

Jada had his arm around my shoulders. An unexpected wave of exhaustion had me leaning into him as I asked Skylar, "Why? What do you expect to find there?"

"I don't know. Don't you want to see the place they arrived? It all feels so unreal. If we hadn't read your mother's diary if she hadn't said straight up, "We are aliens," I'm not sure I would believe it now. I just want to see where it happened." Skylar waved his arms as if presenting a looking glass into the past.

"Grace, how were you able to keep your necklace? We tried to hide our cuff, but they knew exactly what they were looking for. They must have read the diary and the research journal; they must know all the stones came from one Keystone."

"The journal!" I stood up straight, pulling away from Jada. "The journal talked about the properties of the Keystone. The government has both the journal and the diary, so they must suspect that we can communicate through them. That must be why they took them."

"I never saw the journal so I don't know what it says, but they would want to study a stone that has no precedent on Earth," Jada said.

I kept forgetting that he wasn't with us this summer, and I wondered how much he knew of what had happened.

I shivered as a strong wind blew in from the ocean behind us. In the front seat, Shim shrugged off his jacket and held it out to me. I ignored the offer.

"Let us in." I pleaded with Skylar. He fell back into his seat and Jada and I quickly climbed in and slammed the door behind us.

I rubbed my hands together as I continued. "I don't know how I kept the necklace. Luck really. We had two new agents. They weren't with us in Vegas. They knew about the Helios, but they didn't seem to know about what happened this summer. As soon as they arrived, I switched my necklace around so the stone was at the back of my neck. All they ever saw was the bronze torque. They asked my father about the necklace, and he said it was my mother's, and she had taken it when she disappeared."

"But she went missing after the Helios grabbed her, so the government knows it and thinks the Helios have a Keystone." I glared at Shim as he made his first contribution to the conversation.

"Another reason why we need to go back to the house where we are protected. Right now, we are where my father and I were shot at just yesterday. The Helios could be watching us right now." I pounded my fist on the back of the vinyl seat.

"Shim, she is right about that. We can't just sit here anymore." Jada said as he scanned the parking lot. It seemed we were all alone, but were we really?

VanEkman rolled back out of the parking space, the brakes squealed, then the van lurched forward, halting with each gear change as Shim tore out of the parking lot at the speed of a racing green turtle.

"Look," Skylar continued to plead his case, taking a minute to look each of them in the eye. "If the Feds are going to move us all or split us up—this could be our only shot."

Shim stopped the van at an intersection with the ocean at our backs. Going left would take us back up Highway 17, back to our parents and the smothering custody of the government. Going right would take us into Happy Valley in the Santa Cruz mountains, into the unknown and maybe into the net of the Helios.

Intellectually, I knew Skylar was right. We had to take advantage of this unexpected freedom and check it out. But the illusion of home and family that I thought I had found with Breeze and Skylar, and Jaxon, and Shim, especially Shim, was peeled away, leaving me shivering and exposed. Emotionally, I was exhausted beyond reason and logic and just wanted to go back to my dad. But I was outvoted.

"Fine, whatever," I said, crawling into the back of the van.

Shim swung the wheel right and I hunched down in the back seat in silence as he navigated through the city of Santa Cruz. I cracked open the back window, trying to breathe in the healing salty air as I pretended to study the muraled walls and sun-bleached buildings of the lazy coastal city. I still had a catch in my breath as surf shops and meditation centers gave way to quaint village streets when Shim turned inland and left the coast. My body shook and rocked with the van as it reached its top speed of 45 MPH.

"Did your parents tell you anything about how they arrived on Earth?" Breeze leaned forward to ask Jada in the front passenger seat.

The engine whined as the elevation rose from sea level and we entered our first grove of redwoods. The noise must have been too much for his hearing aid to combat. Jada leaned closer, then shook his head and pointed to his ear.

Breeze gave up and waved a "never mind" then turned around to Jaxon, who was sitting beside me. He had Duchess in his lap, her back compartment flipped open to expose the solar panels and he was aiming them at the wide strip of light now coming in the windows.

"Jaxon. Did your mom talk to you about it?" She yelled the question.

Jaxon snorted and lifted Duchess out of the way as he leaned forward, resting his arm on the back of her seat. "Kindle told us Jack Shit, as always."

"Not true." Shim shouted over the engine noise. "She talked about Nadun and her father being a hotshot mayor of a town called Neran."

"Oh that, that wasn't really telling us anything, that was her getting even with Micah for trying to muzzle her." Jaxon's tone held a hint of admiration for his mother's act of rebellion.

Watching Jaxon's fingers brush Breeze's shoulder, a pang of envy flushed through me. I looked at the driver's seat. But all that was visible was the back of Shim's head and one shoulder. I kept thinking about some other girl's finger brushing that shoulder and threading her fingers through those curls. A wave of nausea swept through me and I tried to think of something else. With a sad groan, I settled deeper in the seat, a spring poking me in my butt through the cracked vinyl of the seat. I listened to the twins comparing notes on what they knew about all our parents' arrival on Earth—which was very little.

The van slowed as it whined through a curve. Dark shadows from the trees blocking out the sun matched my mood. There was one thing that would make me feel better. I fingered the broken chain that should have been holding one side of the stone to the necklace.

"Jaxon, do you have pliers in there?" I indicated the mini toolkit in Duchess' backside.

He raised a copper brow then saw the chain. Digging into the kit, he grabbed the pliers. Trying to keep my hands from shaking, I held the stone and the two pieces of chain while he worked the pliers.

"Did you know?" I couldn't make myself add any detail to my question. But I didn't need to. He understood, and I knew the answer when he wouldn't look at me. Jaxon had known Shim had another girlfriend. Maybe everyone had—but me.

"These two pieces need to be together. It's not a perfect solution, but it will hold for now. We will hit it with some solder tonight and the necklace will be as strong as ever—I promise, Grace." Jaxon spoke with a sincerity I had never heard from him before and—was he being metaphorical? Maybe not, I thought as he added, "Shits messed up, Grace, shake it off."

He should put out a sign, "Counseling by Jaxon."

The semi-repaired necklace clenched in my hand, I stared

out the window. I lifted my nose to the opening and took a deep breath. It caught in my chest and I struggled through the inhalation. The smell outside had turned to pine and growing things marinated in the ever-present diesel of Van Ekman. The engine whined in protest at the elevation and curves. By now, I should be used to disappointment. My life was like this van, beaten, but still rolling. This was just one more example of life dumping on me.

No. Anger pushed me until I sat up straight. This wasn't life, this was one guy not meeting my expectations. I had thought Shim was perfect. I had been living in a dream. We had bonded under an unimaginable stressful situation. And I had ignored everything that didn't fit into my perfect scenario. But I had learned my lesson. I'd feel sorry for myself later. Now, I had things to do.

I wrapped the flattened bronze strip around my neck and latched the repaired chain, vowing to never take it off again.

I took a deep breath and leaned into the conversation as Jaxon replied to a question. "Kindle said Nadun was hot and smelly, and everyone lived underground in tunnels. Not quite the vacation destination of Las Vegas where everyone lives in the casinos."

When Breeze saw me paying attention, she cautiously met my eyes and asked, "Grace, what did your mom tell you about her home world, LaDer?"

My mother hadn't even told me she was an alien. Everything I had learned about where she came from and how she got here had been from the diary, and that was the grief-stricken ramblings of a young girl lost and afraid. "She was from LaDer. It's a moon covered in water. Maybe they all live in the ocean?" I cringed. It wasn't lost on me that I seemed to have been told the least amount of anyone about their parents' home world.

As I was talking, I felt the anger bubble up. The Helios had taken my mother while she was scuba diving. She died in their custody, her secrets dying with her. The Helios had stolen her from me, and they were number one on my list of people I didn't trust. The federal watchdogs that had been appointed to keep us safe were on the list too. I was suspicious of their motives and the Helios had infiltrated the government and embedded themselves so deeply we never knew when one of our watchdogs was actually a double agent. No one was safe. I mentally added Shim to the list. I could acknowledge he wasn't evil. But he had lied to me, and he wasn't to be trusted. For that matter, I considered the others. Jaxon had known too. Did the twins? A shiver went through me. What else did they all know they weren't telling me? Could I trust any of them?

Glancing out the window, I saw the road sign.

"It's the first right," I called out. But Shim had already started the turn.

I settled back but my heart was starting to race now. The only thing we knew about the site where they arrived on Earth was that it was in a field and that the Keystone in the necklace had something to do with them being transported here. And that after two decades of trying to recreate the accident that brought them to Earth, our parents had given up on the hope of ever going home. It looked like whatever had brought them here was a one-way ticket.

A huge yellow sign reading "Mystery Spot" with a big black doughnut for the "o" was nestled between lofty coastal redwood trees. Redwoods towered a couple hundred feet over the whole area, clustered in family circles with other trees, their deep green branches reaching out to each other, forcing the man-made products like log buildings, paths, and parking lots, to go around them. The tourist-packed parking area had a carnival atmosphere.

"Welcome to hell," Jaxon muttered.

By luck, a car pulled out right in front of us and Shim eased the van nose in, until there was a jolt and the van sputtered and stalled.

"Good one, bro." Jaxon hollered out, the sound echoing in the lull left from the quieted engine.

Jumping out of the van onto the packed dirt, I looked around. This didn't seem right at all. A long line of people snaked out from the tour ticket booth. A group of teens in the back were laughing and snapping selfies. Short skirts, wooly boots and tennis shoes, bare midriffs, baggy sweatshirts and torn jeans, the culturally diverse group had one thing in common: they were all relaxed and goofing around, without a care in the world.

Unlike us.

Shim was pulling on his backpack when Jaxon stopped him.

"Put her in your bag." Jaxon was clutching Duchess to his chest, eyeing the crowd suspiciously.

"No way. I'm not carrying her."

"Come on, man, I can't leave her here. Some creep will steal her. I'll help you carry the bag."

Shim rolled his eyes. He took Duchess and tucked her into the bottom of his pack before swinging it on. "No, you won't."

Jada was slowly spinning in a circle as he surveyed the tourist spot. "Mom said they arrived in a field. That it took them a while to hike out. This doesn't seem right at all."

We all stared at him in shock. Seems he had a bit more information than the rest of us.

"Did your parents tell you it was the Mystery Spot?" I eyed him suspiciously.

"No," Jada said. "Just a field and hiking downhill—my

mother hates nature, probably why she mentioned it..." He trailed off.

Looked like Jada was keeping secrets. But I couldn't blame him. He didn't know us. I found myself curious to learn more about him. Why did he wear sweater vests? Was he deaf or just hard of hearing? Why did his words sometimes sound muddled? What else did he know about our parents that he wasn't sharing? Could I trust him?

"Grace, that could lead to a field." Breeze grabbed my hand and pointed to a sign marked *Emma's Trail*. It was off from the tourist area and access wasn't restricted by tickets. That did look promising.

I looked at the others, waiting to see who would take charge. I was tired of it always being me.

"We don't know where that goes. Maybe we should get a map of the area?" Shim said, heading towards the ticket booth. My back stiffened, and I had an irrational urge to pop the Know-it-all in the face. Whichever way he went, I was going the opposite.

My mouth stiff, I smiled at Breeze. "I think you found some-thing. Let's check it out." I gave her hand a squeeze and pulled her along with me, ignoring the way she kept looking back for the others. I didn't know if the others followed. I assumed that at least Skylar did when she stopped looking back for them. I didn't know if I could trust any of the others—or if I wanted to. Breeze was okay; she didn't have a duplicitous bone in her body. Skylar was too "in" with the brothers, too eager to please them. He probably knew what Jaxon knew. Jada was new to the group and already keeping secrets. No, just Breeze and me. That would be enough to check out this path. Shim could find his own place to take a hike.

The start of the dirt trail was lined with mud puddles and flanked by a pair of huge redwoods and a yellow sign instructing us to stay on the path. Releasing Breeze's arm, I put my hands on my hips and leaned back. My eyes followed the thick, rust-colored bark up the tree, until my head was tipped back, and I could see the startling blue sky through thick branches. I heard a movement behind me and dragged my gaze away to watch the twins pass and then Jada. I jumped to follow him, not wanting to get stuck in the back with Shim.

The trailhead cut deeply into the side of a hill. We quickly left the sound of the crowds behind us, and with no one else visible ahead or behind, the silent forest started to speak. Birds called to each other, the voices varied and persistent. The groan of branches pushed by a wind that could reach us so far below. From somewhere a bubble of water over rocks. Our footsteps scraped the trail as we ducked under a low doorway cut into a tree that had fallen before we were born.

We had been hiking for twenty minutes when something pulled my attention to an old overgrown path.

"Hold up," I called to the twins.

I stepped over a pair of crossed branches. About ten yards in, the trail disappeared. I searched the surrounding area.

"The signs say to stay on the path." Breeze called, her voice strangled as if the forest would punish the violation.

"What's going on? We shouldn't split up." I heard Shim say.

"Pee break." Jaxon declared.

I ignored them and walked on a few more yards, lifting branches and pushing deeper. I was headed uphill, but water welled up around my sneakers and I slipped. The ground squished under me as I caught my balance, then lifted my foot to step cautiously on the cushioned underbrush, hoping I wouldn't sink into mud.

"Welcome to winter in California." I muttered to myself and dodged another shallow pool of rainwater. I know we needed the weeks of rain to replenish our water reserves in the hopes of staving off drought, but I hated it.

I pushed on through the thick beds of ferns and smaller seedlings. The saturated soil stained my shoes and I gave up on keeping them clean and just tried to keep my footing. Eventually, I caught the path again. Something felt right about this direction, or maybe just being alone, I could relax and just be, not focus on the pain or frustration, disappointment, and shame. I moved forward on instinct, not caring if anyone followed.

I walked another twenty minutes. The old trail faded in and out another half dozen times and I was considering turning back. *Would I even be able to find my way back to the others?* This was starting to feel like a mistake. Then the trees parted.

Leaving the thick grove of redwoods, I emerged from the shadows. A vivid blue sky shone over a field of green grass that was destined to turn golden. Piles of boulders and shrub brush with little white flowers dotted the field. The ground had soaked up as much of the night's rain as it could hold and left the rest pooling. I turned my face up to the sky and let the sun warm me, feeling it seep into my pores and revive me.

"All right, Grace!" Jaxon slapped me on the back. Startled, my foot slid, stopping at a rock. My fragile peace was shattered. Jaxon headed to the center of the rocky field. He seemed unconcerned with the mud and nimbly hopped over the puddles. Skylar followed, screeching as he stepped in a deep puddle. He pulled himself free with a squelching sound.

Shim passed. I narrowed my eyes and he frowned, avoiding my stare. Shoulders hunched, he followed Jaxon.

"This looks like what she described." Jada's eyes were wide, taking it all in.

"And now what?" Breeze asked, looking at me for instructions.

"Spread out and look around?" I suggested. "Maybe we should keep in sight of each other. See what you can find." I pulled out my phone to see what time it was and noticed I had zero signal.

"Like what?" Skylar called back.

"Plants?" Jada suggested.

"Weird alien footprints." Jaxon shouted, then feigned a bored yawn.

"Maybe we will find spiders," teased Skylar. Breeze pouted at him.

"Maybe a stone like the one in my necklace," I suggested, picking my way around one of the larger puddles by walking on the patches of thick grass.

Breeze nodded and switched to trailing Skylar as we all fanned out across the field.

I left them and searched on my own. My mind wandered, and I thought about everything but what we were supposed to be doing.

I don't know how long it was before Breeze called out, "I found something!"

She was at the opposite end of the field, driven off by the brothers. She alternated between waving while she jumped up and down and bending over to examine something. I was the closest and I stomped through the grass towards her, "What is it?"

"I don't know, its stuck," she called back.

When I reached Breeze, she crouched down and pointed to a large piece of metal sticking out of the ground. She reached for it and tugged, and the piece wiggled a little but refused to budge. She let go and I reached a hand around and pulled it. The metal moved a little. I looked around. Jada was closest, a few yards behind me. Jaxon and Shim were behind him, closing fast.

"Jaxon," I called, "bring your knife." I turned back to Breeze. "Maybe we can dig it out."

Jaxon sauntered towards us, Shim following. Skylar stayed behind.

"What you got?" Jaxon asked when he got closer.

I reached down and grabbed the metal, giving it a tug for effect, and gasped as it ripped into my finger.

"Ow!" Blood pulsed from the tip of my finger. Without thinking, I held it protectively to my chest.

The ground tilted.

My stomach plunged like a dip on a roller coaster. Before I could stop myself—remind myself he wasn't mine—I searched for Shim. He reached out, his eyes wide. "Grace!"

Our fingertips almost touched. I stared into his eyes and watched as his body jerked like a marionette on a string, away from me, upward then sideways. I slid, my toes dragging on the grass, before I smashed into Breeze. She grabbed me, her nails digging in as she lurched forward.

Then we both fell.

A strong wind whipped up and before we hit the ground, we were engulfed in the center of a tornado of air and light.

I was spinning like a top—blue sky, green field, brown earth—whirling past faster and faster until it was a blur of color. Nausea rose in my gut. I felt acid in my nose.

Someone yelled and I was hit from behind.

What is happening?

I tried to call out, but the words were ripped from my throat in a scream. I lost my breath as the wind yanked my feet off the ground and threw dirt in my face. I blinked to clear the dust. Dread spread through me as the light intensified. There was a rumbling sound, and I felt a tremble start in my gut and spread outward until I was violently shaking. I was aware of a shift in the space around me. A glow pulsed in the center. Growing until it became a defined opening. We orbited the glow circling it, growing closer and closer as it sucked everything into its hungry mouth.

The brothers fell first. I watched in horror as Shim disappeared, his hand reaching out to me.

Suddenly, I plunged over the edge into a tube of blinding light. Tumbling in a wave at a speed that defied physics. The grass and sky were gone. The glare was blinding, like staring into the sun. Tears streamed down my face as I struggled to keep my eyes open. Fire red and orange gave way to an intense white flare. My eyes burned and a shutter racked my body as I struggled to close them tight enough. I could feel my body flying apart, skin peeling back, joints separating, cells dissolving.

As suddenly as it started, everything stilled. The light vanished and in the darkness, I slammed into something solid.

5

DOWN THE RABBIT HOLE

THE WHIRLING LIGHT and heat stopped as abruptly as it had started. Dirt walls disappeared into total darkness. I landed in a crumpled heap on a hard surface. Sounds were muted and dull. My ears popped, and I heard ragged, gasping breaths. Someone was close. The breath sped up. It was me.

I flung out an arm and struck something hard. A sharp pain radiated from my hand, and I thought the skin on my knuckles split, but I couldn't see. It was so dark I felt untethered, as if nothing connected me to my fingers except that throbbing pain, and I clung to it. Not a sliver of light came through. Blinking hard didn't clear my vision.

I screamed, but no sound came out. I had no air, my chest trapped, the ribs unable to expand. My body struggled to survive while my mind raced to make sense of it all. Images filtered through my mind like shards of glass falling, but they made no sense. Nothing did.

What. Just. Happened?

One minute I was standing in a field on a bright sunny day. The next, I'm hurtling through—what was that, a tunnel? Some underground slide?

I drew in a shallow breath, my toes curled as my body trembled from the effort. I could feel my toes. That was good. Thoughts were slipping like fish through my hands as I tried to focus.

Had I hit my head?

Honestly, I've felt better.

My head spun in the darkness as if churning in a wave until I didn't know which way was up. A fat tear trickled down my face. Down was that direction. I tried pushing up on my arms. My body was so heavy. Limbs struggled to respond before giving out. I smashed face down. As I lay there, other senses kicked in. My nose wrinkled and my eyes watered at the aroma of moist dirt and rotten eggs. I tried my arms again, curling my fingers into warm earth and hard stone as I pushed up.

The heaviness on my back moved.

I screamed and scrambled to escape from under the weight. My muscles contracted and I curled into a small ball against the threat.

Was that a growl?

My mind flashed through all the things that growl and images of mountain lions clawing and bears tearing at me. *I'm going to die* flashed through my mind and I had just enough energy to fight the idea.

A distinctly human moan came from the lump on my back. I reached back cautiously, waiting for the bite, when my fingers encountered smooth, warm skin and cloth.

Not animal! I wasn't alone here! Wherever here was. A sense of relief washed over me.

My fingers scrunch into hair and skitter across cheekbones and familiar lips.

No. It couldn't be the one person I never wanted to see again.

"Shim?" My voice came out in a raw croak. I poked something squishy.

"Ow! Ear!" At the sound of Shim's scratchy voice, my fingers clenched in his hair, and he hissed.

Other noises registered. Someone was sick, my stomach flipped, and I rapidly swallowed, struggling through shallow breaths to avoid the same fate. Something was being hit, no, kicked.

"What happened? Where are we? Grace? Where is Jaxon?" It was the most panicked I'd ever heard Shim.

"NO!" The scream came from farther away.

Closer still, I heard soft sobs.

The distant voice screamed again.

"Shim. Get off me!" I bucked as my hand skittered down his arm. His biceps bulged and what I thought was up became down as he lifted, and I fell off him. In the darkness, his hand searched blindly across my body. He ignored my hand, slapping at him, and when he found my arm, he pulled me to sit. My shattered brain registered a moment of relief. I knew which way was up now. Then panic took over again.

"What happened?" Shim repeated, his voice urgent, his fingers dug into my arm.

"Stop it!" I snapped back in the direction of his voice. I wrenched my arm from his grip and immediately regretted it. My body ached and my skin burned. I ran my fingers up my arm, expecting blisters. There were none, but the skin was scraped raw in places. I felt liquid seep through the seat of my pants and for one horrifying moment, I thought I had peed myself. Then I realized my leg was folded under me, and I was sitting on my damp sneaker. *Thank the Stars!*

I was ridiculous for worrying about wet pants when there was an excellent chance Shim and I would die in the next few minutes.

A light.

A glorious circle of pale light appeared. In the glowing trail, I could see Breeze and Jada-shaped shadows.

I wasn't alone.

The light faltered and fell. A loud curse. The sound of scuffling "What the *Stars* is going on?" The light angled up and lit Jaxon's face with a ghostly illumination.

"Skylar, where are you?" At the sound of Breeze's distraught cry, Jaxon spun the light around. Breeze was limping as she felt her way along a rough, reddish-brown wall of rock.

Was this a sinkhole? No, a sinkhole would have soft sides and an opening above. Maybe a cave?

Breeze was clutching a rock wall covered in chisel marks. A low ceiling of the same surface was right above her head. As her cries turned to sobs, Jaxon jumped over a large boulder to get to her. He took the light with him.

I didn't like the returning darkness. I reached for my phone in my bag. Then I remembered I'd left my bag in Van Ekman, thinking I wouldn't need it for a short hike.

Would I ever learn?

Shim was making shuffling sounds behind me, and I heard the scrape of skin on fabric and then a glow from his ever-present penlight.

"Thank the Stars," I blurted out. As mad as I had been with him, I would curl up in his lap if I could get closer to that light.

"Shim, did we fall down a sinkhole?" I couldn't stop the habit of turning to him for answers.

"Oh, um—" Shim took several shaking breaths before responding, "I—I don't think so. That passage was too long to be a sinkhole or—."

"Or, what? Is it a cave?" I asked, the sting from my wounds making me sound demanding.

"I don't know." He pushed away from me. "I've never seen

anything like that before. The lights, the heat—No. NO! This is crazy, it can't be—"

"What?" I demanded.

"I think, no—it can't be, well, maybe—" Shim argued with himself. With a shaky whisper, he turned to me, "I think it was a wormhole."

"Get out!" That's the most ridiculous thing I'd ever heard.

"I know! It's impossible, but I don't know how else to explain it."

My mind raced. I'd never heard of anything like that, except in Sci-fi shows. "I didn't know we had those on Earth."

"We don't."

Someone moaned on my other side.

Shim leaned over me, the glow from his light spreading until I saw Jada struggling to sit up about ten yards away.

Jada list to the side and fell over. I left Shim to his crisis-of-science and crawled on hands and knees to help Jada. My body trembled at the effort to move.

Jada was covered in dust and dirt and had a trickle of blood down the side of his head. He was next to a large boulder and was struggling to sit up. I held out my arm and as he pulled himself up, I got a better look at the side of his head. "You are bleeding."

Jada blinked at me. He looked dazed, "What happened?"

"Can you stand?" I asked, brushing off some of the dirt on his clothes while checking for further injuries.

He ignored my question, then responded, "Help me up."

Could I stand myself? I sat back on my heels, the muscles in my thighs screaming. I planted my hands and pushed up my hips, my head swam and the ache between my eyes intensified. But after leveling myself for a few steady seconds, I ignored the ache and pushed to my full height, wishing I could roll to the side and take a nap. Instead, I turned to Jada.

Climbing his hands up my arm he stood, wobbling. His balance worse than mine. I caught him as he started to keel over.

"Maybe you should stay down. You have blood on the side of your face." The wound didn't look deep.

Jada ignored me and cupped his hands over his ears.

"Grace!" Jaxon called out, his tone urgent.

I turned towards the sound and immediately regretted the action as my head spun. I took a breath and motioned for Jada to follow me. Shim was standing now, and he lent Jada a shoulder as the three of us picked our way through the rocks.

Jaxon was crouched next to a shaking Breeze, his arm around her.

"Skylar, Skylar, Skylar," Breeze chanted quietly.

"Help her!" Jaxon demanded when he saw us. His face was desperate, his loud voice setting off another set of wails from Breeze.

"Let me see, is she hurt?" I asked as Jaxon pulled her tighter into his arms. Shielding her from us.

"Jaxon, let her go so we can see if she is hurt." I pulled on his arm, and he growled at me before relaxing his grip.

"Skylar." Breeze let out a cry and then turned into Jaxon's arms and buried her face in his shoulder.

Jaxon's eyes widened and he froze for the briefest moment before tugging her closer. His phone dropped to the ground, leaving us in darkness.

Shim was pointing his penlight in a slow circle around the room. My eyes followed the beam of light around. Stone walls, a low rock ceiling with huge chunks missing, piles of rocks and uprooted grass in the center. The space wasn't large. Skylar wasn't with us. It was just the five of us here. Wherever here was.

"Shim, light." A note of hysteria in my voice. I didn't have a fear of the dark. But there was something so oppressive about this space. I was choking on the dark space.

Shim took his time shining his light in our direction. I ignored the need to snap at him and instead crouched beside Breeze, my muscles hating me.

I checked her over for wounds. She didn't seem to be bleeding anywhere, and I didn't see any lumps or bruising, though it was early for that.

"Breeze, he isn't here." I rubbed her arm. She shook her head and faced away from me. "Maybe that's a good thing. Maybe he is up on the surface still and can call for help." I hoped I was right. I hoped rescuers would break through the stone above our heads and pull us safely back to the sunny field in Happy Valley.

Breeze buried her face deeper in Jaxon's shoulder. I stood, wobbled, and turned to face Jada and Shim. We clustered around the light like moths.

"Up?" Shim challenged. His light was unsteady, flickering with motion and I realized his hand was shaking. I squashed the urge to commiserate with him. I had to work with him, but I didn't have to care.

"I don't know. Don't you think we—fell down something to get here?" I stuttered through expressing the idea and then, for emphasis, pointed to the lumps of grass and rocks scattered around us.

"It was a wormhole." Shim said, his voice a whisper as if he was sharing national secrets.

Jada made a motion with his hands and caught our attention.

"Passage." His accented voice was rougher than usual. "We fell through the passage. It was just like my mother described."

"What passage?" A chill shivered through me.

"The passage that brought them to Earth," Jada said.

I gasped. My body went numb as my mind rejected what I was hearing.

"That could be it." Shim was nodding.

"No, no it can't be it." I insisted.

"No, really, it makes sense. The light, the heat, the feeling of falling while traveling a long distance. It had to have been a wormhole that brought them to Earth." Shim insisted and launched into a detailed description of how wormholes worked.

"No, it can't," I said, my voice cracking and louder than I had planned. "It can't have been a wormhole that brought them to Earth. Because if we fell through the same wormhole, then we aren't on Earth anymore!"

6

INTO THE DARK

"IS that what you are saying? That we aren't on Earth anymore?" My words echoed through the dark room.

Shim blinked at me, dawning realization expanding on his face in the penlight.

Jaxon cursed.

"What do you mean we aren't on Earth?" Breeze hiccupped.

"It was just the way my mother described it." Jada said. Closing his eyes, he dug a finger into his temple.

When Jada opened his eyes again, I asked, "Are you saying that after our parents spent decades trying to get home, we accidentally activated the—what did you call it?"

"The passage," Shim whispered.

"—The passage. Are you saying we activated the passage and ended up where they came from?" My jaw dropped open.

"Not possible," Jaxon said. Tone flat.

"How would that even work?" I asked Jada.

Jaxon's gaze jumped back and forth between our faces.

"There is science behind it, but it doesn't matter

now. *Now* we are trapped underground, in a mine, on an alien planet." Jada sat down hard.

"Nadun is a moon, not a planet," Shim corrected.

"Who the hell cares!" Jaxon yelled. Breeze whimpered and flinched, and Jaxon lowered his voice to spit at his brother. "You don't believe this crap, do you?"

I crouched down as my vision wavered. Everyone was looking at me, and I took a minute to collect myself and try not to pass out.

Breeze started crying again, or maybe she had never stopped. Her face was a mess of dirt-stained tear trails as she leaned against Jaxon.

We are going to die.

Once the thought took hold, it pounded like a pulse between my ears as my mind raced through all the ways we could die. None of them are painless.

Something occurred to me. "Who has a phone?"

"Why?"

"Check if you have a signal, then turn it off." If Jada was right about where we were, then this was a useless waste of batteries, but the sliver of hope I was holding on to wanted the phones to light up with a signal so we could dial 911.

"Nothing," Jada confirmed. He stared at the picture on the screen for a minute and then powered off.

Breeze drew in a shaky breath and pulled out her phone. Her breath caught in excitement as the phone searched for service and then gave an error message. She silently powered it down and slid it back in her pocket.

"Why should I turn my phone off?" Jaxon challenged. "You could be wrong, and we could get service somewhere else." Agitated, he shined the light in my face.

It felt like a blade of glass piercing my brain, and I winced, scrunching my eyes. "We are obviously underground—somewhere. Until we know where we shouldn't waste our batteries, we may need every second of light to get to the surface."

"Oh, my Heavens! Oh, my Heavens!" Breeze wailed.

Jaxon shot me an ugly glare.

"It's just a precaution. I'm sure we won't need it."

"I've got this, too." Shim held up his penlight.

"Hold on." Jaxon gently extracted himself from Breeze and jumped up. He grabbed the back of Shim's bag and spun him around.

"Watch it," Shim said as his brother shoved him.

Jaxon pulled something out of the bag, and a second later, a glow filled the circle where we stood. Duchess was in the center, with her eyes glowing a demonic red.

"I just charged her up. We should get at least four hours from her. I'm sure we won't need more than that."

Shim snorted. "Jaxon, that's a great idea."

"It happens," his brother said with a roll of his eyes.

Shim perked up. "And I can test her new wheels. I wanted to use NASA's Rocker-bogie mobility System, but she didn't have the right suspension, so I used the same wheels as the rover—"

"Yeah, yeah, yeah, it's amazing, it's incredible. Now can we move before we starve to death? I'd like to get out of here and back home before Mom has something else to go nuclear about." Jaxon was all bravado, but his voice trembled.

"Why are we going anywhere? We should wait here to be rescued." A puzzled look broke through the terror on Breeze's face and she sniffled.

Was she right? Was I panicking for no reason?

"You can't think of staying here." Jada looked around the chamber, shock apparent on his face.

"I'm not leaving." Breeze stuck out her lip.

"I'm not staying," Jada responded with a tilt of his head.

"We're not splitting up." I shook my head at both of them.

"Maybe we should look around. See if we can find anything," Shim suggested.

"Yeah, let's do that. Jaxon take Duchess. You, Breeze, and I will check this direction." I motioned off into the darkness on my left. "Shim, you and Jada go the other way." It seemed a good way to separate from Shim and keep the stay-go factions apart. "Keep in view of each other's light and shout if you find something."

Breeze leaned heavily on my arm as we shuffled slowly down the tunnel. I kept glancing back, afraid Shim and Jada would disappear. Breeze pulled my sleeve. "Grace, do you think Skylar is okay? I can feel him here." She pounded on her chest. "He will find me. He will get help and dig down to us and rescue us. I know it." Breeze straightened as her idea took root.

I wasn't so sure.

I glanced around at the reddish soil and grey rock. I suppose the rocks could be blocking our phone signal, but we had been in a field on a bright sunny day. There was no shaft of light in the sky. No big hole open to the surface or cave in the rocks around us.

"Grace?"

"What?" My impatient response bounced off the walls and echoed ahead of us.

"What are we looking for?" Breeze asked. She made a muffled squeak as Jaxon led Duchess around a crop of rocks, and we were left in the dark.

"I don't know exactly. Maybe that piece of metal from the field. Or the rock it was stuck in. Or something showing a way up." I trailed off. I really didn't know. Was that piece of metal important? Was that what made a difference in activating the passage?

"Why bother? Skylar is going to find us." A look of peace

settled over her face that I found more disturbing than the crying.

"Duchess, come." The little mechanical dog followed Jaxon's voice, its new wheels smoothly crawling over anything in its path.

Breeze switched over to Jaxon, clinging to his arm as the three of us shuffled several yards to the end of the large, round chamber.

In the red glow of light, I could make out a few clumps of grass, a dirt floor, and walls of rock. There was nothing else. We walked for several minutes, searching for something different, when suddenly there was a void in the wall, a dark opening the size of a double door. It was a tunnel leading out of the chamber.

Taking a breath, I followed the beam of light. The tunnel had a low ceiling, just a foot above our heads, and was barely wider than my outstretched arms.

"Here is something," Shim called out from the opposite side of the chamber. "It's a wide tunnel, about twenty feet across, with a ceiling as tall as the one we are in."

"We found one, too, but it's much smaller," I called back, sharing the details of our tunnel.

Jaxon cursed loudly, the sound echoing off the chamber walls. "How are we supposed to know which way to go?"

"We should go with the large tunnel. It must lead to something," Shim decided. I frowned. That logic made sense, but I hated agreeing with him.

"We are staying here." Breeze stomped her foot. "Help will be here soon."

Stars, I wish she was right. I wanted to believe it. And Breeze may not be able to make decisions without her twin, but she had her moments of insightfulness. What if this was one of them? I thought about the rock cavern we were in and the dark tunnels stretching from each side. If we left, it might take help longer to find us. If we stayed and help didn't come—I shuddered.

Jaxon scowled at Breeze, red flushing his pale, freckled skin. "Breeze, that's a rock ceiling above us and there isn't enough debris for this to be a sinkhole. Where is help supposed to come from?" He held her arm gently but firmly.

Breeze turned her head and pulled her arm away from Jaxon. She moved to my side, wrapping herself around my arm.

We returned to the others, meeting back in the center where we had arrived. When we got under Shim's light again, Breeze quickly transferred herself like a moth to his arm.

"We should go down the tunnel we found. It is wider and has the best chance of leading somewhere populated," Shim immediately declared.

Jada was shaking his head. His gaze focused up. When Shim tapped him for backup, he was startled, as if he had just realized we were talking.

"Populated?" Jaxon seized on the word. He moved into Shim's space. "Just who do you think lives underground? Squirrels? Rabbits? Are we looking for Mole people? Do you think they have a cell phone tower? For *Heaven's* sake, it's a freak'n cave." He pushed his brother back, peeling Breeze's hand off Shim's arm and wrapping it around his own.

"Don't fight," I said in a whisper. I felt exhausted and if it wasn't for the dark scaring me spit-less, I would curl up in a corner and take a nap until this nightmare was over.

"We are not on Earth," Jada said. He was rubbing his ear as he spoke.

"What do you—" Jaxon's hotheaded response was cut off as Jada continued.

"It would be suicide to stay here. There are thousands, probably hundreds of thousands of miles of underground tunnels.

Some have been closed for centuries. Our bones would never be discovered."

A chill wracked through me. *Stars, he was morbid.*

Despite the uncomfortable warmth of the room, I shivered and rubbed my arms. We had to leave. We had to find help before our batteries ran out, and we were trapped underground in the dark.

"Are you trying to scare—" Jaxon started to say when Jada interrupted him again.

"We must make it to one of the underground towns." We all paused, wondering if Jada had finished. I took the time to contemplate my potentially short-lived mortality.

"And what if you are wrong?" Jaxon demanded.

"What if I'm right?" Jada retorted.

The words floated between us, seeming to take all the air out of the space. I deflated like an old balloon, sinking into every ache in my body and soul. I didn't want to believe him, but we couldn't risk it. Help wasn't coming.

Jada's hands were wrapped around his head, massaging his face around his ear.

"Jada, is your head hurting? Let me look at your wound." His eyes were closed, and he ignored me until I touched his arm, and his eyes flew open.

"Jada?"

He took an unsteady breath, and then his face dropped. "I hit my head, and it damaged my hearing aid. It's given me an awful headache, but the dizziness is worse. And—" he paused as if this pained him the most to admit, "—I can't hear anything but static."

I looked him in the eyes. "Will you let me take a look? Can you understand me?"

He nodded. "I'm usually very good at reading lips, but with

the darkness and the headache, I'm having trouble. I would appreciate your help."

While Shim and I examined Jada, Breeze laid out her case on why we should just stay put and wait for help. It didn't make a lot of sense and as she spoke, her voice got softer and more tentative.

"Jada." I put my hand on his shoulder, and he looked up at me. "The cut isn't bad, but a lump is forming. I think you hit something pretty hard. Do you think you will be able to walk?"

Jada shrugged his shoulders, then winced. "What choice do I have?"

A cold fist of worry churned in my stomach. If Jada couldn't move on his own power, we were going to be in even worse trouble.

Before we had even finished with Jada, Shim started to lobby to follow the larger tunnel.

"I've got an idea," I said. I pulled Shim's penlight from his hand and, crouching down, turned it on and laid it on a bare stretch of floor. The round tube sat there, then slowly rolled across the rough ground towards Shim's tunnel, the light flashing across the walls as it did. "That way is down. And our tunnel is up."

Shim blew out a tense breath.

"Up it is." I decided. "Shim, take point?" I tried to make it into a question and not a command.

"Fine." Shim frowned. He swept his pen light off the floor and pocketed it. "Duchess, come."

As we started to exit the chamber following the red glow, Breeze was lagging. "Wait."

"Breeze, we can't stay—" I protested. I was on my last scrap of patience.

"You're wrong, but," she looked around, "I don't want to stay here on my own, so—" She took off one of the dozens of brightly colored friendship bracelets on her wrist, picked up a rock, and wrapped it with the bracelet. "Breadcrumbs, so Skylar can find us," she explained.

Very clever.

"You gonna do that the whole way?" Jaxon mocked. "How will you know where we started if we do come back this way?"

She shook her arm in front of his face. "Order of the rainbow." Her voice was shaky, but she seemed to rally around her new mission of marking the trail. She crouched down and placed the rock with the thin red cord near the tunnel entrance.

Fear smothered me as we left the chamber and I had to force myself to put one foot down and then the next. In there, we were the closest to where we had come from, even if we didn't know how to get back. Every step felt like it was taking us further and further away from our goal of getting home. But until we knew how we got here and where we were, that chamber provided nothing but false security.

Gulping hard, I hurried to follow the others and the red glow down the tunnel, the darkness swallowing the path behind me.

MUCH LATER, the path split and the tunnel broke off in two directions. A metal plate was mounted at the mouth of one tunnel. It was a sign!

We all got excited until we realized the text had long ago peeled up and cracked, making it unreadable.

"What's our plan?" I asked under my breath. Shim glared at me.

"You sent us down this path. What's your plan?"

Usually, he didn't sulk, but nothing about today was usual.

What do you have in your bag?" I asked.

"Not much." He shook his head. "I got lazy and didn't even think about packing supplies. I just have the first aid kit, a couple of bottles of water, a few power bars." Shim passed a pair of power bars and a bottle of water to Breeze, asking her to split them up.

"What do you think?" Shim asked.

"Do you think that is an E?" I asked, smoothing my finger down the residue from the letters on the sign. The plate was more rust than metal, and Shim raised his brow at my wishful thinking.

I abandoned the sign and sank to the ground. *Thank Stars, we at least found some proof of life.* I shuddered. I'd never feared the dark or small spaces, but my skin was prickling, and in the darkness, every sense had heightened to a painful level since we arrived. "I can't believe how long this tunnel went with no open branches until here. I was starting to wonder if it was a cave."

Shim humphed in agreement and reached for me, then stopped himself. "You doing okay?"

I nodded, irritated that he would ask. What was I going to say? I felt dizzy. I was sick from the heat, exhausted, and more than a little freaked out. And I know it was petty of me, but I was still angry at Shim and really didn't want him around me being all charming and caring and supportive.

"What do you want to do?" Shim asked.

I pushed aside my initial snide response and thought for a second. "Let's take a long break, then do a roll test again. We should keep heading up." I hoped the test would direct us down the tunnel with the sign. I liked the comfort of feeling we were following signs of civilization. But heading up felt like the right choice, and the one thing I had learned over the last year was to trust my gut.

"Okay," Shim agreed quickly, but something else troubled him.

"What is it?" I asked, trusting that he would notice things I might miss.

"Have you noticed it seems to be getting hotter?"

I nodded. "I thought caves were supposed to be cool?" I pulled my sweaty shirt off my skin, fluttering the fabric.

"I think it's the rock. The walls feel warm. They are probably heating the tunnel."

"What do you think it means?" I asked.

He shrugged. Shim's body language should have its own dictionary. He could convey more information with a squeeze of his shoulders, raised brow, and the tilt of his head than most people could with a whole speech. And I hated that I spoke that language.

"Shim, how long is your penlight going to work?"

Shim drew in a breath. "It's a new LED, so eight hours, twelve at the most." According to him, we had been going for about four hours, and Duchess would be running low on juice soon.

"So, eight to twelve hours with the penlight. Then we have the phones. The lights won't be as strong, but we have four, and if they were at least half charged, we should get 4 hours out of each. So, about 28 hours of light?"

Shim nodded, his face grim. "If we ration, our water will last about as long. It isn't much. But at least we know where we stand."

"Hopefully, we will be on the surface soon, and we won't need to use up all our resources."

Hopefully.

I heard that word echo around in my head, reverberating like our voices bouncing off the solid rock walls of this tunnel. Hope is all we had

7

THE OFFICE

WE RAN the penlight test again. It rolled away from the tunnel with the sign. Knowing that way was up, so we took that path. But I was already wondering if I'd made a mistake. The walls were rough and covered in smaller tick marks, maybe from pick-axes. Narrow, my shoulders brushed the rough surface, sending shivers down my spine. Shim and Duchess took a tight corner, and for a few seconds, the light disappeared again. The darkness rushed in, and every nerve in my body went on hyperalert.

A bead of sweat rolled down my spine, and my heart pounded as alarm bells went off in my head. "You okay, Grace?"

I jumped. It was Jada's voice. He tugged on my sleeve and wrapped an arm around my waist, and I felt anchored.

"Thanks."

The red glow filled the space, and Shim and Duchess came back around the corner.

"What's the hold-up?" Shim scowled at Jada, pointedly staring at the arm.

"Nothing." I automatically replied.

"Not nothing. You're going too fast." Jada's voice was harsh. He gave my waist a gentle squeeze before letting go.

"Yeh, sorry." Shim glared at Jada.

"Stars, Shim, are you trying to lose us?" Jaxon slugged his brother's arm.

Shim winced.

Duchess's red glow illuminated the surroundings and reflected off something sparkly down a black hole. In some places, the walls were bursting with veins of minerals. Shim would turn on the penlight, and the whole tunnel would glitter. Jaxon could name a few of them from his study of the Keystones, but most of the rocks were a mystery.

We started moving again. More side tunnels, sometimes chutes would protrude from the ceiling, from higher levels, but they were always clogged with rocks.

Duchess was moving slower and slower, and exhausted as I was, I didn't mind until the red light suddenly faded.

My heart raced in the darkness.

A scream.

"No—"

"Hey! What did you do?" That last was shouted in my ear as I was shoved from behind. I felt utterly lost in the dark space despite knowing what was around me seconds before. My head spun, and I forgot which way was up. Panic flushed through me.

Then Shim's penlight flicked on.

I couldn't control my groan of relief from slipping out.

The faces clustered around the light were grim. As Jaxon carefully tucked Duchess back into the backpack, we had a minute to realize our future if we didn't find help soon, and it settled like a cloud over us.

After that, no one was willing to stop for long. We paused at several more branching tunnels, following the same logic each time and always taking the one that headed uphill.

I waited for Breeze as she wrapped a light blue cord around a rock. My eye followed the light growing more distant.

Shim shouted.

We hurried to catch up with Shim, but he had run ahead and disappeared behind a stack of rocks, leaving us in the pitch-black tunnel.

"Again? What the hell, man!" Jaxon yelled. I don't think I would ever grow used to the adrenal punch that coursed through me every time the light snuffed out. My hands trembled as I searched my pockets for a phone I knew wasn't there. An involuntary cry was on my lips when Shim suddenly returned.

"Sorry, I got excited and forgot I was the only one with a light."

"I would like to take a turn with the light." Jada's tone was still prep-school proper, but his voice was weak, cheeks flushed. He leaned heavily on the wall and sweat beaded on his dark skin.

"Yeah, sure, but you have to check this out." Shim was excited. The rest of us less so as we trudged after him.

Shim led us to a pile of rocks tucked in an alcove on the side of the tunnel. They were irregular-shaped and the same color as the rock walls but stacked in a pattern that formed a wall about as tall and wide as a shipping container. And placed in the center was an old, rusted metal door listing sideways.

"Oh, my Stars!" Jada exclaimed.

The door had a rusted lock on it. Which I thought was a sign that we shouldn't disturb it. Shim had other ideas and picked up a large stone, aiming it at the lock.

"What are you doing!" I grabbed at his arm. "What if someone is in there?"

"Then I'll ask them how to get home!" Shim extracted his hand from my loose grip.

"Ain't likely to be anything in this pile of rubble," Jaxon

pronounced as he slammed the lock with a rock. The aged link cracked and fell to the ground.

Shim peeled open the door and disappeared inside.

"Wait—" the words of caution slipped from my lips as Shim disappeared inside.

"No, no, no." Breeze's mantra was unnerving in the void.

Shim reappeared and motioned. "Come on."

Fear neutralized any curiosity I might have. But my desire to follow the light overrode even fear.

"Woah, what is all this stuff?" Breeze's response piqued my hope, and I forced myself to the door's threshold.

Jada pushed in behind me, propelling me into the room. The inside was a cross between an old, abandoned hunting shack and an office. Torn pieces of fabric hung on each wall. There was a table, a couple of rickety chairs, and stacks of boxes made from some type of hard plastic. The boxes were small enough to fit down the tunnels we had been traveling through. The whole space was about the size of an airstream trailer, with three stacked rock walls, the back wall chiseled out of solid rock, and a rusted metal roof, like the door. And it was all covered in a thick layer of rock dust that matched the walls.

"Well, I guess no one is here." As far as signs of life went, I wasn't impressed.

"Doesn't look like anyone has been here for a long time." Shim was trying to dig in a box one-handed while holding his penlight out in the open for the rest of us to see by.

"Is there a phone?" Breeze asked. She released Jaxon's hand so he could sort through boxes with both.

"Doubt it. This stuff is seriously ancient, like the 1950s, well, not our 1950s, but really old. It looks like it's been abandoned for years."

Jada was inspecting a small grey box, tapping the top, when

suddenly, a glow of warm light filled the room. Shocked expressions turned into a cheer.

"Thank you, Edison," I said, applauding, and Jada took a little bow.

"Well, probably not Edison...." Shim was all over the discovery, tilting the box on every side to examine it and turning it on and off, with an outraged scream from the group each time, until I finally demanded he stop.

Investigating the shack was much more manageable with the light. Jada was examining the fabric walls when a section fell on Jaxon, covering him with dust.

Jaxon cursed, angry. He grabbed the cloth and yanked it. There was a loud rip and pop, and the whole top of the wall came crashing down, including some rock. I crouched quickly and put my arms over my head for protection.

When the dust settled, a pile of debris covered the side of the room.

"Anyone hurt?" I called out. Everyone responded with grumbled negatives.

The fabric hadn't covered a wall but a stack of storage shelves covered with cans and bottles.

"Look at this," Jaxon pulled one of the bottles off the shelf. "What does it say?" The printed text looked like scratches and hash marks.

Shim pulled it out of Jaxon's hands and studied the label intently. "Grace, does this look like the marks that were on the back of Arie's watch?"

This summer, we found an unusual watch owned by the twin's father, Arie, who Shim also learned was his father. The timepiece had a completely unique system of measuring time. The specialist we took it to said it didn't measure time like a standard clock; it wasn't even based on a 24-hour clock. On the back, Arie had engraved the words' finding home' in English and a line of what we thought at the time were decorative hash marks. We later learned it was a language from his home world.

"Shim—Stars." I looked closer at the bottle, and the nagging fear I'd had since we had fallen down this rabbit hole opened to a chasm of dread. The patterns on the label looked just like the marks on the watch.

We definitely aren't in California anymore. Somehow, someway, we had been transported to our parent's home world.

I looked closer at the label. "What did Arie say when you gave him back the watch?" Shim tensed and shook his head, eyes down.

"You did return it, didn't you?"

"Kindle was right. He didn't want anything to do with me. I kept thinking he would contact me and I could give it back then. But he never did."

"Oh, Shim—"

"Hey, there's more of those bottles. Do you think it's drinkable? I'm dying here!" Jaxon licked his lips as he eyed one of the bottles, oblivious to our discussion.

"Leave it alone." Breeze pulled the bottle from Jaxon's hand.

He grabbed it back. And they started to argue about the safety of doing a taste test.

Jaxon won by prying off the top of the bottle and, after a quick sniff at the contents, took a big gulp, ignoring our startled gasps to stop.

"Oh, my *Stars*," he moaned, clenching his hand around his throat as he started to sputter and then convulse. Breeze screamed and pulled him to her, sinking with him to the floor.

"Jaxon, are you okay?" she held his face in both hands, then grabbed our last water. She was about to pour it down his throat when he started laughing.

"You ass," Breeze shoved him off her lap.

Jaxon rolled on the floor, snickering. "It's...fine... It's a little weird, not exactly water." He took another swig from the bottle and swished it back and forth in his mouth. "It is a little thicker and slightly metallic, but all together, a good vintage." He went to drink more, and Shim stopped him.

"Let that sit for a while and tell me how you feel in twenty minutes. You idiot, what were you thinking?"

Jaxon turned the bottle around and showed us the back. "I was thinking anything that had a picture of a kid drinking and a sealed lid was probably safe." Sure enough, the back of the bottle had a picture of a toddler enjoying the beverage. "And I was thinking that someone is going to have to try it because we don't have any water left, and we obviously aren't going to find help here, so.... why not me? Was I wrong?"

Jaxon's face was scrunched tight in a scowl as his brother gave a tight headshake.

"You are welcome." Jaxon put the cap back on the bottle and joined Breeze in going through the rest of the shelves.

We split like pool balls. Breeze and Jaxon pored through the shelves of bottles and metal tins of maybe-crackers and food we couldn't identify that had a utensil stuck on top that looked like a chopstick and a spoon.

"Oh yeh." I pulled the lid of one of the big plastic boxes on the floor. "We've got blankets."

"Which would be much more exciting if it wasn't 100 degrees," Shim called over his shoulder. I shrugged. They were in better shape than the fabric that draped the walls.

"Hey, look at this." Coughing at the cloud of dust he stirred up, Shim pulled down the blankets curtaining the other side of the room and revealed a whole wall of buttons, nobs, and blank monitors.

"Sure, that's more exciting than blankets." I rolled my eyes at Shim.

Jada and Jaxon tried pressing every button, and nothing turned on. There was no power in our shack.

"I was hoping we would find something to recharge Duchess with." Jaxon frowned.

"Look, more lights." Breeze held up another box full of slimmer versions of the baseball-sized box light Jada had found. Jada picked one up, blew off the dust, and then turned it on the same as he had the larger lamp. He then clipped it to his shirt. The warm glow in the room doubled. He switched it back off.

"Excellent," Jada said. Breeze beamed a smile at him, which he tentatively returned.

"What is all this?" Jaxon pulled a heavy-looking box off the bottom shelf full. It was full of metal signs. He flipped through them. The signs had icons warning varying levels of danger along with more hash marks. "Oh, man." Jaxon hit one side of the box, and it threatened to topple the shelf.

"Watch it." Shim snapped at Jaxon.

"It's that language again, isn't it?"

Jada jumped back from the wobbling shelf. "It's probably Teran, though it might be a dialect of Nadun."

"What do you mean?" Breeze demanded.

"Well, I'm assuming they would have signs in the main language, Teran, but since we are on Nadun, they may have used a local dialect," Jada explained, his tone patient like he was explaining again that birds fly and fish swim.

"Are you sure we aren't on Earth?" Breeze's voice trembled and she turned wide, watery eyes to Jaxon. "Tell me it isn't true."

Jaxon looked like he would rather do anything other than answer that question. His face scrunched up like he had eaten something nasty, and he turned away.

"Of course, it's true. Where did you think all this stuff came from? It's not anything you would find on Earth." Jada tilted his head and studied her in disbelief.

"Don't scare her!" Jaxon shouted. Walking over, he shoved Jada up against the wall of consuls.

"Jaxon, let him go. He is right. This is Nadun. We are on our mother's home world," Shim said.

Breeze whined as she crouched down, hugging her legs. Her response seemed to enrage Jaxon more.

"No! NO!" Jaxon grabbed the corner of the table, flipping it up and smashing it against the wall, the old wood shredded like matchsticks. The main light and the box of portable lamps sitting on the table flew up in the air, and the metal signs scattered. We all watched the arc of light spinning before it crashed on the floor and thankfully stayed lit. The smaller portable lamps followed a similar path, the box splitting and the lamps flying against the far wall.

Breeze screamed and covered her head.

Jaxon stilled. He looked stricken as he saw Breeze cowering on the floor.

Jaxon cursed, then picked up one of the lamps and stormed out of the room.

I rushed to check on Jada, worried that he had gotten hurt when Jaxon pushed him against the wall. He shrunk back when I got near. Guilt washed through me. I held up my hands, palms out, reaching to help him. He let me pull him up.

"I'm so sorry," Shim muttered, refusing to look at Jada. "He gets really, uh, committed to ideas and isn't good at disappointment."

"Should we go after him?" Jada asked, a little uncertain.

"Maybe I should. It's my fault he got mad." Breeze whispered.

"It's not your fault," Shim insisted. "Don't ever think it is. Jaxon's got to get a handle on his temper, and that's on him. Just leave him. He'll be back—probably regretting the last few minutes when he's calmed down. Shim turned suspicious eyes to Jada. "I'm more interested in hearing what you know about Nadun."

Jada's eyes widened. I could see his mind spinning. I'd gotten so used to our parent's evading answers; was he going to tell us the truth? Could we trust him? I had to remind myself we had just met Jada.

"It's complicated," Jada said.

He was stalling. If he thought he could wait out Shim, he was in for a lesson. I might be mad at Shim right now, but he was one of the most patient people I had ever met. Even if he sometimes made me feel like a mouse being watched by a cat.

Jada shifted nervously. Yes, he could feel the pressure.

"We appear to be trapped *in* an alien world with no idea about how to get home. I'm sure we can take the time to listen to your explanation." Shim said in a deadpan tone.

Jada shifted from one foot to the other. He ran long brown fingers through his hair, mussing it further and leaving trails of white dust. "I don't know what I can tell you."

Shim eyed him incredulously. "You're kidding, right? You want to hold out on us?"

"No. No, that came out wrong." Jada shook his head in frustration. "I mean, I have fragments. I don't really know anything." He started to pace, watching his feet as he talked. "My parents wouldn't tell me much about the place they came from. They had this stupid idea that if I don't know anything, I'm safer. But I've known for a while they were not from Earth, so I've listened. Especially when they had fights." He snorted. "It's amazing the things people will say around the' deaf kid,' he made air quotes with a look of disgust.

I gave a wry smile in agreement. Once we all knew what we

were listening for, we learned a lot more information from our parents.

"This summer, while we were in hiding and you were all missing, my sister Amber also went missing. My parents thought she was safe at college, but she had come home for a visit and the Helios grabbed her. We got her back, but after that, they wanted us to have some basic information in case something happened to one of them."

Shim and I shared a glance. Basic information would have been very helpful this summer.

"I know which colony in the Federation they were visiting when a passage opened up and they got trapped on Earth—it was Nadun. I know Nadun is a mining moon. My mother hated it here, the heat and claustrophobic tunnels, but she's a scientist, like my father. They were all about the precious stones and minerals that could be studied here."

"But this could be any tunnel. We might have fallen into a hole in Santa Cruz." Breeze said.

Shim gave her a side-eye, still on the ground with her arms looped around her legs. He shook his head and turned back to Jada.

"What did she say about how they got to Earth?" Shim wanted to know.

"My mom thought it was a wormhole that brought them to Earth. She mentioned the wind and light." Jada leaned down and started picking up loose lamps, piling them back into the box. Weaving a little, he stopped and put a hand against the wall.

"Are you okay?" I asked, concerned. I had been feeling dizzy, too, ever since we arrived, but I thought it had more to do with the heat and the dust.

"I think the blow that damaged my hearing aid is worsening my vertigo. And I'm straining to read everyone's lips in the dark

—which I hate doing. I don't understand most of what you guys are saying." He trailed off.

I got it. Well, no, I didn't. But I felt like I'd been on a spinning tea cup ride through a haunted house ever since we had entered the tunnels. How much worse to not hear people talking or if something was close by?

"This is so insane. Grace, what are we going to do?" Shim looked at me expectantly.

I didn't know.

"Do you think you can get that working?" I nodded to the panel of monitors, and Shim shook his head.

"There isn't any power anywhere in this shack. Just these lights, which I'm assuming are battery-operated.

"Then I guess we are going to have to have a long rest here for the a–" I paused. Was it night? Day? "–for a couple of hours. Whatever we need to get our strength back and then stock up and keep looking."

"Looking for Skylar?" Breeze asked hopefully.

"Come on, Breeze. Get over it!" I immediately regretted snapping at her, but I was exhausted and beyond finished, "We need to keep looking for help."

"And let's hope they aren't like the people on Earth," Shim added.

"Why?" Jada asked.

Shim looked grim, "Cause we've seen what they do to aliens on Earth."

Somehow, against all the odds, we had done the one thing our parents hadn't been able to do in twenty years of trying. We had opened a passage back to *their* home world. Now, we had to do it again and find a way back to *our* home world. If we couldn't, we were destined to the same fate.

8

BACKWARD FORWARD

HOURS LATER, I was still staring up at the rock ceiling of the storage shed, my exhausted head spinning from one catastrophic scenario to the next. Even though it would be useless, I yearned to check a clock. I hated not knowing what time it was. Could I stop pretending to sleep? Was it morning?

Stars, this place messes with my head.

Flipping over, I rubbed my cheek against the hot, itchy blanket. I tried sleeping right on the ground, but it wasn't cooler. At least the blankets added padding.

Self-doubt swept through my mind like a rip current. Maybe Breeze was right. Maybe we should have stayed in the chamber where we arrived and experimented with the stone, chanted at it, or said some magic words until the passage opened again. Maybe I should have spent more time looking for that ragged piece of metal that cut my hand so deeply it still throbbed. Or looked for something, anything, that would give us a clue to how we ended up here or how our parents had gotten stuck on Earth.

"I can feel your head spinning like a hard drive over-processing." Shim's gruff voice sent a shiver down my spine.

"Shut up. I'm mad at you." I growled, then blew my hard-line stance by whispering. "What are we going to do?"

"I'm so sorry." Shim's voice was choked.

What? What did he–*oh*.

"Not that. What are we going to do about being stuck on Nadun? How did we get here? How is this even possible? Why does this stuff happen to us?"

Something scooted across the floor and a soft touch brushed my arm. In the darkness, time seemed suspended and every thought in my head spilled out of my mouth like I was speaking to the old Shim. The one I was so in sync with that we could look across the room and read each other's thoughts. That Shim knew me. And I thought I knew him. Obviously, that wasn't true.

I flicked off his hand, glad I didn't have to look into his eyes as I did it. Why couldn't someone grow ugly to you once you break up with them? Had I broken up with him?

"By the way, we are totally done." I tried to keep my voice steady. To reinforce my message, I scooted my blanket further away.

"Ah, yes. Fair." His voice resigned.

"Fine."

"Fine. And, back to your first question, I have no idea how we got here. This isn't covered in any of the science classes I've taken." His voice was stressed. "It doesn't make any sense. Our parents tried everything to get home. We heard Micah tell the others he had been researching and testing for years. And that's why the government retook the stones, more testing. The only common denominators I can see is your mother's necklace and the field in Santa Cruz. But it doesn't make sense."

I rolled in the direction of his voice. "It's got to be more than just the stone in the necklace. I've been wearing it since my mother disappeared, and this has never happened before."

"Maybe you had to wear it on the field or touch that piece of metal?"

"My mother wore it to that field a dozen times and it never triggered the portal. And how was the metal a part of it? I barely touched it before it cut open my finger." We dropped into silence. Eventually, I spoke again, "What if Breeze was right? What if we should have stayed and waited for rescue? But, if a passage was going to open up spontaneously, wouldn't it have done it while we were still there?"

"Yes," Shim said.

"And I don't think the answer was on Earth, or our parents would have found it."

"True."

"So, maybe it's here on Nadun. Other passages had to have opened up in the past. We know other people made it to Earth. Maybe people from Earth made it here, and they have some kind of record. But how are we going to find it when we don't speak the language?"

"Maybe my grandfather can help?" Shim offered. "My mom says he was someone important. Like a mayor or something in the new city Neran, wherever that is."

"Wow, you got more info from your mom than I did from my dad." I thought about it. "It's been twenty years. That's a long time. Do you think he will still live in the city?"

"Kindle said her fathers been the mayor for decades. She named me after him, so I guess we go and track down a mayor named Shimmer. It's more to go on than our parents had."

"When our parents arrived on Earth, the government wanted to experiment on them, and the Helios hunted them to discover the secret to opening the passage so they could invade Nadun. Maybe Nadun will be nicer to guests. Alien guests." We both snorted with humor.

"Will you guys shut up," Jaxon's voice carried across the

darkness along with a mechanical whine. Before the lights turned out, I saw him curled up in a nest of blankets with Duchess in his arms like a big metal teddy dog.

"Sorry," I whispered.

A swear drifted across the hot room.

"Grace." Shim spoke so softly I knew only I could hear him. "I wish I had one of the stones, so we could communicate through them like we usually do, I really want to know what you are thinking. But I need you to know I'm so sorry—it's not—"

"No, Shim. You really don't want to know what I'm thinking." I rolled away and rubbed my cheek on the scratchy blanket.

Shim continued. "I wasn't trying to lie to you. I screwed up. I'm really sorry."

I made a strangled noise and was about to tell him to shut up when he added, "But we can do this. As long as we are together, we can do this." My breath caught. Facing insurmountable odds on your own world seemed a lot more manageable than doing it trapped underground on an alien moon where you don't speak the language. I have a greater appreciation for my mother now and what she went through.

I hope Shim is right.

Sometime later, I woke up to the sound of retching.

I wondered what time it was and what was wrong with my dad. The intense darkness confused me for a minute until my memory rushed back.

Sitting up, my hands searched for the portable light when a glow came in through the bent metal door. Jada was leading a quietly crying Breeze back into the office.

"Breeze, what is it?" I rushed to her and tripped over Shim.

"She is okay— just don't eat the crackers," Jada assured us as he helped Breeze sit back on the boxes. He handed her a bottle of the drink we had found, and she eyed it suspiciously.

Jada pointed over to Jaxon, who was curled up on the floor sleeping. He looked fine. She took the bottle, sipped cautiously, swirled some in her mouth, then went to spit but couldn't figure out where to do it. I pointed to an empty box, and she spit into it. After doing that several more times, she finally swallowed the liquid. Sighing, she returned the bottle to Jada with a quiet thanks and lay down with her back to us. Pulling out her phone, she started flipping through pictures with a sniffing sob. I thought about stopping her, conserving the battery, but realized it didn't matter now we had the light boxes.

"What happened?" I asked Jada. He gave a shrug and then settled back onto his blankets before speaking. His words, as always, were carefully selected as if he had crafted them in his mind first.

"I woke with her light. She had opened a tin of crackers and taken a bite. She immediately rushed outside and was sick. She said it burned her mouth, but she didn't swallow. But we should watch her, food poisoning takes up to 28 hours to kick in."

I nodded. Poor Breeze.

Oh, Stars! We had no food, and we'd used up all of Shim's water. My heart sank. We had to keep moving to try and find help before we starved. At least Jaxon hasn't keeled over from drinking the stuff from the bottle.

"What's the noise?" Jaxon complained.

"Breeze got sick eating the crackers. They're bad."

Jaxon shot up off the blanket and rushed over to Breeze.

"So, no food. Guess I better pack up as much of the drink as I can." Shim pushed aside the tins of crackers and lined up the empty water bottles from his pack.

"Do you think that's a good idea?" I watched him load his bag with opaque glass bottles, then struggle to fill the used water bottles with the liquid. I reached over to hold the plastic steady.

The milky white viscous liquid swirled in the bottle. It was beautiful.

When done, Shim replaced the lids on all but two of the bottles and handed me one. "Well, Jaxon is alive. Breeze tried it. And we've nothing else to drink. Happy breakfast," Shim toasted, tipping up one of the bottles and taking a sip.

I nodded and did the same. The warm citrusy flavor rolled across my tongue, tart and a tad bitter. Thicker than juice but not as thick as a gel, the fluid was refreshing, and I found my attention sharpening as if I'd had three cappuccinos but without the jittery side effects. Not bad. At least it didn't have a tag reading "drink me" on it, though I certainly felt like I'd fallen down a rabbit hole.

Everyone was up now, so I put down my bottle and clapped my hands together in forced cheer. "Okay, we are going to keep heading up this tunnel. We were lucky to find a place to rest and something to drink. But we still need help, and we aren't going to find it here. We should all bring lights, and Shim has all the drinks packed he can carry." My initial cheer was waning.

"We should each take a blanket." Jada inserted.

"Why?" It was so hot I couldn't imagine wrapping a smothering blanket around me.

"A blanket isn't just for warmth. It's a rope, a sleeping mat, a tent, camouflage." Jada's voice trailed off, but I got the point.

"Good idea. I can cut off pieces and braid them into straps so we won't get hot carrying them." Shim offered.

While Shim got to work, I addressed my pressing issue with the group. "If you have to do anything, um private...um bathroom-related," I could feel myself blush as I looked at the guys. "Boys go down the tunnel. Girls go the opposite direction." I awkwardly pointed out the door. "We'll leave when everyone gets back. Don't go too far," I cautioned.

Breeze and I headed up the tunnel together. She was quiet, her shoulders slumped. Even her hair had lost its perky bounce.

I handed her the light, "Do you feel better?"

Using my free hands, I finger-combed my hair and twisted the ash and green strands into a loose knot at the back of my neck. I would kill for a hair tie.

"No." She sniffed. I looked at her with alarm. "I won't be sick again from eating that disgusting cracker. I just..." she trailed off. "I'm so stupid I can't even function without Skylar. And when I try to do something on my own, I almost poison myself."

"That is not true," I insisted. Looking for a big boulder that hid the view of the other lights. I found a low one that would work and took the light from Breeze, balancing it on top of the rock so we wouldn't be backlit, and indicated she should go first. "You are as smart as Skylar. You've just always let him make all the decisions. It takes practice." I added, continuing to talk with my back to her.

"Maybe." I heard a zip, and she popped up beside me and indicated it was my turn. We switched places.

"What about you?" she asked over her shoulder. "Have you forgiven Shim? You know, I don't understand it," she carried on without waiting for my answer, "he is a good guy and very hunky if you like the short muscly type. I just don't understand why he didn't tell you he had a girlfriend. I know this year has been a little crazy, but we spent the whole summer together. There was plenty of time. Or even since then." Breeze continued on with all the same arguments that had been weaving through my head over the last day. Only, interestingly, I was never to blame in her version of things, not like in my head where my fault was the root of every excuse.

"Done." I stepped out from behind the rock and picked up the lamp. We made our way back to the storage alcove.

"Well?" Breeze demanded.

"Well, what? I don't understand it any more than you do."

"But what did he say when he explained it?" Breeze asked.

I could tell that she was getting into using my love life as a distraction. But I wasn't going to confess that I was the one who had refused to label our status. Refused to listen to Shim's explanations. Not now, and not this summer. How could I explain to Breeze that whenever he wanted a deep discussion of our feelings or future, I had this urgent need to run? I couldn't even stand to talk about his past, or I guess current, girlfriend. Shim had tried. I felt justified in not wanting to hear his explanations, but really, I was resisting the desire to bolt from the room. Which, considering where we are right now, would be dangerous.

So, I shrugged.

Breeze looked puzzled. I didn't have any answers, not for any of it, and not for how I was feeling. So, for now, that would have to do.

9

SIGNS OF LIFE

I WAS STRANGELY reluctant to leave the storage shed and its illusion of safety. Back in the tunnels, we fell into a routine of walking for a couple of hours, taking a short break to drink, then walking some more. Time was relative, measured by stops and starts. Thankfully, no one got sick from the drink.

We passed an increasing number of metal signs mounted on the tunnel walls, none of which we could read. At first, we stopped and studied them. After a while, someone would just call out "sign." Eventually, we ignored them. Several tunnel intersections had hard plastic monoliths standing like bouncers at the entrance. All the tunnels at these intersections were closed off with cave-ins. The terminals' blank viewing screens and buttons had less life than a tombstone.

It felt like a deliberate move like we were being funneled towards something.

We were on our third stop since leaving the offices when I realized I wasn't hungry. I should be. I hadn't eaten since yesterday. But whenever I felt that hollow echo in my stomach, I sipped the drink, and it disappeared. Maybe that's what the slogan on the back of the bottle, next to the picture of the baby, said. I turned to tell Shim of my discovery.

"Oh no! We have to go back." Breeze gasped, sprang to her feet, and ran back down the tunnel into the darkness.

"Breeze, wait!" Jaxon chased after her. Grabbing my blanket off the floor, I followed. It took a while to find them in the dark. When we did, Jaxon was straddling Breeze's back.

"Jaxon, get off of her," Shim yelled at him.

"I can't!" Jaxon's voice broke. "She wouldn't stop running. I had to tackle her. She ran right into a wall and got up and kept going. I think she is bleeding. Please help." Jaxon was worse than me at asking for help, but his face was furrowed in worry as Breeze bucked and he tried to hold on and not hurt her.

"Breeze, what is it?" I sank to my knees beside them. Breeze was twisting and writhing, smacking her fists into the ground. When she couldn't dislodge Jaxon, she crumpled, burying her face in her hands.

"I left it." Sobbing hiccups made her body tremble. "I left it in the shack. I left it. I'm going to be trapped here, alone, without him. Forever. And now. I. Won't. Even. Have. A. Picture."

She left it? Oh, no. Her phone. She left her phone in that storage office shack. She had been looking at photos of home and Skylar and her father, and she had put it down when we went to the bathroom. When we came back, she must have forgotten to pick it up.

"Please, please, we have to go back. Please." Her sobs were reduced to whimpers. Her pain was exhausting. We couldn't go back. I knew that, but I couldn't say the words aloud. Deep in my soul this awful pit of fear had been ripping open since we first fell into these tunnels. It had been rising, drowning me in a tight grip that made breathing a struggle. And right now, my throat wouldn't let me choke out the words.

We can't go back.

I wanted to cry too. But I had this niggling worry that the fear would take over if I started, and I'd never move again. So instead, I took the coward way out. I lay flat on the ground next to her, and I let Breeze cry for me. I lay next to her, listening to her sobs and her self-doubts, her anger with herself for abandoning Skylar, her fear that she would never see him, or her father, or Earth again, her fear that she couldn't survive here. And in my head, I cried with her. Dry-eyed, I cried out my anger at abandoning my mother's memory, at not understanding what she had gone through on Earth. My fear that I would never see my father again. My self-doubt that I was able to survive here.

"I could go back and get it." Jaxon rolled to his side and reaching out, he brushed Breeze's bangs out of her wet eyes.

"No!" Shim cut off Jaxon's offer. "How would you find your way back to us? Breeze ran out of bracelets soon after we left the shack and we have taken dozens of random turns since then. You will never find us again." Jaxon scowled as his brother vetoed his offer.

"I suppose we could all go back. We might be able to find it." Jada's comment was unexpected. He had been the biggest advocate for moving forward.

"No" Breeze's faint whisper was followed by a delicate sniff. "It's too risky. I don't want anyone to die." Rolling towards Jaxon, she buried her face in his chest. We sat in silence, the light boxes bouncing shadows on the stone walls around us. Eventually, the crying stopped, and Breeze fell asleep. Jaxon lay perfectly still, letting her use his shoulder as a pillow. Jada and Shim had settled against the wall opposite one of the collapsed side tunnels.

I woke in darkness to the sound of movement. Switching on my light, I saw Shim crouched in front of the rock pile blocking the side tunnel. The stack looked like all the others we had passed, time and erosion crumbling the ceiling as the ground tried to reclaim the tunnel.

Shim tilted his head to the side as if he was listening for something.

"What are you doing?" I whispered as I sat up. Scooting on my hands and knees across the dirt of the tunnel floor, away from the others who were still sleeping. I settled next to him. Shim leaned in, and this time I heard it too. A faint scratching. There was something on the other side.

"Oh, my Stars. Is someone there?" At my shout, Shim swung his head towards me.

"Shhh, we don't know who or what it is." Shim gasped as a light leaked around the stone, coming from the other side of the cave-in and seeping into our dark tunnel.

We both jumped to our feet.

"Should we—what should we do?" The instinct to tear through the rocks and scream for help was strong, but what if it wasn't help? I was suddenly reminded that on this world I was an alien, and on Earth, we didn't treat aliens very nicely.

"We are running out of options. Unless you have a sci-fi transporter, we need a rescue. We need to find out who is on the other side of this tunnel." Shim started shifting rocks and I helped him.

"What's going on?" Jaxon asked behind us. I glanced back. All three were awake and watching us.

"Something is on the other side." Before I finished speaking, six hands dove in next to us and soon we had uncovered a large boulder that blocked the tunnel. Smaller rocks had filled in around the sides, but there was a person-sized gap at the top. When Shim went to climb to the top of the boulder, I stopped him.

"Give me a foot up, I can get further."

I was excited and nervous as Shim boosted me up and I inched into the darkness across the top of the boulder, the rough surface digging into my hip and gouging my stomach. Crumbles of dirt trickled from the ceiling. I wrinkled my nose to hold off a sneeze. Light from the other side illuminated the hand holds in the rock and I pulled myself along with my arms. I froze when I heard a buzzing sound.

"Shhhh," I called back to the others. I strained to hear. In the silence, my heart pounded so loud I wasn't sure I could pick up anything above it. Then, whisper quiet, there was a faint snicker of sound. Far off, but most definitely not from us.

Life, we have found signs of life.

I grabbed the rocks in front of me and pushed them back, like I was swimming the Butterfly through the rubble. The stones cut into my smooth palms and scraped my knuckles. But I pushed on, flinging rocks behind me.

"Watch it!" Jaxon shouted behind me, but I kept swimming.

Something shook and hail-sized pieces of debris rained from the ceiling. For a minute, I worried about a cave-in, but then I was too excited to care.

From somewhere behind me, Jada yelled out, "Hello?"

Soon the rest were doing the same, calling out greetings and cries for help.

We kept digging but we had only moved three feet into the pile of stone. How far did it go?

I heard the sound again, much closer now, and stopped so I could listen. More distinct now, though still faint. It was a voice, close by, and a motor, like a car or a motorcycle, continuously revving its engine in the background.

"I think it's people," I gasped, and we doubled our efforts.

We were getting close. I focused on one area near the top that with looser, easier to move stones. The first colossal boulder I slid across the top of had another boulder behind it and I pulled myself along until only my legs hung out behind me. I pushed and tugged at rocks until I had cleared enough room to slither forward. There was an empty cavity behind that boulder before another wall of rock. The others were still shouting, and I made a motion with my hand for them to quiet down.

I turned towards the light and listened.

"It's definitely voices" I called back. A shout of excitement behind me and the next thing I knew, Shim was slithering up next to me, both of us now wedged into the tight spot. I try to block out the noise behind me and focus on the sounds from the other side of the rock. Someone was talking but I couldn't quite make out the words.

"Shush," I called behind me, then turned back. I could make out the words now. "There is a lot of machinery noises, but I can hear male voices. They are talking about hunting for something, no someone." Fear knotted in my gut. What kind of people hunt other people? Shim's eyes widened at my words. "Maybe this is a bad idea?"

"Maybe they are looking for us?" Shim's face screwed up into a mess of doubt as I listened and continued to repeat what I heard. "Something about 'runaways' and 'invasion,' and I think they said 'transport.' Is that what you heard?" I checked with Shim. He was gaping at me in complete disbelief. "What, can't you hear them? Did you hear something different?"

"Grace, I can hear them. They aren't speaking English. I don't understand a word they're saying."

"What are you talking about?" I paused and listened again. "There, right there, it's a guy's voice, and it said, 'capture' and something about 'tracking a portal opening' and 'stopping an invasion,'" I paused, the words I just repeated sinking in.

Maybe I misunderstood?

"I'm only catching a few words. I have to get closer." I reached further into the cavity. If I could just push that last rock out of place, we might break through. But it was slightly beyond my fingertips and with my arm extended so awkwardly, I didn't leverage to push.

"Can you get that rock?" In the confined space, I tried to shift to point out the rock that was blocking my access to the other side.

The others started shouting and calling for help again behind me, and I could tell they were still digging because occasionally, one of the stones they moved caused a cascade and made the stones around us shudder and adjust. This was getting dangerous.

"Grace, you aren't listening to me. I can hear them speaking, but I can't understand them. They aren't speaking English. How do you understand what they are saying?" Shim smooshed up against me. His chest was leaning on one of my arms, and his lips were close to my ear. Minty, hot air blows across my face as he speaks. The rocks above us shuddered and powdered us with dust. We quickly tucked our heads and covered our necks as best as we could.

My fingers brush the metal at my throat, my mother's necklace. Coughing, I sputtered and asked, "Do you think it's this?" I indicated the flat strip of bronze. It was from my mother's home world, and we know the stone can help us communicate with each other.

"Maybe. What else are they saying?"

I strained to hear. There were two voices on the light side of the rock, they were much closer now. I repeated what I heard.

"It's two guys. The first one says, '—can't fail this time... forces ready to move, they just need to know how to open the passage'. The second guy said, 'It was the same reading as last time. It's either a spy or the invasion has started.'" I swung towards Shim. "Do you think they are waiting for an invasion from Earth?"

"Why would Earth invade?"

"—wait, there is more." I pushed forward, bracing my hand against the wall of rock in front and leaning in "—have to learn how it works before Earth invades. The Helios wants them alive." My eyes widened and I lost my grip. All of my weight slid forward, landing on the rock wall, breaking through.

As my head and shoulder burst through to the other side of the rocks, my hands scraped painfully across rough surfaces, trying to support my weight. I turned my head to avoid face-planting and my eyes met those of two stunned men in grey uniforms. The room was brightly lit and loud with machinery and huge pieces of mining equipment.

The man on the right recovered quickly and, with a shout, lunged at me.

I scrambled for purchase and pushed backward into the darkness.

He grabbed my hand and pulled. I was dragged forward into the brightly lit room.

"Shim" I screamed. I felt an arm wrap around my waist and pull me back. Fingers dug into my arm as I wrenched it free.

My body recoiled so fast that I exploded out of the crevice into the dark tunnel. Stumbling backward, I fell over a discarded rock and landed on my back.

"Grace, what is it?" Breeze asked.

"It's people," Jaxon exclaimed. "Hey, we are here." He shouted into the hole.

Jada and Breeze joined him.

"No," I gasped and then collapsed into a coughing fit. "Stop them," I wheezed as Shim emerged from the hole. "Stop them. It's..." I coughed again and croaked out, "It's the Helios."

Even saying their names caused me to shudder. We encountered the Helios group this summer when we learned they had been killing off the people that had helped our parents when they first arrived on Earth. They were the group that kidnapped my mother and faked her death and the ones that ultimately killed her. But they were back on Earth planning an invasion—probably of Teran. Were there Helios on Teran too?

"Are you sure?" Alarm tightened Shim's features.

"They said," I gasped for breath, "the Helios are trying to capture us and make us tell them how to open the passage."

Just as I finished speaking, a loud explosion came from the hole and the rock pile shuddered and settled looser. Our tunnel shook and chunks of debris rained on our heads. I crouched and covered my neck.

Across from me, horror streaked across Breeze's face.

Someone screamed as the large boulder exploded into a pile of rubble. Shrapnel pinging our faces. The walls shook again and more debris crashed down on us.

"Run," I yelled.

We snatched up our lights and blankets, Shim grabbed his backpack, and we raced down the tunnel. Away from the falling rock. Away from the increasing noise and light. Away from the only help we had found since we arrived, and away from, if they were the Helios, what I'm certain would have been the end of us.

A STITCH CRAMPED MY SIDE, and I gasped for breath. We had been running flat out for at least thirty minutes, but they were catching up. They must have had some kind of machine to move the rock as fast as they did.

There was a shout behind us and the sound of falling rock. I could hear an engine rev. We had no time to spare. I clamped a hand to my side and kept moving.

There were more and more metal signs with pictures

warning of dire peril ahead—at least, that's how I read the icon that looked like a stick figure falling off a cliff. If we had passed a side tunnel, any alternate route, I would have taken it. The first thing we saw that wasn't a rock or a sign was a rusted stack of metal stretching from floor to ceiling. The pile looked like a tetanus nightmare. Shim stopped and examined the wreck.

"It's an elevator," he marveled.

"It's a deathtrap," Jaxon concluded, kicking the wire mesh door that seemed to be held up by a single metal hinge. The door tilted and slid sideways. Inside was a narrow platform; the middle rusted through.

"Come on," I urged them, "they're right behind us."

We rushed down the tunnel. More boulders blocked the route until scrambling over them was the only way forward. I don't know how it was possible, but the heat felt so much worse than yesterday. Maybe I was winded from running, but it was getting harder and harder to breathe. I stopped to gasp in air again, leaning my hands on my knees, when I realized there was an orange light coming from the tunnel ahead.

"What is that?" Breeze danced towards the light like a moth to a flame. We all followed, transfixed by the shimmering glow. The heat grew until I felt my hair singe and the skin on my face dry until almost cracking, and still, we moved closer to the light.

Jaxon arrived first at the entrance to the chamber. I could see his skin glowing in the light. Breeze pushed past him; Jaxon grabbed her from behind as she wobbled, and he pulled her back. She raised her arm, blocking her face. Shim and Jada slid carefully in behind them and peered over Jaxon's shoulders.

"What is it?" My nose twitched at the scent of hot metal and overcooked eggs. Putting my hands on Shim's shoulders for balance, I stood on tiptoe and leaned in to see into the chamber.

Oh, my Stars. It wasn't a chamber. The tunnel ended as if a giant monster had taken a bite out of it. The other side of the tunnel was at least thirty feet away, across an open chasm, and at the bottom was a churning lake of fire.

"Lava." Shim wiped the beads of sweat dripping down his face.

The walls of the crevice were smokey black and covered in ridges of smooth fins. It was a long lava tube, and it cut right through our escape route. The heat was scorching my face, and I fell back.

The others pulled back too, leaving just Jaxon at the mouth of the chamber, transfixed, watching the red-hot flow below.

"What do we do? They are going to catch us!" Breeze's voice rose in volume.

"The lava cuts right through the tunnels—we must be close to an active volcano." Jada sounded breathless.

Oh, my Stars, a volcano? That was a terrifying thought. But it made sense. That was why the tunnels had been getting hotter and hotter.

"It's horrible! We can't jump that." Breeze's statement sounded like a question.

I blinked at her, the heated air drying my eyes out and I had blinked to peel my eyelids off them.

"It's beautiful," Jaxon declared, diffusing the panic building among us. He tore himself away from watching the flow to join us. "But we aren't getting across this way."

My skin was tight and itchy, like a bad sunburn. I wanted to get as far away as possible from the lava flow, but the only option we had left made my stomach churn.

"Come on." I forced myself to turn and race back the way we had traveled.

10

THE LIFT

"NO WAY." Jaxon eyed the rusted elevator as if it would attack him.

"The Helios are going to be here any second. Do we have an option other than the elevator?" I asked, drawing in a shuddering breath at the sound of a motorcycle in the distance.

Calling it an elevator was glamming it up. It was more of a platform lift with a broken metal door and a pair of bent cross beams on each side, the edges eaten away by erosion like moths on wool. We were on the bottom level of the lift, and I cautiously leaned in and directed my light up the shaft. It only penetrated a dozen feet before the darkness swallowed it up.

"Maybe we could go back down the tunnel and try another direction," Breeze said.

"We've walked miles, and most of the other tunnels were closed off by rocks." I gazed down at the corroded floor plate, it looked ancient.

"If the Helios capture us, they will torture us for information on opening the passage. They aren't going to believe that we don't know how to do it." Jaxon said, his voice bitter.

So, this is our only chance if it works." I tapped my toe on the rusty cage.

"Couldn't we hide?" Breeze pleaded.

Jada grabbed her arm. "Let's look for places in case Shim can't get this moving."

"Don't go far," I said.

Shim was buried deep in the alcove behind the lift. He had found an engine that must run the thing. With a massive knot of dread choking me, I kept watch down the tunnel. The sounds of a motor were now accompanied by falling rock and the ground vibrating.

"Jaxon, give me a hand." Shim's voice was muffled.

Jaxon disappeared into the alcove. Less than a minute later, he and Shim came out from behind the engine, covered in the dirt.

"Well?" I asked cautiously.

"It's amazing," Shim gushed. "This drum looks like it's centuries-old, and..." he trailed off at my glare. "Well, no. It doesn't work. I don't think there is any power working anywhere on this level."

"So, we are trapped." I choked out. A sense of dread spread through me. The Helios will capture us.

"Not exactly." Shim scrunched his face up like he did when he was thinking of having to tell some terrible news." See, this is a cable system, but it has a manual override with a pulley system."

Voices were coming down the tunnel. I spun towards the noise and then back to Shim. "What does that mean? Are we taking the elevator, or are we trying to hide?" I asked, my tone hinging on desperate.

"Elevator."

"How—"

"Elevator." Shim insisted. I didn't even have a breath to

think about it. I either trusted Shim, or I didn't." Jada, Breeze, come quick."

Shim pulled open the door, and Breeze and I piled in first, squishing as close to each other and the edge as possible. Jada followed us in. The lift platform was already cramped, and our lights shining in each other's faces was haunting.

"Jada, get ready to pull that rope," Shim instructed.

I repeated the comment so Jada could read my lips, and we both reached up to the steel rope. That was going to hurt. My hands were already raw from climbing over the rocks. I whipped the blanket roll strap over my head and ripped the strap into four pieces. I quickly wrapped one around each of my hands and handed the other two to Breeze, who helped Jada wrap his hands.

"I'm not getting in there. You guys are always telling me I'm reckless—" Jaxon shook his head." This is a death trap. There is so much rust we'll break through the floor. Or the old wires will break and we'll plummet to our deaths. But it's more likely we will get trapped between levels or crushed by a cave-in. NO, nope, nope, nope. Not doing it." Jaxon shook his head and backed away.

"Okay," Shim stepped back from the lift. "I'll tell you guys how to operate it, and you can go up that way. Jaxon and I will try and find a place to hide."

My mouth dropped incredulously. "Are you crazy? We are not splitting up. There is absolutely no way we would find our way back to each other. Then we would never find a way home. Do you know why our parents survived on Earth? Because they stuck together—we have to do the same."

An engine growled. It was so close.

"Jaxon," Breeze said in a strong, authoritative voice. "Jaxon, you get on this elevator thing right now because I'm not losing any more people that I love. Do you understand me?"

Jaxon blinked, stunned, and then leaped onto the lift. He crowded right up next to Breeze and stared into her eyes. Shim looked flabbergasted but followed, wedging himself in and pulling the rickety door closed behind him. The hinge broke off on the backside, but the latch still connected, and when it did, there was a click.

"Okay, pull that lever." I pulled on the stick Shim indicated. It had something like a clutch at the top and I had to use two hands to squeeze it. There was another shift, and the lift swayed.

"Huh, that worked." I was not impressed with the surprise in Shim's tone. Shim added," now pull the cable down. I'll pull up on this one at the same time, and it should raise up," I repeated to Jada what Shim had said but stopped halfway through and swung back to him.

"Should?" I asked incredulously, my heart racing.

"It's my first time overriding an alien elevator system to manual mode."

"Deathtrap," Jaxon squeaked out, his eyes wide.

Breeze raised a shaking hand and placed it over Jaxon's mouth to shut him up.

I could hear distinct voices coming down the tunnel and the roar of an engine.

"Pull!"

Jada, Shim, and I all heaved on the cables simultaneously. Someone shouted as we lifted off the ground. I cringed as the shrieking metal seemed to scream, "here we are." We awkwardly fumbled over each other, grasping the cable and pulling. The lift groaned and whined and continued to rise up into the hole in the ceiling. Just as the last sliver of the tunnel was left behind, the light and noise in the tunnel increased. Boots slapping the ground, lots of them, engines revving, voices shouting, it was terrifying.

"Turn out the lights," I held my breath as everyone quickly extinguished their lamps.

The sound faded away as we continued to rise into darkness until on all sides we were encased in solid rock. No one on the lift spoke. Heavy rasps of breath filled the space. The cardio was making my heart pound in my ears. Someone shuddered and pressed so closely together I felt it through my whole body.

As we pulled on the cables, the lift's counterbalance kicked in and we started to pick up momentum as we climbed. Sweating from the exercise, it took a few minutes to realize it wasn't as hot here in the shaft. It was still very warm, but I didn't think my skin was going to peel off my body anymore. Every so often, the air would shift, not quite a breeze, but I wondered if we were passing by other tunnels. There were no platforms.

It was at least twenty minutes, and I don't know how far we had come, before Breeze whispered, "Are we safe? Can we please turn on the lights? Just one. I-I can't breathe."

Immediately, a light flipped on.

My vision whited out and I rapidly blinked until it cleared. The first thing I saw was Jaxon leaning over Breeze, coaxing her to slow her breaths.

"That is better. Felt like I was going to fall into an abyss when the lights were out." Jada said. His voice echoed up the shaft.

"Want to take turns?" I asked.

Jada nodded. "I'll go first."

I let go with a sigh and stretched my aching arms. My whole body was shaking from an adrenaline crash. I hugged my chest, gave a quick squeeze for courage, then shuffled a couple of inches across the scarred floor until I was next to Shim. "You better wrap those hands."

Shim gave me a grateful look as I took over his cable. He

flexed his hands; his palms already had red welts and were starting to swell. But he quickly wrapped them and took the cable back from me.

The two boys picked up a rhythm and we were traveling at a good pace. I was just thinking there seemed no end to this shaft when abruptly the lift came to a stop.

"What now?" Shim grumbled as he gave another tug on the cable, but it wouldn't budge.

I cautiously looked over the gate, careful not to touch it. My stomach swirled as I looked down. "There's a landing."

The ledge of perforated metal was barely the size of a truck bed. The landing sides were caged in with rusted chain link fencing, and the only exit was an entrance to another, larger lift at the other end.

I looked back at the others. Jada and Shim were flexing their hands, their breaths still ragged. Jaxon had an arm around Breeze, whose eyes were scrunched closed.

I guess I needed to investigate.

Turning back to the landing, I lifted the door latch. The hinges screamed, then gave way completely. I held the door as it came loose in my hands.

"Here." I passed the door back to Shim, who leaned it against the wall.

I made a tentative step out onto the landing, slightly more motivated now to leave the rusty elevator before it disintegrated around us. I had to look down to avoid weak patches in the perforated metal floor. I tried not to think about the dark void below. I was suspended in the stone elevator shafts, the lifts like charms hanging on a necklace. Swaying, I grabbed at the metal wall, my finger breaking through a rust spot, and a piece of the cage crumbled and fell down the shaft. Vertigo made my head reel. I hate heights.

"Don't look down," Shim called.

His comment wasn't necessary. I quickly covered the distance between the lifts, trying not to imagine the floor crumbling beneath me. The door was open, and after a toe tap to make sure it wasn't going to move, I entered the elevator carriage. This one was more solid. The platform was shaped like a big square bucket, and there was less danger of scraping our skin or catching a limb on the sides of the shaft.

"Come on," I called to the others.

One by one, they cautiously made their way across the bridge. The bucket swayed each time someone stepped in. I was bracing myself for the exertion of pulling this larger lift up the shaft. The car was double the size of the last one. I adjusted the wraps on my hands, and Jada and I stood ready, but the cables were above the lift.

Shim came last and immediately started examining the switches on the wall. "Yes!" he fist-pumped the air and hit a button. A dim greenish glow lit above us, and the lift slowly began to rise on its own. Startled, I braced my feet. Shim pushed another button and the lift stopped. The lip of the lift was about six inches above the landing now. Shim forced shut the half door, pushing on the oxidized hinges that groaned until they latched and sealed the base of our bucket. The top was open and exposed to the rock walls of the shaft.

"Look!" Jaxon pointed to the lift we had just left. The platform was slowly receding down into the shaft again. The cables that we had used to raise the lift whirled.

"Go!" I hissed at Shim. He pushed the button again, and our lift began to rise at a snail's pace, much slower than the original lift we had raised by hand. Inch by inch, we ascended. Our eyes were glued to the landing. Were the Helios coming up?

Were those really the Helios? Like the ones we knew from Earth, the ones that had captured and killed my mother?

I took a breath as the landing slowly receded from view, and the stone shaft above us swallowed us up. We were safe for the moment, but what were we going to do?

"I don't understand how the Helios could be both here and on Earth," I whispered.

Shim looked away from the button panel." From what you said, this group wants to invade, so the group back on Earth was right to plan for an attack."

"Each of the groups wants to invade the other's home world. And now, they are both after us because they think we know the secret to opening the passage." I slid to the floor and leaned back against the bucket. My body was too exhausted to move, and my mind couldn't stop running.

"But we don't know how to open the passage." Breeze's voice sounded like a six-year-old's as she tugged Jaxon to the floor with her, pulling his arm tighter around her shoulders and curling into his side.

"No, we don't. But if we want to go home, we need to find out how before the Nadun Helios figured it out and blocked us, or worse." Even as I said it, I winced at how grim I sounded.

The others fell silent as we watched the lift inch its way up the dark stone walls.

We had been looking for help. Now, any time we saw some-one, we would wonder if they were going to help us or hurt us? Could we trust anyone?

One thing is for sure, we couldn't survive here on our own. We had to find someone that could tell us how to get home. On Earth, any knowledge about the passage was top secret, but the two guys I'd heard talking worked for the Helios and they knew about the passage. They knew about Earth. They said whatever readings had happened when we came through had happened before. Someone must have come through the passages before us. Someone else knew the secret of how we could get back home.

$$\infty$$

THE EXCRUCIATINGLY SLOW elevator continued its climb. Jaxon was sitting opposite me, his feet almost touching the other wall. His head tipped back, and a snore escaped his lips. Not for the first time, I envied his ability to sleep anywhere. Breeze had squished between us, her head in Jaxon's lap, hands covering her face, and her feet in my lap. Shim knelt in front of the control pad, still studying the controls but not touching them. Jada sat cross-legged next to Shim, his thoughtful gaze on the three of us. I gave him a half-smile which he didn't return.

"You're very close." I had to strain to hear his whisper above the scraping and grinding of the metal lift rising.

I nodded and shrugged. Until today, this summer has been the most trying and challenging experience of my life. Losing my mother had been sad. Moving all the time and not under-standing why had been depressing. But being on the run with Shim, Jaxon, Breeze, and Skylar while we hunted down the truth of our parent's origins had tested everything I thought I knew about myself.

I was alone most of my life, only feeling like I had a home, a place I fit when I met the brothers and the twins this summer.

"Why did they keep us away from each other?" Jada asked.

"I think they thought it was safer if we were split up."

"I was jealous when I heard you had met." He looked down, embarrassed. "Not that I wanted all the difficulties you had, but...you had each other." His eyes went to the moving wall above me, so I couldn't say anything to him until he looked back. I waited. When he returned his eyes to my face, he continued. "I've known for a while what they are."

His statement confirmed a suspicion we had had since we first learned of his existence.

"Aliens?" I asked. That word made me nervous.

Jada nodded." I used to get so angry at my father that he would never let me meet you or talk to you."

"But why would Micah do that?" I gasped. So much pain could have been avoided if we had known the truth and had each other to talk to.

"He didn't want to be found out by others. Proven a hypocrite." Jada's laugh was bitter. "He demanded that the others never tell anyone. Not their spouse, not even their kids. But I found out. If it makes you feel better, my siblings didn't know. My younger sister is just a baby, and my older sister had already left home. She found out this summer and it almost cost her life."

"That's so unfair," Resentment flared. But it wasn't Jada's fault he knew, and we didn't.

"Yes," Jada agreed. "My father always has an agenda, a way of twisting everything to his purposes. He made me feel like it was my fault that he had to tell me because of the stones."

"I don't understand," Shim commented. Sitting back on his heels, he angled himself so Jada could see him as he listened in on our conversation.

"I've been deaf since birth. My father's research is all around that stone." Jada pointed to the stone in the necklace around my neck." He knew what the stone could do and wanted to use it to experiment with me, test if the communication would work with someone with no hearing. And it does." Jada closed his eyes and his face relaxed into a look of awe. "I heard their voices in my head. His and my mother's, they were so distinctive and different. It was incredible."

I smiled. I knew what he meant. Once we found out the stone was a conduit that allowed us to talk to each other telepathically, we had used the stones exclusively for safe communications. Shim and I spent hours talking on them. I looked down, and my smile faded until the government took the stones away and now, we only had my necklace.

"I was so excited to meet you," Jada continued. "Then I messed it all up."

"What?" my head snapped up.

"I must have done something. You were leaving without me," Jada said. "I shouldn't have been upset." He shook his head." I guess I've known about you and wanted to meet you for so long, and when I did, you were all so close I felt like an outsider."

I didn't know what to say to that. I always felt like I was the one who was the outsider.

"As soon as we learned that Micah had a son our age, we've wanted to meet you. My dad said you were deaf, so I've been learning sign language so we could talk." I admitted. It was silly to burden him with my attempts to communicate.

"You have? Wow! How much do you know?"

"Well, it's not much. I heard that not everyone likes to read lips, and I wanted a chance to say—" I trailed off and lifted my hands and signed, "hello, my name is g-r-a-c-e."

Jada smiled. Then I pointed to Shim, who roughly repeated my gestures with his own name. Jada's smile deepened. It felt good to have the misunderstanding past us. He kept looking at me. The stare should have been too much, but the intensity was a connection. Something I hadn't felt with Jada before now. His face grew solemn again, and he hesitated, directing his next question at Shim.

"Is Jaxon mad you found out who your bio dad is?"

Shim snorted and quirked up a brow. "Jaxon is just mad—all the time. He doesn't need a reason. Logan, our dad," Shim stopped and frowned, "my stepdad is like that too. Very volatile. It's hard-wired into him, this volcano of anger. Logan loves to feed the rage. I always wondered why I never felt it." Shim gave a self-conscious shrug. "Jaxon struggles with it, but he is so different from Logan. I wish he could see that." Shim fell silent.

I was about to ask Jada what else he knew about our parents when the lift ground to a stumbling halt, jerked and started to drop.

11

THE SHAFT

THE LIFT DROPPED and then immediately jerked to a stop. My scream puffed out in a whoosh of breath at the impact.

Shouts sounded around me. I tensed and clutched Breeze's feet. The lights flickered. Shim had fallen forward onto his hands and knees, and the carriage went dark.

I scrambled for the light clipped to the front of my shirt and turned it on. A glow filled the metal box.

"Why did we stop? Make it go!" Breeze pleaded.

Shim righted himself and returned to the control panel. Pushing several buttons, we waited. "Oh no." Shim smacked the board with the palm of his hand. "There is no power at all. We're—we're stuck."

I was unnerved by the terror on his face.

Panic choked me. As long as we were moving, I kept the claustrophobia at bay— pretending the darkness wasn't just waiting out of site to consume me. With no movement, the blackness pressed in.

Breeze blinked up at me, her face distorted as she curled herself into a ball. Even Jaxon, braced for attack, was looking at me expectantly.

I stood on shaky legs and unclipped the light from my shirt. I extended my arm far above my head, trying to see deeper into the void above our carriage. The glow only spread a few feet.

Above the half walls of the carriage, rock surrounded us on four sides. I could have touched the shaft walls easily, but I had a paralyzing fear of putting anything outside the carriage for fear it would get ripped off.

"Shim, lift me up." I automatically enlisted his help.

Jada shook his head. "I'll do it. I'm taller."

He squatted down and indicated I should climb on his shoulders. I guess he was right, but it was awkward touching him, let alone stepping onto his thigh to straddle his neck. I was clumsy and embarrassed by the time I settled on his shoulders. He didn't notice and slowly rose to his full height, and the top of my head easily extended past the ceiling beam and through the debris into the open area above the carriage. I stretched my arm with the light. With the added height, I could see a couple of feet higher up the shaft. All four sides were rock as far.

Wait. One patch was darker than the rest. It was just out of range of my light, but the darkness had a different texture. I strained to see deeper, leaning in my torso brushed some of the debris off the crossbeam.

"Watch out," I called.

Jada coughed. My base wobbled. I grabbed the cross beams for support. They felt solid. More debris rained into the carriage.

"What are you doing?" Jaxon snapped.

"I can see something. I need to get closer." My arms straining, I slowly pulled myself up by the steel beams, trying not to dislodge more material. Soon I was standing on Jada's shoulders. I twisted and sat on one of the beams, my feet dangling below me. *Don't look down. Just keep climbing. Just keep climbing.* I mumbled to myself. My heart was pounding as I studied the wheels and cables of the ancient mechanical equipment, looking for a safe place to put my hands. Finally, grabbing my courage, I pulled my feet up and leveraged myself to a crouch and cautiously straightened.

With the light at the tips of my fingers and my arm fully extended above my head, I could see a ledge above. It was maybe a dozen feet above us, but the darkness beyond was deeper.

"Shim, come up here." I urged.

"Where are you going?" Jada asked a panicked edge to his voice.

"I just need him to double-check something," I called down.

A minute later, Shim's head emerged on the other side of the mechanical equipment. He was faster and smoother climbing to the top than I had been, but still the carriage jolted and swayed.

When he was standing on crossbeams across from me I pointed my light up. "Look."

"Is that a tunnel entrance?" Shim strained his neck to get a better look.

"I think it is. But how do we get up there?"

Shim shone his light down around us and examined the equipment. His eyes widened. "This stuff doesn't look very good."

"Can we climb up the cable?" My already taxed body shuddered at the idea even as I said it.

Shim contemplated the cable and then pulled his wraps out of his pocket. Carefully covering the entire length of his hands, he stretched them out and I tied the ends.

Taking a calming exhale, Shim jumped. Grasping the cable two feet over his head, he wrapped his legs around the lower length. The carriage swayed with the motion.

Screams came from inside the carriage, along with an angry shout from Jaxon. "What are you doing up there?"

I crouched down, grasping at the crossbeam and praying to the Stars above that we weren't all about to plunge to our deaths.

A snap sounded high up in the shaft, and then a mumbled "ouch" from Shim.

I put out a hand to steady myself on the crossbeam. Shim didn't slide. He sort of fell back to the roof, one leg plunging into the carriage. His face was a tight grimace. I let go of my death grip on the crossbeam with one hand and grabbed his shirt to steady him. His clothes were shredded—rust embedded into the cloth and drops of blood starting to dot the fabric.

"I'm okay," he steadied himself, and when he had his balance back, he showed me his hands. The rusted cable had cut through the binding, almost to the skin. "We can't climb the cable."

"Yeah, got that." I lowered my voice. "I don't know if you heard, but something snapped at the top when you did that."

Shim's eyes grew wide, and he looked up into the darkness.

Okay, new plan.

I leaned down into the carriage. Every lamp was on, and Breeze had her arms and legs wrapped around Jaxon like a boa constrictor. Wide-eyed and staring up at me, Jada was braced beside them, on one knee like he was ready to race his way off the lift. "Jada, how tall are you?"

Jada's mouth dropped open, "Is that really important right now?" At my glare, he relented, "five-foot-ten, why?"

"Jaxon, Breeze, how tall are each of you?"

Jaxon cursed and gagged as Breeze choked him. She lessened her grip and Jaxon asked, "What the hell is going on, Grace?"

"No time. Come on, how tall?" I demanded.

"Five-foot-five," Jaxon spat out.

"Me too," Breeze whispered.

I thought for a minute. It would have to do. "Grab the blanket rolls and get up here." They blinked up at me, and I started to pull back up, but they weren't moving. "Hurry, this thing is going to fall any minute."

There was a scramble beneath us and within minutes, Breeze's head popped up next to me. She handed up the bedrolls, which I looped over my shoulder as Shim helped her climb up.

Their combined weight started to tip the carriage, one side scrapping against the shaft wall. A shrill scream came from inside the elevator. We carefully rebalanced, each taking a corner.

Jaxon came up next. "Jax, what was that sound?" I gave a choked laugh as I tried to swallow down my anxiety to tease him.

"It was Jada."

"No, it wasn't," came the response from the carriage.

Jaxon scoffed and muttered as he and Shim braced on the cross beams and leaned into the carriage. They each grabbed one of Jada's hands and pulled until he was sitting on the crossbar. His eyes were wide with horror as he looked at the rusted mechanism that had, until this point, been carrying us up.

"How are we not dead already?"

I gave a weak chuckle. "It gets worse." I pointed up into the darkness.

With all our lights focused, the opening of the tunnel above us was visible.

"We have to get up there. Fast." I pointed my light at the cable. "Shim tried to climb this, and something snapped up above." My voice was shaking. My heart was pounding from the adrenaline racing through my system. I took a shallow breath as I outlined my insane plan.

"Jada, if Jaxon gets on your shoulders and Breeze climbs on top, I think she can reach that ledge."

Jada stood up. "Yes, it is better that at least one of us makes it."

In shocked silence, we all stared at Jada. That hadn't been my intention at all.

"Are you insane?" I pointed between all of us. "We all make it. That is the only plan that works." I stared Jada down. The doubt on his face made me push ahead. "Breeze takes the blankets with her. If she can find something to secure them to, great. If not. She just has to be strong enough to hold them while she lowers a rope of blankets to Jaxon. He climbs up, and they will both be strong enough to anchor you while you climb Jada. Then Shim and I will go last."

Jada looked doubtful.

"This will work," I said. Trying to convince myself.

Jaxon studied the distance and then looked back at me. "Still not your craziest idea, Grace." He moved quickly into position, and the whole carriage jolted and slammed into one of the walls. There was another snap above us, and something fell past us, landing inside the now-dark carriage.

"Careful," Shim snapped at his brother. Jaxon flipped him off. Shim and I slowly moved to the opposite side from the other three. I held the cable with my wrapped hands for balance but was careful to keep my weight on the outside edge.

Jada found his footing on the edge of the metal frame. Bracing his back against the shaft's wall, he gently pushed. Someone whined as the carriage swung slowly away from the wall and stopped when it pressed against the opposite side of the shaft. I gasped out the breath I had been holding.

Jada squatted against the wall, his knees looking like steps, and motioned for Jaxon to climb up. Staying carefully on the cross beams, Jaxon moved, so his back was to Jada, who put his hands on Jaxon's waist and balanced him while Jaxon stepped up onto each of his thighs, his movements now slow and measured. Jada ducked his head, and Jaxon was sitting on his shoulders.

Breathe, I reminded myself and struggled to pull in air as my free hand dug into the rock as if it could anchor me. Someone was making a low whining sound. I think it was Breeze, but it might have been me. I don't think I've ever been more afraid in my life.

Jada held up a hand. Jaxon grabbed it with one hand and, pushing on Jada's head with the other, he slowly rose to a standing position. His back against the wall. Both feet braced on Jada's shoulders.

He was so close. The ledge was a couple of feet above Jaxon. Hope rose in me. This could work.

Jada's face was stony as Jaxon's shoes dug into his shoulders. I know the wall gave them slightly more balance, but it was terrifying to see the wide gap behind Jada's feet.

"Okay, Breeze, move in front of Jada, same as I did," Jaxon said. Breeze moved, and Jada's eyes widened in alarm. He couldn't hear Jaxon. I tapped my mouth and started to repeat every word Jaxon and Breeze said. Jada's eyes stayed glued on my face. The car slightly adjusted as she moved into position, but now that Jada knew it was coming, he shifted his balance.

"Here," I handed over the blankets, and she slipped the straps over her shoulder. There was a moment of confusion as she tried to figure out if they would be better in front of her or behind her.

"Back," Shim said, "You're going to climb facing them."

Breeze's eyebrows rose, but she blew out a breath, making a strangled sound, and looped them to her back.

Jaxon talked Breeze through every movement as she climbed the boys like a tree. Twice, hands got caught in blankets. But eventually, she was slowly rising to stand on Jaxon's shoulders. Leaning against the wall became a problem as she had nowhere to go to balance. It was more of Jaxon's muscles that kept her from falling than balance, and when she was finally standing, both of the boys were sweating profusely, their skin growing wet and slick. At the bottom, the strain on Jada's face was tremendous. He blew out breaths of air with each move Breeze made, but his white-knuckled lock on Jaxon's calves was solid. By the time Breeze was standing on Jaxon's shoulders, she was able to fold over the edge into the tunnel entrance.

"Argh—" I screeched. Shim shouted in alarm as her weight loss caused the carriage to pitch.

My fingers dug deeper into the rock, nails cracking as I found my balance. The carriage steadied. A fine tremor had set into my legs, but I held on, waiting for an eternity until Breeze's head came over the ledge.

"Hey," she shouted down to us with a choking laugh. "It's a tunnel." Breeze burst into tears, trying to speak through them as she continued, "but there is nothing here I can tie anything to. I don't know what to do. Help."

I was about to talk her through it when Jaxon's voice interrupted me. "Breeze, baby, you can do this. Listen. How wide is the door? Can you brace your feet on each side?"

A tense moment followed as she disappeared again. "Yeah. I can do it." Her voice sounded calmer even as she sniffed back tears.

"Okay, tie the straps together from the bags."

"What about the blankets?" She asked, confused.

"No, just the straps. Use that knot I taught you and loop the end you keep and wrap it around your hand."

"Jaxon, are you sure she can hold you?" Shim called up, worry stressing his voice.

"Yes," Jaxon said confidently. "I know she can do this."

We didn't see Breeze again. Several minutes later, a rope of the braided straps dropped in front of Jaxon. It only went to his waist, but he coiled it around his hand and reached up with the other hand to climb the rope. I nodded to Jada to let go as Jaxon slowly pulled himself off Jada's shoulders.

The carriage shifted harder this time, and Jada's hands, free now, scrambled for a hold on the rough rock wall behind him. By the time the three of us had regained our balance, Jaxon was pulling himself over the ledge.

I took a shuddering breath as I looked over at Shim.

It was another eternity before they both put their head over the ledge. "You ready?" Jaxon shouted.

"Yes," we all shouted back, impatient.

Jaxon disappeared and a long rope made of blankets dropped down the shaft. "Grace, you need to go next."

"No, you go." I shook my head. I couldn't leave Shim behind.

"Is someone going to climb the damn rope?" Jaxon shouted.

Shim made a frustrated noise in his throat, "I'm a stronger climber than you, Grace. I don't know how long that rope or the elevator will last, and if something happens, the last person up needs to be fast. Now move it." As if to emphasize his point, the carriage shifted, dropping a couple of inches. If that happened again, none of us would make it.

Panicked, mad at Shim, my adrenalin spiking, I reached out and, with a growl, grabbed onto the rope. Jada boosted me up and as my feet left the ground, I heard the carriage clang against the wall and a quick shuffling as the boys moved to rebalance.

As I slammed against the wall, it took all my concentration to hang on and a lot of my rage to haul myself up. I wrapped the rope around my leg and hand over hand pulled upward. Sweat slicked my skin, my hands were slippery. I felt like I was moving an inch at a time, but I came to a knot and used it to pull myself up, then another knot. Breeze was calling down something annoyingly encouraging. My breath was wheezing, and I kept repeating my *just keep climbing* mantra. About that time, the rage wore off, and my muscles were trembling in fatigue. I reached the tunnel entrance. Stretching one arm onto the ledge and clinging to the rope with the other, I pulled, muscles straining. So close! My fingers grasped at the floor, slipping in the dirt, skin tearing at sharp-edged stones. Breeze grabbed onto the back of my shirt and my pants, she pulled, and I strained and slithered until I collapsed face down in the tunnel.

Relief flooded me, and I burst into tears, gasping, I breathed in the dirt, choked and sneezed and laughed all at the same time. Rolling onto my back, tears streamed down my face. I can't believe I made it. My arms were vibrating, the muscles spasming.

"Grace," Jaxon groaned. With a strength that came from the remnants of rage I felt for Shim, I pulled myself together and rolled toward Jaxon. I'd barely noticed crawling over him and now saw that he was braced with his feet on each side of the crude opening and had the blanket wrapped around his waist. His face was flushed with exertion as he strained. A long brown arm came over the ledge, and Breeze was leaning precariously out, trying to help Jada get up. He seemed stuck on the edge and unable to hear our directions. I grabbed his wrist, braced my foot next to Jaxon's, and pulled. The three of us were able to drag him into the tunnel.

Relieved of the pressure on the blanket rope, Jaxon quickly rubbed his hand on his pants, then braced himself again and called the all-clear to Shim. The carriage clanged against the wall. I had to see if he was okay. Before thinking about what I was doing, I leaned through the opening and looked down. Shim was dangling from the rope. My head swam, and I fell back. Jaxon was straining again, and Jada was helping pull up the rope. Soon Shim's arm was reaching over the ledge, and I grabbed it and pulled. Muscles straining and bulging, he pulled himself cleanly up and over the edge.

I fell onto my back and stared at the ceiling. We made it.

Shim stretched out on the dirt floor next to me. "Grace..."

"Shut up."

12

THE LAKE

WHAT WAS THAT NOISE?

I sat up so fast that it took a minute for my body to register the motion and respond with a wave of pain and nausea.

Every single inch of me hurt. Had I been thrown from a moving truck?

Swaying in the low light, I tried to remember where I was. Someone lay slumped next to me. I tried to poke them. Maybe whoever that was could tell me what had happened. But my arm refused the command, my hands tucked up under my armpits and I remembered our terrifying climb up the elevator shaft the night before.

Wait, was that yesterday? Were there days if there was no sun? And what had woken me?

Someone left a lamp on, bleeding a thin line of light over Breeze's sleeping form and barely lifting the pitch-blackness of the dark cavern.

I looked around for what had disturbed my sleep. This tunnel wasn't as hot as the ones on the lower levels; the floor was cooler and the ceiling smoother. Both were still rock, but they had been chiseled flat, and the corners were neat ninety-degree angles, feeling more like a room and less like a cavern.

The ground trembled.

Ah, an earthquake—a small one from the feel of it. Did they call them earthquakes here? Maybe they were called nadun-quakes? Or something else?

The ground trembled again. It couldn't have been more than a 3, maybe a 3.5. We were used to them in California, and since the ceiling didn't rain down rock, it must be reasonably safe.

I lay back down.

Then I heard a metallic ping.

Ping.

Ping.

Ping.

Rapid-fire snaps came from the direction of the shaft, followed by a whirling sound.

A lamp turned on beside me, and Shim sat up. He aimed his light at the dark shaft, and we watched strands of elevator cables slide past, followed soon after by the sound of metal impacting metal. I flinched as a barrage of rock and metal flew by followed by the sound of a considerably greater impact.

"If that was the cable that held up the lift—" Before I could finish, there was a loud, long screech, like nails against a never-ending chalkboard. The sound was familiar from when we had ridden the carriage.

It went on and on.

It woke the others.

"What is it?" Breeze squinted her eyes as she held her hands over her ears.

The sound carried on, growing fainter but still going as the carriage dropped. How deep was the shaft? I started counting in my head like I was waiting for thunder.

One Mississippi, two Mississippi, three Mississippi.

I must have counted wrong because I got to thirty Mississippi, and there was no crash. The sound just faded away.

"Jaxon, get back," Shim reached out and pulled back his brother, who had his head over the edge. Shim's shirt rode up, showing the new white bandage in the center of his toned chest, contrasting sharply with his dark skin and flanked by bruising under his ribs and old road rash scars down his side.

"Couldn't see anything," Jaxon said, frowning.

"Watch for falling rock, you idiot. Someday you're gonna get your head knocked clean off your body." Shim snapped.

"Was—was that the carriage we were in? Falling?" Breeze asked.

Shim nodded. "Try to get some more sleep." He caught my eye as he lay back down, facing me.

Slowly, the others returned to their strips of blankets and everyone turned off their lamps, except Breeze.

I sat frozen, looking down at Shim. He was shaking—no, I was. My entire system was flooded with adrenalin like I'd touched a live electrical wire. Everything felt messed up inside and my mind raced. I wanted to yell, but I was too tired. I wanted to scream, but I had no voice. I wanted to run, but there was nowhere to go. And I was angry at Shim. So angry. I considered pushing him away or demanding he move. But my soul, tired of limping alone through this crisis, yearned for its other half. My heart was in mourning and I wanted to curl up in his arms and weep.

I broke eye contact to glance at the dark doorway we had emerged onto this level from. We had changed from the people we had been on Earth. And I was beginning to realize we may have a long way to go before we could get back home.

If we could get back.

The idea of being trapped here forever shocked me almost

as much as the realization that almost dying was starting to seem normal.

Eventually, my exhausted body won over my racing mind, and I collapsed back down, turning away from Shim, into a restless sleep.

∞

THE NEXT TIME I woke up, the others were already up and stretching, cataloging injuries, and packing up supplies. Not that we had much.

I walked far enough down the tunnel away from their lights and switched mine off before taking a bathroom break. It was spooky in the dark, my heart racing, and I finished quickly and returned to where the group was waiting for me.

These tunnels were different. Besides being wider, conduits and cables were snaking through the ceiling, and I'd passed several signs on my way.

"Where's Shim?" I asked when I got back.

Jaxon pointed in the opposite direction up the tunnel. "Found one of those tombstone box things that had power."

My pulse quickened, and we walked in the direction Jaxon had pointed.

Up ahead, Shim was hunched over a terminal that hummed with lights. The tall metal arch set into the rock wall like a portal that led nowhere.

We were almost there when a tremor vibrated through the walls.

"Wow," Breeze said, her hands spread wide like she was riding a wave. "That was bigger than the one last night." A stream of dust trickled down the wall, and an occasional small rock plunked harmlessly to the ground.

"I thought the tremor last night was from the elevator falling?" I steadied myself with a hand against the terminal. I shivered. Small earthquakes usually didn't bother me, but something about being underground with an unknown amount of rock above my head—I decided not to dwell on that.

"Our weight in the elevator probably splintered the cables, then when the tremor happened, it was just too much and—" Jada made a downward motion with his hands.

As soon as the shaking stopped, Shim bent back over the monitor the metal arch was protecting. A few lights were on, and a large square message was blinking. The lettering was bold and red, and it looked like a warning—but for what? The text was the same hash marks we had seen on the drink bottles underlined by a moving white chevron.

He pushed buttons and cleaned off surfaces for several minutes.

Even though we had slept, I still felt exhausted, limbs like jelly from the climb up the shaft and rattled from the stress of being trapped in an alien world. And while I was still so mad at Shim, it seemed a ridiculous waste of energy at this point.

I should talk to him. Hear his side of the story. My head told me it wouldn't change anything, but my anxiety over our situation made me want to give in and let him apologize and we could go back to being the type of friends who worked really well together and weren't stupid enough to get romantically involved.

But my heart wasn't on board with the just friends idea and before I could grab his shoulders and cry on his neck, I forced myself to ask.

"What did you find out?"

Shim shrugged, "Unless you've learned to read Nadun. Nadunish? Nadun-es? Or do they speak Teran?" He let out a choked laugh that turned into a sigh. "Grace, we know nothing."

I slumped beside him.

He leaned into the monitor, his forehead clunking on the surface. I heard him whisper. "We almost died in an elevator shaft. An earthquake or a cave-in could crush us at any moment. No one would ever find us. And there's nothing I can do."

Shim straightened, and in a move more characteristic of Jaxon, he kicked the bottom of the terminal in frustration. I saw him clench his fist like he would hit the wall, then looking at the rock wall, thought better of the idea and flexed his fists several times instead.

I wasn't sure if I should stop him or join him.

"Grace, I am so sorry." Shim started, and I cut him off.

"Shut up." Even though I thought I was ready, I wasn't. And I couldn't believe he wanted to discuss this now.

"No, not this time. You have to listen."

"Listen to what? Your excuses?"

"My explanation."

"Why? Is it going to help us get home? Shim," I wanted to grab onto the front of his shirt with both hands and shake him and then yell at him not to touch me. I was so confused. "Is your explanation going to help us get out of these tunnels and find help?"

"No," he conceded. "I know we have to get home before the Helios find us. But this is important too." His voice rose.

"You had all summer and this fall to explain to me why you were dating, or whatever we were doing, with me, while you had a girlfriend."

"You are my girlfriend. You are who I care about."

I glared at him. "Then you lied about having this other girlfriend?" My mouth tensed. I couldn't believe his audacity.

Shim hung his head, "No, that was true. It's complicated."

"What the hell? You know what, I don't want to hear it!" I said, my head pounding.

"Um, you guys are kinda loud." Breeze interrupted. I had

forgotten we had an audience. "Hey, is that an arrow? Is that the direction we are supposed to go?"

Both Shim and I gaped at Breeze. She was pointing to the moving chevron under the blinking red notice. Sure enough, when you thought about it that way, it looked like an arrow pointing up the tunnel.

Shim raised his head and let out a bellowing cry at the ceiling. He picked up his backpack and stalked off in the direction the chevron pointed.

"Good job, Breeze," I muttered under my breath, stomping after Shim.

THE OTHERS TOOK the directional chevron as a sign of hope.

"We are going to see Skylar soon!" Breeze crowed as she told Jaxon about her plans for when they got home. Jada looked lost in thought as he walked.

"Hurry up." I called to them.

That's when the big one hit.

I tripped at the first shiver. Before I had time to catch myself, the next rumble shook the floor and slammed me against the rock wall. I covered my head as slivers of rock and dust rained.

Someone shouted.

Shim raced back.

"Grace, are you okay?" I don't know how he was moving. The ground was still rippling beneath us.

I nodded, "I'm fine."

"Up ahead—a large chamber—it should be safer there." He panted out before racing off to help the others.

I ran for the chamber.

The walls were undulating, and every other step hit hard as the ground rose to meet me. I jumped over several larger rocks that had fallen across the chamber entrance. The tunnel ended and the floor abruptly changed to a metal walkway over a dark lake of water.

I slowed and wrinkled my nose at the gassy, stagnant smell. But there was no time to stop.

"Come on!" Breeze rushed past and barely spared a glance at the enormous room.

The shaking still rumbled through the chamber, the lake gurgling and gasping until a spout of boiling water and gas shot into the air.

Up ahead, Breeze screamed as she avoided the spray and then skirted a vertical conveyor belt in the middle of the metal bridge. My eyes followed the path of the industrial-looking conveyor, up, up, up the circular shaft cut into the rock. Artificial lights radiated from islands of illumination lining the walls of the lake.

Jada caught up and hurried past me. As more spouts gushed from the lake into the air.

Lights shone on the opposite end of the bridge, beckoning me. They glowed the same greenish hue that gave everything in here a ghoulish, mossy look. Our shoes clanged and clomped on the metal treads as we raced like bugs to the ghostly glow of the zapper.

Breathing hard, I pushed on, passing the halfway point, where the frozen lift seemed poised on the brink of purpose. There was a hole in the bridge where buckets dipped in to fill with water. The back of the buckets had controls and a flat area for cargo. I'd never seen anything like it. It looked like it still operated, but the mechanics were rusty and repaired with only patches holding it together in places.

I looked back, and Shim and Jaxon were fighting. Again.

They had made it a couple of yards onto the bridge. Behind them, the tunnel was raining down rock.

The ground shook again and I wanted to find a door frame to stand in or a safe place to hide. The whole chamber rumbled restlessly, punctuated by the spurts of water.

I was almost to the other side when, with a crack, a stream of fire shot up in front of me, melting a section of the bridge.

I gasped as steam burned across my skin.

"The waters on fire!" Someone screamed.

Another spray shot up behind me, and the spray burned my back.

"Run!"

Pushing forward, I jumped the hole in the bridge.

In a chain reaction, fire raced across the surface of the lake. As if it was a live, sentient entity, it hissed and snapped at us. The previously harmless geysers of gas were now blowtorches shooting flames into the sky. They burned and scorched the air, and when they crossed the bridge, the structure started to bend from the heat.

"Watch out." Jada had reached the other side and turned. At the look of horror on his face, I twisted and looked behind me.

The whole lake was a blazing boiling pit of fire.

Jaxon and Shim made it to the halfway point before a super-heated geyser of fire shot up between us, halting their progress forward. As they turned to go back, the bridge behind them collapsed into the lake of fire, blocking their retreat.

They were trapped.

"Shim," my call was swallowed up by the roar of the inferno. I tried again, yelling louder, "the lift!"

Breeze screamed as a section of the railing next to the brothers fell into the scalding water.

Jaxon teetered on the edge, his arms windmilling. Shim

grabbed his brother's shirt and yanked him back. In one quick motion, he used the momentum to throw Jaxon into one of the buckets. He looked back at me, his face a wreck of raw emotion.

Shim's words from earlier echoed in my head. As *long as we are together, we can do this.*

We had to get back home to Earth, and we couldn't do that if we split up.

But the brothers were trapped. The blaze was ravenously hungry, feeding off the gas that the tremors released. The flames grew bolder and taller as if they consumed the air around them.

Shim and Jaxon had to go.

Shim stared at me a second longer than was safe. Our eyes locked.

An hour ago, I'd been done with him. Now, I couldn't bear to let him go. With Shim and I, it hadn't been fate or an immediate, passionate attraction. It wasn't always comfortable, and there were a lot of times where we hurt each other. But I trusted him. We were friends and had each other's backs. Always. We were stronger together.

His eyes stayed on me until the last possible minute.

Then he threw himself onto the lift with Jaxon and the bucket started to rise. I watched it rise up and up until the brothers were swallowed by the darkness above.

Hands pulled at me. I was lost in a wave of emotion, yanked and spun like I was underwater and didn't know which way was up.

I forgot how to breathe.

I numbly stumbled along, following Jada. There were lights, stone walls, a noise like an alarm. I had a vague sense that Breeze was on my other side, clinging to me, while back at the lake, a piece of my soul had ripped loose and lifted away.

For the first time, I didn't think we would make it home.

13

SPLIT-UP

SHIM

"WHAT THE HELL, SHIM!" Jaxon slammed his hand repeatedly against the side of the metal bucket. "What the Stars were you thinking?"

I ducked a foot but missed the elbow that slammed into my left pec as Jaxon lashed out. Jaxon struggled to flip over in the confined space and the rusted metal surface rang like a bell at the impact of his foot. With nowhere to go, I curled in to protect my core. But the damage was done.

What were we going to do now? I'd messed up, again. I should have found a way to stay.

I hugged my legs tighter against the clenching in my stomach. How was I going to find Grace again? We couldn't pick up a phone, pull up a map app, or even ask anyone for help if we ever found someone to ask. We were completely alone. And been chased by the Helios, known killers—at least they had been on Earth.

The familiar sinking sensation of failure landed on my shoulders and pressed me deeper into the curved bottom.

Jaxon pulled himself to the rim of the bucket and craned his head and upper body over the side, trying to spot the others.

The bucket tipped, a jerky movement that interrupted the gentle oscillatory motion. Skin scraped across rusted metal as I slid into Jaxon, my hands scrambled for purchase. I got a view of the fiery lake below growing distant.

Heart racing, I quickly leaned back and balanced my brother's actions.

As always.

My head thunked against the opposite wall. I closed my eyes just for a second, trying to breathe.

Stars, I was so stupid!

Before Jada and Breeze dragged her off, I'd stared into Grace's eyes and, once again, I hadn't been able to say the right thing.

It was my fault she wasn't safe. I'd messed up. The alarm went off the minute I hit the controls for the bucket lift. I should have known something like that would happen.

I had to fix it. I had to fix something.

I opened my eyes and shook my head to get the hair out of my eyes. The mechanical box mounted above the free-hanging scoop caught my attention. It was hard to resist the urge to crawl up there and take a closer look. The mechanisms of every piece of tech I'd examined on this moon was so different from what you would find on Earth. They seemed to follow the basic laws of mechanics but I couldn't wrap my head around them.

The bucket shook again and reminded me of the fragility of our situation.

Since arriving, the other lifts we had ridden were more of your traditional mine elevators, though exceptionally long. This wasn't a lift. This transport was closer to a vertical bucket suspended belt conveyor. They probably called them something else here.

I hated not understanding how something worked. If you

don't know how it works, you can't fix it. And I couldn't fix any of this. I was practically useless here.

I slammed my hand down on the metal surface in frustration.

We had traveled well past the point where we could see the fire from the lake below. Jaxon kicked out as he twisted, still trying to see into the dark abyss below us. His foot skimmed past my nose.

"Watch it," I growled, tired of fighting.

"You watch it," Jaxon shot back. In the light of my lamp, I could see his twisted-up face, mottled red and ready to blow.

"Jax, please stop moving." I hated that my voice whined as I added, "Don't tip us—please."

I clutched the edges of the bucket as it swung. The scoop was large, the size of an excavator, but the space cramped, especially with Jaxon kicking and flipping around.

"Why'd you drag me onto that damn bridge?"

I hadn't. But Jaxon would pick a fight with a rock when he got frightened. Unlike me, he was fearless—most of the time, but he hated water and anything to do with it.

"You'd rather have stayed in the tunnel with the ceiling falling on us?" I reasoned. I don't know why I bothered.

"I'd rather we were not on this damn planet."

I tried not to say it, but "—it's a moon."

That set him off again.

"And why did you throw me into this–this–thing? I could have made that jump."

I took a breath, unclenching my jaw. "You could have jumped over flames shooting twenty feet into the air with a rusted bridge buckling under you—surrounded by a burning lake?"

"Maybe." He shot back. Then his face dropped like a major power outage. He slumped down to the bottom of the bucket.

"They're all alone, Shim. What if something happens to them without us there? We don't split up. We don't." His voice wavered.

It was a gut punch.

The black cloud of fear rising inside me since I hit the button on the conveyor choked me as we lifted higher and higher into the unknown. He was right. I shouldn't have done it.

We don't split up. We can do anything if we are together, even find our way home, but only if we are together.

14

CLOSE ENCOUNTERS
GRACE

MY BODY KEPT MOVING, but my head was back at the fiery lake, watching Shim disappear into the darkness. Jada turned back to glare at me. I knew I was letting him down, but I couldn't pull myself together.

I tried to remember Shim's last words to me. What were my last words to him? Was it something in anger? Is that how we end?

Stumbling along behind Jada, a horrible thought struck me.

This is what happened to my mother when they got stuck on Earth. We should never have left the tunnel we first landed in. We should have just stayed and kept trying things. Anything. Until the passage came back. My mother was trapped on Earth for twenty-five years. I couldn't do that. We can't get stuck here. We had to get home.

Breeze had wanted to stay in the tunnel. She was right. Again. This was all my fault. I was the one that had the stone. I said we should leave. I picked the direction to go in the tunnel that led to the lake that split us up.

No, that was the one thing I hadn't done. The chevrons had

directed us. I thought it would lead to some sign of life. *Not this.*

"Grace, snap out of it." Jada looked pissed. "Breeze, can you still hear the alarm?" Jada asked.

I was surprised to realize Breeze wasn't clinging to me. She was holding me up. Her hands dragged me along even as tears streamed down her face.

Breeze nodded, "It's still going, but it's farther away now." And like a switch, my hearing kicked back on. A smoke detector-like bell rang behind us.

"How long has that been going off?" I asked, turning to Breeze. Her mouth gapped open.

"The alarm went off as soon as the lift started," She shot me a nervous side glance. Under her breath, she added, "about the same time you checked out."

"This way." Jada hesitated at a branch in the tunnel and then picked the one on the right and kept moving. Breeze nudged me to follow.

I picked up my pace, and we caught up with Jada.

I let go of Breeze and touched Jada's arm.

Jada jumped in surprise but turned towards me as he kept moving. "Are you okay now?"

"No," I answered honestly. "Where are we going?"

Jada shrugged. "People follow alarms."

Breeze grabbed Jada's other arm. "But maybe they could help us. At least they could tell us where the lift goes." The lights mounted along the walls flooded the tunnel and I could see hope in her eyes.

Jada was shaking his head before she had finished speaking.

"Police respond to alarms. If these Helios are in charge, and as bad as you say, then we don't want them to find us before we can find someone to help. Especially since we need to know where that lift goes."

We kept moving at a brisk pace. Shouting had left my throat dry and scratchy. I uncapped the lid of my bottle and took the smallest sip.

We had another problem.

Shim had all the bottles of that drink we found. We each carried a plastic bottle we had refilled earlier. Mine was still half full. Jada's had a little bit more. Breeze was almost out. I guess we had an even greater reason to find help, but how could we ever trust anyone?

Desperation flooded my body like it was injected into my bloodstream. My body felt permeable, like the darkness inside and outside had linked and the barrier of my skin was irrelevant.

We had traveled a long way and the alarm had faded. The topography changed. The lights lining the corridors disappeared and we switched back on our lamps. They bounced spookily off massive outcroppings of rocks.

The ceilings were taller now and there were more nooks and alcoves and rough-hewn tunnels. The path we were traveling turned from smooth to rocky. Somewhere, we had made a wrong turn and ended up in an area where fewer people traveled.

I heard a noise. Someone was behind us.

We were passing another alcove entrance, this one tucked back behind a peninsula of rock, and I would have missed it entirely if I hadn't turned at the sound.

In the distance was the distinct sound of running feet, a way behind us, but drawing closer.

"Wait, someone is following us!" I hissed at the others. Spinning around, I squinted into the darkness. That was the scuff of shoes.

Could it be the Helios? Should I switch off my lamp or should we call out to them? What if they weren't someone we wanted to meet? If we turned out our lights, would they just pass us by?

I had less than a minute to make a decision.

"Breeze, check out that alcove. I'll go get Jada." Not hearing me, he had kept walking and was several yards ahead of us.

Something I'd noticed about Jada since we had arrived on this moon rock was that he didn't like to be in the front or the back. I suspect not being able to hear made him feel vulnerable in either position. But he was in the lead now because he was still angry with me and keeping his distance.

Sprinting, I grabbed his arm and spun him around. Like an idiot, I looked away and pointed back down the tunnel where the footsteps were coming from. "Someone is coming." I hissed, looking back. His eyebrows raised in question. I could hear the single runner's footsteps were joined by booted feet, lots of them.

We had to hide.

"Someone's coming," I repeated. Jada's eyes flared. Grabbing his arm, I hauled him back to the alcove Breeze had disappeared into. I hoped this was a good idea.

When we got inside, the chamber was dark.

It was a dead end.

"Grace," Breeze hissed.

I spun around. She wasn't there.

The entrance ramped down with solid walls of rock rubble on either side. Suddenly, Breeze stepped out from behind the wall of rubble and motioned to us.

We raced over. It was a fake front. From the backside, the solid rock was brilliant masonry work with tiny holes cut out so you could see through to the alcove entrance.

We threw ourselves behind the blind and had just turned off our lights when the running footsteps approached.

My breath blasted in and out like a leaf blower, but it was drowned out by the pounding of my heartbeat.

I bent over, hands clenching my trembling knees as I struggled to breathe. I realized I was close to one of the peepholes and I leaned in, closing one eye to peer through the crack. The jet-black darkness of the tunnel entrance lightened slightly, then faded back to black as the lone runner passed the alcove.

The chorus of boots grew louder and louder.

The steps of the runner returned, skidding across the gravel as they entered the alcove that led to our chamber. The sound of rocks scraping together. Something shuffling. I squinted through the peek-hole and followed the sound. I could barely make out a faint blue glow. Curiosity had me shifting until I was leaning around the corner of the stone wall to get a better look.

From the shape, I guessed it was a boy. I got the impression he was tall, but his head was in shadow.

"Oh no. This isn't the one. Oh, Stars, no, no, no." His chant ended in a whisper.

Whoever he was, he was frantically searching the opposite end of the alcove as the *ka-dunk, ka-dunk, ka-dunk* of clomping boots grew closer, echoing in the small chamber.

"Here," I hissed.

I had no idea what possessed me to call to him. It was one of those moments where you just followed your gut. It's something I learned from the ocean. On the water, you had to trust your instincts. And right now, mine were screaming at me that we had to help this boy.

Before I thought about it, I stepped out of the alcove and flashed my light on, off. That was all it took. The boy hurtled towards me. I grabbed his arm, and in the exact second I pulled him around to our hiding place, he extinguished his light. Stones were still rolling across the ground from how fast he had moved.

And then the marching boots arrived.

"Check in there." A gravelly voice sounded from the tunnel.

My swallow sounded loud and so did the ragged inhale through my nose. I opened my mouth to breathe, worried the sound would give us away.

I felt the press of the boy's trembling body next to mine. His hand gripped my arm.

Footsteps stopped at the alcove entrance while a storm of boots thundered past. Pinpricks of light came through the peepholes in the wall.

A crunch of rocks. Someone sliding.

"You see the kid?" a woman's gravelly voice asked.

"Nah. Nothin' here." A gruff male voice replied.

"Check the back."

"Do you think the kid is one of them?"

"Maybe," Gravel responded, "the Helios know something. They've got us tracking down every lead. Though, if it was an alien invasion, I'm not sure why the enemy would send a kid."

"Nothing in the back." Gruff paused, and scuffing sounded. "Yeah, it's more likely it's just a runner not wanting to register."

"The alarm sounded, so he probably went up the lift to Bashita. A team will catch him there."

Gruff groaned. "That's going to be so much work. Why bother? We rarely catch any of them."

Gravel laughed; it wasn't a pleasant sound. "That's about to change. We've got eyes on the inside. Our friend helped us tap into two of their security monitors. Next time their retrieval squad throws a welcome party, we'll be greeting them as they leave. This time, we'll catch young Blaze. We'll catch them all."

"That will be something to see. But why catch him? Isn't he usually a good source of revenue?"

"Since he took over the payments, he's been shorting us. Not sending the full amount. And they want to see what he knows about the workers' strike—what are you doing?" Gravel snapped.

"I'm taking a break." There was a shuffle of feet, and a bright light filled the cave. "We've been chasing down leads for hours. I'm exhausted."

"You'll get a permanent break if the Helios catch you sitting on the job. You do not want to cross them—" A scuffing of boots muddled the voices, "...they have someone embedded in our unit. That's their way. I just haven't figured out who it is. Until we know, you better not get caught slacking off."

A rock shifted under me and I wobbled, planting a hand on the ground. What if the people in the chamber heard me? I swallowed a gasp as the boy's fingers dug into my other arm.

The voices came closer, and I stopped breathing altogether. Every muscle in my body tightened, preparing to run. The pinpricks of light had faded, and I couldn't see anything in the dark.

"Stars, you're right. They are brutal. You hear what happened at the unregistered prison? They razed the thing to the ground. No one walked out, not even the guards. That's our own people! Can you imagine what they would do to a group of spies?"

"That's exactly why we have to find them. With a workers' strike looming, we can't be worrying about aliens."

"Aliens! What an age we live in." Their footsteps faded away, following the direction of the receding marching boots.

Behind the wall, none of us moved.

It was minutes, maybe longer, before the boy shifted. His hand on my arm relaxed, and he let go. "Who are you?" he whispered. The faint sound was like a shout in the darkness.

"My name's Grace," I breathed back.

"I'm Jeu'l."

We sat in the darkness for several more minutes before he

spoke again. "I think they are gone. Thank you for helping me. Are you unregistered?"

Breeze's whispered *Shhh* interrupted us. Then she added, "What is he saying? Can you understand him?"

The boy jumped and the sound of feet sliding on rock was much louder than our voices.

We all froze and listened in the dark. The boots didn't return.

A glow came from the boy's wrist. His light source was some type of watch on his wrist. "Are there more of you?" He demanded in a harsh whisper as he backed away, a hand held in front as if to ward us off.

"It's okay." I slowly slid from the hiding spot. My body was shaking from the adrenalin crash, and I tried to use a soothing whisper, "These are my friends Jada and Breeze." I motioned for the others to come out of hiding. He eyed Breeze up and down quickly and dismissed her as non-threatening. When Jada stepped out, Jeu'l's eyes widened.

Both boys looked about the same age, sixteen, but Jada was at least a head taller than Jeu'l. And to be fair, the confusion on Jada's face as he tried to understand what we were saying did look like anger.

"I can understand him," I told Breeze and Jada. Hooking a finger on my mother's necklace that we had learned this summer was a translator. It was amazing it still works after decades.

"Jada and Breeze can't understand you," I said to Jeu'l.

"Where are their linka, and why is yours so ancient? I think my mother had one of those models." He said, leaning in to look at my necklace.

I shrugged, I didn't want to explain about the necklace, and I wasn't sure what a linka was. Unsure what to do next, I waited for him to say more.

And he did. Then, we couldn't get him to shut up.

∞

"SO, every sixteen-year-old has to pick what they are going to be for the rest of their lives?" Breeze asked, her voice rising. She hadn't warmed up to Jeu'l.

At least a half hour had passed since the marching boots had left. The feeling of a metal band around my chest had released enough that I could breathe. The others also felt bolder. We sat on our strips of blanket, watching Jeu'l in the glow of his linka as he talked. I liked him. There was something in his nature that was inviting and friendly.

"Years? Do you mean age? Yes, it is mandatory. The Law of Registration requires every teenager in the Federation to choose. For some, there is no choice." His face was glum.

I relayed his answer to Jada and Breeze. This process was time-consuming, especially when his translator would pick up what I said and he would make corrections, which I would translate, and he would then correct again.

We went in circles.

"Stars, Grace, that is so unfair," Breeze said. She was sitting cross-legged, tapping her empty bottle on her leg. "If you don't have a place in a Learning Center, which sounds like college, you are forced into unpaid labor camps? That's—that's slavery!"

I was about to repeat Breeze's comment, but Jeu'l was already nodding animatedly, his linka having translated what she said, "It's called the Age of Consent. You can also join the military, but you usually have a family member in politics to get a position." I repeated what he had said, and Jada pulled on my leg, turning me slightly so he could see my mouth in the glow of the light.

"Why do you do that?" Jeu'l asked Jada. He spoke directly

to Jada. It was so strange, I could not only understand what he was saying, I could even hear his accent, a lilting one, like a French mashup up with something else. He waited for me to translate.

I was trying to figure out what to say when Jada responded. "I'm deaf," Jeu'l cocked his head in confusion. Jada continued, "I was born unable to hear." He put his hands to his ears and shook his head. "I can read lips, but it is so dark it is hard to see what she is saying."

Jeu'l reached forward and touched the lamp clipped to Jada's chest. The room lit up, and Jada blinked at Jeu'l, who was examining the lamp. With the added light, I could finally see Jeu'l. Even kneeling in front of Jada, he was noticeably shorter and thinner, with toned muscles, like a runner. His hair was styled into dark brown spikes shot through with green.

"Hey, you have green hair like mine." I was shocked.

Seeing Jeu'l's hair made something constrict in my chest. I knew my hair color was genetic. My mom had it to. I missed recognizing something of myself in another person. Recently, I found I had forgotten little things about her. I ached from the loss.

"Of course," he laughed, "I'm from LaDer too. Well, my mother was. I got her hair and height. My dad was Teran, and I got my name and skin tone from him." He waved his hands, showing off the olive skin of his arms.

"Does everyone on LaDer have green in their hair?" I was fascinated by the idea.

Jeu'l cocked his head suspiciously at me. It took me a minute to realize how stupid and dangerous my questions were. "Don't you know? Haven't you ever been to LaDer?"

My mouth dropped open, and I tried to think of a plausible lie. Breeze chose that moment to break in again with another question we should have known the answer to, "but I don't understand why they put the law in place. Why can't everyone choose what they want to be?"

"Because we are dying." Jeu'l shrugged like the answer was simple. "The government denies it, but the law is just another form of population control. Once they outlawed procreation–"

"Wow, wait. You can't have babies?" I was stunned.

"No. It's illegal to get pregnant without government approval. They put that in place when I was a child. My parents already had another child, my older brother. They would have been put to death if I had been born after the law passed."

"Both of them?" Breeze gasped after I finished translating.

"Well, it wouldn't be fair to put just the woman to death for getting pregnant. Sometimes it takes two. How is it that you don't know all of this already?" Jeu'l looked at us strangely. "Where did you say you were from?"

I stiffened and my stomach knotted as I tried to think of how to answer the question.

"Grace, can I have some of your drink?" Breeze changed topics and I sighed in relief. She waved her empty water bottle. I handed mine over.

"Do you have extra? I'm parched. They've been chasing me all day." Jeu'l asked.

I translated and Jada offered him his bottle.

"Jada," Breeze whispered, "are you sure you want to share? He's a—" she hesitated and avoided looking at Jeu'l as she whispered, "—an alien. He could have, you know, diseases." I groaned as I knew that Jeu'l's translator would have picked that up.

Jada deliberately handed his bottle over.

Jeu'l took it with a warm smile at Jada, then held it up in the light, examining the milky fluid through the clear plastic. He watched Breeze drink from my bottle and followed her actions.

Taking off the cap, he took a tentative sip. His eyes widened, and he pulled the bottle away to look at it again.

"This is Eloa! Are you sure you want to share?" At Jada's nod of encouragement, Jeu'l took another sip and closed his eyes as he swallowed.

Capping the bottle, he handed it back to Jada. His voice was reverent as he thanked us. "That was so very generous of you."

"You know what this is?" Jada asked.

"Yes. I've only had a few drops before when I was a child. It was a special occasion. But I remember. You've been so kind to share this rare bounty." Jeu'l cocked his head at us, eyes squinting," but you don't know that, do you? You don't seem to know what you have, and I suspect you don't know where you are." Jeu'l returned to his earlier question, suspicion growing in his eyes. "You aren't runners—what are you?"

15

BASHITA

SHIM

THE FIRE below faded to darkness and the shaft we were traveling up narrowed. Tunnels branched off, each with conveyor systems connecting like spider webs to ours. The pale glow of LED-like lights illuminated the intersections. Metal shuddered as we passed over a switching station that redirected our bucket into one of the tall side tunnels.

Our ride angled off the main path, swinging more than the other buckets with our added weight as we entered the tunnel. Shivering, bumps raised on my sweaty arms. A feeling of wrongness spread through me as we traveled farther away from Grace.

Up ahead, a short platform was on one side of an approaching intersection. We were twenty feet off the tunnel floor.

Could we make that jump?

I didn't know how we would make it back to the others, but maybe the horrible imbalance that was growing in my gut as we traveled away from them would stop.

The platform was about as wide as my skateboard. It was doable, but could Jaxon make it?

Maybe.

The drop to the tunnel floor afterward might be a problem.

Before I could decide, there was a short drop and clang, and the bucket automatically transferred to yet another conveyor system and the platform was out of range.

Hopes dashed, I sunk down and resumed memorizing interchanges. Was that the fourth switch to the left and two to the right? I'd lost count contemplating the jump.

It was becoming obvious that there was no easy place for us to get out of this one-way ride. And even if we did, these were service tunnels, and we had no way back to the lake, to Grace and the others. We were going to have to ride this one to the end.

Dreading what was at the end of this line, my thoughts raced—what was happening to them? Had the Helios found them? Did they have enough to drink to get to safety? Who would help them? We had to find a way back home, but how would we do that if we weren't together? And even if we were together, how were we going to find our way back through the tunnels? Is this what my mother went through when she was trapped on Earth?

My head jumped from one worst-case scenario to the next. It felt like it was going to spin off my neck and my jaw ached from grinding my teeth.

This was all my fault.

Usually, Grace would make all these decisions and I got to support her and stuff. She would come up with some crazy plan, something I would never think of. Then, I would balance her out with the pure logic and mechanics of the situation. And it would work. We worked.

I didn't have a plan, didn't even know how to come up with one.

Logic and mechanics. Those were my things.

The mechanics of this massive conveyor system was a true

feat of engineering. Everything was aged but patched and maintained and still running. I tried tracking the exchanges and understanding the pattern of why some buckets would head in different directions.

As we traveled through the tunnels, we rose in elevation. We changed levels frequently and all the intersections and tunnels we passed now were lit with floating ball lamps.

I'd completely lost track of where we were and it was impossible to know how long we would be traveling, so I decided to get some rest and slid down to the bottom of the bucket next to Jaxon and fell asleep.

"Hey, you!" I woke up with a start.

"What are you doing?" Jerking up, I blinked in the darkness.

Jaxon pulled his head in, "there's someone down there."

I yanked him back and took his place. The bucket swung, and I clung to the edge. A single figure was below, lit by the strobes around an interchange for a lower conveyor system. The figure was dressed in all grey, from their boots to their helmet. A black belt strapped around their waist held something that looked like a weapon, and a silver visor covered their eyes. Red beams were coming out of the visor, bouncing around the tunnel, as the figure searched for the source of the shout.

"Let me see." Jaxon climbed my back, and the bucket swung wildly.

"Stop it." I managed to gasp out as my stomach did a pipeline swirl, and we hovered on the edge of flipping. When we swung back, I turned and grabbed Jaxon, pulling him down to the bottom of the bowl and quickly switching off our lamps. Jaxon snarled and scratched at me. It was like trying to hold a feral cat. I quickly put a hand over his mouth.

"That's a guard." I winced as he bit me. Pulling my hand back, I shoved him away. From the ambient light in the tunnel,

I saw the trapped fear on his face as he kicked out and struggled to the rim. By this time, we had passed into another tunnel, and I knew the figure would have disappeared from view.

Not for the first time, I wondered why I kept trying to help Jaxon. It always made me feel bad, and he didn't want help.

Why was I still trying to save him from himself?

Jaxon never thought before he did stuff; he was pure impulse, guts, and raw emotion. His anger ruled his head again and again.

I was done.

The minute I thought it, guilt clawed at me. Every time I wanted to give up on him, I saw my mom's face looking down at six-year-old me telling me "Jaxon is your responsibility. He is your *fila*. Keep him safe. Keep him out of trouble. Shim, I'm counting on you."

It was the only thing she had always believed I could do.

So, I kept doing it because I was the responsible one. It was a full-time job trying to keep Jaxon from blowing up the world. And there was never a payoff.

My mom and stepdad blamed me when Jaxon got in trouble and told me off when I tried to keep him out of trouble. I never won.

I was a complete and utter failure. Everyone knew it—even Grace.

The darkness clawed at me, and I switched back on the lamp.

Grace had been my one true friend. And I messed that up too.

What was wrong with me? Why did I let everyone push me around, like my opinion, my feelings, didn't matter? Why was I such a doormat?

Miserable, I clung to the hand that stung from Jaxon's bite, knowing I deserved it, and tried to find a corner to hide in the round bucket.

"Sorry," Jaxon grumbled. Looking up at him I saw the remorse on his face. He cursed, "You know how I get. I'd just hoped...you know, that it was someone that could help us get back to them."

I shook my head and looked away. The thing was, when Jaxon wasn't letting his anger control him, the little shit was an awesome brother. He knew our dad treated me like crap and favored him, and he always found ways to help me get what I needed—except football, I got stuck playing that. But he helped me sneak into the computer and art classes I wanted to take and covered for me with the folks.

I couldn't let him think this was all his fault. Flipping back around I studied him in the low light.

"It's okay. I'm sorry too. I should have, I don't know what, but I'm sure I could have done it differently." I said, trying to make him feel better. "But you gotta think first, man. The Helios are here, chasing us. They may not be the same guys that tried to kill us and who killed Grace's mother, but they are the same group. We don't know what they look like here. Anyone could be a threat."

"I know. I know. I'll..." Jaxon stopped short of a promise we both knew he wouldn't keep and sighed.

"We have to stick together now, or we will never find Grace and Breeze and Jada again." I pleaded with him.

"But what are we doing? Where are we going?" Jaxon's face was a mashup of misery and frustration.

"I don't know. We have to find people that look like they don't work for the government or the Helios. Then we can figure out where we are and start trying to find a way back to the others."

"That is going to take forever," Jaxon said.

"Yeh, it is." I stared at him, trying to will some common sense into his thick head. He glared back. Eventually, he got bored of the staring game.

"Fine, whatever." Jaxon's chin jutted out as he crossed his arms and continued to glare at me.

Sighing, I sunk deeper into the bucket. I might have dozed off, but when I opened my eyes next, I realized I could see Jaxon better. He was snoozing with his arms wrapped around Duchess. His hair was sticking up like an orange safety cone, severe against the pale skin and freckles. He was a mess of dirt and torn clothes. I'm sure I looked just as bad.

Outside our bucket, the light had brightened enough to see the rock ceiling in detail. I kicked his foot and he woke up. We switched off our lamps, rose up on our knees, and looked over the edge.

"Wow, that is—" Jaxon cut off mid-sentence.

"Oh, my Stars." I croaked out as the bucket exited the tunnel into a cavern so massive I couldn't see its end.

The noise hit us in a wave, a cacophony of sounds from people and machines. It was overwhelming after the empty echoes of the tunnels. Domed dwellings, like cliff swallow nests, cover every surface of the walls. I leaned back. At least a thousand feet above us, maybe as tall as that skyscraper in Dubai, daylight trickled down from a hole in the ceiling. It must be massive, but from here, it was the size of a pinprick. Lining the side of the cavern were floating opaque globe streetlights, emitting a warm sunshine glow. We passed by one, and I reached out a hand, brushing the cool surface. It rippled, the globe bounced like a bobber in a lake, then resumed its original position.

Ridged platforms at odd angles delineated levels, and dwellings dropped like stalagmites from under each terrace. Streamers of colorful flags wrapped around thick cables between buildings. Bridges crisscrossed haphazardly between levels and arched up to the next. There were neon signs and strobing lights, and human-looking people—everywhere.

"Shim, look at that." Jaxon grabbed my arm and pulled my attention back to the ground below us.

A man in a robe walked onto a stack of placemat-sized platforms. A waist-high lever, which looked like a boat tiller, emerged, and he put his hand on it, and the platform took off, going up vertically, then suddenly shifting horizontally. We ducked as he flew past and joined the stream of other people and cargo drones heading the same direction.

No one had noticed that our bucket was swinging more than the others, but I wasn't sure how long that would last. The buckets in front of us were passing close to an empty bridge.

"Can you make that jump?" I pointed to the bridge.

"Of course." Jaxon sneered at me. I put on the backpack. The basket tipped as we poised at the lip, waiting.

I counted out, "One, two" Jaxon jumped from the bucket, and I continued speaking to the empty space beside me. "Three."

Landing with a clang in the center of the bridge, my legs were a little wobbly but firm, and I glanced around. I was alone.

"Jaxon?"

"Shim!" I ran to the edge of the metal bridge.

Jaxon dangled from his fingertips. I flattened to the platform and reached down, snagging his wrists. Rolling, I pulled until I grabbed the back of his pants and yanked him up to the bridge.

Jaxon quickly bounded to his feet. "I had it under control."

"Uh-huh." I dusted off my jeans as I stood.

I was relieved to see that nearby, two lifts had gotten tangled together and the commotion had distracted everyone from noticing our plunge.

"Come on." I pointed down the busy street. Until we knew where we were going, it was best to get lost in the crowd.

∞

"UGH," Jaxon complained as he stepped in another pile of garbage. We had left the tidy top levels of the city and descended several floors, trying to get someplace we wouldn't be noticed.

Besides smelling like rotten food, the sun didn't reach this far down, and half the lamps were out, with the working ones casting a greenish glow. But more shadows made it easier for two teen boys to avoid notice.

Considering there were three times as many people on this level, we should have been able to blend in, but everything about us didn't fit, from our torn jeans to our hair.

An older man spat on the ground and said something I didn't understand; he eyed us suspiciously as we turned down another maze-like street.

"This sucks."

"I know. We have to find translators without drawing attention."

"No shit, but no one is wearing a necklace like Grace's." Jaxon bared his teeth at a woman who I think was cursing at us.

"Come on." I yanked his arm and dragged him along when he wanted to stop and confront her. We wandered for some time before we came across a market street with hawkers at kiosks and rows of shops.

"Have you noticed everyone has a cuff? I think they are like smart phones. I've seen people talking on them, I saw a projection coming out of one while the man was looking at it, like a TV, and two people clicked theirs together, and something happened. We need one of those." I told Jaxon.

"Give me a second," Jaxon said.

"Wait." But Jaxon had already popped his hoodie up and

disappeared into a busy shop.

Shit, that's all we needed. Jaxon was a good enforcer, but he had no subtlety. This summer, when we were using a mannequin to learn how to pick pockets, Jaxon had been so bad everyone laughed, and he had punched the dummy. That would be a bad start for our first day in—wherever we were.

That oily feeling of wrongness washed through me again as Jaxon came back at a run.

"Come on"

We took off. There was a shout behind us.

We didn't stop until we were several levels up and had covered up our clothes with some cape things we'd found on a clothesline. At least all the aliens looked human. Most were wearing strange goggles and had face masks which would be suitable for hiding our faces once we found some.

Jaxon handed over his prize; a six-inch flat strip of pink plastic with a clear coating on one side.

"Are those kittens?" I studied the colorful cartoon animals.

"Don't be picky. Do you know how to make it work?"

I examined both sides. I'd seen someone slap a flat bracelet onto their arm, so I tried that. It curled around my wrist with an uncomfortably tight fit, locking at my pulse point, and flared to life. Then it died and slid to the ground.

"Yeah, that's how I found it, saw it fall off a little girl's wrist." Jaxon picked up the bracelet and wrapped it around my wrist, squeezing the two ends together until it pinched my skin.

"Ouch." The screen flared to life, and I forgave him. With my free hand, I played with the features.

"Hey, what are you kids doing there? Move on." I about jumped out of my sneakers as a woman yelled at us from a window above.

Looking up, I called out, "sorry."

"Dude, did you understand her?" We walked awkwardly

with Jaxon's hand still clamped around my wrist, holding the cuff on. Jaxon looked hopeful.

"Sure, didn't you?"

"No, man, not a word."

"That is crazy," I examined the cuff as we hurried along. The woman had sounded like she was speaking in oddly accented English. If Jaxon didn't understand what she said, the translation must not be audible. Maybe analog—or digital, but it would still have to convert the sound to waves at my wrist, and Jaxon should have been able to hear it.

I needed to examine the cuff closer to figure it out.

"I can see you wanna go all mad scientist on this but save it for later," Jaxon grumbled, pushing away from me.

I snorted. I might have the mad scientist hair, but I did have some sense of priorities.

We had wandered into a residential area. As soon as Jaxon let go, the cuff fell off. I picked it up and stepped to the side of the path, out of the way of the heavy foot traffic. It was less path, more country lane, winding around a two-story, cone-shaped house that touched the level above and looked like a school for Smurfs. Handing the bracelet to Jaxon, I took off my backpack and rummaged through it until I found the first aid kit. Then I held my wrist out. Jaxon pinched the two ends of the cuff together and I used a band-aid to hold the ends of the cuff together. It worked.

"You can keep holding my hand," I offered.

"You're too ugly for me. I have standards," Jaxon pushed my arm away, and the cuff stayed on.

I laughed and drew in what felt like my first deep breath since we had left the others. We could do this. "Let's find out some information."

"Can you read signs and stuff too?"

"No. I didn't expect to. Grace couldn't. But I can understand what people are saying." We wandered back towards the central market area but farther down, where the streets were more crowded. People and stalls lined both sides of the pedestrian path. A cacophony of sing-song voices tried to lure people to come into the shops. Some hawkers were people, some mechanical humanoids, and others just tented signs with voices coming out of them.

"What's that one?" Jaxon pointed to a young man dressed head to toe in silver; even his face was painted, singing a hip-hop-style lyric.

I slapped down his pointing arm. "Jewelers."

"What about that?" He pointed to a mechanical girl our age wearing little more than a bikini that changed colors as she sang a cabaret song. I slapped down his arm but then stopped. We both gawked as her clothes went transparent. I don't know how long we stood there before I shook myself and pulled Jaxon away.

"No, really, I think she can help us. She seemed really nice," Jaxon said.

"Her bits tell you that?" I asked.

"Yes. Didn't even need a translator."

"What about that one?" I nodded my head to an old lady the next block down. She wasn't saying anything, but she had a singing sign outside her door:

> *Feeling dusty? Feeling down?*
> *Need a drink to cheer your frown?*
> *Got a question? Got an itch?*
> *Discretion has just your fix.*

I did a rough translation to Jaxon. It didn't rhyme.

"Yeah, sure, I'd much rather talk to that old raisin." Jaxon rolled his eyes and followed me into the shop named Discretion.

The room inside was dark. As my eyes adjusted to the lower light, I spun in a slow circle looking for threats as Waters had taught us.

It looked like an old dusty cantina. It was dark inside and the few customers were sitting at tables. A short counter was against the side wall with racks of bottles behind it.

I took a tentative seat at the bar. Jaxon climbed up next to me. We were in the shadows but close enough to the door to run, if needed.

"What can I get you?" The old lady had followed us in. She had heavy lines around her face and walked with a cane made of a thin metal pipe. She had a post-apocalyptic look with a long tunic and goggles on her head over a beige scarf that must have been wrapped twenty times around her head and neck. Everything on her was sand-colored, even her face.

"Not sure. What's good?" Stalling, I tried to hide the shock I got every time the translator worked. I didn't know what to ask for, but I knew we didn't have any way to pay for it. "Can we get some water?"

"Pay first," she said.

"We have to pay for water?" I tried not to let the surprise in my voice give away that we had no idea what we were doing.

"Huh, not from around here, are you? You a runner?" She asked, her eyebrows disappearing under her goggles.

I must have looked panicked because she tapped my arm. "Don't worry Ber. I won't turn you in. Got a son myself, about your age. Didn't get into the Learning Center." She looked sad.

"Two waters on me—" her eyes narrowed, "just this once."

"Thanks," I said.

"Don't order something you can't pay for." She huffed and disappeared into the back.

"What was all that?" Jaxon demanded. I shushed him.

She returned and plunked down two square glasses half full

of a brownish liquid.

I grimaced at the site, almost forgetting to ask my question. "So, where is here?"

She cackled.

"You mean Discretion? It's my shop. Been around as long as Bashita's been free." She said proudly. Her voice was gravel, and the translator gave her a thick accent like cockney English, but she ended everything on an up note as if she was replying with a question instead of an answer.

"Bashita?" I asked cautiously.

"Yeah, Bashita, this is a free-workers town. You boys sure are fresh." She chuckled. "Now you look, Nadunese, but your friend doesn't. Too pale. He from Mirah or LaDér?"

"Mirah," I latched onto the name quickly. "He's quiet. Lost his translator."

"Did he? Well, he would have thrown his linka away, of course, as it would have a tracker in it. Everyone knows that. Can't even steal one unless you know how to turn off the tracker. And you could get arrested for that."

My eyes bulged, and I tried not to look at the cuff on my wrist. She smiled knowingly at my twitch and eyed the pink band wrapped around my wrist. With a laugh, she started to turn away. "Wait," I called her back. "Say someone wanted a... link...a linka without a tracker in it, is that possible?"

She smiled slyly. "Don't order something you can't pay for." A customer called her from one of the tables, and she went to help them.

Jaxon was hitting my arm, and I turned to shush him.

"Look," Jaxon said. I followed the direction of his gaze. Behind the counter, on the very top shelf, with all the expensive-looking drinks, was a small bottle with a picture of a laughing toddler drinking from it.

Maybe we did have something of value we could trade.

16

FRIEND

GRACE

WHAT ARE YOU?

Jeu'l's question ricocheted in my head. *What are we?* I didn't know how to answer that. *We are from Earth.* But our parents were from here-*ish,* Jada's parents were from Teran, my mother from LaDér, Jaxon and Shim's mother from Nadun, and Shim and the twin's father from Mirah.

But we were also the aliens the authorities were looking for.

"Let me clarify." Jeu'l said, tone cautious. "I know you aren't runners. The penalty for violating the Law is strict, and something learned from young, and you know nothing about it. Only one of you has a translator. You don't know about Eloa, the most sought-after ritual drink in the Federation. In fact, you seem to know nothing of the Federation or the colonies. You aren't from here."

I stopped translating.

A year ago, I didn't even know other worlds existed. A year ago, I didn't know Shim, Jaxon, Breeze, Skylar, and Jada.

A year ago, I was all alone and I didn't know the biggest secret about myself.

"We are aliens. We are from Earth. And we need your

help." An hour ago, we didn't know Jeu'l, and I never thought I would have trusted anyone from this world. But we had to trust someone, and my gut told me this was a good place to start.

"*Stars!* I knew it!" Jeu'l jumped up, eyes wide. He started backing away; the air vibrated between us as I watched his face process what he had learned. I expected him to keep backing away until he ran screaming to the authorities.

He looked up at Jada cocking his head to the side. "I felt something was different about you. Something was special." He looked at Breeze and squinted. "You ask strange questions and don't know anything you should. You'll have to work on that, or they will catch you." And while I was still trying to process that he wasn't going to turn us in, Jeu'l began firing questions at me: Why did you come? Are you invading? Oh, Stars, I drank from your container—am I going to get some alien disease?

I was repeating everything to Breeze and Jada, but Jeu'l was going so fast, I stopped translating, and we just watched as he paced in front of the false wall, deep into a long explanation about something—the words were translating, but they didn't make sense. I shrugged at Breeze and Jada. Maybe he was in shock.

Jada stepped forward and blocked his path. Jeu'l was drawing in gulps of air, his body shuddering. Jada slowly raised his arms, watching Jeu'l for permission. He gently placed his hands on either side of Jeu'l's shoulders. Jada slowly breathed in, held the breath for a second, then blew it out in a long exhale, "one-two-three, breath in, one-two-three, breath out."

Jeu'l locked eyes and followed what Jada did until his breathing calmed and evened. "Good" Jada squeezed his shoulders and released him, stepping back. Jeu'l's eyes followed.

"Are you okay?" I asked. Uncertain if it would set him off again.

Jeu'l blushed and looked down. He shook his head. "I'm

sorry. I'm so embarrassed. I've never met...well, anyone like you before. You helped me and now you need my help, and I just went *mada* on you."

Occasionally, words didn't translate, but I thought I knew what he meant.

"I feel like I've been going... m-m-mada?" I tripped over the word, "ever since we got here."

Jeu'l cocked his head at me, "but you came here to meet us? Or to invade?" His eyes widened as he looked between the three of us, undoubtedly thinking what a pathetic invasion we made.

"No, no, neither actually. We aren't supposed to be here. It was an accident." I told Jeu'l about falling through the portal, leaving out the part about the stone and everything we had done to make it to this level in the mines.

"Could the old stories be true?" Jeu'l whispered under his breath.

"What stories?" I leaned in.

"It's nothing, really. Warring worlds and ancient families of guardians are stories you tell children to make them eat their meals."

"Maybe—" or maybe not, I thought. Was this the break we were looking for? If we could find someone who knew those stories, would they also know the way home?

"But you are lucky to be alive. I was told the lowest mine levels, especially anything close to the volcano, were sealed cycles ago." Jeu'l interrupted my musings.

"A volcano? Is that what that was?" Breeze's eyes bulged.

"The authorities restrict the deepest levels to only government access. There are rumors there are labs there. Some people talk about their grandparents working that deep, but they haven't mined down there in recent memory." He looked thoughtful. "Did you set off the lake lift alarm? It's good you didn't take the lift. It is old and very dangerous."

Oh no.

"Where does the lift go?" I asked, evading his question.

"It's the quickest way to Bashita. But the authorities control the city, so everyone has to use the long tunnels to get there. The lift was closed decades ago when the fires started with the Phataling." At my confused look, he blew out a frustrated breath. "They push something into the ground, force out gas, and capture it for energy. But it made the moon unstable, and they've been having quakes and fires since they started. The Terans don't care. They are going to tear this moon apart." Jeu'l raised his hands into fists and shook them at an unseen enemy.

After I repeated what he had said, Breeze and I shared a worried look. At least we now knew where the brothers had gone.

"There are two others in our group. They went up the lift, we had to find them, and we needed to figure out how to get home. We—" I sighed, my whole body compressing in on itself. "We need help."

Jeu'l patted my hand. He hesitated before offering. "You do. It is dangerous here if you aren't familiar with the mines. Thousands of runners die each year thinking they can come to Nadun and disappear into the mines. I would like to help you as you helped me. The UNR might know how to find your friends. They took me in, after I showed my worth, and gave me a place. I can introduce you to them."

"Are they safe?"

Jeu'l seemed to be carefully choosing his words. "Strength is everything to the UNR, so if you are strong, you are safe. However, the authorities have probably issued a bond for your apprehension. If anyone finds out you are more than a runner, they will not be able to resist turning you in for the bounty. They might even see it as their chance to stop running in exchange for information. It won't be safe to tell them where you are from."

"UNR?" I asked.

"UNR is the top unregistered gang."

Gangs? I didn't like the sound of that.

"They are okay, and, oh, I have an idea of how we can get you in." A broad grin spread across Jeu'l's face. He rubbed his hands together and asked Jada for another drink, forgetting about his concern for alien diseases. At least it was a start.

We have made a friend, maybe.

"THIS IS INSANE. Seriously. We're not really going to follow this guy, are we?" Breeze asked. Grabbing Jada and my arms, she spun us around to look at her.

We had rested before we left the alcove. But we hadn't been able to talk among ourselves. I just assumed the others were as relieved as I was to find a friend.

Jeu'l was out in front now, keeping up a running dialogue on the history of The Federation that we were ignoring. His singsong voice lingers over each L.

"We don't know this—guy." She waved her hand. "He could be Helios. He could be working for the government. He could be leading us to get mugged. We don't know!"

"But that is the problem, isn't it? We don't know!" Jada waved his hands as he spoke. "We don't know how to return to the passage that brought us here. We don't know where the brothers went after they arrived in Bashita. We don't know who to trust or how this world works."

"But why him?" Breeze's face settled into a frown.

I swallowed the tightness in my throat and turned to look for Jeu'l. His light was fading into the void of pitch-darkness. A shiver of fear raced up my spine at the idea of being alone again. No, we couldn't trust Jeu'l, but we also couldn't lose him. He was our only lead to finding something that could help us find the brothers and find a way home.

"If the people chasing us are also chasing Jeu'l, then he doesn't want to be found by them either. And he knows this world, knows the tunnels and the legends or knows people who will." I didn't know what else to say. I didn't have proof.

I studied Breeze's face in the glow of the lamp. Shadowed and pinched, she looked miserable as she gave a shrug and slumped.

"I guess we have to try."

"We aren't giving up on Shim and Jaxon. We are going to find them, and we are going to find a way home. I promise."

Did she know I was lying?

How many times would I fall into the trap of believing that what I wanted superseded the circumstances?

As if Breeze read my mind, she put her hand on my arm and said "We have to believe Grace. That's what will make it happen."

This girl.

Jada was nodding.

Both of them. I don't know what I would do without them. The glow around us increased like faith was letting in the light.

"Is everything alright?" Jeu'l was suddenly standing next to us, the glow from his watch lighting our faces.

Jada couldn't understand him, but somehow, he knew exactly what to say.

"Sorry, we were delayed. We appreciate you coming back for us."

Jeu'l smiled up at him. "It was my pleasure. Where was I? Ah, yes, so a millennium ago, Teran colonized its moons Nadun, Mirah, and LaDér. Centuries later, something catastrophic happened, I don't know what, but Teran lost the ability to travel to the colonies."

I linked arms with Breeze and we trailed after the boys.

JEU'L SKIPPED around a couple of large rocks in the path. He was looking for something. It was the only time he stopped talking. Then, and when he waited until I repeated what he had said to Breeze and Jada and he was convinced they were part of the conversation.

"The moons developed autonomous cultures and economies. LaDér is my home, it is all water. The surface has these tremendous storms, so we learned to live underwater. It is so beautiful—if you like water." He smirked and reached out to touch my hair, letting the green strands slide through his fingers. "Our diet of phytoplankton is rich in chlorophyll and has resulted in genetic variants...are you sure you aren't from there?"

I shrugged. What could I say? I'd already told him we were aliens. I knew he was suspicious, but it seemed more dangerous to tell him we were only half-alien. Accidentally falling through a portal was unfortunate. That your parents had done the same thing—feels less and less like a coincidence.

We traveled slowly down the tunnels, frequently pausing so Jeu'l could brush the dust off pieces of rocks and study them as he searched for something.

"On Mirah, they live in the sky in floating cities and use wind to power everything. I've always wanted to visit." He looked at Breeze, "You look like you could be from there. If anyone asks, you should say that you are."

Breeze gave a tentative smile. We already knew that her

father was from Mirah, but it was helpful to know that she could pass as being a citizen.

"You know what Nadun is like, though it has become more dangerous as the workers prepare to strike." He kept up his search of the nearby rocks while he waited for me to repeat what he had said.

"How about me?" Jada asked.

"If I were to guess, I would say you are from Teran." He studied Jada from the top of his gelled head, which was now hopelessly matted with sweat and dirt, to his scratched and scarred sneakers that had been immaculate just days ago.

Jada nodded that he understood, and Jeu'l frowned.

"It won't make you popular. Terans are not liked. After hundreds of cycles alone, the population of Teran exploded, and they had used up all their resources. In a last-ditch effort, they used everything they had left to reestablish contact and supply lines with the colonies. At first, we were eager to profit. For decades we supplied the Terans with everything they needed. But it was never enough. They bribed governments, assassinated people that stood in their way, and manipulated the colonies into joining them in a Teran-ruled Federation."

We took a side tunnel, Jeu'l stopping at every nook and examining the entrance while he talked. "But I have to admit I am biased. My *pata* is Teran, and he has left me with a predisposition to distrust them."

"What are you looking for?" While this story was fascinating, I was growing frustrated with our slow progress.

"Markers for the path we must take." Jeu'l replied, then shook his head and stepped away from the rock that he had been examining and hurried further down the tunnel.

"How did you get here?" Breeze asked after I had translated.

"My mother got sick. I had to drop out of studying for my

exams, and by the time she got better, it was too late to qualify for a Learning Center. I thought I would have more time, but the authorities went after my mother and new-father for harboring me."

It sounded barbaric. Imagine becoming a criminal for allowing your teenager to stay with you. Shim, Jada, and I would all be required to register if we lived here.

Oh Stars, I hope we don't have to live here.

"So, I ran. I proved my worth and got work with the UNR. Every colony and Teran has an underground system and gangs of unregistered. No one can go solo, and if you could, where would you go? Who would you work for? No one is allowed to hire you unless you can prove your status. Your options are: go to school, pay to join the military, or work for ten cycles in the unpaid labor camps."

"I'd like to take door number four," Jada shook his head.

Jeu'l stopped and turned to him, then burst out laughing. Jada smiled.

"Ah." Looking past Jada, Jeu'l's eyes lit up and he rhythmically tapped his head and chest a couple of times quickly. I had seen him do the ritual before and wondered what it meant.

Jeu'l whispered, "Thank Stars."

Reaching up to the rock on the top left corner of the alcove's entrance, Jeu'l brushed off the dust, and a small, engraved square appeared, blended into the natural rock around it.

"This is it! Do you see? Secret, ancient directions. A square means there is a passage. A line is a hiding wall. I thought the alcove where we met had a square, and I was in too much of a hurry to finish cleaning and see that it was only a line. Crossed lines mean danger."

Jada ran his hand over the square mark. "How do they keep them secret?"

"Most Nadunese don't know about them. Old-timers have

many secret stories. I'm not supposed to know. I had a friend—" he looked down, a little bashful, "well, I knew someone that told me about them when I became a runner." He got flustered again.

"That is so cool," Jada injected. Jeu'l smiled at him and indicated we should all follow.

As we entered, Jeu'l studied the walls. Inside, the wall curved, snaking back farther than the alcove we had been in before, and soon we lost sight of the entrance. Nothing seemed different in this tunnel from the others. Near the end, he crouched down and searched a pile of fallen rocks. We helped in that awkward way you do when you don't know what you are looking for.

"Got it." Jeu'l pointed to a ledge he had revealed about a foot and a half off the ground. He cleared the debris on the floor below it. "Best to go headfirst." He dropped to all fours and shined his light under the ledge, then slid to his stomach across the smooth rock and disappeared.

"Oh, whoa," Jada said. He crouched next to the opening and Breeze and I squatted next to him as he shined his light on Jeu'l.

"You coming?" Jeu'l called, his voice muffled.

"I'm not doing that." Breeze immediately said. "Nope, nope, nope. Not happening."

"Why do we have to go this way?" I looked at the others. My eyes were bugging out of my head.

"This is the fastest way to the town. The other tunnels take a long time and are monitored. I have to get back quickly." Jeu'l frowned. "It's okay if you are afraid. I understand. I can try and come back and find you after I deliver my message. But that might take a full cycle, longer if they send me out on another run." Jeu'l worried his lip between white teeth. "I am concerned about you staying here alone. I think we have limited time to establish your story before the UNR finds you."

My inner voice was listing a million reasons why crawling into a crack in the floor of a tunnel on an alien planet was a bad idea. Most of them had to do with getting stuck, earthquakes, and crawly things.

A Bad. Bad. Idea.

Had we been on this world for one day or two? And so far, we have met more enemies than friends. We had to find Shim and Jaxon and, so far, Jeu'l was the only person we had met that I felt we could trust, the only one who knew how to help us.

Breeze was shaking her head.

"Breeze, we have to try this." I tried to inject optimism into my voice.

"Uh, no, we don't." Breeze said.

"You want us to stay here in the dark, with no food or water, and hope that someone else comes along to help us?" It wasn't really a question. I was slightly more frustrated with the circumstances than I was scared to enter that small dark crack in the earth.

Breeze whimpered.

Jada was crouching down, ready to go after Jeu'l. But he couldn't go next. He was too big, and if something happened, he wouldn't be able to hear our directions for help.

We had to do it, and I had to do it first.

I grabbed Jada's shoulder. He looked up. "I'm first, then Breeze. You come last." He frowned but nodded in agreement.

I hated this.

I crouched down, my heartbeat picked up, and my breathing got tight. I took some calming breaths. Then, I pointed my light into the crack and moved to lay on my stomach. There was a shoe ten yards away—Jeu'l crawling on his belly. I followed, pulling myself along on my elbows through the dust. The rock closed around me.

As I crawled, I got lost in my head. Emotion boxed me in.

Anger was pushing me along as I wiggled my hips and toes. If Shim hadn't gotten on the lift and left us, we wouldn't be in such desperate need of resources. We wouldn't need to spend time finding him and Jaxon instead of searching for a way home. Most importantly, I wouldn't need to crawl under this rock if he hadn't lied to me, pretending to be my boyfriend, pretending we were something that we weren't, something special, while he was dating someone else.

Okay, that was a total stretch, but I held on to my anger. It blocked out the fear.

It was uncomfortable and exhausting crawling on my stomach. The ceiling height changed, and I had enough room to get on my hands and knees. I tried it and immediately cracked my head on a rock. Dropping back to my elbows, my light got buried in my shirt.

Darkness.

Okay, that was worse. Panic bloomed in the void.

Let me out, screamed on repeat in my head, and I panted from exertion and fear. I fumbled for that anger that had been so good at distracting me. As I pulled myself along on my elbows, following Jeu'l's feet, I reminded myself I was angry at Shim. He was a cheater. He had been cheating with me. Oh, Stars! I hadn't even thought of that. I was the other girl.

That jerk!

I wiggled further under the rock. We had probably gone twenty feet, and I could hear Breeze's heavy breathing behind me.

Stars, what if we were all crushed under here?

You are angry, I reminded myself. I was angry at Shim at making me the other girl.

But I wasn't. So, it was hard to keep pretending.

I hadn't wanted to talk to him about it because I was hurt. I tried to push *that* thought aside because the hurt was too close to fear, and fear was telling me to curl up and close my eyes until I woke up back on Earth.

Nope, have to find that anger again—what was I angry about? Shim. He messed up my perfect illusion. That little bubble Jada had been so jealous of. I thought we were something extraordinary. I've never had that before in my ordinary life.

Every movement stirred up a cloud of dust and I pulled myself through it. It felt like a metaphor for my life.

Breathing shallow, my heart started to race again, and I tried to distract myself from choking on the fear.

I'd never had anything close to a perfect life. My parents had always acted like bandits on the run. I now knew it was because they were aliens on the run. We always had to make do. Not make waves. Leave abruptly. Sacrifice friends. We were loners. And after my mother was gone, we were just lonely.

A wave of sadness enveloped me, suffocating me like the rock was sucking the air from my lungs. Forty feet, and the path was narrowing. I took a shuddering breath and tried to find my anger to fuel me to keep moving. Maybe I was angry at my dad? But it wasn't his fault I was here. He was just a poor Earth boy who fell in love with a green-haired alien. True, he had left me this summer to fend for myself. But he hadn't meant to. Maybe I was angry at Shim, no, that made me sad too.

My elbows hurt. The skin rubbed raw from the sharp rocks. I stretched an arm out in front of me and almost touched Jeu'l's shoe. Twisting my neck back, I had just enough room to see Breeze struggling along behind me. The glow of light behind her must be Jada. I rose up on my bruised elbows and moved on.

My mom, I was angry at my mom. She had lied to me all my life about who she was. I'd always thought she had left. But she really hadn't. She had been captured and killed by the Helios.

That is how I knew how evil they really were. The government. Now I could get angry at them, but it did no good. Everyone we met had been drones following orders.

The channel through the rock had narrowed to just three feet wide and just enough height to pull myself along on my elbows. I couldn't see Jeu'l's feet anymore.

Where did he go? Panic set in again, and I diverted it back to anger. The Helios. Now that is a group I could get angry at. They were ruthless killers that had hunted us on Earth, killed my mother, and somehow they were on Nadun. And from what we had overheard, they were just as ruthless as the Earth-based group. How could two groups with the same name exist in these different places and have the same function? That was important. And when I wasn't trying to survive, I would have to think more on it.

I pushed my light out further to try and see Jeu'l and realized I was looking at a solid rock. The channel ended abruptly. Where did Jeu'l go? I pulled myself closer until I was hanging over a huge hole. It was black as pitch.

Holy Crap! Dead end. We were going to die.

I was diving into a deep panic when Jeu'l's face appeared below, glowing from his wrist linka thing.

"You did it."

17

———

ELOA

SHIM

"CAN WE TRY THAT?" I pointed to the top shelf where the bottle with the picture of the happy toddler had a place of honor.

The old lady looked up, and when she saw where I pointed, she snorted.

"Cheeky brat. You can't afford that."

"How much does it cost?" She gave me a sum in kuri. Guess that was the local currency. I don't know why I was holding my breath, I didn't know what a kuri was, but I could multiply.

"So, it's hard to get?"

"Runners usually annoy me, stealing and begging, but you ask questions. You amuse me." She cackled at her joke.

After a long pause where I tried desperately not to fidget, she sighed.

"It's not hard to get. It's impossible. I am one of a few in this town who has it," she leaned forward and whispered, "it's a miracle in a bottle. More nourishing than mother's milk, it can sustain a worker in the mines for a month with no food, heals wounds, and kills disease. It's the foundation this moon was built on—and it's impossible to find. I have people here that would sell all they own for a drink. You see it just sitting there?"

She pointed up to the shelf, grabbed a stick that looked like a police baton, and poked at the bottle. A greenish light like a force field shot up around the shelf, the rod sizzling as she held it against the green light.

Patrons in the bar behind shouted. One called out for her to quit playing with the fresh ones. She ignored the mumbled complaints from customers.

Pulling back the stick, she chuckled, amused with her game, as she blew on the end that was smoking slightly.

My body was trembling, adrenaline pouring through it from the shopkeeper's performance, but I was used to working through the rush. Bracing my hands on the counter, I leaned forward, muscles coiled in case this all went wrong. When we were eye to eye, I said in a low, even voice, "and what would a bottle be worth to you?"

I didn't move a muscle. Jaxon moved to my back as I stared down the wily coyote. Her eyes widened at my words, then narrowed as she studied my face.

It was a performance our mentor, Waters, would have been proud of and I wish Grace and the twins could have seen it.

I didn't flinch as I stared at the woman.

She stared back at me.

This was something. This could work.

Or it could blow up in our faces. I didn't know which direction it was heading, but I stared back, unblinking.

Her eyes never left mine.

Don't move. I breathed low and deep.

She tilted her head, eyes still locked with mine.

I raised a brow.

She gave a small smile. It reeked of knowledge and danger. It reminded me of Waters.

I knew then that she was more dangerous than I had first thought.

She broke eye contact and nodded her head down the long bar to a hallway at the back of the room. She smirked and headed in that direction.

I slid off the stool and followed.

It felt like the whole bar had gone silent behind me. Were they all watching? I was glad Jaxon had my back. As we approached the back area, I hesitated for a second at the threshold, then crossed over into the darkness.

The long hall was chiseled out of rock. The only light came from the front bar and I could make out doors of different sizes. At the end, the old lady opened a door and light oozed into the hall.

She stood at the edge of the light and motioned us in with her hand. "You're in it now, boys, no backing out." She cackled again.

The horror movie narrator in my head screamed, "run!" and I gave myself an internal pep talk as I tried to keep all emotion off my face.

I moved cautiously into the back room. It was just a workspace with an additional exit, like a loading dock. Or an escape route.

A couple of thugs and three workers were packaging something that I quickly looked away from. Everyone looked up as we entered. The two enforcers reached for weapons strapped to their chests.

The shortest person in the room was a man—maybe a woman—they were obviously in charge. I think they were younger than the original coyote, as I'd started to think of the old lady from the front, but with just as many wrinkles. They had on the same dingy-colored clothes and were wrapped in multiple layered headscarves and baggy tunics.

The shorter coyote's stare followed the old lady as she backed out of the room. She did her cackle thing again and told the group. "These boys *say*," she emphasized that one word, making it clear that she didn't believe us, "they got a source for Eloa." Then she shut the door.

Shit.

The short coyote didn't speak. They just studied us, their expression neutral under layers of wrinkles.

I willed myself to stay still but couldn't stop the shift from one foot to the other. The silence was getting to me, and I had to stop myself from breaking it.

Finally, they spoke.

"You selling?"

I was so relieved I almost thanked them, but I tried to play it cool. Without looking, I knew Jaxon was glaring at them with his resting bitch-face.

"Eloa."

"How much you got?"

"A bottle," I raised my hands and indicated the size of the bottle and ignored my pulse trying to beat its way out of my chest.

They flinched. Yeah, that was defiantly a flinch.

"We will have to test it." Their voice was neutral as if they couldn't care less one way or the other.

"Okay." I agreed.

They offered me a price. Based on the old lady's price per glass, it was a fraction of the *kuri* I'd calculated the tiny bottle in the bar would have cost.

So, I took a wild guess and asked for twenty times their offer. It seemed a good place to start as I had no idea what a *kuri* was.

"Oh, and I want double if you break the seal to test it."

Their nostrils gave the barest of flares. Oh, yeah, they liked the idea of an unopened bottle.

We settled on ten times the originally offered price in *kuri*, plus two clean communicator-linka things, two changes of clothes, and a map.

Jaxon just stood next to me, eyeing the workers and pretending he understood what was happening. I thought about asking for a place to stay and information on the mines. But when I saw their eyebrows go up at the map, I realized I'd made them suspicious, so I stopped there.

The short coyote muttered about linka being expensive and how I was taking advantage of them. It reminded me so much of Waters, I had a pang of homesickness but quickly squashed it down.

As near as I could tell, the short person and the old lady were middle-level merchants. The muscled enforcers didn't work for them. They just happened to be there on business and didn't like being startled. The Muscle left once their purchase was made.

I could respect that the short coyote had tried to rip us off. A merchant has to make money and I didn't care if we were under-paid as long as we got what we needed. But what did bother me was that now six people knew we had access to Eloa.

The short coyote said it would take a while to gather what we had requested, which I didn't believe, but they arranged for us to come back in a little bit with the bottle for the exchange.

I'd made it real clear I only had one bottle, and *Thank Stars* they hadn't tried to search us. Under the cloak, I had four bottles left in the bag on my back, but I wasn't going to open it up now and let them see.

I was concerned about Grace and Breeze, and Jada not having anything to drink, but right now, I had to focus on our current situation.

When we left the shop, I took off at a jog and started turning down a lot of random streets. I knew Jaxon would follow. Hopefully, we can lose whoever tailed us. We just needed to get far away enough to make sure...

"We've got a tail," Jaxon said.

I was expecting we would be followed, but Jaxon hadn't spoken in so long that the sound of his voice startled me.

"Which one?" We made the next turn.

"Big guy nose hair."

I grunted, remembering him from inside the bar. A hulk of a guy with big clumsy fingers. He wouldn't be very fast. "The others are probably there too. You ready?"

Jaxon didn't respond, but as soon as we took the next turn, he passed me and I tried to keep up.

He zigged zagged down side streets and made several level changes before looping back. I was relieved when I recognized the start of the market again and saw the stalls were still up. Jaxon made quick work of dipping behind a distracted merchant's stall. I followed and we crawled under the display table.

Surrounded by the long lengths of gem-colored fabric curtaining the table, we caught our breath.

"That lost the big guy; dude was more fighter than runner. I don't know about the others," Jaxon said.

I thought about that. What if they grabbed us before we could get back to the shop? We needed a backup plan.

A scrap of beige fabric fell to the ground. Reaching out, I snagged it and dragged it quickly under the table.

The merchant was caught up in gossiping with his neighbor. "Neran thinks, since they are the capital, they don't have to pay their share, Bagana too, sure leaves a strain on Bashita. That's why the workers are striking!"

Neran–that is where our grandfather used to live. I tucked that bit of information away for later.

"Take off that cape thing," I said to Jaxon. He narrowed his eyes and I added, "Please."

Stripping off the backpack and cape, I pulled out one of our bottles and wrapped it in the fabric. I'd seen a few people wearing these slings with babies in them. Fat little faces and feet sticking out. Of course, they had theirs over tunics, but hopefully, no one would notice my jeans under the cape. I tied the fabric and slipped it over my neck and across one shoulder.

Not bad.

Pulling the cape back on, I handed the backpack off to Jaxon.

"Put it on, then put the cape over." Jaxon was so amused at my little bundle of joy he complied without complaint. That wasn't going to last long.

"Jax, I want you to stay here."

"What the hell?" Jaxon aimed a punch at my arm.

"Hey, hear me out. We were lucky they didn't search me last time. I go in there again, and they might. Then we have nothing. Nothing to bargain with. And so many things could go wrong, they might not want to pay, Nose Hair could cause trouble—"

"Yeah, that's why we stick together. Isn't that what you went on and on about earlier?" Jaxon's voice raised with each word.

"*Shhh*," I said, hushing him. "Yes. We stick together. If you are here, you'll be close, and I've got backup. If you are in there with me, we would both be trapped in that back room."

"Together." He spits out the words with clenched teeth.

I cursed.

He glared.

The light on my communicator thing lit up and started blinking red.

Crap!

"That's got to be some kind of tracker." I ripped it off and tossed the bracelet deeper under the table.

"Come on. I guess we are both going."

Jaxon was smug. I was pissed. We tried to look natural, crawling out from under the table. The merchant was watching some authoritarian-looking guys in uniforms arriving at the end of the market.

We walked the several blocks back to the shop and the sudden loss of my translator made the noises and voices that I could no longer understand disorientating. I was relieved when I saw our old coyote standing at the shop door. Her eyes disappeared into the wrinkles of her face as she cackled and clucked at us. With no idea what she was saying, I just smiled and nodded.

"Stay here." I tried again. "Please." For all the reasons I mentioned before, I really hoped Jaxon listened this time. There was a long silence where the noise of the market filtered through the unspoken argument we were having.

"Fine. But I'm going in there in ten minutes. So, you had better make it fast."

I left Jaxon behind and stalked across the street. The old lady waived me in. She was saying something I didn't understand, but when she motioned for me to take a seat, I sat down on a stool at the bar, this time facing out, watching the rest of the room.

I saw Nose Hair come through the door in the back. He looked winded. I smirked. He glared back at me, then flicked one of those big hairy knuckles my way before turning back to go through the door again.

Great.

When I got to the door, Nose Hair grabbed the collar of my shirt with one hand and patted me down with the other, paying special attention to the bottle strapped across my chest, then he dragged me down the dark hall. He was talking the whole time, but I had no idea what he was saying. I'm sure it was something about how happy he was to get help with his afternoon exercise 'cause he knew he really needed to focus on his health. Oh, and how glad he was to see me again.

We got to the back room and he didn't knock, just opened the door and pushed me through, still holding onto the collar of my t-shirt. The short coyote and one the workers were the only ones left in the workspace. Nose Hair grunted something and shook me in front of them like he was a dog that had caught a squirrel.

I waited until he had the attention of the others, then I reached up and grabbed his wrist, breaking his grip. I pushed my thumb into the back of his hand and twisted and folded his hand backward until he was crouching on the floor and yelling. A little more pressure and I would break his hand.

I looked at his boss. The short coyote chuckled and made a motion for me to let him go. With a sigh of disappointment, I released Nose Hair and took a quick step back.

A big hairy hand swiped at me. He snarled and looked like he was going to come after me. The short coyote made a noise, calling him off and, with a glare, he turned and stomped out of the room.

Now, we can get down to business.

Well, soon.

I showed I wasn't wearing a translator.

The short coyote shook their wrinkled face and pulled a flat object out of the package on the table. They held it out with one hand and motioned with the other. I hesitated, then pulled the baby out of the sling. There was a sharp intake of breath when they saw the bottle.

Guess I'd caved early on my price. I hated being undercut.

I put the bottle on the table and took the wrist cuff. While they inspected the bottle and made happy sounds, I slapped the cuff on my wrist. It wrapped around, but nothing happened. No lights, no translation.

Frowning, I tapped at it.

The short coyote snorted and grabbed my wrist. I watched the sequence of screen swipes and taps they made and hoped I could duplicate it. The cuff lit up.

Immediately, I was able to understand the questions being fired at me. Where the bottle came from? How long have I had it? Was there more?

"Found it," I said. There was a long silence as we stared at each other.

"Are there more?" They asked, voice slow and patient—but the look in their eyes was not.

"No."

They pushed for more information. I had them show me how to turn on the other linka and show me where the tracking was turned off.

They asked where we were heading. I asked them where the map was. I had expected the folded paper kind. They eyed me suspiciously, then showed me how to pull up a map on the linka, where I was, and how to use voice activation to say where I wanted to go. They waited while I picked a destination.

"Bagana," I said. That was the first thing that popped into my head and wouldn't give away our true destination. The linka map showed the route, including where to get transportation. Nice!

I asked about a few of the other menu items we had gone through to get to the map. They eyed me suspiciously, muttering "fresh" under their breath, and showed me the other options.

They finally got tired of playing tour guide and declared our business done.

I demanded the *kuri* payment and clothes. They muttered "fresh," again, and a couple of other words that I was glad didn't translate and shoved the package at me. Then they showed me how to pull up the credits on the linka.

I guess that would have to do. They might be completely scamming us, but I decided I'd pushed my luck enough today.

Backing out of the room, I opened the door behind me, cautiously stepping through. Nose Hair was waiting, but when I moved towards him, he stepped back involuntarily, stopped himself, and glared.

The path down the hall was clear. I quickly left the shop, picking up Jaxon outside and ignoring my nerves and the sweat pooling under my arms, I pulled him along in my wake.

I wanted to get as far away from that shop as possible.

18

THE CAVE
GRACE

OH, *thank Stars.*

I was never so happy to see someone's face. I scrambled for the hole's edge and let my momentum carry me down headfirst. It was like falling down a chimney, and I felt like Santa as I landed in a crumpled pile on top of Jeu'l. He pulled himself out from under me and grabbed my arm, dragging me free of the hearth-like opening. Then disappeared back up the chimney to meet the others.

I rolled onto my back and tried to slow my breathing. My eyes darted around the room. The chamber had a tall ceiling, but maybe I'd lost perspective. Knowing I was still underground freaking me out, and I tried to get my head back together.

The Helios were evil—My parents did the best they could—I was hurt, not mad at Shim. I could do this. Look at what we have come through so far.

Things were bound to get better.

They couldn't get worse.

I really shouldn't have thought that.

"All here. Good!" Jeu'l said. Jada was sitting up, covered in dust but looking eager to explore. Breeze collapsed next to me, her whole body trembling. I suspect that the tug of war going through her head in the crawl was similar to mine.

She looked wrecked.

"A couple more of these shortcuts, and then I've got something amazing to show you. Something I think you have never seen before." Jada bumped me with his foot and indicated I should repeat what Jeu'l said. On autopilot, I complied.

Jeu'l looked us over. "I forgot it takes a while to get used to being underground. At first, the bypass tunnels feel like traps. After a while, you realize they are escape routes and freedom. Here" he handed me Jada's bottle, "just take a small sip. We need the rest to buy linka for Jada and Breeze."

"Linka?" I repeated the unfamiliar word. He had mentioned it before. I forced myself to sit up and take a small sip.

He flashed his glowing wrist cuff at me. "Linka."

"How are we going to buy something like that with half a bottle of this?" I swirled the milky liquid in the plastic bottle before taking another drink.

"You have no idea what this Eloa is worth—that's it." He cut me off and handed the bottle to Breeze, making a motion that she should take just a little.

I thought about objecting to having Jeu'l take over, then realized it was a relief.

Jada and Jeu'l got us up and moving. Breeze didn't want to move.

"Why are we doing this again?"

"We are trying to find our way home," I said.

"And how is following this stranger going to do that?" Breeze asked.

I couldn't answer her.

I thought Jeu'l might be hiding something. But I didn't think he was a bad guy. I just hoped the people he was taking us to would be better than the Authorities or the Helios.

In the end, Breeze's fear of being left behind, as if I would ever do that, was greater than her fear of moving forward.

I didn't tell her, but that was the only thing that got me moving too.

We went through several more escape passages and drops and down many levels lower than where we had started, where I had last seen Shim. I was adjusting to the small space and the bypass tunnels evoked a downgraded fit of panic each time instead of a full heart attack.

The last drop landed us in a cave, not a tunnel. The raw rock untouched by chisel or drill. We passed through two more caves before arriving at Jeu'l's surprise.

"Turn off your lights." Jeu'l requested. As our eyes adjusted to the darkness, pinpricks of light emerged, dotting the cave ceiling and walls like stars. They illuminated the lake underneath which bubbled and glowed. The room was humid, and as we stepped in further, I placed a hand on the wall to steady myself. The wall felt warm and slick with a mossy substance—a tiny light wiggle just inches from my hand.

"What is it?" I reached out a finger.

"Don't touch," Jeu'l chastised. "Bioluminescent insects. They are safe but very delicate."

I reluctantly pulled my hand back from the glow and turned around to study the chamber. It was about ten feet high and three times as long. We were standing at one of the long ends at the very edge of the pool's beach.

"Hot springs keep the room the perfect temperature for them. They provide just enough light for moss, mushrooms, and Eloa to grow. Though, Eloa doesn't need much light. It's proof that the impossible is possible." He gently fingered what looked like a purple aloe vera but with feathery tendrils on the ends. They were growing in patches along the floors and walls.

"The earliest colonists found Eloa and realized it could be

replanted in mineral-rich soil. It kept them alive for centuries after they were isolated from Teran. But most of the minerals it needs to thrive are gone now, over-mined. Eloa refuses to grow above ground. Most people don't know this cove is here, or I'm sure it would have been harvested and shipped off-world." Jeu'l said. He sounded sad.

When I finished translating, Breeze said, "Thank you. This is amazing."

Jada stared at Jeu'l. "How do you know all this?"

Jeu' l's cheeks flushed, "I had a Learner that loved botany. They dreamed of coming here and studying these plants. It is why I chose to run to Nadun instead of going to one of the gangs on Teran, where I grew up."

Mini-waves of water from the bubbling hot springs lapped at my dusty toes as we walked the water's edge. Glowing centipedes wiggled under the crystal-clear surface. A movement caught my eye.

"What is that?" I pointed to the far side of the pool at a small moving lump that hung from the roof.

Jeu'l stepped closer and followed the direction of my finger. "Ah, that is a bat. So rare! It's too hot for them to stay in here but they love the insects. See how the tips of its beak glows, it's the luciferin in the bacteria from the worms."

Three-quarters of the way around the pool, we came to the exit. As we reluctantly left the refuge, we flicked our lamps back on.

"It's not much further." Jeu'l promised.

The next few drops were severe. We had left the cave system and were back in tunnels, and I finally felt like I could stand up straight without smacking my head on something. We came across more and more signs of civilization, a terminal like the one that had pointed us to the fire lake. Signage with directions we couldn't read.

The tunnels were now lit by faint halos of light that bloomed out from the ceiling, leaving gaps of darkness between. We switched off our lamps as Jeu'l led us to a spiral staircase carved into the rock. We descended down a level, then abruptly, the stairs straightened out, and we descended two levels on a ramp before the winders narrowed and twisted into another deep spiral. We passed many dimly lit tunnel entrances that branched off the stairs.

Suddenly, a young man appeared. Ignoring us, he cut in front of Jeu'l and briskly descended the stairs. He was dressed differently from Jeu'l, who had on baggy gray pants and a short tunic. This man wore fitted pants and a vest in a black material with a sheen of gold. The man got off at the next level and disappeared.

We heard steps behind us, and a woman passed us. She was similarly dressed to the man, but her clothes were brown with a short fringe around the edges of the top. She got off at the next level.

"Grace, there are people here," Breeze said in a loud whisper. I shushed her as we passed a man and a woman. The man had a baby strapped across his chest. Jeu'l hesitated as we approached, but when they motioned for us to go ahead, he quickly passed them.

"Jeu'l there are families here?" I asked.

"Of course," he seemed surprised. "When you run, there is no going back. But life goes on, and people work, live, and have babies as best as possible." Jeu'l picked up speed now, descending faster on the wider, more even steps.

"Grace, I don't like this." Breeze crowded in on me, clinging to the hem of my shirt.

Sometimes Breeze reminded me of the angel that sat on your shoulder and said all the things you were thinking but were afraid to voice. I didn't like that either. We had made first contact with a single alien. Were we ready to meet more? But it would all be worth it if someone here knew how to find Shim and Jaxon and get us home. Jeu'l said he would help us, and so far, he has. Would that change when he got back with his own people?

Having nowhere else to go, we hurried after Jeu'l, descending another ten levels before Jeu'l left the stairs and quickly snaked down a wide twisting tunnel. We hurried to follow him, passing through an archway and coming to an abrupt stop.

We had entered a large cavern and were immediately blasted by the sounds of a bustling city. Jada, Breeze, I stared. "What the—"

"Is something wrong?" Jeu'l had continued on and when he realized we weren't with him, he came back.

"What is that?" I pointed out the general direction of the metropolitan sprawl.

We were near the top of the cavern, looking down, like being in the nose-bleed seats at a ballpark. Where was the light coming from? I looked up and several floors above us, huge lights emitted a glow that shone down like sunshine.

"You mean the town?"

"Town? That is a city—underground!"

"Yes. This is where we will get help. Come on." Jeu'l motioned eagerly for us to follow him.

I gawked like the worst kind of tourist as we trailed behind, trying to look at everything at once. We passed curved-glass fronted shops, offices with business names posted over the door in a script I couldn't read, and homes with children playing around them. The buildings lined the walls like thirty-story-high swallow's nests, then stacked on top of each other. Going up and up and connecting with other buildings by sloppy metal scaffolding and makeshift bridges.

Finally, Jeu'l left the stairs and crossed a bridge into a rowdy marketplace. As I followed, I looked over the edge of the railing and could see several levels of the city below us.

The market engulfed us. Row after row of brightly decorated stalls, barkers shouting offers, and the smells of herbs and sizzling grills as vendors cooked up dishes they handed over after linka tapped together. The noise of stomping feet on metal, music, laughter, shouting vendors, and buzzing machines was overwhelming after the quiet of the tunnels.

"Look out." Jeu'l pulled us out of the way, and we gaped as something flew by carrying a box. It dropped it off at a merchant, paused for payment, then leaped into the air again.

There was a variety of clothing, though loose tunics and layers of scarves were the dominant styles. A variety of people, young, old, short, tall, dark and light skinned. And every so often, I caught a glimpse of green hair, and I would crane my neck to follow them with my eyes.

Breeze stopped to finger the different types of cloth as one of the vendors. "Silks and cottons and linens, just like home."

"Look at this!" Jada called us over to another booth displaying hundreds of different styles of linka, from sleek modern ones to antique ones that looked a lot like my necklace.

"What do you think?" Jeu'l asked, bouncing on his feet with excitement.

"I think it's a little overwhelming," I admitted.

Jeu'l laughed, "Welcome to *Bina*!

19

TRUTH AND TRAINS

SHIM

MY HEAD HITTING something hard woke me up. I was lying on a platform made of hard mud or terracotta. That must have been what I hit my head on. Pushing up to sit, I looked out at the view. The whole underground city was laid out in front of me in the twilight glow of artificial light.

We had spent hours evading the henchmen tailing us when those old coyotes sold us out. We finally lost them about the time we figured out how the map on the linka worked. I managed to find a transport hub and we headed to a nearby neighborhood so we could watch it. We climbed to the roof of an abandoned building to get a better vantage point. Secluded, with a bird's eye view of the station, it was a perfect place to rest and watch the city pulse with life.

Jaxon was snoozing next to me. He was supposed to be standing guard.

The little shit wouldn't even follow simple directions.

We were never getting out of this alive.

I suppose I should give him a break. It was my fault we were in this city. But the main reason I didn't want to wake up Jaxon and call him out for sleep on duty was I didn't want to deal with his messy temper. On a good day, Jaxon's tank was full, ready to explode—I'd become an expert at fixing holes in the walls of our Las Vegas house. And this wasn't a good day. I was starting to worry that he was hurting himself on purpose. I didn't know what to do. But if he didn't get his shit together, he could end up in jail, or someplace worse here on this alien world. I needed to make sure that didn't happen.

It was so frustrating. I know taking care of Jaxon is what my mother Kindle and stepfather Logan expected of me, but it felt so unfair.

My family sucks.

I smacked my palm to my head and groaned as I remembered how much I had hurt Grace by pulling her into our sick family games.

Brittany was a good friend. It had been her idea to let our parents think we were more, and for a while, it worked. Her super strict father financially backed all of Logan's real estate deals. When we started to fake date, Logan was ecstatic and let me drop football to spend more time with her—what I actually did was take a college coding class while Brittany spent time with her girlfriend. Win-win.

When Kindle told me she was going to tell Grace I had a girlfriend, I knew I had to confess. Kindle wanted to drive a wedge between us, but I'd done so much worse. Worried Grace wouldn't understand I'd waited too long to tell her the truth. Grace might have been the one to break up, but I'd been the one to break us into pieces and I didn't think there would ever be a way to put us back together.

All this expository information was making my head hurt.

I looked out over the city as the lights slowly changed from a dim twilight to a morning sunshine and the city woke up.

"Hey, wake up. We need to get moving." I thumped Jaxon on the shoulder. There was no response.

With the faux-morning light, I could see the gates opening on the transportation hub that was our destination. The system was similar to an enormous international airport, with gate checks and ramps going a million different directions.

I got a look at one of the transportation vehicles in the light. There was no engine compartment, just a wedge-shaped nose. It resembled a Maglev with multiple compartments that hovered off the ground. I watched as hundreds of people went through secure gates and formed orderly lines, then quickly climbed aboard the train-like structure.

Where was it going with no track?

The train broke away from the platform with a slight wobble and a ramp similar to a draw bridge lifted the carriages, pushing them into a vertical line. It looked like a rocket about to take off.

There was no ignition, just a jolt, then the train shot up the shaft to the circle of sky above and disappeared over the edge.

"No way! Check that out," I shouted.

Jaxon woke up and shot up to his feet, instantly ready to run. "What is it?"

"The train, it has no tracks and it goes vertical!" I scrambled up beside him, grabbing his shoulders with excitement.

"You woke me up so you could geek out over an engine?"

"Vertical Jaxon!"

Jaxon put his back against the back wall of the alcove and slid down the wall, curling his head into his chest. He went back to sleep.

"Don't go back to sleep. We have to go." I repeated.

I was watching people arrive at the station and noticed that most were carrying what looked like respirators. Maybe we should pick some up before we tried to get on the train.

"Where are we going now? And what stinks—did you fart?" Jaxon said, his voice thick with sleep.

"It's probably the recycled air down here. And we are going to Neran." I'd put off telling him our destination. He wasn't going to like it.

"What? That's on the surface! We can't go up there...we...we have to get back to the lake." Jaxon said. He sounded fully awake now.

"They won't be at the lake anymore. If they were, the Authorities would have caught them. We have to go to Neran. I told Grace about it. She will know to look for us there."

I had told Grace about my grandfather, Kindle's father, being the mayor or something like that in Neran. She knew his name, Shi'mmer. Like mine, though I'd never pronounced my name that way. If we couldn't find Grace, Breeze, and Jada, then we needed to go somewhere they would expect us to go and wait for them.

"Then we stay here. Ask around and find out more about that lake and where the tunnel off the lake goes. Then we go back and search for them. It's kinda claustrophobic underground, but I'll get used to it." Jaxon stood up and then leaned aggressively into me to emphasize that he expected to get his way.

"I know you're upset about leaving this city. Here, we know the others are somewhere below us. Someplace close, even if there were hundreds of miles and maybe even hundreds of levels between them and us. We know where we saw them last. But that's the problem. They aren't staying there, they can't. They had to move on or they would have been captured when that alarm when on. They are moving on. And we don't know where they are going —they don't know where they are going."

Jaxon swore. He closed his eyes and drew in a deep breath.

When Jaxon opened his eyes, I nodded my head towards the transportation hub. "Look at all those guns at the station." People in gray combat gear were checking identification at one of the gates. "Looks like she called the Authorities on us. That is our departure gate." I studied the map on the linka on my wrist.

"Where did you tell her we were going?"

"That other city the merchant mentioned, Bagana, wherever that is."

"Nice." Jaxon was silent for a minute as we both watched the Authorities searching everyone who entered that gate. "I hate when you are right. We need to get out of town before they expand the search."

"Yep," I said, relieved Jaxon wasn't going to fight me anymore.

"You sure the tracker is off on these things?" Jaxon shook his wrist with the linka.

"The authorities would be up here if they weren't." I guess when we bought our tickets, we would know for sure and find out if the Kuri credit in the linka was real.

Jaxon scraped a hand over his face and yawned. "Fine, whatever."

We pulled ourselves together, packed up Duchess, and took sips of the Eloa, holding back now we knew how valuable it was. Then we climbed down to the path that was heading for the transport hub and further away from Grace.

I SETTLED back in my seat on the train. With the absence of engine vibration, I was left sinking into the hum of my anxiety as the full containment racing seat with harness sucked me in.

"Shim, what is this," Jaxon growled at being tied down.

"The most amazing ride of your life."

Jaxon rolled his eyes and muttered "geek" under his breath as he strapped in.

The transportation hub looked to be the newest building in

Bashita. The whole thing, the technology, the design, was different from the rest of the city. This city was a pallet of dusty browns and rusty reds, accented by colorful pennants, flags, and fabrics. The train and hub were a cold white metal with grey detailing. Clean industrial precision. And it looked like the trains ran on time as a voice came through a speaker and announced departure.

"I'll be glad to leave the underground. It's so claustrophobic," Jaxon muttered, crossing his arms and closing his eyes.

"I don't mind that, but not having a sun or sky, don't people miss looking up and seeing clouds?" I was watching our fellow passengers.

We had made it through the gate, skirting security and finding a side entrance. Inside we found a shop selling respirators. We bought two and they were in the bag tucked into the webbing under my seat.

Everyone else on the train was strapping in their possessions and themselves and pulling on their respirators.

I frowned. Should I pull ours out?

A polite, detached voice came over the speaker again. "Respirators will not be needed for our trip today as we will be safely cruising at (she mentioned a speed that meant nothing to me) within a secure environment."

The guy in the seat behind us snorted. I looked back. He was slipping a respirator on over his head and looked like Darth Vader.

Quickly, I reached down to grab ours, the harness clamped tight across my chest, pulling me back. I fumbled to unlatch.

The voice over the speaker started counting backward from ten.

"What the hell are you doing?" Jaxon gaped at me as I freed the buckle and reached for my backpack stowed in the webbing under my seat.

"Nine – eight — seven," I tugged on the zipper and pulled out the masks. "Six – five – four" I zipped it shut again and shoved the bag back into place and I thrust one of the masks at Jaxon. Watching me bug-eyed, he quickly slipped the mask on. I hesitated for a second, trying to decide if I should put on my mask or the harness first. I jammed my arms back into the harness and quickly shoved the sides of the buckle together.

"Three – two – one." The latch caught on my harness, and the train immediately tilted back, the front end elevating to a full 90 degrees. I grabbed at the mask, just catching the strap as it tried to follow gravity and escape. I pulled the respirator on and laid my head back as the momentum slammed me back into the seat and we shot forward.

In less than a minute, we had cleared the ocular opening high above the city. I blinked against the harsh sunlight. Our vertical ascent ended as the train curved ninety degrees and then, without a track, started to run along the ground. We were on the surface of the moon inside a large dome. The remnants of an abandoned city were all around us. The train sped through the decaying remains. It looked like a game rendering of a post-apocalyptic city in stasis. The enormous dome was mostly opaque with sand and grime built-up on the surface.

The train moved quickly through block after block of destruction and within minutes arrived at the edge of the dome. A series of locking doors opened for us. We entered an airlock and as it sealed, my ears popped. We must have gone through some kind of decompression. The outside doors opened, and the train moved.

As if a race gun had gone off, the train shot out of the airlock. The vibration was strong the first few minutes, and then the ride smoothed out.

Outside of the dome, it was incredible. Sand piled up on the side of ancient ruins. People must have lived out here before they moved into the domes and then underground.

Someone behind me patted my shoulder. I pulled myself away from the window.

"Good reflexes," joked the Darth Vader passenger behind us, his voice muffled by the mask. He must have seen my last-minute fumble for the mask.

Darth Vader stood up and took off his mask, and so did the man beside him. I thought I was seeing double. My eyes shot back and forth between the twins.

"Thanks." My nerves tingled at talking to someone. Like it was forbidden, and maybe it should be since we hadn't had much luck meeting people since we had arrived.

The brothers had left their seats and were swaying in the aisle along with a few other passengers who were stretching or looking for items in their stored luggage.

Jaxon yanked the respirator off his face. "What's the deal with the masks?"

The first brother gave a bitter laugh. "You must not have caught the story. Now they have all our resources the Terans are trying to kill us with incompetence."

The other brother nodded and picked up the conversation as he stretched. "They've had two trains break down this week. One forced all of its passengers out at Myrta. That dead city has had a crack in its dome for centuries. Only half of them survived until rescue arrived. The other broke down in an airlock. There was a malfunction, they had to decompress the whole train, or it would have blown the dome. Only the ones with respirators survived." The first brother pulled down a bag and handed it to the second, who thanked him and started searching through the bag.

The first brother resumed the story. "Now, everyone wears

respirators through departure and arrival. You must be fresh from the mines if you haven't heard that news."

I grunted thanks.

The second brother gave a sigh and turned to the first. "You're right, it's not in my bag, my linka must have dropped off at the station or at home."

"Don't worry, I'll take care of you." The first brother patted his mirror image on the shoulder. It was a kind gesture and the other brother accepted it and the support as if he expected it.

The twins returned to their seats and settled in.

As I twisted forward again, I felt decidedly unsettled by the exchange. The kindness. The support. It was obvious from their actions that the brothers looked out for each other.

What would that be like?

Jaxon punched my arm. "Take a look at that."

As he nodded out the window, I rubbed my arm and studied his profile.

"Look," he hissed.

Blinking at the brightness out the window, I studied the sandy landscape of Nadun. A terrain like the desert surrounding our home in Las Vegas. But our desert had life. Here, I couldn't see anything living, not even a blade of grass.

"What am I supposed to be looking at?"

Great dunes stretched out on either side to the train. The sand wasn't beige. It was rust and browns, sienna, umbers, sulfur yellow, explosions of colors.

I was speechless at the beauty.

"Woah, are you seeing this?" Jaxon breathed. I followed his gaze and finally spotted the dark spot racing towards the train, a cloud of sand following. Closer and closer the vehicle came until, at the last minute, it slid and settled into a parallel path with the train. It was—something—like a huge UTV-motorcycle hybrid. It had three over-sized non-pneumatic tires chewing up the sand and an open roll cage. Painted all black, an orange pennant with a black cross flapped behind the vehicle.

"What is that?" It was right outside our window, just feet from us, matching the train's speed. I studied the driver, bent forward over the bike, wrapped in thick, fitted protective gear from heavy boots to a full face shield with a built-in respirator and helmet on their head. The shielded face turned casually toward the train. I could feel their stare. The vehicle shot ahead, racing the train. Faster, faster.

Out of nowhere, a dozen gray vehicles with white canons mounted on top converged on the hybrid. Some were hovering, others had the dust still spewing around them as they sped onto the scene.

The hybrid vehicle suddenly decelerated to a stop, the drivers arms rose off the handlebars as dozens of weapons were pointed at them.

The train flew past the scene.

"What was that?" I asked aloud. Everyone on the train was leaning towards the left side to watch.

The brothers behind me shared glances. The first one finally spoke. "The Teran forces. They round people up that they suspect could interrupt their flow of exportation but that was an extreme response. They are getting worse."

The train continued towards the next dome. We left the scene behind and passengers resumed their seats.

I turned forward again. On either side of the train, there was nothing but dunes as far as the eye could see. Up ahead, a series of mountains rose from the horizon, and before them was another dome. Our route bypassed the dome. Huge modern metal walls were erected around the dome, and dozens of hovering grey vehicles circled the walls. The train approached a platform away from the fortress.

The cabin fell silent as the train stopped. The doors didn't open, and no one stood up. I held my breath, waiting to see what would happen. A couple of people in uniform rushed to the last car. A few minutes later, the train started up again, and everyone gave a collective sigh of relief.

"So are you headed to Neran? What brings you there?" I jumped at the sound of the first brother's voice. I twisted backward to address him.

Outside the window, barren ground pockmarked with holes, each with huge piles of stone and debris next to them, raced past.

I didn't want to hesitate so long to come up with an excuse that it looked suspicious, so I quickly answered with the truth. "Yes, visiting family and you?"

I tried to sound casual like we chatted up aliens every day.

The train passed a quarry, almost as deep as the mountain next to it was high. A trail wrapped around the outside, and rusted machines lay abandoned everywhere.

We finally reached the mountain and a tunnel consumed us. Everything went dark in the cabin.

"Us too. Distant family." In the darkness of the tunnel my ears popped and the brother's voice sounded unnaturally loud.

Small lights flicked on over our seats. We were in the tunnel for several minutes, and I looked around the cabin. The dozen or so passengers in our carriage were snoozing or reading from their linka. A couple talked quietly with each other. There wasn't anyone close to our age. That made me a little nervous. We were conspicuously different from our fellow passengers.

"Is it normal for families to live in different domes?" I didn't want to draw attention to us by asking too many questions, but I was so curious about how they lived.

The second twin tilted his head as if deciding how to answer, then replied, "when we hit the Age of Consent we had to choose to run or comply. Luckily, we had been accepted at a learning center for mining engineering and we were sent there. Together." He shared a look with his brother. "It was several cities away from our families and we aren't able to get home to them very often. But as you know, everyone leaves their families at that time, either to join a learning center, the military, or a work camp—or to run."

I nodded as if I knew what he was talking about.

From the minute I heard the word *engineering*, my curiosity was eating at me. "So can you explain—" The whooshing sound of the train leaving the tunnel drowned out Jaxon's groan and I took a chance and asked every engineering question I had been dying to know since we had arrived on the moon.

We chatted for several minutes until I noticed that up ahead was another city. The crystal clear dome sparkled in the harsh sunlight, and as we got nearer, I could see bright green colors and tall buildings in white. Neon signs flickered through the dome, and everyone in the cabin started speaking excitedly as they put back on their masks.

"What is that?" One of the brothers pointed to the blockade of vehicles surrounding the airlock. Armed figures were outside the vehicles, their masked faces studying the train.

"Is that not normal?" I risked a glance at Jaxon who was waiting like me for the answer.

"No, it certainly is not. They must be looking for someone pretty important."

I glanced at Jaxon and we shared a concerned look.

We sat looking forward, not speaking and trying not to stare at the armed guards. The train was allowed to pass and enter and pass through the airlocks. Just inside the dome, it stopped at a colorful platform.

"They didn't stop us outside." I risked asking. Jaxon tensed beside me.

"No. You can see why." The brother nodded his head at one

of the armed guards on the platform. No, there were two—three, and another two standing at the exit.

When the doors whooshed open, most of the passengers in our car got off. The guards stopped several of the younger passengers, asking for ID.

The older man that had been sitting across from us stepped carefully off the train onto the platform. A group rushed up to him, welcoming him with ritual taps to their heads, faces, and chest and looping colorful scarves over his shoulders. Boisterous music played, and everyone was laughing and smiling.

The empty seats in our compartment were quickly filled with relaxed and smiling people wearing comfortable clothes. We all buckled in again and put on our masks, and the train took off. Exiting the city was like leaving joy behind, and the people on the train slowly fell silent. Just a few voices were murmuring in the back.

According to the list of stops, the next one was ours. We entered a series of canyons. The parched ground's surface cracked with giant fissures. The wind rocked the train. Huge jagged rocks rose against the butterscotch-colored sky, standing guard over the landscape, eroded from centuries of brutal winds.

Nothing lived. No roads. No trees or plants. There weren't even animal tracks recording life. We traveled through the canyons at high speed, leaving a trail of dust behind the train. It took at least an hour at this speed before we exited the canyons, and the terrain returned to the normal Death Valley-like appearance.

Passengers returned to their seats and started to pack up their belongings.

Off in the distance, something shimmered.

20

BINA
GRACE

A DRONE BUZZED PAST. I missed a step and stumbled as I watched it join a freeway of flying things up near the cavern's ceiling.

"This is Bina?" I asked, overwhelmed by the noise and size of the city after the quiet of the tunnels.

"Yes, it is an old Nadunese word meaning 'free'."

"This is amazing," Jada shouted as a man flew past on a flat platform with a waist-high handle.

"This feels dangerous. What are we doing here?" Breeze pushed between Jada and me.

"I thought you understood." Jeu'l's brows creased. "You need answers, and you can't find them in the tunnels. The cities below ground are tightly controlled. You will certainly be discovered by either the authorities or the UNR. If either of them suspects you are—" he glanced around and made a motion with his head like he was pointing away from the city, but he meant much further away. He lowered his voice to a whisper, "—you will be in serious trouble. People disappear when the Authorities take them. And the UNR will not hesitate to barter you to them." Jeu'l looked more nervous now than when he was being chased.

I translated to Jada and Breeze before he continued in a loud whisper.

"You don't have linka. You dress strangely. You know nothing of the worlds. These things will get you noticed. You'll be noticed."

Breeze shuddered.

"So why did we come here?" Jada asked after I translated. He sounded curious and far more trusting of Jeu'l than I felt at this point.

"I needed to come here for my work. And you needed to get out of the tunnels before you got lost forever. It happens."

A chill washed over me. I dreaded taking this next step, but I feared getting lost in the tunnels more. I swallowed hard and leaned in closer to Breeze and Jada. "Is it safer here?"

Jeu'l hesitated before replying. "The city has its dangers, but you will have a better chance of finding your answers here."

Jada nodded, "So, what is your plan?"

"First, we have to hide you, then get you clothes and linka from one of the other moons. People will think you are fresh runners. You will still have to deal with the UNR eventually, but you will be less interesting to them as yet another runner."

Breeze grabbed my arm, her fingers pinching into me as I translated. "How are we going to afford these things?"

"Eloa." Jeu'l nodded to Jada's bottle.

"Someone will pay for a half-empty plastic bottle we've all drunk from? Are you kidding?" Breeze's eyebrows shot up.

"Even the small amount you have left will get you what you need. And I have a very discreet friend who will help." Jeu'l frowned. "But we must hurry. I have an urgent message to deliver, and your risk of discovery increased tenfold the minute we stepped into Bina."

My stomach lurched at the thought of returning to the tunnels and wandering lost. A shudder went through Breeze next to me.

"So, do we go?" Jeu'l asked.

I hated this. Even though he made it seem like we had a choice, I wasn't feeling it. I glanced at the others. With a nod from Jada and a whimper from Breeze, I agreed. "We go."

Jeu'l turned and headed down the path into the city and deep into the labyrinth of shops. With my pulse racing, I hurried behind him, hoping this wasn't a big mistake.

BREEZE GLUED herself to my side as we pushed through the loud market, and I clutched her arm back just as tightly as I tripped around brightly colored fabrics laid out on the ground and skittered past hawkers shouting. I cringed as a flying thing came too close to our heads.

It took us a long time to get through the extensive market before Jeu'l turned and left the cavern to head down a side tunnel. With the low ceiling, we didn't have to worry about things flying at us, and it was quieter but still wider than the tunnels we had traveled through to get to Bina.

The shops here were smaller, less formal, and interspersed with homes. Rickety tables sat in front of some with people-watchers sipping beverages, and neighbors stopped and chatted with them.

People. They looked almost like someone I would expect to see in a busy city on Earth. They dressed differently, of course, and everyone here had more lean muscle as if they worked hard with their hands to survive. It was friendly, but with a tension, like they were surviving, not thriving.

The desperate edge pulsed through the whole city.

Huddled close, we avoided eye contact as we followed Jeu'l, who wove through alley-like tunnels at a speed I could barely follow. He finally left the street and entered a shop.

Stopping outside, chest heaving, I tried to catch my breath. This city smelled of warm dirt, grease, and sweat balanced by an umami scent I couldn't identify.

"Why here?" I asked aloud. There was nothing different about this shop, it had the same faded sign in a language I couldn't read hung over a rounded door frame. There was a tall threshold, like on a ship. And a small strip of yellow fabric stuck to the side of the door frame, almost like someone snagged their shirt on a nail as they passed. I had seen the same strip on other shops. An ancient man sat on a metal stool at the entrance. His eyes were faded but sharp, and they followed Jeu'l as he entered the dimly lit space.

"Do we have to go in there?" Breeze huffed out a pout.

"I'm sure it will be fine." Jada's voice wavered.

My nerves were stretched so tight I was surprised I wasn't vibrating. My instincts were still telling me to run at everything new. I forced myself to follow Jeu'l into the darkness.

After the dim light of the tunnel, it took a second for my eyes to adjust to the brighter interior of the shop. It wasn't fancy. Two walls wore mismatched fabric tapestries and faded pennants were strung across the low ceiling. A customer sat nursing a drink at a high table that functioned as a bar.

We moved in further, and Jada ducked under a hanging decoration. Two tables were squeezed into the space beyond the bar. I wondered if we should try and sit. A young woman, heavily pregnant and not much older than Jada came out of the back.

"Jeu'l?" The pregnant woman's face lit up. She shuffled towards us.

"What are you doing up? You should be resting." Jeu'l

hurried to meet her.

"Oh, *nish-nash* you all are trying to keep me down. You're as bad as him." She angled her golden blond head to the older man at the door, who grunted back. "Acting like I should put up my feet and do nothing. I've work to do; a business doesn't run itself." She narrowed her amber eyes. They were the same color as Shim's. A wave of longing washed over me.

Jeu'l made the ritual series of taps with his hand on his head, forehead, and chest, which she repeated before they reached for each other and hugged over her extended belly.

She eyed him, "Why are you back so soon? Ah, you have brought me something interesting, haven't you?"

Jeu'l raised a brow and looked around. The pregnant woman shook her head and motioned to the back.

We followed her through a door into a dark storage area, another door, and into a private residence. Each room, carved from rock, led to the next room and the next. We finally stopped in a small but comfortable living space.

The woman nodded that we should sit. The rock ceiling had been painted white and a light hung from the center, casting a warm glow over the room. Embroidered tapestries lined the walls and in the center of the room was a long, low table surrounded by cushions.

Suddenly exhausted, I eyed the soft squares, yearning to drop into one. This space was the most welcome I'd felt since arriving on Nadun.

"Let me introduce you. This is Win." Jeu'l pointed to each of us and gave Win our names. I didn't understand the tapping thing Jeu'l had done, so I rocked, shifting my weight from one foot to the other, and gave a small wave.

Win cocked a brow at my greeting but smiled warmly at each of us.

"Sit, sit," she encouraged. "Can I bring you something to

drink?"

"You sit." Jeu'l demanded, "I'll get it." He left the room. Leaving us alone with the pregnant—alien.

When Win eased herself onto the low stool, the rest of us fumbled with the floor cushions until we finally settled around the table. After an eternity of smiling awkwardly at each other, Jeu'l eventually returned with a beautifully decorated shot glass, five banged-up metal glasses, and a matching pitcher. He poured what looked like water from the pitcher into the metal glasses and handed one to each of us. We waited as Jeu'l, and Win raised their glasses to their foreheads and said, "thanks."

Breeze, Jada, and I cautiously did the same, being careful not to spill. Then we took a sip. It was warm water. I drank deeply. It had a metallic aftertaste and was very disappointing after the Eloa. I then realized how long it had been since we'd had water. We should be sick from dehydration. Maybe the Eloa was a miracle drink.

Win smiled expectantly at Jeu'l. He pulled Jada's bottle from the inside pocket of his tunic. "I know you've stopped working as a taster with the baby coming, but I've found something unique. It's Eloa, of course, rare enough on its own. But this blend has been aged more than twenty, and it is unbelievably smooth."

Jeu'l poured an eye-droppers worth, a minuscule amount compared to what we had been guzzling, into the delicate glass. He capped Jada's banged-up plastic bottle and, using both hands, handed the shot glass to Win with his head down, eyes towards the floor.

Looking skeptical, Win took the glass and contemplated the liquid. She held it up to the light and tipped the glass sideways and back to see the color. Pulling it close, she sniffed and smiled. Closing her eyes, she slowly sipped. I could see the muscles in her mouth working as she chased the flavor with her tongue.

Win moaned. "Incredible. The impact is so intense. That little tang you get when it first hits your tongue is only found in the Bagana region. It's the minerals in the ground that seep in. It's been refined and processed, but by hand, they managed to maintain a thick, luxurious texture. And this was from plants in the wild. No farm could grow this. You can taste the individual notes only present at the height of a harvest at the hottest of temperatures. It is much older than twenty. A hundred at least, maybe more."

She laughed and, using her finger, wiped the inside of the glass clean, then patted her belly. "The baby likes this–where did you find such a treasure?"

Jeu'l shook his head. "You know I cannot reveal my sources. Are you pleased?"

She rolled her eyes and shook her head as if to say he was an idiot.

"I don't have provenance. Will that be a problem? And—I need to be paid in advance." Jeu'l asked.

"No, it would be worth more with a bottle and label, but this will sell, and it won't be a problem to buy it outright. It is highly concentrated. Do you have all that to sell?" Her eyes widened as if the amount in the dinged plastic bottle was beyond her imagination.

Jeu'l looked at me, asking for permission.

I glanced at the others, then nodded slowly, agreeing to the sale.

Breeze was watching wide-eyed, not understanding a word. I could only guess what she thought was happening. Jada was studying the pregnant woman. He kept glancing between her and Jeu'l a confused look on his face.

Jeu'l and Win negotiated a price, and when both seemed satisfied, Jeu'l paused and turned to me. I quickly agreed on the price, having no idea how much a kuri was worth.

I realized Jeu'l could have just negotiated a secret selling commission for himself or could disappear with the money, leaving us as uncomfortable guests of Win. But in my gut, I knew that wouldn't happen. Even though we hadn't known Jeu'l long and knew little about him, I felt like our experience escaping the Authorities bonded the four of us together.

I could be completely wrong, but it felt right. And my instincts were all I had left to find Shim and Jaxon.

Win got up and shuffled from the room. She returned moments later with a linka. She slapped it on her wrist and wrinkled her nose in disgust. "I hate wearing it with everything swollen." She tapped on the surface, then Jeu'l and Win touched their linka together, and one of them chimed.

Jeu'l looked at his and smiled. "Done."

"What else do you need?" Settled back into her chair.

"Do you think Tenny is around today?" He urged us up, and we scrambled to follow him to the door.

"I saw him being chased by several UNR this morning, over by the well. You need to watch out for him. He isn't trustworthy." Win arched her brow.

"True, but he is resourceful."

She shrugged. "As we all must be."

Jeu'l hurried us out of the shop. He tipped his head at the older man on the stool by the door and nodded toward the market. The man shook his head. And Jeu'l quickly turned in the opposite direction.

We followed.

I was hopeful after our stop. Maybe we could get our linka, quickly find Shim and Jaxon, and then find a way home. Could we do this today? Before the UNR found us?

"Jeu'l, where are we going?" I stepped up beside him several minutes later as we entered an older-looking, more run-down section of the market.

I disliked being dragged around in the dark. I appreciated the risk Jeu'l was taking to help us, but our lives were on the line, and I needed to know what was happening.

Residential areas mixed with shops here and some stores looked like little more than a pile of products by the door.

"What was all that back there? How do you know Win? Can you trust her?"

"You need money. Win's family is one of the few reputable sources of Eloa at this level—in Bina," he clarified at my confused look, "If we had tried to sell that much at other places, we would have been lucky to walk out alive."

"Really? It's that valuable?" I asked.

"Yes. Her shop is heavily guarded. Besides her grandfather at the door, her brothers own the shops on either side. She can have twenty men in that room in seconds with a shout."

I didn't think twenty men would have fit in that room. I remembered that Jada and Breeze had only been able to follow my side of the conversation with Win, so I caught them up.

"How did you meet her?" Jada asked.

Jeu'l sighed. "That isn't something I can discuss out in the open. Just...I trust her. Hurry, now we have *kuri* we can get clothes for you all and *linka* for Breeze and Jada, and then I'll take you to the UNR. They already know we are here, so we don't have a lot of time before you'll have to be presented. I'd like you to understand what they are saying if they split you up."

Jeu'l walked on, oblivious to the horror on our faces as I repeated his words.

"HERE" Jeu'l took Jada's wrist and tapped through a few screens on the linka.

Jeu'l had stashed us in an empty stall in the back corner of the market. We weren't visible, but we could people-watch. Then he disappeared with our money. For hours we waited for his return.

Was trusting him a mistake?

I'd done that. I wanted to believe so much that we had found an ally that I'd let him lead us to a town where we would probably be captured and I'd given him our only asset. I couldn't even look at Breeze and Jada.

We had all retreated into silence as the market thinned out, most of the vendors packing up and leaving. Cleaners were sweeping the street when Jeu'l finally returned with several cloth bags.

My jaw dropped open when I saw him, and my mental planning frenzy of what to do next ground to a halt.

Breeze jumped up and raced to Jeu'l, giving him a hug. Surprise and regret washed his face as he apologized over and over. Only I understood him when he explained his employers had kept him waiting when he had gone to relay the messages he had brought. As a result, it took much longer than expected to complete the shopping and return to us. He wouldn't tell us any more about that. Jada was all smiles, and when Jeu'l clasped his forearm, he eagerly returned the greeting.

Breathing became easier, and my shoulders sagged as I immediately dismissed all the resolutions I'd made to do things differently if I had a chance.

Jeu'l pulled out of the bags he had bought for us. We all got new linka. Jeu'l said they were clean with no transmitters — something I would never have thought to ask about. Breeze's and my linka were smooth flat strips that wrapped around and linked on the other side when slapped on our wrists. Jada's was a solid cuff, like a fighting bracer, made of something that felt like thick rubber. White like ours, but extra wide with a latch at his pulse point. The inside of the cuff was covered with thin round pads that, when the cuff was locked, stuck to his arm like a second skin.

"This one has special features, it costs more, but I was hoping it would work for you." He looked at Jada when he talked but waited for me to repeat what he had said before he continued. Tapping a few more screens, Jada jerked in surprise, looking down at his arm.

"Did you feel that?" Jeu'l asked.

Jada didn't respond.

I tapped on Jada's arm, and he looked up. "Jada, did you feel that?"

"I felt something, like pinpricks or marching ants of electricity up my arm."

Jeu'l frowned at Jada. "But you still can't understand me?"

Jada squinted at him. "What?"

"Jada," Breeze tapped his arm to get his attention, "you still can't hear us?"

Jada read her lips and shook his head.

Jeu'l frowned. "It should work. It's the most advanced model—"

Jada interrupted. "I'm not getting words, but I can hear something like static in my head. How is that possible?"

"Deafness is common on Nadun. The mining machinery wrecks your hearing. They can cure most of it, but these were designed for severe cases. This device translates the same as ours. It transfers the translated words to the pads that use your skin as a conductor to get vibrations to your ear. It's more technical than that, but I did not study engineering." The line on Jeu'l's brow deepened. "I thought it would work."

Jeu'l smoothed the tunic sleeve down Jada's arm and tugged it into place. Before giving us the linka, we had each been given a new set of clothing. We looked very different now.

As he had handed them over, he told each of us our cover

story, and we practiced them as we learned how to use the linka.

"Do I have to wear this?" Breeze asked as she pulled the sides of her pants out until it looked like she was wearing a wingsuit.

"I am concerned that if anyone finds out the truth about where you are from, they will turn you in to the Authorities in exchange for leniency in their own sentence." Jeu'l shook his head. "Your story would be too irresistible."

Turning back to Jada, he adjusted the band around his wrist again. "I don't understand why you hear static. Maybe the device is calibrated wrong or confused about your language. It's programmed for every known language and even some dead ones, but it makes creative leaps in meaning when it doesn't know the language."

I was shocked. Their technology could make creative leaps. That's AI. And it occurred to me that if our language was known, then the Authorities must know a lot more about the people of Earth, than the people of Earth knew about them.

"I will keep trying. We will find a way to communicate." Jeu'l promised.

After I translated, Jada turned to Jeu'l and made the sign for "Thank you."

"What is that?" Jeu'l watched the motion.

"It's sign language. Some people on Earth who can't hear use it to communicate."

"Again, please," Jeu'l insisted to Jada, who repeated the motion. Jeu'l copied him, and broad grins broke out on both faces.

Jeu'l's linka beeped, and his smile disappeared.

"They've found us. We are out of time."

21

———

NERAN

SHIM

THE FIRST GUARD vehicle came into view as the shimmer of light on the horizon turned into a series of domes in various sizes clustered like soap bubbles.

Outside the domes, giant warehouses stretched for miles. Large, industrial-looking cargo trains were stopped in front, and enormous cranes unloaded shipping cubes. The cranes moved the containers across a football-sized field, then hooked them to small ball-shaped drones that rose to an honest-to-Stars spaceship hovering over the city. I popped my seat harness, dropped to my knees, and got a better look at the ship.

The massive ship in the sky was the size of a flying aircraft carrier. The drones with the containers looked like moving ants positioned around the exterior and locked into place before the ball vessels zipped back to the surface and picked up new containers.

As it approached the first group of grey vehicles, the train's sudden deceleration drew my attention back to Neran. The Hummer-like ATVs and the hovering vehicles were barricading the warehouses, which also blocked the approach to the airlock. A platoon worth and more were approaching the train from both sides. I heard a quick intake of breath behind me. The brothers were whispering behind their masks.

I resisted looking at Jaxon. Were they searching for us? Wasn't this an extreme reaction for two runners? But, to them, we weren't runners; we were alien invaders.

I held my breath as the vehicles took up a flanking position and followed the train to the airlock before finally waving it through.

I let out a gasp as the doors of the airlock slid shut behind us. The airlock popped and released, and we proceeded freely into the dome.

Shaky and on edge, I studied the neighborhood we were moving through, looking for threats. Old shipping cubes were doubled up and stacked like Legos with gaps of green between them. Children waved as the train went by. They looked like human kids, except for their clothes, long tunics, tapered pants, and scarves, all in the explosion of colors of the dunes.

My mind raced as we crawled through the city. Would guards be waiting for us at the exit? How could we evade them?

The city was layered with domes inside of domes. We entered an internal airlock that was little more than the opening and closing of doors around the train. The next bubbled dome was more congested, more business-like, with buildings crowding the sky, curving to follow the dome's edge. Parts of the dome were clouded like a giant sunshade.

The next few airlocks and domes were similar, with a crowded suburban mix of residential and commercial areas. With each new dome, we stopped at a platform and let people on and off. And each one held more and more guards.

The closer we drew to our destination, the faster my heart beat. Since the city noise couldn't permeate the train cabin, I imagined that in the silence, the whole train heard the rock band beating in my chest.

The airlocks became minor formalities until we entered the dome at the center of the enormous city. Here two distinctly different building types battled it out. The predominant style was a mass of curves and cupolas low to the ground and built of natural stones. Their vibrant colors ranged from rust to gemstone, and great arching windows opened up to the outside. Towering over them and dominating the sky were tall white towers with sharp edges shooting up like arrows until they almost pierced the dome above.

At the center of the beautiful glistening city, the train angled underground into a tunnel and descended into darkness. As my eyes adjusted, the harness tugged at my chest.

The environment outside the train changed completely. High fences covered both sides of the track, and beyond the barriers were dim, run-down neighborhoods with thick clouds of particles floating in the air. The buildings were damaged and hobbled together with hand-made bricks patching the graffiti-covered ruins. Orange squares of cloth with black Xs hung from a few windows. As the train crossed a busy street, a thin force field barrier repelled the crowd on the streets. I could feel their eyes following us. Many of the pedestrians wore masks.

The train took another quick dip down. Sliding through the darkness, the lights flicked on in the cabin again. People around us seemed immune to the mass of humanity bubbling under the surface of the glistening city. They were closing linka and repacking bags they had pulled from under their seats. The train slowed again. The lights dimmed and immediately came on full brightness as we pulled into a platform swarming with guards.

We were almost there—what would we do if we got stopped by guards? I took a shuddering breath, closed my eyes for a second, and then popped them back open.

"Hey guys," I stood up and turned to the brothers behind us. "Is there another way out of the station?"

The brothers were startled by my questions—so I quickly follow-up with them. "Like you, my brother lost his linka, and he is wearing one of mine. We just don't want to have to deal with the hassle of trying to explain all that to the guards. You know how they can be."

The second brother nodded. "I was worrying about the same thing myself. We have a friend that works here that I think can help. Why don't you follow us."

Jaxon and I shared a look as I pulled my backpack on and put my cloak over it then we followed the brothers off the train. They headed for the back instead of moving to the front with everyone else. One of them was furiously tapping on his linka as they went.

"Shim." Jaxon grabbed my cloak and yanked me back.

I shook off his hand and spun around, walking backward through the train aisle. Eyes wide, Jaxon mouthed, "are you sure we can trust them?"

I pointed out the window and mouthed back. "You got a better plan?"

We followed the brothers off the back of the train, skipping horizontally to another platform where two more trains were disembarking. We almost lost them in the crowd but caught up again as they steadily made their way to the back of the station where the trains were entering. I hope they didn't plan on walking down the tracks back to the surface.

A minute later, they jumped down on the tracks and crossed three sets. It looked dangerous, but we followed. No rails protruded from the ground but cleared debris showed the path the trains arrived and departed from.

Climbing up to the platform on the other side, we were

alone, near the back wall of the station, opposite from where security checkpoints had been set up at the exit.

I jumped at a noise behind us. A short door set in the wall cracked open, and a voice gave a muffled call.

The brothers hurried for the opening. They ducked and slid through and we followed.

We crammed into the dimly lit service corridor, bending to avoid the low-hanging pipes and lights. The brothers excitedly greeted the maintenance worker, an old friend, and explained why we had decided to exit this way. After the greetings, we hurried down the corridor until we came to another door.

"This is your stop. Be careful, it's not the safest area, but the Authorities won't be around. They like to pretend this part of the city doesn't exist."

We said our goodbyes and the brothers headed off to catch up with their friend.

We opened the door and stepped out into the stinky, dirty underbelly of the glittering city above.

"THIS IS DISGUSTING." Jaxon grit out.

"Don't flip out," I warned him as I tried to think through what we were going to do next.

Like we had options.

We had been pushing through the crowd for over an hour. There were people everywhere. Mostly walkers in this section of town, but every so often, someone would fly overhead in one of the personal transport platforms. We were sticky with sweat and exhausted and completely lost because, for some reason, our linka weren't working.

"They need to f-ing get. Out. Of. MY. WAY." Jaxon's voice rose, and I glared at him.

"If we just keep going, I'm sure we can find something."

"What? What will we find? What are we looking for?"

Stars now was not the time to tell him I had no idea. Jaxon must have read the uncertainty on my face.

"No way. I'm done." Jaxon stopped walking. I turned in time to see a woman crash into him from behind. She shrieked and something broke when her bag hit the ground.

"You are causing a scene," I said through gritted teeth.

"Hey, you stop that!" a man shouted from a shop. Out of nowhere, a guard appeared. The black linka on the guard's wrists started flashing yellow as she raced towards us.

I grabbed Jaxon's arm and quickly dragged him off the street and into the crowded subterranean city.

After several minutes of weaving in and out of buildings, we found a door off an alley to duck through. We were alone for a minute.

Woah, this room stank. I turned the light up on my linka up and tried to figure out where we were. Low walls were lining one side of the room with holes in the floor between them—Oh geez.

"It's a bathroom."

"More like a pissroom." Jaxon pulled his shirt up over his nose. "What the hell are we doing here Shim?"

"You don't know what a bathroom is for—"

Jaxon glared at me.

I took a deep breath and choked. I couldn't take it. "Out."

Outside, our staring contest resumed. I finally caved and admitted I didn't know what to do.

Jaxon stared back at me—for a long time. I started to squirm.

People were coming up and down the alley, but we had relative privacy as Jaxon ground out, "Then why did we come here, to Neran?"

Back to that again. He was the most stubborn person I had ever met, exceeded only by my mother's intractable nature.

"I mean, we need to find our grandfather, but I have no idea how to do that. The maps aren't working on the linka the coyotes gave us. I can't just hit up a search engine and figure out who the past mayors were. We are going to have to ask someone." I didn't know who to trust."

"Those dudes on the train seemed okay."

"Yeh, and I wish like hell I'd asked them, but if I had, and they couldn't be trusted, then the Authorities would know exactly where we are going."

"So, we need to break it up."

"I'm listening."

"Just don't ask for too much info from one person."

"Well, we have to start somewhere. Let's try the shops. If we buy something, they will talk to us."

"Waters 101"

I grunted in acknowledgment and headed back to the main street.

We spent a bit of time going in and out of skeezy shops, buying handfuls of excellent candies and dubious jerky-looking sticks. Soon we had a bit less kuri but learned about the Agara Hara.

The name wasn't translating but from the description, it was either a library or a historical center.

We also found out why the linka wasn't working. The shopkeepers were in a lather about it. Seems whenever the Authorities cracked down on an area, they also put out a dampening field.

Our search took longer than expected as we were constantly skipping around to avoid the Authorities. The brothers were wrong about that; they were everywhere. Guards randomly stopped people and checked bags. We even saw a pair beating on a man who looked like he could have broken pool cues over their head, but he was just taking the beating while they asked over and over, "when is the strike?"

Jaxon tipped over a pallet of electronics and yelled, "free."

The commotion from the mad grab had distracted the Authorities and given us, and the man being questioned, a chance to get away.

We needed to get off this level.

When I saw a lift going up, I jumped on it. As we ascended, we broke free of the crowded back alley-feeling neighborhoods and emerged into a more open area. I tried not to gawk, pretending I knew what I was doing, but it was overwhelming. If Bashita was the equivalent of an eighteenth-century English cottage country, then Neran was a twenty-third-century futuristic Singapore with its modern building and its cutting-edge technology.

I immediately tried to activate the map feature on my linka. It worked!

Using voice recognition, I butchered the words several times before saying "Agara Hara" in a clear enough accent that the linka recognized what I was asking for. A route was mapped out for us to follow. It looked like it was on this level but on the opposite side of the city, and it would take ages to get there.

"Three o'clock," Jaxon said. He was sitting in a moss-like ground cover, angling Duchess' solar panels to capture the natural light filtering through skylights from the surface. If he could charge her batteries, we wouldn't have to keep dragging her around like a broken toaster.

We didn't have watches here, but I knew what he meant. Keeping my head low, I glanced up through my bangs. A pair of guards set up a checkpoint at the top of the lift. How had they found us so quickly? It seemed every place we went they were one step ahead of us.

"I see them." I thought about the trek we had to make. Using public transit with all these checkpoints was just too risky. We would have to walk there.

"Come on."

Jaxon rolled Duchess back into the bag. His back was tight with tension as he pulled on the backpack.

"I hate this, Shim." He said, his voice a growl. I didn't respond.

I hated this too.

AS WE WALKED up the front steps of the Agara Hara, I organized my search plan. We had two things to find. The first should be a quick online search: who was the mayor of Teran back when my mom lived here? If I could get something other than the mapping and payment features working on my linka I would have looked it up myself. The second search would be more difficult, we needed to know more about the history of the tunnels and anything strange about people disappearing in them. That might take a bit more time.

The Agara Hara turned out to be a dusty old museum that, based on the number of visitors, everyone had forgotten about. After bribing the librarian, her name was Pyre, with Eloa, we found ourselves settled in a nook at a standing desk in the back of the museum flipping through a touch screen of archived content at a terminal similar to the tombstone ones.

Finding our grandfather, the mayor, took a lot longer than expected.

"I'm not sure of the exact conversion from Earth time to Nadun time—which uses Teran standard time. The other words, "hours," "days," "months," are all translating. But Kindle told me that the days here are longer, 28 hours, and they only have six days in a week, and 13 months in a year. What do you think?" I asked Jaxon.

"I don't think—I know this is boring." Jaxon sat on the floor and pulled out Duchess and set her spinning around the tables.

The location of where Kindle's father was a mayor was also an issue. Each city had dozens of districts, and each district had even more neighborhoods, and every neighborhood had a council representative, like a mayor, that ruled the city under the Terans. We didn't know which neighborhood Kindle had lived in. At least we knew when. She was thirty-six years old and had left when she was fifteen. Wait, she said she and Grace's mom were the same age; that would make her fourteen when she came to Earth twenty-seven years ago.

"How old is mom?"

Jaxon was on his hands and knees doing a slo-mo race with Duchess whose batteries were still not charged.

"Thirty-six."

I did the math in my head. Forty-one. Kindle had been lying about her age, how had I never figured that out before?

Frustration crawled along my skin, battling the homesickness I'd been denying. She had done it again. Every time I peeled back a layer of the Kindle puzzle, thinking if I could get to the core and understand her, maybe she could understand me, I found an even deeper mantel of protection. It constantly kept me unsettled, as if she wanted me to be on guard all the time.

"She lied." I turned to look at Jaxon.

He studied my clenched jaw and then shrugged. "She must have had a good reason." He turned back to Duchess.

"She always has a' good reason,'" I said under my breath.

I couldn't figure out how to turn on translations for the interface software so I had to translate the results through my linka and decide if they were relevant. It was taking forever.

"I'm going to make that librarian help us."

"Is it safe?"

"If we don't, we will be Kindle's real age before we get out of here."

Jaxon grunted and I went to find Pyres.

About an hour later, we were close to having what we needed. I had bartered a bottle of Eloa for Pyre's help. She was thrilled. We quickly found a Nadunese who was a junior city clerk of the Bash district in our time frame. His name was Shi'mmer.

"Junior clerk?" I arched a brow at Jaxon, who had stopped by to check in. He shrugged and wandered off again.

Pyre and I spent hours sifting through old archives on her terminal's multiple screens. I guess she was the equivalent of a Teran researcher. There was no way using the translators in our linka we could have sorted through as much data as fast as she did it.

Pyre also clued me in on the Terans, who were basically in charge of everything on Nadun that involved production or making a profit.

"Safety and worker rights, they leave up to us," Pyre said, the sour look on her face showing what she thought of that.

She found an article in an obscure journal that had been banned and buried in the archives. The headline read: "Passage opens, tunnels collapse. Three dead, six students missing."

The papers talked about a passage opening up to an alien world as if that was no big deal. Did this world know about aliens? About the passage to Earth?

"Where—" I grabbed Pyre's arm, and she jumped. I quickly stepped back and tried to calm my racing pulse. "Does it say where they were when they disappeared?"

Stars, if we could find that out, even what level, maybe it would help us get back there, get back home.

"No, just that it was an ancient pit mine that had been closed for a decade. They closed the whole level again afterward, citing a cave-in risk."

"Had you heard about this before?" I asked, fishing for more information from Pyre. If everyone on Nadun knew about the passage, maybe they would know how to open it again so we could get back to Earth.

"No. Cave-ins are always a risk. You hear about them all the time, but the passage—" Pyre's voice trailed off as she continued to read the article but she didn't appear to be in shock like I was.

"This happened right after the last worker's revolt, or it would never have been published. We had six months of blissful freedom, where we were strong and united. We were free. I'm sure no one outside of Nadun ever heard about this. I mean, there have been conspiracies for centuries about ancient blood stones that open passages to a sister world."

I flushed and dropped my head as my heart raced. Ancient blood stones? They had to be talking about other keystones. How many varieties of stones did they have that could open up a wormhole? If the rumors had gone on for centuries, we weren't the first to pass through to this side. Were there rumors about this back on Earth? People from Nadun, other than our parents and that guy, Tar Xanon, that had found them when they arrived, that had taken the one-way trip?

Oh, Stars, what if it was a one-way trip? Our parents never found the way back.

"Can you imagine us being tied to an alien planet that way? Ridiculous." Pyre was still snorting out laughter, oblivious to me, frozen in fear at her side.

When I could choke out a question, I asked. "Do you know what a blood stone is?"

"Never heard of it. But we mine thousands of minerals and

precious stones, some so rare they haven't been found in centuries, but that doesn't mean they don't still exist." Her snorts of laughter died off. "A stone that opened a passage to an alien world, the Terans must have been terrified. What if they lost control of the colonies? What if there was an invasion? That's what they tell us they need the Helios for, to protect us from an invasion from the stars, when all the Helios really does is torture and terrify citizens."

Even though it confirmed my suspicions, it was still a shock to learn the Helios functioned the same on Teran as they did on Earth. I wanted to ask more questions about them but thought that would look suspicious. So instead, I asked, "What happened to the parents of the kids that disappeared?"

"Doesn't say. They were probably told it was a tunnel collapse," she checked an article. "There were two Terans, two LaDerian, a Miran, and a Nadunese that disappeared."

My heart sank. If our parents hadn't found their way home in twenty-seven years, what made us think we could?

22

THE UNR
GRACE

WE BARELY MADE it back to the market before being stopped by a dozen huge guys. Every one of them looked like they swallowed linebackers for breakfast. They had thick necks and muscled bodies as if all they did all day was work out and retrieve things—like us.

"Show us your ID." The widest one stepped forward and latched onto Jada's hand.

"I was just taking them to report to the UNR. I found them wandering in the tunnels." Jeu'l pulled up his ID on his linka and showed it to the short man.

The man glanced at it and then looked at Jada. "And where is your ID runner?"

Jeu'l sighed.

I STARED at the metal bars that made up our prison. Jeu'l was right. The gang had heard of our arrival. We had been able to sell the drink without being tracked. But Tenny had turned us in after he made a bit of profit off us.

"Grace, growling won't change anything," Jada couldn't stand fully in the cage, so he watched me from where he sat on the floor.

I stared at the guy with his back to us. I didn't like him. One of the other guys called him a name my necklace had translated to roughneck, but my linka had called him a dozer. Maybe my necklace translator needed a software upgrade after spending twenty-five years on Earth. It was weird having two translations running through my head, but I wasn't taking off my mother's necklace.

Dozer's long hair hung in a thick braid down his back. His dark shoulders exploded out of a tight black vest, and his pants looked painted onto bulging leg muscles. It must be a uniform. It was the same clothes we had seen others wearing. How long had we been here? We'd been fed three meals, and when the lights went out, as Jeu'l said they would at the end of a cycle, we'd slept. At least they let us out to use the semi-private toilets several times.

Yesterday, when the retrieval squad surrounded us, I had to fight the urge to run. While they marched us to the detention center, Jeu'l explained in a low, calm tone where they were taking us and what to expect. Eventually, they split us up and threw us into these cells.

And now, they just left us sitting here. Shim and Jaxon were Stars knew where and we still didn't have a way home. I paced the two steps our cell allowed, clenching my hands to resist yanking on the bars, groaned and turned and repeated the action.

"Grace, stop! Please, you aren't helping." Breeze said from the cage next to mine. Her voice muffled from where she had it buried in a pillow on Jada's lap. She refused to open her eyes—she said it made her feel like she wasn't really there, so she didn't panic.

I gave the bars another growl and a pout, then slumped next to them, leaning my arm against the divider that separated us. Breeze blindly reached through the bar, and I grabbed onto her hand and squeezed. The quakes inside me calmed enough I could take a stuttering breath.

It was disturbing to see both her and Jada in their new clothes.

Back in the alley behind the shop, Jeu'l had insisted we put them on immediately. He said all the fresh runners arrived in a state of shock, so us wandering lost would be believable. While we pulled on the clothes, Jeu'l explained their purpose and the cover stories he had made up for each of us.

Jada wore a long sleeve tunic and loose pants in a thin grayish fabric that Teran's favored. The tailored pieces fit him well. I was wearing a sleeveless, super flexible swimskin. The light-weight material was like nothing I'd ever worn before—shimmery green with a texture of hexagons that looked like scales. It was stretchy and felt fantastic on my skin. I'd turned my necklace around so the bronze strip lay on my neck and the stone was hidden under my hair. Breeze looked, well, she looked like a flying squirrel. She wasn't happy. Jeu'l said most people from Miran's wore wing suits but being smaller than most runners, Jeu'l hadn't been able to find something that fit her.

I thunked my head against the wire bars. Stars, I don't know what we would have done without Jeu'l. The backgrounds he gave us worked, and once the retrieval squad saw how we were dressed, they accepted our story and dragged us back so we could be properly processed through the UNR.

The room held several other cages with runners. All their faces tense, angry, fearful. The way I felt.

The door swung open and slammed into the wall. Every eye turned to the man who entered. Tall, in his early twenties, he stomped in with a twisted sneer.

"You fresh-uns ready for judgment day?" Clapping his hands, his shout woke the runners who were sleeping. I didn't trust a person who laughed at their own jokes. The other guard rolled his eyes, and the two of them went about opening the cages so we could step out. In some cases, they pulled kids from the cells. A boy in grey coveralls tried to run. We heard his shoes stomping up the stairs just as more boots sounded, and two retrieval dozers came in with the boy suspended between them, his feet still spinning in the air.

"We have a volunteer to go first," A sneering dozer shouted. "Any other volunteers? No? Don't worry; you'll all get your turn."

They filed us out of the room and up the stairs. The three of us complied with their directions and tried to stay together. More vested dozers joined the group at the top of the stairs, and they shuffled us through the halls. We passed other people; most stepped out of the way and stared. We entered a hallway open on one side to a huge pit below, surrounded by balconies and openings on each level, all packed with men and women. The guards made us stop and turn toward the crowd, who cheered when they saw us. A few of the other prisoners waved. I studied the group cheering. Most were a little older than us and dressed in black and brown pants and vests that seemed to be the uniform of the UNR. Some people had thick pads stitched into the knees of their pants. Others wore fingerless gloves. They were in a good mood as if they were attending an entertainment event.

The dozers moved us along. Sneering Dozer took the lead and called back ominous threats if any of us tried to run. "Remember, this is why you came here."

We entered a barely light hallway and then descended several sets of stairs. Eventually, we came to another door, and as it swung open, we were pushed out onto the floor of the pit. It was blindingly bright. As I blinked, I recognized the form, it was an arena, and we were the show.

I spun slowly in a circle, blinking as my eyes adjusted to the light. We were now on the ground floor, looking up at the crowd. My stomach sank as the shouts and jeers of the guards were amplified by the boisterous crowd.

We followed the guards across a stage to a row of benches. Breeze and I tried to sit together in the back row, but a large girl with shoulders like a bodybuilder and a skinsuit like mine squeezed between us. Jada was in front of us between two boys that looked like brothers and matched his height and build. I tried to move back to sit by Breeze.

"Volunteering?" a dozer asked. I quickly sat back down.

Lights covered the ceiling, and I could see the space wasn't as huge as it first seemed, but it was tall, like a basketball court or a theater in the round. There were a few rows of seats on the elevated stage, but the rest of the three hundred or so attendees stood or draped over balconies to see better.

A spectacular waterfall ringed by plants and vines started at the ceiling. It gently cascaded down one side of the pit, riding over natural rocks, down carved channels, and softly chiming as it pinged into metal bowls embedded in the wall. The water pooled into a stream that split one-third of the theater from the other at the base. The smaller section was on a raised base with benches full of people, except for a small section in front with a large empty chair in the middle. I expect the King would sit there if this were a medieval joust.

As I thought it, a guy a little older than me in a sleeveless black robe came out, followed by a similarly dressed older man who was at least thirty. The crowd grew quiet.

The older man stood in front of the chair, the younger next to him, and they both theatrically threw off their robes to reveal uniforms similar to the others, with gold chains covering their vests.

As the older man stared up at the crowd, the water stopped flowing down the wall. When it had grown silent, he turned his attention to us.

"Welcome, Runners. I am Ferno, and I lead the UNR." He paused, pleased with the cheers and shouts, letting them fade out before continuing. "This is Blaze, and he will lead you after I age out." There were a few shouts, but the audience was notably less enthusiastic.

Blaze? Why did that name sound familiar to me?

Before the answer came to me, Ferno continued. "We were all once like you. We found a home here, in Bina, and in the UNR. Each member brings something to make us stronger. Today, you choose what you will give.

"We invite you to demonstrate your strength. Tell us why we should take you in." His narrowed eyes felt like a knife to the gut, "Show us what you have to contribute or work the mines."

I wasn't the only one that shivered. The whole bench trembled with anxiety. It seemed unfair. To do anything other than work the mines, you had to fight. That wasn't really a choice.

Sneering Dozer pulled the volunteer up and shoved the boy in grey coveralls to the center of the sand-covered stage.

The boy's voice shook as he spoke. "I'm from T-T-eran. I'm a f-fast runner. I could be a runner in the mines."

Blaze took over for Ferno, calling up to a man leaning on a balcony one level up. "Foreman, do you need runners?"

"Ay, if he is quick enough." The Foreman called into the crowd for two of his runners. A tall boy and a girl slightly older than Jada jumped down onto the sand floor. Their bodies were toned and conditioned, their legs strong. This was Jeu'l's job. I wondered if he would join the group. I hadn't seen him since we'd been captured.

"Any other runners in the group? We will only do this once. If you want to be a runner, you best join now." A girl from our bench stood and joined the line. Someone scratched staggered starting marks in the sand for each of them. They lined up. "Three laps, no hitting, spitting, tripping," he shook his head, "—just no touching each other, or I'll throw you all in the mines myself. Ready yourself and GO." The four runners took off. The two professionals took the lead. The boy was very good, and he kept pace. The girl was not; you could tell she regretted joining the challenge. She dropped out before the others ended. The professional girl runner was at least half a lap ahead. The two boys took turns edging ahead of the other; they were side by side at the final mark with no clear runner-up to the girl. "I'll take him," the Foreman yelled.

The crowd cheered. Shouts of laughter bubbled up with the excitement of the race.

"A runner and one more for the mines." Blaze waved a hand, and the girl and boy were led off the stage.

The next few kids that stood were easy placements. One came from a family of mechanics and quickly showed that he could fix almost anything. If he was here, Shim would have been good at that, and I got a pang thinking about him and hoped that he was somewhere better than this.

Two girls volunteered for the mines. The next boy said he didn't want to work the mines, but he didn't have any talent that he could think of, so he would fight for a position. He was put aside for a moment. The claiming continued until another boy also said he would fight. The two were pitted against each other. It was sad to watch. Neither was very good, and in the end, one tripped over his own feet. The looser was sent to the mines. The winner crowed dramatically, hyped up on his victory until Ferno silenced the crowd.

"You're not a very good fighter. You got lucky. If you want to show you can sustain yourself, then you must fight one of my squad. He nodded to Sneering Dozer, who stepped forward and raised his hands. The boy's eyes grew wide.

"That's not fair." He claimed.

"Fair? Is it fair that we support you, that you become a burden on our society when you can't pay your share of the taxes?" Blaze was making a point, but he was also a jerk.

I held my breath as the boy raised his arms and looked like he was trying not to puke. It was over quickly. One hit knocked the boy out. Others came forward and carried him off stage. Sneering Dozer preened for the crowd that booed and hissed at him.

The next few teens presented viable contributions and proved them. There was another fight that was far more competitive and captivated the crowd. It was almost Jada's turn. I worried about him and Breeze. I didn't know Jada well enough to know what he could do. And while Breeze was resourceful, but she hadn't been herself lately. I tried to talk to her but got a vicious shove from one of the dozers.

I was desperately searching for ideas of what I could say to show my own worth. What was a valuable skill on this planet? Even on Earth, there was nothing that I could do that anyone else couldn't do better. I'm good at leading people into trouble, getting them trapped on alien worlds, climbing elevator shafts, and solving puzzles, but I don't think those would count as sharable skills—wait. I guess I do solve mysteries. I could say I'm a detective. Do they need those here? And how would I prove it?

"Blaze," Ferno turned to his successor and pointed to a pair of boys racing to reassemble a mechanical engine. "What do you think? Have they earned their place?" Blaze gave them a thumbs down, and the crowd roared as the teens were carted off.

I really didn't like that guy.

The first twin was next; then, it would be Jada's turn.

Twin One stood and declared himself a fighter. Twin Two stood and did as well. That was a dumb move. Now Blaze would make them fight each other.

Then Blaze gave a sly smile and nodded to Jada. "All right, let's see what you can do. You both can fight him."

"What? That's not fair," I stood quickly, and the people around me seemed to shrink back. Breeze stood too, as did half the crowd, but they were encouraging the fight, shouting out favorites and placing bets.

"What's going on? Jada turned to me, confusion wrinkling his features. The dozers pinned my arms to my sides and I was trying to wiggle out of the hold. I stopped squirming and repeated for him what Blaze had said.

Jada nodded, his face serious. "It's okay, Grace. I got this." He stood and turned to Blaze, speaking loudly, "I'm a scientist. A geologist. I study rocks."

Blaze nodded, "we can use those skills. But you still have to fight them." He nodded to the twins.

Jada looked at me again. I quickly repeated Blaze's challenge.

Jada studied the two boys. They were the same size and height as him, but there were two.

Jade turned back to the stage and nodded his agreement. Then, he moved to the center of the stage and bowed to his opponents.

"Go," Blaze said while Jada's head was still lowered.

Twin One rushed him. Jada caught the movement out of the corner of his eye and shot up. He made a clean side step, slicing his hand under Twin One's chin as he surged past. He must have hit some pressure point. Twin One's neck snapped up, Jada stepped around, hooked an arm behind his neck, and assisted the unconscious boy to the ground.

Quickly backing away, Jada focused on Twin Two, who had been trying to sneak up behind him. Seeing his brother down, Twin Two charged, swinging a fist at Jada's head. Cleanly side-stepping again, Jada slapped the incoming fist down onto the second arm raised for a follow-up strike. With both his hands locked down, Twin Two was helpless to defend against Jada's KO chop with the side of his hand to the twin's neck. Jada gently lowered the second twin to the ground. It took less than a minute.

Stunned silence filled the amphitheater, and then the audience roared to their feet, cheering. Jada stood unsmiling, oblivious to the noise and waiting for the verdict. Blaze eagerly jumped to his feet, clapping. Ferno nodded slowly, acknowledging Jada's actions and reluctance to rejoice in the takedowns.

"Acceptable."

Jada was led from the stage.

The audience was distracted and buzzing as the next few teens made their cases and accepted their destinies. Then it was Breeze's turn.

She looked pleadingly at me. I whispered to her, "you can do this. Think of all that Waters taught you," before Sneering Dozer yanked her up and dragged her to the center stage. For some reason, he must have thought she was going to run because he stayed there, pinching her arm in a tight grip.

Breeze winced.

"Well?" Blaze demanded.

Breeze's voice was soft and tentative as she responded. "I'm not made for mines. So I don't think I would like that. I really don't enjoy the tunnels at all, and I don't like the dark." She rambled on and on, and I cringed, putting my head into my hands.

"What can you do?" Blaze asked. He sounded bored and

impatient.

"Well, I'm a pretty good sneak thief, and I think I could probably take out this guy." She tilted her head to Sneering Dozer, whose jaw had dropped open when she motioned to him. He held her so tightly one foot barely touched the ground.

That a girl Breeze!

I watched as Blaze and Ferno laughed, and the audience roared. "Little girl, we don't need thieves, but if you could even knock him to the ground, we would let you do whatever you wish."

Breeze nodded, "Okay." Quick as a whip, she brought her hand up into a prayer position over her head, the motion twisting her arm out of Sneering Dozer's grip. Then folding both hands into a fist, she drove down hard and slammed her elbow into his stomach. Spinning behind him, hidden by his bulk for a second, she reappeared and raced to the opposite wall.

Sneering Dozer was no boy, and he had quick reflexes. He turned and chased her, almost catching onto the billowing sleeve of her squirrel suit as she charged the theater wall. In a parkour move Jaxon would have been proud of, Breeze ran straight up the wall and flipped over Dozer's head. Landing, she slid to a crouch and gave his pants a yank pulling them down to his knees.

Thank Stars, they wore underwear in this world.

Breeze did a rolling spin to get out of the way as Sneering Dozer, now furious, turned. His legs got caught up in the pants around his knees, and with a flailing windmill of arms, he crashed face-first into the dirt. Breeze stood in the center stage with his linka in one hand and his belt in the other. Uncertain about what to do next, she gave a little bow.

The audience roared with laughter.

Two big guys helped Sneering Dozer up and then had to

hold him back as he fumbled with his pants and tried to get to Breeze simultaneously.

"You are..." Blaze stopped to smother a laugh before he could continue.

"Let her go, Blaze." Someone shouted from the audience.

"In all my days..." he snorted and waved his hand. "You can do what you want."

A guard came and quickly escorted Breeze off the stage.

Suddenly, it came back to me where I had heard Blaze's name. I knew what I needed to do.

The next few teens had their say and received their verdicts. Then it was my turn.

I glared at the dozer that tried to take my arm. He backed off, amused. Stalking to the center of the stage, I waited for the crowd to settle down.

"I solve mysteries. You have one, and you need to let me figure it out."

"Really. And how will that help us?" Blaze was back to sounding bored. They all looked restless, as if they were ready for these games to be done. And so was I.

"Because I can save you."

He turned to stare at me. He was waiting for more. I stared, and he blinked back. "You can save me?"

He didn't sound convinced, but he was intrigued.

"Yes," I continued, "I can save everyone else in this room too."

A wave of murmuring went through the audience and a couple of angry shouts.

Ferno jumped up and stepped to the center, eclipsing Blaze. "Explain yourself."

I took a deep breath and put on my game face.

I could do this. I repeated in my head, hoping the mob didn't turn against me. "You've been compromised. Two of your security cameras have been tapped into, and the authorities are waiting to arrest everyone who leaves this room." I pointed to the door I'd seen the crowd enter.

"The exit is over there." Ferno pointed to doors on the opposite side of the room.

"Oh, well, don't go that way." I stammered, changing the door I pointed to.

Ferno leaned over and whispered something to the man and woman sitting on either side of him. They both got up and left.

"Lock down the exit," Ferno commanded, and guards jumped to do his bidding.

"You can't be taking this seriously," Blaze objected. "She is just trying to get out of working in the mines." Some in the crowd agreed, but others were getting restless and looked like they were thinking about leaving.

The woman returned and whispered something in Ferno's ear. There was a furious back and forth before he turned to look down at me.

Ferno's face was calm as he addressed me. "Come along. You'll be working with me. Guards, get the audience out using the emergency exits through the runner's entrance." He turned to look at the crowd, "The authorities have set up traps along the normal exit routes." As the crowd exploded in panicked shouts, he raised his voice above them, "Calm. We have prepared for this. Follow the guards. They will get you safely out."

Ferno, Blaze, and their entourage jumped off the platform and onto the stage. Ferno motioned me to him, and with a wide-eyed glance at Jada and Breeze standing off-stage, I went to Ferno's side and was swept up in his group evacuating the theater. I'd accomplished my goal, but I'd lost sight of the prime directive, don't separate from the others.

I looked over my shoulder and watched Jada and Breeze disappear from sight.

23

——————

FAMILY

SHIM

"I WANT to go on the record as saying this is bullshit."

I scrubbed my hand through my messy curls and sighed. "Noted."

"Is this a wall or a house?" Jaxon kicked at the base of the plain terracotta-colored wall.

"Jaxon, don't get us into trouble before we've even met him." I glanced around to see if anyone had noticed the chunk of broken loose wall.

Representative Shi'mmer lived in the most exclusive neighborhood in Neran. Pyre found an article on his rise to power after his daughter disappeared. The humble clerk had parlayed his grief into an aggressive political career, quickly shooting up the ranks, bypassing the council seats, and becoming the Nadunese representative to Teran.

For decades he had been the most important person on Nadun—even if he was a puppet for the Terans.

The dome sparkled above the exclusive neighborhood of walled-off estates. A line of real grass, the first I had seen on Nadun, ran parallel to the windowless wall in front of us. The only break in the wall was a black square the size of a garage door, framed in a mosaic of blue crystal geodes.

Jaxon kicked the base of the wall again.

"What do you want?" a voice demanded. It was tinny, and I tracked the sound to a speaker on the side of the black square.

"We are looking for Representative Shi'mmer." It felt weird to say my name as the librarian had, with the accent mark, and it sounded strangled.

"Why?"

Why? Cause we're the sons of his long-lost daughter, and we need his help. But I didn't think that would go over well, so instead, I said, "We have a private matter...."

"Urgent," Jaxon injected.

"Urgent, private matter to discuss with him," I said.

"What is it?" The tinny voice sounded bored with us already.

"It's private," I repeated with a roll of my eyes.

"Not interested."

The speaker went silent.

What the heck? I mouthed at Jaxon.

I banged on the black square. "Hello? Hello?"

"Stop that!" The tinny voice was back, angry now.

I repeated what I had said earlier.

"Aaaannnd?" The voice asked.

"Aaaand," I added, "he will want to talk to us."

"No." The voice cut off.

Jaxon lost it.

He yelled, slammed his fist on the door, and started kicking it.

"Let us talk to him, you sack of shit. It's about his daughter." He kept kicking the bottom panel. It started to cave when the door shivered, and a small silver emblem in the center of the square split into four parts. The space between the parts increased until the black squares separated into quarters, and each section rotated forty-five degrees, revealing a center opening.

A man stood in the doorway. His face flushed red. He wasn't much taller than me, but he still managed to look down his wide nose at us.

"Let me guess. You know where she is. You know what happened to her. Ah, right, you are her son—so, she never left, just ran away. And for a little bit of kuri, you'll tell me all about it." It might have been the disdain in his voice, but his accent sounded refined.

The man's clothes looked expensive; a short black tunic with cutouts and thick pants of matt-gold material with a black stripe running down the side.

He didn't flinch at Jaxon's anger, staring him down with a sneer. He looked ready to break Jaxon in half as he continued.

"How dare you come here and attempt to perpetrate this fraud. What are you really looking for? Kuri? Rights to a mine? What petty little thing do you think justifies bringing up painful memories of my sister?"

Jaxon's mouth gaped open.

Jaxon looked at me, then back to the man, then back to me, "Shim, he looks just like you!"

I stepped forward, frowning at what was undeniably an older version of myself. The man's eyes widened as he looked me up and down. His skin was darker, his eyes were brown, not amber, and he didn't have blond highlights in his dark curly hair. But forgetting all that, we could have been twins.

I stepped forward, and the man backed away and put his hands up as if to hold me off.

"What—who are you?" he asked. His veneer of boredom dropped.

We stared, each studying the other's face.

"You had it right the first time, you goober; we are the sons of your long-lost sister," Jaxon smirked as he strolled past the man into the house. "Do you have anything to eat? I'm hungry."

I raised a brow at the stranger and followed Jaxon in, leaving my newfound twin to refold the door behind us.

"Stay! Don't go wandering off, and don't touch anything."

As the man turned to leave, I stopped him. "What's your name?"

He eyed me warily and reluctantly replied. "My name is Byrn."

"I'm Jax." Jaxon waved a hand. "And your younger doppel-gänger is Shim."

Byrn's eyes narrowed at my name. "Of course you are."

"DON'T TOUCH IT," I said for the hundredth time.

Bored, Jaxon wandered out of the luxurious room we were waiting in. I followed—to keep him out of trouble.

The rest of the house was even more palatial.

The place was beyond words.

Our grandfather's residence was in the very center of the main dome. While the exterior architecture was the same natural stone with arches and domes we had seen throughout the city, the interior was sleek and modern, predominately white and gold, with artwork everywhere, from ancient-looking sculptures in gold to landscape mosaics made of precious stones. Large raw gems were displayed in ornate backlight cases—room after room. We had found three pools, two outdoor and one indoor, and more fountains than we could count—each with great arching doors leading to lush gardens.

We had passed waiting rooms, reception rooms, ballrooms, and huge lounges with comfortable seating for dozens of people.

What we didn't see were any other people. Did anyone live here?

About twenty minutes after we started wandering around, we found this two-story white glass wall fountain. The cascading water made pleasant tinkling music; patterns pushed out to constantly change the shapes and sound.

It should be relaxing, and I should be curious about it, but all I could think is *this is where Kindle should be living.*

I know her dad made all his wealth after she left, but still, this would have been her home, her family. And instead, my mother gets stuck on Earth. With us.

I wondered if some of Kindle's fear that something would happen to Jaxon, to us, came from missing out on the security of this privileged life.

In Las Vegas, we have the trappings of wealth, moving from one luxury apartment to another each year, the best toys, and private schools. But it was all a facade, a carefully constructed pretense to project an image of success. Beneath it were credit card debt, foreclosures, and creditors.

"How does it work?" Jaxon put his hand in the water. As soon as he touched the panel, the patterns and the music ended, and there was just the patter of water falling.

I slapped his hand away, and as the music resumed, we heard someone approaching.

"...I was stuck playing nurse to them." It was Byrn, and whoever he was with; they were coming down the corridor toward us.

"Sorry, sir. I thought you were not allowed to leave the premise?"

"That is not the point." His voice rose an octave. "Your responsibility is to take care of the house and the commoners trying to get access to my father."

Jaxon and I raced back to the room we had been left in. We

flung ourselves onto the sofa. If this was his idea of babysitting us, he sucked.

Byrn scowled as he entered the room as if irritated to find us still there. An older man with short white hair dressed in a pressed uniform followed him.

Jaxon and I posed on the sofa as if we had been sitting and meditating the whole time he was gone.

I looked up, feigning surprise at their arrival.

The older man stopped and stared. He turned and looked to Byrn, then back at me. "Astonishing."

With a quick flourish of hands, the older man touched the top of his head, his forehead, his chest, and his stomach, his eyes downcast as he greeted us. "Welcome."

"Hiya." I gave a wave.

The corner of his mouth quirked up. "Hi-Ya," he returned slowly.

Byrn snorted and rolled his eyes.

"I apologize for the delay in greeting you. I understand you wish to see Representative Shi'mmer, but you have come on a day when he is not taking appointments. Perhaps if you would like to schedule a time and return."

"That doesn't really work for us. We need to see our grandfather as soon as possible."

The older man's eyes bulged.

It took a while to convince the new guy we had to see the representative today. I was afraid if we let them push us out to another time, we would never make it back into the house.

We argued a bit, Byrn looked ready to chuck us out the door. Finally, the older man said he had to consult someone. He left. The three of us were still glaring at each other when he came back and asked us to follow him.

Jaxon crowed in triumph. Both Byrn and I rolled our eyes.

We had covered a lot of the residence in our earlier explorations. But, as we followed the new guy down corridors, upstairs, and through courtyard after courtyard, I realized we had been in a kind of formal greeting space. Somewhere we crossed a line and left the sleek architecture in white and gold and entered an area with the richly colored arched architecture we had seen in other parts of the city.

Eventually, we reached a set of enormous metal doors across from an impressive floor-to-ceiling painting. At least, I thought it was a detailed painting of a beautiful white city with sharply pointed skyscrapers piercing the clouds above. Looking closer, I could see it was a mosaic of gemstone squares. It occurred to me. I hadn't seen anything made of wood since we arrived on Nadun.

The four of us waited in front of the doors. The awkward silence distracted me from the skittering of nerves under my skin.

"Enter," an imperial voice commanded from inside the room.

Byrn drew a deep breath as if centering himself and pushed on the center of the door. The set of doors split into four, and each segment spun away, leaving a wide opening.

Three of us stepped forward into the impressive space. My eyes scanned the room. Tall shelves lined the room, displaying objects, art, and framed photos featuring the same man. The center of the room had a half dozen wingback chairs arranged across from each other as if in confrontation. Overhead, a large chandelier made of thousands of raw yellow crystals cast a warm tone to the light over the room.

But, it was empty.

Tapestry curtains fluttered on the far end of the space, and a beam of sunlight proceeded to the entrance of a short, round man. The fabric of his clothes looked expensive. As did the thick, official-looking gold chain hanging from one shoulder, across his chest and belly, and attached at his waist on the oppo-site side.

"Who are you?" He crossed the room towards us. His eyes were cold and unfriendly as they brushed over us, but the look he gave Byrn was worse.

If the stare wasn't enough, his entire demeanor announced he was less than pleased to be interrupted.

"Father." Byrn started, hesitated, and with a glare at myself and Jaxon, he pushed on. "These two *say* they are Kindle's sons." The arrogance was back in his voice, but it felt hollow.

The older man started. His head swung from his son to Jaxon and me. Then back to Byrn.

"Lies! Why did you bring them here?" The representative's shout reverberated in the room.

I was shaking, recoiling like a bell at the impact of his cry. But no one said anything, so knees knocking together, I stepped forward, shielding Jaxon.

"I know it sounds incredible, but Kindle is our mother. She got trapped by a passage in the mines and sent to Earth." I tamped down the urge to run, I straightened my back. "I'd like to tell you what happened."

Representative Shi'mmer studied us. Looking from me to his son and back. Then to Jaxon. I could feel puffs of air blowing across my shoulder as Jaxon's breath caught and blew out. My head was spinning, wondering what the verdict would be.

Days of regret and fear washed through me as I waited. When he indicated we should sit, I gasped in a gulp of air in relief.

"So, tell me about my daughter and how she came to be on Earth?"

Maybe later on, I would ask myself why he seemed more surprised to see us than he was to hear the words "passage" and "Earth." For now, I settled nervously on the edge of one of the high-backed chairs, cringing as dust dropped from my filthy clothes to the plush cushions.

He indicated I should speak.

Where do you begin with a story like this? So, I started with how Jaxon and I had arrived on Nadun with three others, leaving out the part about the necklace since we didn't even know how it worked. How we had been lost in the mines, scared to leave the level we had arrived on but frantic to find water and help. How we wandered the mines for days and found the lake where we were separated.

I told him about our life on Earth how we had discovered our mother's secret, that she was an alien and had been lying to us our whole lives.

Jaxon seemed to have no problems with his nerves. After plopping down in one of the chairs beside me, he interrupted any part of the story he felt I wasn't telling right.

Byrn sat next to his father, body tense and eyes narrowed as he listened.

"How do I know you speak the truth?" The older man demanded when I had finished. His bushy brow arched, his tone both condescending and demanding, and it cemented in my mind that he was Kindle's relative.

I thought about what I could show or say to convince them who we were. Proving it wasn't something I had spent much time considering when I decided to come here.

"Honestly, I don't know how to prove it. If Kindle were here, she would kick us out. She doesn't put up with any shit, and our story—I know, it sounds crazy." I shook my head so hard my hair flew around my head. "We've been trying to get home since we fell through the passage. Everything just got worse when we lost the others—I don't know what to do. I-I-I was hoping you could help us."

Stars, I didn't sound very convincing, and I would have

tossed my own ass out if I'd heard that pathetic story. My stomach clenched up at the thought I'd messed up our one chance to be somewhere that Grace could find us.

A chuckle emerged. Then a deep belly laugh. "That does sound like my Kindle—and like her mother." If I could have, I would have stepped back at the look in his eyes as he stared at the far wall, lost in a raw memory. At my flinch, his gaze narrowed back on me. The old man stood and looked to Byrn, then back at me.

"I can't deny you are the spitting image of my son." He nodded in the younger man's direction. He wandered to one of the shelves and adjusted a photo of himself flanked by taller men in all-white formal wear. His back to us, his voice low. "I've heard of ancient families protecting passages to other worlds. Just legends, but I wonder if there is any truth to them—" He trailed off.

In the blink of an eye, he spun around. The warm smile on his face more unsettling than his booming voice had been. The representative strode back to us, his hand reaching out. I instinctively held out my hand to shake it. Instead, he gave my forearm a surprisingly strong squeeze, and I clumsily clutched his back as he clamped his other hand on my shoulder.

"Don't you worry about a thing. We will find your friends and get you home." The representative said with a reassuring squeeze.

I barely realized we were moving across the tile floor before the older man had expertly led us to the door. As the four panels rolled back, the employee with short white hair appeared.

"Warrem, please find rooms for my grandsons and see to their needs. I suspect new clothes are somewhere on that list." The order was met with a deep bow, but Representative Shi'mmer had already left us at the door and retreated back into the room.

Byrn pushed us out of the room, and the door quietly folded behind us.

"Just because you convinced him, don't think you will be able to get away with anything." Byrn gave me a shove and then left us with Warrem.

We were further down yet another set of corridors before I acknowledged the niggling feeling in my gut that something was off with Representative Shi'mmer's response. I wondered if telling them about the others had been yet another one of my mistakes.

24

TRAITOR

GRACE

THEY LOCKED me in a room with a bed and I was so exhausted I crawled in, and even the crinkling of the synthetic blanket couldn't keep me from falling asleep.

I woke as someone dropped off a food tray. I was so hungry I barely noted the strange textures and flavors. I was halfway through the food before it occurred to me it could be poisoned or drugged. Would they do that now I was working for them? I will likely find out.

Food was brought again and again, and empty dishes were removed. I thought about not eating but couldn't see how it would help anything. I tried talking to the guards, but they were silent.

They left me there for a full cycle.

I had nothing to do but worry. *Where were Shim and Jaxon? Were they together? Would we ever see them again? Was Breeze okay? What job did she get? Was she close? Where was Jada? How was he communicating with people?* And I was worried about myself. I'd hinted I knew more than I did. What would the UNR do when they find out the truth?

The only thing I could do was pace the room, nap, and wait.

It was late the next day when the door opened, and Ferno and his entourage swept in, filling the small space.

I jumped up from where I had been lounging on the bed.

Ferno stared at me, and no one else spoke. He was wearing a scaled-down outfit with fewer ceremonial gold chains. His close-cropped dark red hair had a sprinkling of grey on the sideburns, and his build, while tall, was leaner than the people around him. His eyes scanned me, and I found myself squirming under the intensity of the sharp gaze.

"So, why don't you tell me what happened?" His measured voice was deep and loud in the small room. It unnerved me, and my mouth gaped like a fish as I tried to figure out what to say. Did he mean what happened on Proving day, or was he asking how I got here?

At my silence, he demanded, "Explain how you knew about the trap."

Okay, that narrowed it down. "I overheard."

"Really? Because it looks like only people involved in setting it up knew about it."

Alarm shot through me. "No," I found my voice and raised my hand as if to hold off the accusation. "I heard. About it, I mean." I thought back to my claim that I was some type of detective. "I was sleuthing, looking for things. Sherlock-style observing, I'm good at hiding and not being noticed. I mean, some people might call it snooping or spying. It's not my fault people talk about stuff, secret stuff, while I'm hiding and watching them—while detecting." My voice trailed off.

I was getting sent to the mines. I would never see Shim or Breeze or Jada again, or even Jaxon. And why was I just now realizing how much I would miss Shim? Why didn't I let him explain to me what had happened? And now I'll never know.

"You can stop pretending," Ferno said.

I froze. Did he know I wasn't from...around here?

Ferno chuckled and added, "I know you are not an investigator. I want to know the truth."

I sighed with relief. I was a terrible liar. "We got lost in the tunnels. We heard the Authorities coming and panicked and hid." I was reluctant to bring Jeu'l into this, so I skipped ahead. "Two of them came into the room where we were hiding. They didn't see us. They talked about tapping into security and a trap they had set." I hesitated, this next part was important, but it could also get me locked up for good. "They said they had someone on the inside."

Ferno's face was like thunder. "Yes, we found their monitoring devices in several of our security cameras. Only someone on the inside could have done that."

I was more than a little scared of him right now. Even his entourage had leaned away from the furious energy pouring off the leader.

I bit my lip, and released it. We needed to learn as much as we could about how the Helios functioned on this world. I had to ask. With my teeth knocking together I leaned in and added. "They mentioned that the Helios was giving orders. Is that normal?"

Ferno studied me for so long that I thought he wouldn't answer. "That is very concerning. The Helios are a virus infecting most branches of government. Insidious and deadly. They have spies everywhere but don't usually concern themselves with us. Is that all you heard?"

I quickly nodded.

Ferno frowned and turned to his team, their faces grim.

I hesitated, not wanting to reveal to much, but this was important. "I think the Helios are trying to learn more about the worker's strike."

Ferno's face grew hard. "It will be a cold day on Nadun

before we betray our friends in the Workers Union. But maybe we can help them."

He turned to the man and woman beside him, the same two that had been with him at the Proving. "Can you use her?"

The pair studied me. The woman nodded, and the man shrugged.

"Very well." Ferno turned back to me. "What's your name?"

"Grace, I'm' from LaDer," I blurted out nervously.

Crap. That wasn't at all suspicious sounding.

"Grace from LaDer." He raised an eyebrow as he studied my skin suit and the green streaks in my hair. "Of course. Grace, let's see if you can be useful. This is Ash" He nodded to the woman. She had a soft face and a hard stare. A long white ponytail and a grey vest showing off muscled arms.

"And this is Flicker." The man stood at least a foot taller than everyone else in the room. But the way he looked down on me wasn't from his height. He didn't believe a word I had said.

"You will work with them and try and find out who this traitor is. Be quick about it, we only have a little time before the negotiations break down between the Authorities and Workers Union. When it happens, I want us to be ready to assist them."

Ferno turned and left the room with complete confidence that what he had decreed would happen.

I smiled tentatively at the other two. They exchanged a resigned look and, ignoring me, exited the room. I hesitated, then raced to follow them. I guess that was orientation, and now it was down to work.

I HAD no idea what I was supposed to be doing.

Ash and Flicker viewed working with me as a babysitting job.

After going through several secure doors, waiting impatiently at each to badge me in, they dropped me off at a large security center where dozens of UNR guards watched hundreds of monitors.

The officers gave me a pad and told me to look through the log and find any anomalies. They told the guard at the door to watch me and they left.

Jokes on them, the pad wasn't translating, and I couldn't read anything it said. They were obviously giving me busy work because they didn't trust me. And I was okay with that. I already felt like I was skirting the edge of danger with what I had told them. I would keep my head down and find Breeze and Jada.

I shouldn't have asked Ferno about the Helios. That had been stupid. But I needed to know if the Helios on Nadun were as dangerous as the ones on Earth. And I'd learned people here knew about them, unlike the people of Earth.

I turned to my tablet and tried to look busy. I spent about thirty minutes scrolling through line after line of alien script. It looked like the hash marks on my necklace but in a kind of modern font. I would have an easier time reading grains of rice dancing on the page.

I tossed the pad on the table in front of me.

The atmosphere in the room was serious as the watchers relayed instructions on their linka to guards they were watching on monitors. It felt like an air traffic control booth, intense with the white noise of electronics whirling.

Whenever someone entered the room, they all straightened up and glued their eyes to their section of the monitors that lined the walls on three sides of the room. The bank looked like a larger and more modern version of what we had found in the old shack down in the lower tunnels.

At first the guards stayed focused, casting uncertain glances in my direction. When I didn't leave, they started to relax.

Someone shared a joke. They took turns at what must be the equivalent of a coffee maker in an alcove off to the side—not taking their drinks back to the monitors but enjoying them and a chat with their co-workers there before returning to their desks.

Everyone in the room wore the black vest and uniforms of the UNR but had weapons strapped around their waist. Except for the guy at the table next to me. When he headed to the coffee table, leaving his weapon on the table behind him. I got up and joined him at the coffee counter.

"Hi!" I said to his back, still marveling how everything I said was being seamlessly translated to the other person like it had when I talked to Jeu'l.

The guy jumped and spun around.

"Oh, I didn't know if you were allowed to take a break or talk." He gave a nervous laugh, his eyes flicking from me, and to quickly looked around to see if anyone had noticed him talking to me.

No one seemed to care.

"I guess I am." I smiled and held out a hand. "I'm Grace." He pushed a ceramic bowl-like mug into my hand.

"Hi, Grace. I'm Ember. Are you new? Well," He gave a bashful smile and looked down. "I know who you are. I was at the Proving yesterday. You were amazing." His eyes widened.

I smiled back.

Embers grabbed a pitcher from the shelf in the nook and proceeded to make us both drinks. He poured something creamy and light blue colored into the mug and added a dark and earthy-smelling brew on top. He didn't stir. He held out the cup and indicated I should drink.

The food here had been different in an its-not-going-to-kill-me-so-I'll-choke-it-down sort of way. So I was braced for the coffee to be disgusting. I brought the mug to my lips, prepared to choke it down. I sipped.

"Hey, that's not bad." It tasted like a cold chai latte, only blue.

He looked at me oddly.

"Haven't you had Rooibus tea before?"

I tried to cover my mistake, "Yes, but ours isn't this fresh." He nodded, and I relaxed in relief.

"Yes, it does make a difference when you are on the planet where it grows. It's expensive back on Teran, but here the bushes grow everywhere. It is about the only thing they can grow on the surface. So, what are you working on?"

It wouldn't hurt to tell him if he knew of my revelation yesterday. "The monitor logs. I'm supposed to be checking them for anomalies."

"What, manually? That will take weeks! Who put you on that job?" I shrugged, not wanting to rat anyone out. "Oh, wait, it must have been Ash's idea. She can be so cruel but clever. If you want, I can help you out. It will just take a minute to write up a script that will check them all in less than an hour."

"Really? That would be great!" I smiled at my new friend.

"It's not like they are going to show anything. Anyone who can bypass all this security will know how to cover their tracks."

That made sense.

"What are you working on?"

He hesitated. "Well, I suppose it isn't classified—you know how for months there have been transmission interruptions across Nadun?" He asked. I nodded, pretending I knew what he was talking about. "Well, my specialty is communications, and I've been writing a program to locate the issue's source and work around it. It's been tough, but I'm narrowing it down. I'll have to move to the surface later this week to finish my work. Shame, since I just met you." He gave a shy smile I couldn't help but return.

We talked more about his work, missing his home, and life

in the UNR when Ember stopped abruptly. "I'm sorry, I've been doing all the talking. Are you done? We can look at those logs."

I nodded eagerly and left my empty mug next to his. "We are supposed to wash those ourselves, but no one does it." He shrugged, and we headed back to our workstations. Ember pulled my chair next to his, grabbed my pad, looked at a few details, and started typing madly on his pad.

After a few minutes, he switched to my pad and transferred whatever he had been doing to it. With a few tweaks, line after line of text started rolling on the screen faster and faster.

"It will collect the needed data, then we can analyze it."

"Thank you. You've saved me so much time."

And saved me from having to explain why I can't read.

Embers smiled. "Just let it run. I will get back to my project, and we will check it in a bit." I dragged my chair back to my workstation and put the pad on the surface.

Embers turned his attention back to his own work.

I took the time to study the rest of the people in the room. Watching people work was less exciting than you would think, so I studied the monitors instead. Most were of doors and corridors, some covered sections of the town Bina, and a few were pointed at a city somewhere on the surface—was that a dome? I wondered if the town was on the surface directly above us. Have Shim and Jaxon gone there? The city was huge. We would never find them.

And then I spent some time being depressed.

Ash and Flicker had been happy to drop me off in this room, surrounded by guards loyal to them, with busy work I had no hope of accomplishing. Ferno wanted me to find out who the spy was. I had no idea how I was going to do that. I knew nothing about this world and was spending all my energy faking that I did. But I had to fake it long enough to figure out where

Breeze and Jada were, and then we could find Shim and Jaxon, and then we could learn what the Nadunese knew about activating the passages so we could go home.

It seemed an impossible task.

I don't know how much time had passed when Ember came back to check the progress.

"So, let's look at what we have. It's starting to collect some results, but it still needs time." He flipped through a few screens.

Embers kept glancing over at me and then back to the screen. The third time it happened, I finally asked him. "What?"

"Wouldyouliketogotothepitwithmetonight?"

It took a second for the translator to figure out what he said.

"Go where? Wait, are you asking me on a date?" My voice must have sounded incredulous because he backtracked.

"Well, no, it doesn't have to be. I thought you would like someone to go to the party with tonight.

"What party?"

"You don't know? A couple of days after the Proving, The Pit sponsors a big welcome party. Everyone goes. I can show you. It doesn't have to be a date." He shrugged but kept up his smile.

"All the new people go? The runners from the Proving?"

"Yes, that is the whole point."

I thought about it. This sounded like an excellent chance to try and find the others.

And I'd like to have someone there I knew.

And I liked Ember even though I'd just met him.

And I wasn't technically dating Shim right now.

And even though it felt weird, I nodded. "Sure, I'd love to go on a date with you, and I want to check out the party."

His smile almost split his face in two. "Good. Great! I'll pick you up after dinner." Still smiling, he turned back to the pad. "Most of these are nothing—wait, that's odd. It seems Blaze was logged into the system when the monitors were tampered with. That can't be right."

"Is that not something he would normally do?"

"It's not completely unusual. Let me run another program to make sure there aren't any glitches. Do you mind if it runs overnight?"

"No, please, do it."

He made a few more adjustments on the pad. "Leave it running. We should know more in the morning. It's almost time to finish today anyway—"

There was a commotion at the door, and Ember quickly slid back to his workstation.

Ash and Flicker came in. Trailing behind them was a scowling Blaze.

"So, did you find anything?" Blaze asked, sounding bored with his own question.

I shook my head. "No, not yet."

If he wasn't there, I might have asked Ash and Flicker about Blaze being on the system, but the marks were adding up against him, and until I knew what it all meant, I was going to keep it to myself and, well, Ember.

Ash waved a hand like it wasn't necessary. "You can stop work now. Tomorrow morning you can begin again. Blaze has a question for you."

Blaze rolled his eyes like this hadn't been his idea. He sighed, "I'm here to formally invite you to dinner. Ferno wants me to get to know you..." Before I could tell him how much I disliked that idea, he continued. "I'm so sorry to hear you are unavailable. I'll let Ferno know you turned me down to have dinner with these two instead. Understand?"

Ash and Flicker groaned.

Blaze barely waited for my nod before he turned and left.

I blew out a breath of relief and raised my eyebrows at Ash and Flicker, wondering if it meant the same thing here.

The officers shook their heads and left the security room, and as I hurried to keep up with them, a thought occurred to me. Guilt rushed, and my stomach cramped so hard I was sure I wouldn't be able to eat anything.

Here Jada, Breeze, and I were, safe-ish with access to food and water, and Shim and Jaxon could be somewhere lost in the mines dying.

25

THE OTHER SIDE

SHIM

"I COULD GET USED TO THIS." Jaxon settled deeper into the pool float, a fruity drink in one hand.

I let everything go for just a minute and pretended we were back on Earth at our condo's pool. I lay back and floated next to Jaxon in the cool water, the sounds of cascading water in a fountain nearby, the feel of the sun warming my skin, a scent like jasmine and a couple of other flowers I couldn't identify blooming on the vines surrounding the estate. There were a lot of similarities with Nadun. No wonder my mom had been comfortable in Las Vegas.

We had been at The Representative's house for a week, waiting. There was a lot to do here, so much that I could almost forget why we were here. Almost.

Every day we spent time at one of the five pools on the grounds. This one, the largest, looked like a lagoon with its own sandy beach. We would last about an hour before Jaxon's freckled nose would turn red, and we would retreat to one of the dozens of outdoor shaded living spaces open for our use and fully stocked with drinks and games. Life under the sparkling dome differed significantly from living outside or underground. I wondered if everyone lived like this in the city.

The thought that I should ask Warrem to add sunscreen to the list of items he delivers almost hourly to our suite of rooms gave me pause.

What are we doing here?

With a splash, my feet touched down on the indigo and gold tile lining the pool bottom, and I stood up and pushed my way to the beach, sending a wave of water toward Jaxon.

Jaxon's float flipped over. He sputtered as he found his feet. "You couldn't let it go long enough for me to finish my drink?"

Really, what were we doing here? Grace and the others could be dying underground somewhere. Lost. And we were sunning ourselves and waiting for one of Warrem deliveries of unsolicited daywear and evening wear because it would be unheard of to turn up to dinner with the same clothes you had worn all day, swimwear, shoes, new linkas, sunglasses, and some hat thing I would never be caught dead in, though I probably should have given it to Jaxon as shade. He also brought gear for sports we had never heard of, purse bags, jewelry, multiple pairs of shoes, and lots and lots of scarves, I must have a dozen. Unless rolling luggage turns up, we will never be able to carry all this stuff when we left.

And that's all I wanted to do—find Grace and leave.

I had hoped it would happen quickly after we spilled our story to the representative and enlisted his aid to try and find the others. That is why we came here.

The representative, our grandfather, insisted he had resources far beyond what we could ever hope to achieve. He told us we needed to relax and be patient. He was working on it for us.

Jaxon was completely distracted by a VR mask with a multi-player RPG game. So I waited. I paced the estate and learned everything I could about the fancy tech Warren brought us.

And I waited.

The representative was very busy, and the only chance to see him was at dinner. So each night I put on fancy clothes and choked down a fantastic meal so I could question him on his progress. He always had updates that sounded important, but didn't make sense to me and, more importantly, didn't tell us where they were.

We had come here for help, but I was beginning to feel like one of those lotus-eaters from Greek mythology, and soon we would forget why we came here and never leave.

"Gentleman." The honorific title grated my nerves. It was what Warrem called us, especially when he was dropping lousy news or when something was expected of us.

As I emerged from the pool, Warren held open a towel for me to step into. I made the mistake of stepping into range the first time, and he wrapped me up in it and attempted to rub me dry like I was a six-year-old. I snatched the towel and glared at him through the visor-like sunglasses he had gotten for us.

Warrem calmly proceeded with his announcement. "It is time to dress for dinner."

"Sorry about the pool" Jaxon handed Warrem an empty glass as he grabbed a towel and took off running across the lawn towards our suite.

I looked back at the pool. A cloud of pink and bobbing fruit surrounded Jaxon's float.

Warrem's lips pursed.

"Will we be able to talk to our grandfather tonight? He promised an update."

OG Shi'mmer, as Jaxon liked to call him just to annoy Warrem, wasn't at dinner last night. We had gotten all dressed up and were stuck with Byrn for the evening. He didn't like us any more than Warrem did. Byrn was always at every dinner, picking holes in everything I said. The only person at the estate who liked us was our grandfather. OG was pretty cool.

Damn it; now I'm calling him that too.

"You do realize Representative Shi'mmer is an extremely important man. His time is precious. I'm sure he will deal with you when he is ready."

The answer was ominous and less hopeful.

Not for the first time, I wonder if coming here to get help to find Grace wasn't a big mistake.

DINNER WAS in the informal dining room; every evening it was one of the fanciest meals I'd ever eaten. When we arrived, Representative Shi'mmer was sitting in the center of the low, oval table in an armed chair that looked like a plush throne coated in gold leaf. I hope it was leaf and not solid. The table was surrounded by enough stools and plush benches to seat twenty, but there were only four place settings.

"Father." Byrn swept in from behind us, ignoring Jaxon and me; he headed to his father and made a show of tapping his head and stomach in the ritual gestures we were getting used to seeing but still didn't understand. He seated himself next to OG, and Jaxon and I took the seats across from them.

"What is that?" Jaxon asked, miming the gestures Byrn had made.

Both men stilled and stared at Jaxon, Byrn doing a double take that ended on his father with a raised eyebrow as if to say, "I told you so."

"You are unfamiliar with the goddess Insanna?" If Byrn's eyebrows rose any higher, he'd have to tuck them into the back of his million-dollar, or kuri, shirt. Condescension dripped as he replied to Jaxon's question. "From birth, we are told the stories and raised to have faith in the sun goddess."

"Correction," the representative waggled a finger. "As the Teran's have dictated, the Federation is not religious. The gestures are traditional greetings, nothing more than signs of respect."

"Yes, of course." Byrn's eyebrows descended, and he looked down at his hands as he smoothed the front of his tunic, the muscle in his jaw clenching. "What is interesting is that you have never made the gestures and now claim to know nothing about them. How is that possible? Even if you are from this other world, Earth, as you claim, surely they have similar gestures of greeting?"

Byrn stared us down as if his point was a victory of some type.

"Yeah, we got stuff, like handshakes, bowing, salutes, and bro hugs. Even have a couple of religions with similar tapping." Jaxon shrugged.

"Several? How many religions are on Earth?" Byrn asked. His curiosity seemed to be outweighing his suspicion of us.

"We aren't really religious. But there are like two, three?" Jaxon looked at me with a shrug.

"A bit more than that," I said. I wanted to steer the conversation to the situation with Grace, but this was the first time Byrn's questions seemed curious, like he believed us, and I could see the banter of the discussion relaxing the older men, so I listened and waited.

When the main dishes came out, and we each had our own server, footman, whatever they called the guy who stood behind us just waiting to refold our napkin, I finally brought up the only thing that mattered to me.

"What have you learned about Grace?" I held my breath,

and the table grew silent. The only sound was the tapping of the staff's shoes on the marble floor.

Representative Shi'mmer finished chewing, dabbed the corners of his mouth with a napkin, and after a thoughtful moment, replied. "Well, we know she isn't in Bina. We've had hundreds of guards scouring the city looking for her."

"You sent the Authorities after them?" My voice rose several octaves, and Jaxon looked alarmed.

"Well, of course. How did you expect we would find her? They know her description now and won't stop until she has been tracked down. Besides, we have another lead. She may have been picked up by one of the gangs. We will know more soon." Both older men stiffened and the representative shuddered.

A gang! Oh Stars, what had I done?

Had sending the authorities after them driven Grace and Breeze and Jada into the hands of a gang? What if something happened to them?

I stared in horror at my relatives as I realized they meant nothing to me. Grace and the others were all that mattered. How had I lost sight of that? This was all my fault; I had messed up again, and I feared that someone would get killed this time.

26

THE PIT
GRACE

"SOMEONE IS GOING TO GET HURT."

A couple of boys in the front of the line had started shoving, and others were backing away.

A base beat of music was thumping dust from the walls, and we were still several rooms away, waiting in line. A long line. Clubs here are a lot like clubs on Earth. I hope these tunnels were reinforced.

"You sure I'm dressed, okay?" I tugged at my vest. Ember had picked me up a couple of hours after dinner. I had no idea what to wear to an alien club. But I decided to change out of the wetsuit unitard and into some of the clothes I'd found stashed on a shelf in my room that looked like the standard UNR wardrobe of pants in blacks and browns made of a strong synthetic fabric. I sorted through the pile, choosing stretchy leggings and a vest with laces down the sides. It had been made for someone with a lot more chest than me, so I tightened them so it wouldn't gap. It left several inches bare at my waist, which Ember seemed to approve of from how his eyes found their way there.

"Yes! You look great." I smiled at his response.

"So, do they just open the club for parties?"

Ember shook his head, a lock of blond hair falling into his brown eyes. "They're open every night, but it's a much smaller crowd. It will take us a long time to get through this line." That bashful smile was back, and I would not have guessed the nerdy guy who wouldn't wear a weapon would clean up so well. He looked great with a loose brown wrap shirt that hung asymmetrically off one hip. The front of the shirt dipped into a deep V, calf-long leggings, and boots. Everyone wore boots. They were practical on the rough stone floors.

"So, does the UNR run all of Bina?" I asked, curious about the city and hoping I could learn more without raising suspicion.

"They don't run it. It's a free workers' city. They are not supposed to be affiliated with the official Worker's Union, but they both work with the UNR. The Worker's Union sends runners here, and the Union and the free workers created a system to house and feed everyone. Technically a runner isn't supposed to work for the Union. But there is much to do to keep up with the Federation's demands. It's too much. They are going to break us."

There was a commotion behind us, and we turned to watch an entourage parting the crowd behind us. Blaze and a half dozen men and women passed, heading for a VIP entrance. When he saw me, he stopped.

"Well, Ferno's pet project." He lifted an eyebrow at me.

Ember's eyes bulged, and he bowed his head in greeting.

"You'll never get in waiting in that line." Blaze studied me for a minute, then added, "Come along."

I didn't know what to think of Blaze. Was he all show, or was he more dangerous? But I wanted to find Jada and Breeze.

"Thank you," I replied. Blaze shook his head and then continued towards the VIP entrance. I grabbed Ember's arm and pulled him along behind me. We swept through the entrance and into the club in seconds.

It was smaller than I expected. About a hundred people in a dimly lit room with decorative lines of fire running along one wall. "How do they do that?" I asked Ember.

"It's a projection." Ember ran his fingers through the flames and brought his hand back. I grabbed it and felt the fingers. They were cool. "Ready to go in?"

"This isn't it?"

He chuckles, "No. Brace yourself."

Threading through the crowd, we left Blaze behind and came to a wall. Ember gave it a push, and it slid open with a wave of noise. A rhythm joined the deep base beat: part Bollywood, part Miss Elliot, and all raw throbbing sounds. Ember pulled me to the edge, and we looked down over the railing. We were three stories above a pulsing dance floor the size of a football field with thousands of people grinding away. Balconies below us projected out over the floor, and long sweeping stairs at either end led down to the pit.

"I understand the name, The Pit," I shouted, and Ember's brow furrowed. Putting my lips close to his ear and repeated what I had said.

He smiled and nodded.

"Is this safe?" I indicated the railing.

Ember leaned in close to my ear, "One way in, but many ways out. It is as safe as any place in Bina."

I nodded and looked back down at the dark sea of moving bodies. I was never going to find Jada and Breeze here. I held onto Ember's arm tightly, afraid that I would lose him while standing beside him.

Exhilaration swelled up inside me, and the beat of the music tugged at me.

"Do you want to dance or find your friends?" Ember asked. My brows shot up.

"Friends. But how?" I spread my arm out, and strobes of colored lights crisscrossed my skin.

"Newcomers meet up on the balcony. If they heard about the party, that is where they will be." My eyes lit up, and he laughed. "Friends first. Come on." He grabbed my hand and pulled me through the crowd.

We stopped at the edge of the balcony, and Ember bought tube-like bracelets from a vendor. He slid one over my wrist on the opposite arm from the linka and latched the other one on his wrist.

"What's that?" I shouted at him. He touched the bracelets together. They glowed the same bright orange. He pulled his arm away from me, and the glow faded. He pulls it back, and it flares. "They help you find people. Is that okay?" He looked uncertain now that he had locked it on my wrist. I smiled and nodded my acceptance. I'd rather avoid getting lost before finding Breeze and Jada.

We head down towards the pit. The stairs were made of a stone that glittered in the pulsing lights. The only light on the next level came from glowing colored cubes and benches people were sitting on. The mezzanine was deep, and we filtered through the crowd looking for Breeze and Jada. The farther we got from the stairs and the railing that looked over the pit, the better I could hear. By the time we got to the back wall, I could make out distinct conversations and laughter.

"Grace!" I turned in time to catch Breeze as she hurled herself at me.

The last time I saw Breeze, she had beaten a man built like Dave Bautista and was being led off to whatever her new job was. I clung tighter.

"I can't believe we found you." Breeze used the corner of the scarf she had wrapped around her neck to wipe at her eyes.

"You made it!" Seconds later, I was wrapped in Jada's arms and sandwiched between him and Breeze. Something settled in my chest, a sense of rightness. There were two holes left now to fill; Shim and Jaxon.

After another squeeze that almost toppled us, they released me. Jada claimed a corner seat next to Jeu'l.

"Jeu'l." I greeted him, genuinely pleased to see our first alien again.

"Greetings, you look well. We were worried about you." I sat on a glowing cube across from the boys and Ember squeezed in beside me. "Jada, Breeze, and Jeu'l" I nodded to each. "This is Ember." I made the quick introductions.

"I'm so glad we found you. I connected with Jada and Breeze immediately after the Proving, but once you went off with Ferno, it was impossible to communicate with you." Jeu'l's earnestness to keep us together was comforting.

"So what happened?" Breeze seemed too wired to sit and bounced on her toes to the beat of the music.

I caught them up on my new job. "But, what about you? Where did you end up? How did you get here?" I asked them.

"Jeu'l found me first. I've been assigned to a metallurgy and geology group. I'm trying to find out more about—" Jada glanced to Ember and Jeu'l and finished with "special stones from Nadun."

Breeze squeezed my hand. "I'm so glad to see you. I've been miserable and all alone. They stuck me with the guards. I'm supposed to train people twice as big as me. Everyone laughs at me. Jeu'l and Jada found me a couple of hours ago and brought me here."

"We've been waiting for you. Jeu'l was sure you would turn up." Jada turned to Jeu'l, who signed something to him.

When had Jeu'l learned sign language? I tried to follow what they were saying but could only understand the word "private."

"Ember, thank you so much for helping me find my friends. It's really hot in here. Is there a place to get something to drink?"

"Of course, I'll get you something. Would anyone else like a drink?" Breeze quickly nodded, and the boys shook their heads. "I'll be right back."

As soon as Emory had disappeared into the darkness of the mezzanine Jeu'l turned to me. "Are you safe?"

"I believe so. I'm not sure if I can trust him, but he has been helpful. What about you guys?"

Jada and Breeze nodded. Jeu'l said, "I know the people they are working with and believe they are safe for now, but we need to find out what you came here for and get the three of you out of here as soon as possible."

"Yes. we need to find Jaxon and Shim." Breeze insisted.

"But we don't know how yet." Jada reminded her.

"Until we have found the brothers, we should stay here and learn as much as we can about the stone and how to get home. But we have to stay connected."

"You should not use the linka." Jeu'l cautioned. "Even though yours are unregistered and not tied to your real names, they scanned them when they processed you, and they will be able to listen to any conversations. We should meet at regular times."

"Can we meet here? Ember says the club is open every night." I scanned the crowd to make sure Ember wasn't near.

"Yes, good idea." Breeze squeezed my hand.

"But it would have taken a long time to get in if Blaze hadn't asked us to join his group."

"Blaze spoke to you?" Jeu'l was incredulous.

"Yes, I'm going to be working with him."

"Grace, you have to be careful. I've heard some dangerous rumors about him." Jada said.

"Do they suspect you?" Jeu'l's entire body stilled as he waited for my answer.

"I don't think so." I bit my lip. They were more suspicious of my knowledge than afraid I was not who they thought I was. "Inheriting green hair from Amé Mar'n Thompson of LaDér has, for once in my life, been a blessing."

"Was that your mother?" Jeu'l asked.

"Yes."

"That is a very LaDér name, as is the chlorophyll pigmentation you carry."

"What?" Jada gave Jeu'l a crazy-guy look.

"The green color." Jeu'l explained.

Suddenly I realized Jada understood us. "How do you know what we are saying? I thought the linka didn't work for you?"

"Well, I can read your lips, but I also taught Jeu'l some sign language. He translated the words into Nadunes, and we are teaching the linka sign language. I can keep the visual on and follow what it says. It's a bit awkward, but it works."

"That's amazing."

"I was so relieved when they showed up today. I've been panicked I wouldn't see you again." Breeze said. She grabbed Jada's arm and linked her fingers with mine.

"Okay, I don't know how much time we have but let's make a plan. We meet here each night. We do everything we can to find anything about the brothers, the stone, or a way home. And we make sure no one finds out where we came from. Agreed?" They all nodded.

"Grace, meet us in line tomorrow, same time, and I will show you a way around it. Just in case you don't have Blaze to get you in." Jeu'l smirked.

"Here we are." Ember returned with drinks for us. He settled down next to me. I found myself leaning into him.

"Thank you," I caught his eye. He smiled, then turned to the others.

We chatted for a while about life in the UNR, our jobs and the characters we were working with. The conversation was easy on the surface but littered with subtext and we gleaned information about each other's safety.

Ember didn't seem to notice. His tone was casual when he asked, "Jada, I was curious how you could eliminate your opponents so quickly?"

"Oh, Tae Kwon Do, I've been studying for years."

"What is that?"

I froze and quickly asked, "Ember, will you dance with me?" I handed my drink over to Breeze.

"I will see you all later," I promised. Her head bounced in agreement, and Jeu'l and Jada both nodded.

I headed to the floor with Ember.

I enjoyed dancing. It is usually my favorite escape from anxiety. But as much fun as I had dancing with Ember, there was this aching Shim-sized hole in my heart. Where were the brothers, and how on Earth, or rather Nadun, were we going to find them?

27

THE PARTY'S OVER

SHIM

"STOP PULLING ON IT." I swatted Jaxon's hand as it tugged on his collar while resisting the urge to do the same to mine. Not only did the high collar cut into the neck, but the slim fit made moving difficult. If I had to bend down for anything, there would be a wardrobe malfunction.

The embroidered tunics transformed us, we looked respectable and wealthy, and I felt like a fraud.

"Do you see him anywhere?" Jaxon was now fidgeting with the cloth at his armpits.

My eyes scanned the crowd where it was thickest. The one thing I'd learned about my grandfather was if there were an audience, he would be in the middle of it.

"Why'd we have to come to this thing? I've got better stuff to do." Jaxon whined. He had discovered the Nadun equivalent of an Xbox, another gift from our grandfather, and once he had mastered the controls, he rarely left our rooms.

Grandfather seemed to be warming up to us, unlike Uncle Byrn, who was still a jackass.

"There you are, my boys." A booming voice spread across the room, and the crowd parted to let the representative through. "I've some people I'd like you to meet. They are from Teran and have been very helpful in the search for your friends."

I grabbed the OG Shi'mmer's arm, ignoring the stern look from Warrem. "Have you found them?"

Representative Shi'mmer's smile slipped as he shook off my hand. "Just about. We are so close. That's what I think these gentlemen can help with." His smile was back. Jaxon smiled at him too. It was suspicious. Jaxon rarely made an effort with anyone.

"Representative!" A throuple in matching emerald-colored clothing approached the OG Shi'mmer and ran through the respectful hand motions.

"Ah ha, you came!" Representative Shi'mmer greeted them. Out of the side of his mouth, he whispered to Jaxon and me, "let me get through these greetings, and I'll meet you at my office." He turned away from us and was absorbed back into the crowd.

"How can we get to his office in this crowd?" Jaxon moaned, his hand tugging at his collar again.

"I can get us there." Over the last few weeks, I'd learned a few shortcuts around the compound.

I stopped. Jaxon slammed into my back.

"Ow." He shoved me from behind. But I ignored him. Had we been here two weeks? And we hadn't left the house once? How was that possible? I counted the days and realized it had been a little longer than two weeks—fifteen days by Nadun's standard of telling time.

Fifteen days and we still hadn't found Grace.

Surely Representative Shi'mmer, with all his resources, could have found them in that time. Were we being played?

I started walking again.

Several minutes later, Jaxon asked, "Where are we going?"

"The office."

"I think you missed a turn or two." He was right. "If you got your head out of your ass and paid attention, we wouldn't be lost."

I scrubbed a hand over my mouth, stopping the retort that would start a fight, and headed off in the opposite direction. We had to be close to the admin wing of the complex.

It took longer than expected and several more wrong turns to find the office. As soon as we saw the mural, Jaxon sped up.

"Wait, hold up." I grabbed the back of his shirt, and he gagged and shrugged free of my grip. When he swung at me, I pointed to the door. "Look, it's open."

The door to Grandfather's office was cracked open. The cross of light coming from between the four panels caused the diamonds in the mosaic across from the door to glisten. Anytime we had been by the office, the doors had been sealed shut. Not that we had tried to snoop around. Okay, we tried once or twice.

Even though we got lost, the representative should still be holding court at the party below. Who was in there?

Jaxon and I shared a look, then crept towards the cracked door.

"Is that Byrn?" Jaxon whispered.

I nodded, my eyes not leaving my doppelgänger as Byrn searched the desk in the corner. He pulled an electronic device from his pocket and crouched at the drawer on the side of the desk. It was quick work for him to override the lock. This wasn't his first time using that lock pick. I recognized an expert at B&E.

Footsteps approached.

Byrn heard it and rose to his feet, a scroll in his hands. They did everything differently here; their paper was a thin wafer plastic substance like Tyvek. They also had strange sizes and frequently preferred to roll them instead of cutting them into sheets.

Byrn lifted the back of his tunic and stuffed the roll down his pants.

Jaxon yanked on my arm and pulled me back down the hall, away from the footsteps, and around a corner, where we waited and watched.

The footsteps grew closer. It was our grandfather, and he was talking to someone, probably Warrem.

"Why is the door open? What are you doing in here." Grandfather demanded.

"Well, well, well, here you are, finally." I hardly recognized Byrn's slow and slurred voice—not at all what I would expect from someone who had executed those B&E skills.

"This office is off limits to you." Grandfather said. The angry shout carried down the hall.

We heard a side of these men we hadn't encountered before.

"Can't I have a private chat with my father?" Byrne gave an inebriated laugh. "Take a seat, Warrem; you might as well stay. Wait, have you ever sat in one of these chairs? They are comfy. How is it you follow all his orders and know all his dirty secrets, but has he ever let you sit in one of his chairs?

"You're drunk." The disdain dripped from grandfather's voice. "Sloppy. Useless. And now inebriated."

"Not enough to put up with you, but give me a bit more time, and I'll get there." A clinking of glasses followed Byrn's comment.

"You are a continual disappointment. I don't know why you came back to torment me with your malcontent attitude, but I shouldn't be surprised that you failed again at one of your ventures. You are useless, and you contribute nothing to this family."

Grandfather spit out the words with a hiss.

I didn't understand the spite. Grandfather had been very amicable towards his son.

"At least I'm not a traitor," Byrn said, sounding sober.

I headed towards the door.

"You're not going in there?" Jaxon grabbed at my arm.

"I have a bad feeling about this," I said.

A tremendous crash of shattering glass proceeded, the sound of flesh hitting flesh.

We both raced for the door.

Our grandfather, the great and honorable representative, had his son in a chokehold. Warrem was trying to pull the older man back. Byrn, the larger and younger of the two, had a gash on his head and seemed dazed.

Jaxon and I each grabbed one of the older man's hands and peeled them off Byrn's neck. Freed, Byrn dropped to the tile floor, gasping for breath.

Grandfather's face was a mask of ugly with a side of hell—red and blotched with crazed eyes, lost in his anger. He lunged at us.

"Go!" Warrem shouted as he tried to hold the older man back.

Jaxon and I wrapped arms under Byrn and dragged him from the room.

HOURS LATER, Uncle Byrn was passed out on one of our beds and Jaxon and I were sitting across from each other on the u-shaped bench sofa playing the Xbox-like game while I tried to wrap my mind around the Jekyll and Hyde character of our grandfather.

Was being under the same roof, even with all the doors barred with heavy furniture and the windows blocked, a mistake?

"That was some messed up shit," Jaxon said for the hundredth time.

"Keep it down," I replied.

Jaxon cranked up the volume.

The game had a 3D virtual board that emerged from the ground between us. We were working as partners against six other partnered teams. For only having a couple of days' experience, I had to admit; we were really good.

"He's passed out drunk. It won't bother him—do you think he will be okay?"

Jaxon had been different since we witnessed our grandfather's unhinged attack on his own son. He wasn't talking about it, wasn't likely to, but something was going on in his head.

"He's not drunk. He was faking it." I leaned to the side to avoid a sword swipe from a player behind me. The sensors in my visor moved my player with me.

"Watch the chatter." A sapphire player warned.

"Hey, the fresh ones are good." A gold player, I think it was a girl, said.

A member of the ruby team snuck up behind her and tried to cut her throat. She dipped, elbowed him in the crotch, followed with a backflip that would have been impossible for a human, and stabbed him with her sword. The player fizzled and disappeared from the game, along with his partner.

Jaxon whistled, "Fierce! Do you play every week?" He asked her.

"Affirmative. Except for next week of course."

"What's next week?" I asked, curious.

Mada, you are fresh. "What's next week? It's the race, of course. Everyone will be there."

"What kind of race?"

The gold player laughed and leaned on her staff, then suddenly ducking, she spun the staff and nearly decapitated a blue player. They retreated.

"The race is held yearly. It's projected across the whole planet, a real media event. But that's just the pre-show. The real game is the ten-day course through the most grueling terrain on Nadun. Every step is transmitted across the whole Federation. Everyone will be watching. The contestants become the biggest stars, whether you win or not. Just surviving is the real challenge."

"Have you ever entered?" I asked.

She snorted. "If I had that kind of *kuri*, do you think I'd be here playing against you?" she laughed. "Besides, the race starts in two days, and applications are due tomorrow—better move quickly if you are going to enter." She laughed and flipped up her staff, smacking me across the head with it. I could feel the stinging blow through the haptic tech. "Are we playing or not?"

"Ouch. We are out." I pulled off the visor, shutting off my view of the game.

"You forfeited our game." Jaxon threw his visor across the room.

"I did because we have a lot of research to do. We are going to enter that race."

"You are funny."

"Not joking."

"Why? I love a good ass-kicking race, but that one sounds suicidal. And how will that help us find Breeze, Grace, and Jada?"

"Look, we last saw them in the mines, but Grace is smart, she'll find someone to help, and they will have moved on to one of the cities." I was pacing the width of the room, excitement humming through my body.

"But we have no way of knowing which city."

"So we have to give them a way to find us. A high-profile event where all the contestants will be shown everywhere. Our faces will be famous. And she'll know exactly where we will be in two days at the start of that race." This race felt right, and every cell in my body wanted to get started. "Come on. We have work to do."

28

DIGGING IN

GRACE

"GRACE, I overheard something—you know, that is one of my super strengths," Breeze yelled over the noise as she broke away from dancing with Soar, a cute red-headed guy from her work group who had started showing up every time she was at The Pit, and grabbed my arm. We headed to where the guys were sitting on the mezzanine.

I liked talking at The Pit. The music was so loud no one could overhear our conversation unless they had Breeze's bat ears. We had been meeting every evening, and even though I was exhausted the next day, at least I knew they were safe. If only I had the same confidence in Shim and Jaxon's safety.

We made our way through the glowing bench to where Jada and Jeu'l were having a heated discussion via sign language. I'd learned a few new words, but I needed more to keep up with the speed of their hands. Breeze plunked down on the bench between them.

"I heard Blaze on his linka setting up a meeting for tonight." Breeze leaned in. "He asked the other person on the call, 'why won't the Helios be there?' Then, he set up a time for an hour from now, but I don't know where. What do you think it's about?"

"Blaze was trying to meet with the Helios? Why would he do that?" Jeu'l's appeared shaken by the news.

It didn't look good for Blaze.

"I have something too." I looked around, then leaned in closer. "The logs for the tampered monitors all show Blaze as being logged in when they were messed with. Ember thinks there is something hinky with them and is digging deeper. I've spent the last few days with Blaze, and he is definitely up to something, but—"

Blaze was such a contradiction. He was shallow, arrogant, and infuriatingly vain, but then I'd catch him jumping into a pit to help an elderly worker who had fallen or dropping food off at a single parent's home. We visited neighborhood after neighborhood, and the people all knew his name, and he knew theirs. He would catch me looking at him, and he would preen and ask how his hair looked. It was very confusing.

"I can't explain it, but I wonder if we are wrong about him."

"Breeze, do you want to dance more?" Soar sounded pleased he had found us.

Breeze sighed dramatically. "I guess." She looked over at Jada and Jeu'l to see if they would save her. Jada shook his head and made a shooing motion to her. When she stood up, Soar beamed.

"Great! Everyone is on the floor, even Blaze—he is a great dancer."

"Blaze is here? Where?" I craned my neck to see over the crowd.

Soar pointed to the far side of the dance floor before grabbing Breeze's hand and pulling her towards the music.

I could see him. He was a good dancer. I sat down again, then plucked up my resolve.

"I'm going to follow Blaze." I nodded, trying to convince myself this was a good idea.

Jeu'l frowned. "How?"

Good question. Sneaking around and following him in the dark club, even with all the light effects and neon-homing lights people were wearing, was one thing. But out in the tunnels, he would hear me coming. And what if I lost him?

I spotted the bands on Jeu'l and Jada's wrists. "Hey, are those linked?"

Jada looked slightly embarrassed, but Jeu'l showed off his glowing bracelet and nodded.

"Can I borrow them?"

"Why?"

"I think I might know how to track Blaze."

∞

THIS MIGHT HAVE BEEN a bad idea.

I should be focusing on finding Shim and Jaxon. But I didn't know how to do that. I'd found out the conveyor system Shim and Jaxon had taken from the lake led to hundreds of different locations, the largest being a town called Bashita. But how was I supposed to find him there? He had mentioned a grandfather who was a politician in Neren. I'd thought about going there but when I looked it up I found the city was massive and I couldn't remember anything about the grandfather except he had the same name as Shim. I had this crazy idea that if I won over someone like Ferno, that knew everything that went on underground on this moon, he could help us. Tracking down the person that was betraying the UNR to the Helios would impress Ferno. I just don't know if he will believe it is Blaze, even with the proof.

It had been easy to slip one of the bracelets into the pocket of the sleeveless robe Blaze had carelessly thrown over a bench. Using the homing beacon to track him in the dark tunnels was not. I was backtracking a lot.

I lost him. I stared down a dark tunnel. I should go back.

Suddenly, my bracelet flared, and I heard voices up ahead.

Taking off the bracelet, I tucked it into my bag and turned off my linka, trying not to bump my head on a rock overhead as I crept closer in the dark.

The voices were growing louder, so I must be heading in the right direction.

"Not what we agreed." I moved closer. That was Blaze.

"You said you would deliver them to us. Are you holding out?" Blaze again. Who was he talking about? Who was he talking to? I couldn't hear the other side of the conversation. I risked turning on my linka and using the glow to move around some rocks on the floor and quickly snuffed it out as a light appeared ahead.

"We didn't promise to turn them over to you. We said we would keep you informed." The deep voice was of an older woman's, smooth as silk, confident.

"No, the Helios agreed anyone found in the tunnels was ours. Has been our deal all along."

"Anyone from the Federation. Not spies. Those are ours."

"Are you saying they aren't from—wait—what are you saying?" Blaze nearly shouted.

"Hush, you wouldn't want any of your precious UNR to find you cavorting with the enemy." She gave a deep, slow chuckle. "Oh, you cheeky boy, I adore your naïveté."

"Yeh, you've told me. That's what got me into this mess."

"Yes, yes, it was. Now, this is what I expect you to do; contact me if any runners turn up who aren't what they seem and keep supplying information about the Union. You do that, and no one will ever know about our arrangement." There was a slap, and someone walked away. The steps grew fainter, and I realized they had left.

I sagged against the rock. It was confirmed the Helios were hunting us. How did they know we had arrived from Earth? And now the UNR knows about us. How long would it be safe to stay hidden among them? Caught up in my thoughts, I didn't hear footsteps until someone almost stepped on me.

"Who's there?" A flare of light blinded me. I threw up a hand in defense.

"Grace? What are you doing here?" Blaze's voice was a strangled whisper. "Do you know how dangerous this is? We have to get you out of here."

He switched off his light and grabbed my arm, pulling me behind him as he moved briskly down the tunnel, away from the Helios. We made several turns before he stopped and switched back on his light. Why was he wearing sunglasses in the dark?

I waved my hand in front of his face. "How can you see?"

"Night visor. Don't you have one?" Blaze grabbed my waving hand.

I shook my head, and Blaze groaned. "Could you at least try to act like you're from here? Do you know how much trouble you would be in if she found you?" Blaze turned a corner and started hauling me down another tunnel.

A chill went down my spine and my mind reeled. What did Blaze mean by that? It sounded like—no, he couldn't know we were not from Nadun.

"How am I acting? And, where are we going?"

Blaze snorted and shook his head. "We will talk later. Now, we are going back to the base. At least there you will be safe, for now. We can figure out what to do tomorrow."

29

THE RACE

SHIM

"IT IS unfathomable how you talked me into this." Byrn had been complaining all morning.

I'm not sure how we talked ourselves into doing it! When I'd hatched the plan yesterday, my gut had told me this was it. But everything I read about the race made this one of the worst ideas I'd ever had. All-terrain vehicles at neck-breaking speeds race across a planet full of unmarked pits and mines, with racers ganging up to disable each other. Half the race teams usually drop out on the first day, and the number of racers killed increases yearly.

But we didn't need to race. We just had to enter, hoping all the publicity would capture Grace's attention. And hope having our face all over the vids didn't backfire and get us captured by the Authorities—or worse, the Helios.

I'm not sure how far Grandfather's protection reached or if we even had it anymore.

Joining this race was dangerous.

But so had been my stupid plan to find my grandfather.

A shudder shook me as I remembered his behavior last

night. His face screwed up with malice and glee, and his eyes unhinged.

And I had told him about the others.

This had to work. Grace, Breeze, and Jada had to find us before the authorities found them.

"I can't believe you talked me into sponsoring you." Byrn leaned back against a vehicle and crossed his arms. He was pretending we had given him a choice. I don't know why he was trying to save face in front of a sales bot.

"You're *mada!* Teams have been preparing all year, making alliances and training, and you want to sign-up days before the race? But go ahead, get yourselves killed. I'm not going to stop you." Byrn winked at the sales bot, who didn't move.

"Oh, over there." Something caught Jaxon's eye, and I followed.

Everything we had looked at was stock—the same light-weight materials and buggy-style tube frames on three or four wheels. It was remarkable how similar some of the tech was to Earth-tech and it made me wonder if the passage was used more frequently than anyone knew. I could identify most of the parts and systems, so I should be able to rebuild them, but there were a couple of systems I'd never seen before. I couldn't wait to get up to my elbows in the engine and see what made them work. I wish we had more time.

I skirted one of the popular three-wheeled UTV-style motorcycles.

"This is it." Jaxon lovingly stroked the hood. He was standing next to a sweet-looking four-wheeled vehicle with high-cut body panels. It wasn't quite a truck style, so it would still fit in the car class, but we could fit five people inside.

My heartbeat quickened. This one might work.

"Pop the hood."

"Clarify." A bunch of lights spun on the sales bot's body as it tried to comply. It turned to each of us and ended with Byrn.

"He thinks he is a mechanic and wishes to look inside the engine." Byrn was not happy to be here, but we couldn't have gotten this far without him. Registering for the event, which they called the Great Race, required extensive forms, proof of where you lived, and references, not to mention a huge chunk of cash or kuri. Then we had twenty-four hours to present our race vehicle for inspection. But first, we had to find one.

Two hoods popped open on the vehicle. That was different. I stuck my head under the one in the front. The sales bot hovered beside me, explaining the systems and how they integrated, then repeated the lesson when I got to the back.

"This will work," I told Byrn.

"Of course, it will. It's the most expensive one." I raised an eyebrow at him, and he added. "And my father will be pleased to pay for it. Though, he won't ever know he paid for it."

I hated thinking of myself as a blackmailer, but that's what we were. Even with the money we made from selling the rest of our Eloa, we still needed Byrn's help to make up the balance required to enter the race.

While Byrn had slept, we took the scroll he had found in Grandfather's desk, the one he had almost died to hide and threatened to tell Grandfather he had stolen it. I was not proud of what we had done.

When we told him we had hidden it and wouldn't get it back unless he helped, Byrn had put on a display of temper rivaling his father's but held himself back from the edge of violence.

Jaxon seemed unnerved by the behavior of our uncle and grandfather, which surprised me. But he had backed me up.

There had been a subtle shift in our relationship since we

had met our family. I couldn't pin it down to anything, but we were now working more as a team.

I closed the flaps that covered the engine and latched them down. We had a lot to do. We were just hours away from having our faces and names splashed across every screen in the Federation.

It may not be the most brilliant plan. But it's the only one I could come up with.

Once Byrn accepted he had to help us to get the scroll back, he delighted in spending his father's money.

Between him and Jaxon, I felt like I was missing an inside joke.

Striding out of the private showroom, Byrn laid out the plans for the rest of our day. "We have publicity vids being shot in an hour, the vehicle will be moved by carrier there, then taken on to Bashita, and we will meet it in the morning. We have to get the rest of your gear as quickly as possible."

I stopped listening as Byrn droned on. My mind churned through some of the emergency survival supplies I wanted to get, just in case. Backpacks, climbing rope, night vision glasses, and other items I wished I'd had our first time in the tunnels.

My ears perked up when Byrn said, "—immediately after the shoot, we leave for Bashita. We should have arrived last night, but we can still catch the welcome party tonight, which will be transmitted everywhere in the Federation. The real publicity starts in the morning. You boys are slipping in at the last possible moment, and even that wouldn't have been possible if the other team hadn't been forced out."

I looked up from the list I was making. "Why were they disqualified?" The workers union team, which we learned used a large orange cross on a black background as their emblem, being disqualified, had angered a lot of people.

"It's common for the Authorities to revoke privileges to keep the workers in line." He said it casually, like he condoned the action. I guess he did since he and his family profited from the Teran's strict control on pricing and access.

From the limited time we had been on Nadun, I'd noticed the tension peaking between the workers and the Authorities. This was about more than just a race.

"The workers union claims there is the mistreatment of mine workers and colony resources. They will eventually strike, maybe try an uprising. They're waiting for public support—which they are close to having."

His hands were clenched, but his tone was bored and distracted. It made my stomach turn.

"Don't you have any loyalty to the world that made your family rich?"

"The Terans made my father rich. I had nothing to do with it."

His attitude was disgusting.

But I felt like an absolute hypocrite after spending a week in the Representative's luxury villa and now taking a private flight to Bashita.

I was a fool for relying on my grandfather to find Grace and the others. A fool to tell them as much as I did. I hope I hadn't gotten them killed. The sooner Jaxon and I can find them, or they find us and can get off this rock, the better.

Later that day, as we flew low over the desert floor into Bashita, I got an excellent aerial view of the terrain of the racecourse.

"I was reading about the course." Jaxon leaned over me and pointed to the city. "The track starts outside the dome, there. It runs across the desert for a short while, dips down into that valley, and then up into those hills."

I followed his finger as it traced a path that quickly left civilization behind and snaked through a crevice as wide as the

Grand Canyon and then up and over dunes that rivaled mountains. There was no life, only the remains of ancient ruins and mining debris.

I hope Grace finds us before the race starts and not after. This was some of the most dangerous terrain I'd ever seen.

Thinking of hazards, I asked Byrn, "Will you get into trouble for helping us?"

He didn't answer, and I turned back to the view.

Several minutes later, he whispered so low I barely heard him. "It's not about me. The betrayal is deeper than a damaged relationship with his son. He cares not for his people. My father's loyalty has always been to Teran. That is where his power lies. But now they have raped our planet of all its resources; they have run out of use for us. And him. His time is waning. It makes him angry and unpredictable, and a temper that has always been a detriment to his career, maybe his downfall."

I was surprised. Byrn's statement was passionate and protective and treasonous if heard by the Authorities. It almost sounded like he—was it possible he backed the workers union?

Once that thought occurred to me, I started to look at him differently.

The shuttle gently descended through the retractable roof of a smaller dome next to the central city dome. Within minutes we were whisked from the shuttle to private transportation into the city and up to the penthouse of a high-end hotel.

Byrn warned us we had only an hour to prepare for the party, then he disappeared.

Jaxon dropped to one of the wide bench sofas and pulled up a vid on his linka. "Whatcha doing?"

"I want to see if the media is covering us already. Tells me how much of a show I need to put on tonight."

"Good idea." I sat across from him and spent the following twenty minutes scanning coverage.

"Shim—" Jaxon's voice broke my concentration. "I don't see our faces anywhere. Our name and pictures are on the main race site, but there are so many racers it's not enough to get noticed."

"That's a problem—we entered too late."

"Maybe we could win and then get noticed?"

"Against teams that have been driving this terrain their whole lives? We haven't even researched the hazards. Besides, driving the full race would take at least ten days. Something tells me we don't have long before the worker's strike. We need to get off this world before they do."

"You really think you can get us home?" Jaxon grabbed onto my arm. "You wouldn't leave the others—"

"No way! We all go, or none of us go. But, yeah, I think I figured it out. Remember when that librarian was talking about conspiracies?"

"No, but I was bored out of my mind and not paying attention."

"Thanks for the backup." I deadpanned.

Jaxon shrugged.

I continued. "Well, she mentioned legends about ancient blood stones opening passages to a sister world. I think that sister world is Earth."

Jaxon sat up. "You think the Keystones are the blood stones? They have those red blotches on them. But if so, why didn't the passage open again for our parents?"

"I think it's literal. Like real blood is needed to activate the portal. Remember, the artifact you found in Portland had a spike on the top. And both Grace and her mom were bleeding when they triggered the connection. I think we need to put blood on the stone in Grace's necklace to open the passage."

Byrn's voice drifted down the hall towards us. "I'm going to have a drink before we go."

"Shit!" Jaxon and I jumped up and raced down the hall to our room where the matching luggage Warrem had bought remained unpacked.

We had a bigger problem than wrinkled evening clothes—we had to figure out how to ensure every eye and camera were on us this evening.

∞

"I'VE GOT IT," Jaxon said as we arrived at the event. "I'll tell them I know someone in the race is cheating. Then the reporters will want to interview us." He jumped out before I could tell him that was a terrible idea. I hurried to follow.

Byrn was already out of the vehicle, waving to the media as if born to be famous. And the media loved him, so we stuck close.

While trying to smile and make sure every camera got a good shot of my face, I hissed out of the side of my mouth at Jaxon. "That is the stupidest idea you've ever had. They will kick us out of the race."

Jaxon cursed.

We both kept waving and whistling to the crowd until another vehicle arrived, and the media turned to them.

"What are you talking about?" Byrn asked as we left the arrivals area and walked a lit path toward the venue.

"Jaxon had a bad idea," I responded.

"Well, I don't see you coming up with any good ideas," Jaxon pushed back.

"Ideas for what?"

"To get more views and get pictures of our faces transmitted further," I replied.

"That is why you are doing all this? I thought you made up that story." Byrn looked shocked.

"Wait—" I stopped in the path, ignoring the crowd that flowed around us. "You don't think we are really searching for our friends? Do you even believe we are related?"

Byrn snorted. "No. Of course not. Neither did my father."

"Why did you help us? Why did you let us live with you?"

"The esteemed Representative of Nadun probably thought you were a spy from Teran testing his loyalty. You wouldn't believe what he would do to prove that. If you lived with him, then Warrem could monitor everything you did."

"And you?" I asked. The event faded away, and I held my breath waiting for Byrn's answer.

"You really don't know what's in that scroll you took from me, do you?" It was Byrn's turn to stare at us.

"We told you, man. We can't read your language, and the linka only translates a few words at a time, slowly." I tried to keep the frustration out of my voice.

Byrn started laughing, it was a deep belly laugh, but it grew in volume and pitch until he was bent over, hands on his knees, trying to catch his breath.

"Shim, what's going on?" Jaxon looked panicked but waved to all the media as they turned to watch.

"I don't know but keep smiling for them. This might get us more coverage." I smiled for the cameras while keeping an eye on Byrn.

"Oh, Stars—" Byrn wiped his eyes as he regained his composure and breath. "I steal the biggest state secret ever, and it's taken from me by a pair of idiots that don't even know what they have."

"Hey, who are you calling idiots?" Jaxon demanded.

"If that's your name, then use it," Byrn replied. It didn't make sense, but something else he said did.

"That scroll you took was that valuable?"

"I'm not in the habit of risking my life and throwing away my family for things that aren't important."

I'd like to tell him he was pretty sucky as far as family went. But I wanted to know what he had taken and what he planned on doing with it. I didn't want to have any part of something that would hurt people.

I studied Byrn. His face was determined, his calm confidence stilled the fidgety energy he usually displayed. Maybe he had been pretending to be a wealthy playboy since we met him, but my gut told me this Byrn was the real one. This was important to him.

I pulled the scroll out of my pocket and pushed it at him.

"What are you doing!" Byrn's eyebrows rose, and he glanced around us before grabbing the scroll and shoving it into the pocket of his leggings. "I can't believe you are carrying it around in your pocket. No wonder I couldn't find it in your luggage."

"Well, now you're carrying it around, so what happens next is on you. If you don't believe we are family, don't believe our story, then you have never had an interest in helping us find our friends. So, take what you want and go away. Thanks for helping us get in the race. We will take it from here." My lip curled up in disgust as I turned to walk away.

Byrn grabbed my arm. "Why would you give up a life of luxury to enter a race that will probably kill you? And why would you give up your only leverage?" Byrn sounded utterly bewildered.

I held back the urge to hit him.

"If we are telling the truth, then you know why we would give up everything to find our friends and go home." Too disgusted to look at his face anymore, I stalked off. Jaxon fell into step beside me, and we left Byrn on the path on his own.

This was yet another thing to add to my long list of mistakes.

Why was I surprised that everything about my family was a facade? And Byrn was the fakest of them all.

Unfortunately, the media had no interest in us on our own, and we entered the venue with little fanfare.

Inside it was loud. The live band fought to be heard over thousands of people talking. Everyone knew someone, and we were not anyone.

The room was a huge dome, at least three stories high, and the rounded walls were lined with colorful glowing gems and crystals. It was a living geode. A large crystal ball, diamond bright and the size of a car, was the centerpiece of the room, and hundreds of raw crystal chandeliers hovered high above our heads, floating like clouds to wherever they were needed.

I wanted to be excited, but all I could think was that I'd foul up our chance to find Grace. What was wrong with me? Storming off wouldn't be the biggest mistake I'd made since we arrived on this planet, but it could cost us the most.

"I'm sorry—"

"Nope." Jaxon bumped my shoulder and pushed me along. "You did the right thing. We are better off without him. If he doesn't believe us, well—" he cursed.

I appreciated his unexpected backup. We pushed into the crowd.

Why was he being so supportive?

"What happened?" I shouted at Jaxon, hoping he could hear. The noise level significantly increased the deeper we moved into the room.

"Just now?" Jaxon looked at me like I'd lost my mind.

"No. Yesterday. You've been acting weird, all nice and supportive. It's confusing me." I shook my head.

As expected, Jaxon didn't reply.

A band started a fast-beat song, and it became impossible to talk.

Jaxon hitched a shoulder and indicated the other side of the room. The raised stage for presentations was empty, so we climbed the steps up and stopped near the lone podium. I hope a camera will be focused here.

"What?" I asked, getting nervous. This wasn't like him.

Jaxon sighed, "It's not a big deal. It's just—" he grabbed a handful of red hair and yanked on it while he bit his lip. "It got to me—the fight. You know—I—that's me! I get that rage in me, that ugliness. And it's genetic, right? Did you see how he lost his mind and hurt Byrn, his son? He would have killed him if we hadn't stepped in. I don't want to become that. I don't want to be like this—angry all the time."

I was at a loss for words. Anguish and fear contorted his face, and he looked away.

This was Jaxon being real with me and he needed to know the truth.

"Jaxon, you aren't like him. You're passionate and protective, but you don't hurt people."

"I hurt you, sometimes. I don't mean to, I realize it later, but it happens."

I scanned the room while I thought of what to say. He did hurt me, sometimes, and I take it, but I often wonder if I should have to. It may be time for both of us to change. "Do you want us to keep fighting?"

"No!"

"So let's not. We don't have to become our dysfunctional parents. We don't have to live their lives over again. We can choose a different path."

"That's what I want, but how—"

Byrn rushed up on the stage. "Thanks, Stars, I found you!"

"What do you want?" Jaxon glared at the older man.

"Is what you said really true? Are you my sister Kindle's kids?"

"Yes!" How many times would we have to say this?

"And you would do anything to get your face transmitted around the Federation?" Byrn held his breath, waiting for our answer.

I turned at Jaxon. He shrugged, then I looked back to Byrn and gave a slow nod. Maybe he did believe us.

"I have a way. It will cause a big disruption, may even cancel the race, but I don't think the Authorities will take you. It's me they'll focus on. And you will get a lot of media coverage—are you in?"

30

EMBER'S DISCOVERY

GRACE

THE NEXT DAY I was pouring over the monitor logs with Ember, trying to spot the anomalies, but my mind kept wandering to the events of last night.

It bothered me that Blaze treated me like a child and hadn't answered any questions I asked him. I would have stomped off on my own, but that would have proven his point, as I had no idea where I was.

But what scared me, what had run in a loop through my head since he dumped me at my room last night was his demand. "Could you at least try to act like you are from here."

Chills had ran through my body and my arms broke out in bumps. We thought we had been so clever in covering up our unfamiliarity with...everything. How could he know?

I guess I had been a bit evasive when Blaze asked about my home on LaDér . And his exasperation when I hadn't known how to pay for my lunch with my linka. Then there was the time I almost walked off the edge of a pit, not realizing the marked lines on the floor were warning signs. Our disguises relied on people not looking too deeply at us, and Blaze had me under a spotlight.

Ember jolted me out of my musings when he jumped up from where he sat, scanning the logs. "I think I found something."

"For the two monitors to be bugged, they had to each be manually turned on and off. Four separate logs would need to be deleted so we wouldn't see who was doing it."

"They logged in from a different terminal each time and used Blaze's credentials. But this is the interesting part. When they erased the files, we were in the process of changing our access protocols. Only a few people had the new protocols. Now, everyone uses them. But when this happened, only a handful of people were doing it this way."

I sat up, the front legs of my chair crashing to the floor. "So we find out who knew the new protocol at that time and narrow the list of suspects?"

"Yes! It won't be easy, but Ash should be able to get you the list."

"Ash?"

"Yes, she handles the role out of new security procedures. I've dug through the backend of the system. I can't find any other anomalies. Is this enough for you to go to Ferno with?" Ember worried his bottom lip.

I squeezed his shoulder, "I hope so. If Ash can back it up." But was Ash the right person to go to with this information? If only a few people knew the protocols, wouldn't she be one of them?

I felt a twinge of guilt as Ember rubbed his hand over his eyes. He had spent hours reviewing the results of the programs he had run for me. I owed him.

"I had no idea it would take this long. I should have known you'd be trouble when they asked me to keep an eye on—" Ember's teasing voice choked off as he realized what he had said. "Uh... I mean.—" He stammered, but it was too late.

I stilled. Removing my hand from his shoulder. "They asked you to watch me?"

"Oh, Stars Grace, I'm sorry. I should have told you the minute I realized you weren't a threat. But I didn't want you to think I just liked you because I was supposed to... I mean, I do like you, but I would have even if they hadn't told me to—I have no idea what I'm saying." His voice trailed off, and he slumped in his chair.

The door to the security room opened, and Blaze stuck his head in. "Grace, we need to leave."

I picked up my bag and paused in front of Ember. Not sure what to say, I finally settled on a quiet "thank you."

Ember groaned, but as I moved away, his hand grabbed my arm. He said in a barely audible whisper, "Grace, be careful. Not everyone here works for the same side. Watch out for yourself."

I gave a curt nod and pulled out of his grip. Message received.

I brushed past Blaze and he gave an exaggerated sigh. I needed to be careful. Ember was right.

BLAZE HAD PICKED me up late, and we were the last to arrive for Ferno's lunch meeting. Ash and Flicker, flanking Ferno at the table, were already eating when we arrived.

These lunches were more of an inquisition than a meeting. I had no idea how anyone could eat.

Ferno was smart. He knew everything about this city and the surrounding area, the interconnectivity between the communities, and all their weaknesses. And he was fearless in leveraging this information.

Ferno was also concerned. Bina vibrated with restless

energy. The UNR was at a heightened security level and readying its defenses. Everyone was holding their breath, waiting for the Workers Union to make a move.

Something was coming.

Blaze glared at me. I took a bite of food, but my throat closed up and wouldn't let me swallow. Was he going to mention what had happened last night? He kept watching me with a smug look on his face.

The conversation turned from strategic relationships to security. I was trying to take another bite of the burrito-looking thing that was my lunch when Ferno asked if Ash was feeling better.

I looked up.

"Yes, I haven't had a flare-up in cycles. I'm back on the schedule full-time."

"You were sick?" I blurted out.

Everyone turned to look at me. Ash glared.

"She was sick last week." Blaze's eyes narrowed at me.

"So, you were sick before the Proving?"

Ash looked offended, and only after an elbow from Blaze responded, "Yes, for several cycles."

My head tried to piece it all together. If Ash was the one distributing the new protocols, and she was sick, was Flicker covering for her? Is he who I had to talk to? My gaze shot to him. The tall man was distracted. His head bent low over his linka.

"Ferno, they are here," Flicker said as he looked up from his linka.

"All ready? Do they want to catch us off guard by arriving this early?" Ferno frowned and wiped his hands on a cloth napkin.

"I don't know. Do you want to make them wait?" Flicker stopped, half risen from his chair.

"No. Let's finish them." Ferno rubbed his hands together and pushed up from the table. "Blaze, you coming?"

"If you can destroy them without me, I need to complete a project with Grace."

The leader nodded, and he left with a wolfish grin.

I watched them going, wondering when I would have a chance to talk to Flicker again. Maybe I should turn this information over to Ferno and let him sort it all out.

But that didn't feel right, and with this high-security level, he had enough on his mind. I'll figure this out. Then I'd have some leverage to get help finding Shim and Jaxon.

BLAZE WAITED until we were twenty feet off the ground on one of those platform transporter things before he brought up the subject I'd been dreading.

"So, how long before you slip back to Earth? Have you completed your mission on Nadun?"

I lurched away from him, and only his quick reflexes kept me from flying backward off the metal plate. My heart raced as he tugged on my belt, my arms windmilled, and I struck him in the head. Ignoring the blow, he yanked me back to the center of the platform.

"Stars, are you suicidal? Should we check you for poison pills?"

"I'm not a spy!" I had my hands twisted up into the front of his robe, and they and his hand on my belt were the only things holding me up as my legs trembled and my whole body shook from the adrenaline rush of being discovered and almost dying. I was too scared to look up at him.

"Well then, what are you? You aren't from Nadun or LaDer. We know that."

"Everyone knows that?" My breath caught as I looked to see if he was serious.

Blaze rolled his eyes at me. "Why were you following me last night?"

"I thought *you* were the spy."

The shock on his face was genuine.

"What do you mean?" Blaze relaxed his grip but still held me steady.

I thought about it. This I could talk about without confirming his suspicion of me. I didn't know who to trust. But all the clues pointing to Blaze, assured me he was probably being set up.

"Your login was used to mess with the monitors," I slowly relaxed my grip on his lapels and told him what Ember had found in the logs.

"So, Ember is working for you? How did you flip him so fast?" He ran his eyes up and down my body.

The ass. I scowled at him. Embers tracks were all over the research we had done, so anyone would know he was involved. But I decided then that I wouldn't tell Blaze about the protocols. Not yet. I needed proof.

"Fine. Back to my original question, how did you find out about the meeting, and how did you track me there?" Blaze cocked a brow.

I reached down into his coat pocket and pulled out the club bracelet. "I have the matching one. When I overheard you were going to meet someone, I slipped this into your pocket and tracked you."

Blaze's eyes widened. "That is the most ridiculous—do you know how dangerous—the price on your head." He caught his breath. "The Helios would give me anything to get a hold of you."

I was aware of how dangerous the Helios were on my side of

the portal. But why do the ones on this side want us? We had done everything we could to avoid them!

"Why do you think I'm a spy?"

"You have no history. Anywhere. Do you think that we don't verify the background of every runner that comes here? It would be easy for the Authorities and the Helios to plant spies. We check each runner's age, their families, and the situation on their home world. We are not just limited to Nadun. The UNR is everywhere."

Did Jeu'l know they did background checks? Maybe that was why he wanted us to leave as soon as possible.

"Even without the check, your ridiculous lack of knowledge about many things, like the Law of Registration, the Age of Consent, what it means to Age out, even how to use your linka. That is what gave you away. And your friends."

A chill rushed through my body, beading up goosebumps on my skin. He knew about Breeze and Jada? Were they safe? What about Shim and Jaxon?

I drew in a stuttered breath. "What are you going to do?"

I was aware of what I'd barely avoided admitting, but I needed to know, were the others at risk too?

"I'm still considering my options." Blaze released my belt and I swayed on the platform, my breath in my throat. I managed to squeak out a question. "Why were you talking to the Helios?"

The platform lowered and automatically headed to a dock where a line of people waited for transport.

Blaze lowered his voice and sighed. "We can't talk about it here, but it's my job."

31

THE REBELLION

SHIM

THIS IS NOT what I had in mind.

Getting our faces on screen is one thing, but being tied to a rebellion—We should have gone with Jaxon's original idea.

"Hold it up closer to your face," Byrn whispered the instruction, and I raised the open scroll next to my face and stared out at the shocked audience. The party music stopped abruptly. Some bozo in the back was laughing, but the rest, several thousand eyes, were turned to us with a mixture of shock and horror.

We had gone from alien spies to instigators of an insurrection.

When Byrn told us his plan; to reveal the scroll's contents to the partygoers. He should have mentioned what those contents were. And as we couldn't read the language, I didn't realize the enormousness of the act—until he started speaking.

"Representative Shi'mmer, my father, is a traitor." His linka projected his voice out over the crowd.

He repeated the statement until he had the media's attention.

"I have the proof." He pointed to the scroll in my hands, and

I used the back of my hand to push back my hair so it didn't block the media's view of my face as they looked at the scroll.

"This document contains my father's signature, along with the Teran and the Federation representatives in a secret treaty with an *alien species* to pay them a ransom tax."

A man shrieked, and the crowd rumbled in. They swelled forward, pressing closer to the stage. "What are you saying?" someone shouted.

Byrn raised a clenched fist. "You know the Federation is bleeding our resources away, leaving our children hungry, our workers broke, our planet on the brink of environmental collapse, to pay for their power and domination." Byrn paused to make sure the audience was hanging on his every word. "But we have discovered they are also secretly siphoning money to an alien race!"

Gasps from the crowd followed the announcement.

"Byrn," I tried to get his attention. "What are you doing? Are you sure about this?"

The older man cocked a brow at me and gave a crooked grin. I had deja vu; I'd seen that determined look in the mirror.

I blew out a nervous breath and adjusted my grip on the scroll.

"Teran sold out the workers of Nadun. It betrayed our trust. For too long, we have been willing to do their dirty work for the illusion of safety. For too long, the rich, like my father, have sold out the workers of Nadun. They devalued the lives of workers to get rich."

The cool and aloof guests now had an edge of fury. They surged, hungry for more. I watched a woman in the front with a gemstone studded gown with sleeves that projected like wings above her head. She was tugged this way and that by the crowd until the wings sagged and crushed over her shoulders. Men ripped open the collars of their tunics. Decorations were ripped from the wall, and glasses were thrown to the ground and trampled under fancy shoes as the crowd compressed.

A motion near one of the entrances drew my eye. The gatekeepers checking invitations had disappeared, and swarms of people in black and orange filled the doors, pressing in toward the main floor.

"Are we going to continue to allow the Terans to dictate our lives? Are we little more than a puppet to their authoritarian reign?" Faint shouts peppered the crowd, and the low growl of disquiet rumbled louder. "They pretend the Federation is a place of equality, but we know the truth—it is Teran's rules, Teran's concerns that rank above the colonies time and again."

Shouts came from the audience. The new group in black and orange was louder, more vocal, and angrier. Shouts rang out.

"Enough!"

"Stop the Terans!"

"No more!"

Someone shouted something about a Union, and I thought I heard the initials UNR, but the increasing volume of the voices was canceling each other out.

The media, having doubled in quantity, were in an uproar. Several commentators gave a play-by-play of what was happening to their audience. My arms sagged, and I ignored the ache and tried to raise the scroll closer to my face again. Suddenly, I felt a hand on my elbow, supporting me. Jaxon stepped to my side and helped me hold the scroll high.

"Now is the time when we stop allowing the Terans to dictate our lives. Now is the time of the Worker!" Byrn ended his speech with a shout and raised his fist into the air.

The crowd roared.

Fists pumped the air.

Shouts of "Workers Unite" translated through my linka, but

the rest was garbled. The black and orange-clad workers mingled in the crowd, riling them further. The media turned its cameras to the audience. Someone was trying to burn a Federation banner.

"Come on," Byrn directed us to follow him, and I dropped my arm in relief. He dragged us off stage to where a group of people in black waited. They surrounded us, and I quickly rolled up the scroll and tucked it into my tunic pocket. As we descended into the crowd, I felt tugging at my arms, back, and hair. My scarf yanked on my neck, and I ripped it off. The press of people was so tight my feet left the ground, and I was carried along. I caught a glimpse of red and snagged Jaxon. We locked elbows, creating a raft as the crowd swelled and surged.

Byrn got farther and farther ahead of us. We lost sight of him for a minute as we were pushed out of the building into the night. I regained my footing and realized we were next to him again.

Lights strobed the building, sirens sounded, armored vehicles screeched into the grounds, and people in grey swarmed from the vehicles. Red beams from silver visors scanned the area. Weapons drawn, they entered the building.

Before we could hear what happened, the people in black that still surrounded us ushered us down several dark alleys and quickly loaded us into a vehicle. As the doors closed, we heard the first shots.

Slamming against the door as the driver took a hard turn, I caught my breath and had the presence of mind to ensure that Jaxon was safe. He was facing me, holding his arm close to his body and swaying with the vehicle's motion.

Relief washed through me. We were not okay, but we were together.

"What was that? And who are these people?"

"That gentleman was your uncle starting a rebellion. You

have just witnessed history," said a voice from the front of the vehicle.

I stared up front and then over at Byrn. We bobbed and swayed. The vehicle had a suspension system like something we would expect to see at the race tomorrow, but the inside looked like a van.

"Sorry, nephew, to drag you into this, but you did ask for help."

Oh, sure, now he believed we were related.

"This is not what we had in mind." I didn't want to say too much in front of strangers. Did Byrn know them?

"It's okay. You can talk freely. I've told the Union about you and your friends. They will keep an eye out for them." Byrn's dark face flushed with excitement. He crowed to the man in the front seat. "Did you see that crowd?"

"I did. That couldn't have gone any better if we had planned it."

"You got lucky!" The woman in the driver's seat shot back at Byrn, not taking her eyes off the front of the vehicle.

Another woman on the other side of Byrn slapped his stomach with the back of her hand. "You could have called us in earlier. When we lost touch with you, I thought the old traitor had caught you, maybe killed you."

"He almost did. My nephews saved me. He's never gone that far before." Byrn shuddered.

I understood they were talking about Grandfather. They all seemed to know him much better than we did.

Could I even call him Grandfather now that we knew he didn't believe we were related? This was very confusing.

"So you work with them?" Jaxon asked.

"Byrn's been deep undercover as—himself." The others in the vehicle laughed at the man in the front seats joke. "But his work is just getting started. Byrn, I'll let you say your goodbyes."

The others turned away and started to talk amongst themselves.

Byrn's face was serious. "He is right. It is not safe for you to go where we are going, and you have your mission to accomplish."

"So you've been spying on your father?"

Byrn nodded. "Growing up, I sat in the family villa and thought the luxury was owed me. I believed the lie that I was entitled to something I'd done nothing to deserve. I didn't know how corrupt he was, the damage he'd done by his complicit obedience to the Terans and the Federation. My life was shallow, and I just knew my own wants."

Byrn sighed and gave a lopsided grin. "But I met a friend who made me look deeper, and when I went through a dark time, he and his family were there in a way my family had never been. I spent more and more time with them. They live in the mines in a town called Trin. I saw how hard their life was, never seeing the sun. Injuries and lack of compensation. The despair. One day when we were back in school, there was a cave-in. The whole town was buried. They thought there were survivors, but the Authorities felt production would drop if they tried to dig anyone out, so they left them to starve. I went home and raged at my father. This time when he lectured me on my responsibilities, I saw how hollow his words were. I realized he was the traitor..."

Byrn's words cut off as the vehicle slowed. It was dark outside. "Sorry, I went a little long there, and now we have run out of time. But I wanted you to understand how important what you helped me do tonight was. We have to break their power. We have to regain our rights to control our own lives.

The Workers Union started a rebellion, and we couldn't have done it without you."

I was at a loss for words.

"So, this is your stop, boys." The voice from the front of the vehicle drawled. The door opened, and Jaxon and I climbed out. Byrn didn't.

We were in a large warehouse, parked next to our race vehicle. Behind it was a repair bay, and off to the side, a small living area.

"You should find everything you need. Good luck in the race tomorrow, and good luck getting home. Tell my sister—" Byrn stopped and shook his head, "tell her I wish her a good life."

The door slammed, and the vehicle sped off through an open bay door which slowly slid shut behind it.

32

REVELATIONS

GRACE

I HAD to tell Jada and Breeze the UNR knew about us. And I needed to decide what to do next. Should we stay here until we find Shim and Jaxon—or run?

I hesitated at the top of the spiral staircase leading to the security area. As my mind was spinning through options, it didn't miss my attention that most of the problem was my fault. If I had gotten a low-level job like Jada or Breeze and kept my head down until we could find the brothers and find a way back to Earth, we would have been fine. But I had managed to gain the attention of the two people we most needed to avoid; Blaze and Ferno.

The blow hit on my lower back, shoving my hips forward. My arms flew wide as my body hovered for a second in open space. My fingers scratched at the rock walls as I tried to catch a handhold. I pitched forward with a scream.

I crashed into a curved wall and bounced off. My legs twisted as I spun. There was nothing underneath me then I slammed into the hard stone edge of a riser. I tried to curl into a protective ball as I kept moving. The spinning continued, and I hit another hard surface. I don't remember what happened afterward.

∞

"WHY ISN'T SHE WAKING UP?" I struggled to open my eyes at Breeze's nervous voice.

"She will. Give her time. She's banged up pretty bad, and we will have to watch that deep cut over her eyebrow, but otherwise, she is fine. Not even a concussion."

"She looked dead when I found her." Ember's voice trembled.

I struggled to lift my lids. I had six pairs of eyes staring back at me.

"Look!" Jada said with a wide grin.

My tongue felt swollen, and I could taste blood. It took a couple of tries, but I was finally able to ask, "What happened?" My voice shook.

"You fell." Breeze was sitting next to me, holding my hand.

"She was pushed," Jada said. His tall frame crammed into the narrow space between me and the wall.

Jeu'l was beside Jada and asked, "Why would someone push her?"

I tried to shake my head to indicate I didn't know, but a vice-like pain clamped down on my head and neck. When I didn't respond, Ember spoke up. "She found something, a lead on who tapped into the monitors. Grace was going to ask Ferno about it."

I tried shaking my head again and stopped, whispering instead. "No. I didn't ask him."

Where were we? I turned my head slowly and studied the other occupants of the room. They were not moving.

"It's the morgue." Blaze smiled.

"What?" I tried to sit up. My head swam at the sudden movement and thunked back down on the metal table. That explained the weird smell and why no one on the other tables was moving. I glared up at Blaze. "Why am I in a morgue?"

"Well, we wanted to get you medical care quickly, and the coroner was the closest doctor. Should we have waited?"

Jada scrunched up his nose. He demanded of Jeu'l, "Is this normal?"

The shorter boy shook his head. Then Jeu'l shrugged, "Well, Blaze is right. It's closer. Getting her to the medical center would have taken much longer."

"And they would have been happy to help you after they took blood work and confirmed your identity." Blaze cheerfully chipped in again. He raised an eyebrow at me. "That what you want?"

An older man I didn't know came into the room. "You can take her whenever she is ready to get up. Preferably soon. I've got a body to get back to." He slipped a huge plastic apron over his head and walked past the room's video screen on his way to one of the other tables. He flipped it on. An announcer's voice on the screen started talking about an event on the surface. It was loud and annoying and more than my head could handle.

I closed my eyes and asked, "How did you guys get here?"

"Ember found you and called Blaze. Blaze brought you here and called us." Breeze still had a death grip on my hand. I heard a saw whirl and cringed.

"Thought you might like your friends with you when you explained to me what you had found." Blaze shrugged. "And in case you died."

I rolled my eyes at him and cringed from the spasm of pain that shot through my forehead. I carefully touched the skin above my eyebrow. It was covered with a very thin strip of tape.

"Don't touch." Jeu'l warned. "It's theraskin. It will take a couple of hours, but you will heal without even a scar."

"That!" Blaze said, with an accusatory finger pointed at me. "That right there. You don't know about theraskin—that's your problem!" Jada and Breeze tensed up beside me. Ember just looked confused.

I took a deep breath and looked at the coroner. He had his hands full, literally, so relying on the loud party on the video screen to block out what I was saying, I hissed at Blaze, "We are doing the best we can. You have bigger problems to worry about than a couple of aliens."

"Ha!" Blaze exclaimed.

"Aliens?" Ember asked.

"Oh no." Jada groaned and put his face in his hands.

"You do have a spy—and it's not us." I slowly pushed up to my arms. I was sore, but my head was starting to feel better, though I could already tell it would be hard to move from all the bruising in a couple of hours.

His face clearly showed he didn't believe a word I said.

"A real spy. It's in your leadership. Ember and I found out they used your login to tap into the monitors." I said.

"You already told me this." Blaze looked bored.

"Yes, but the protocol used at the time it was done was only used by a few people. Ash would be able to give us a list of who knew about it. But as we heard at lunch today," I paused. Was it just today? I continued, "Ash was out sick. So, who would have completed a protocol switchover if she was gone?"

"Flicker would have taken it over." Blaze sounded less sure of himself now.

I swung my legs off the table and tried standing. My feet were steady. "That is what I thought, and when I mentioned the timing at lunch today, he avoided looking at me and changed the subject, and then this evening, I got pushed down a flight of stairs."

"Three flights," Jada said.

I shuddered and felt the outline of each stair on my spine. I corrected, "Three flights of stairs. All I wanted to do was ask Flicker who had the new protocols—but this was his reaction."

"You don't know it was him who pushed you." Blaze didn't sound convinced of anything at this point.

"No, but it's a good place to start looking; only be careful." I indicated the cut over my eye.

The amusement was gone from Blaze's face as he considered my words.

"Grace." Breeze tugged on my elbow. I ignored her and kept my glare on Blaze.

"Grace." Breeze's tone was more urgent.

"Aliens?" Ember was having trouble wrapping his head around having met an alien.

"Grace!" Breeze yelled.

My head throbbed. I turned to her. Eyes wide, she pointed at the video screen, and I followed the direction. On the screen, an extremely well-dressed man was standing at a podium. He looked very familiar though I'd swear I had never met him.

And next to him, wearing an expensive-looking tunic and holding a scroll next to his face, was Shim.

BLAZE GRABBED my hand and rushed us out of the morgue so quickly I didn't have a chance to thank the doctor.

"Was that your friend on the vid screen? Is he like you?" Blaze demanded, dropping his mocking tone. I hesitated before answering.

Ember broke in, "I don't know what is happening, but we

need to get to our stations and be prepared for what happens next."

I didn't understand.

"Grace, your friend just started a rebellion." Jeu'l said from behind me. My eyes widened. I was so surprised to see Shim. I hadn't been listening to what the transmission said.

Blaze led us down several corridors and stopped at an interchange. People were rushing in all directions. An alarm was going off somewhere. We were in a section of the compound I had never seen before. Blaze turned to Ember. "You should go to your station."

Ember hesitated.

I turned to him. "It's okay. Thanks for your help." I hugged him, and he seemed surprised by the gesture. A second passed before he hugged me back and then rushed off down one of the side passages.

Blaze gestured to Jeu'l. "Are you coming with them?"

Jeu'l hesitated, but Jada didn't. He answered, "Yes."

Blaze opened several more secure doors, and we left rough rock walls behind. We stopped in an empty corridor with a smooth floor and decorated walls. He dragged us to the middle of the hall and swiped his linka at a massive panel in the wall. It slid sideways to reveal a large elevator.

"Where are we going?"

"I can get you to Bashita and then on a maglev that will take you to the surface. Then you have to find your own way to the race."

"Race?"

Blaze groaned. "How have you survived this long?"

I scowled at him.

Blaze stepped onto the elevator. "I'll tell you on the way. Are you ready to leave or not? This may be your only chance."

We dove into the elevator before he finished speaking.

I panicked when I patted my neck and couldn't feel the stone in the necklace. Had the chain broken off again when I fell? Jada noticed what I was doing and discretely pulled my hand to the back of my neck, where the stone was dangling. Not wanting to call attention to it, I left it there.

Blaze was distracted by swiping his linka on another panel inside the lift.

"This okay?" I whispered to Jada and Breeze.

They nodded eagerly.

"You have an elevator? Where does it go?" Jeu'l's tone was curious.

"This is Ferno's private elevator to Bashita."

"It goes all the way?" Jeu'l gasped, probably thinking of all the times he had to make the journey on foot.

"With a few interchanges. It should take a while, so we have plenty of time for you to tell me the rest of what you know so I can decide if I should turn you over to the Authorities when we get there." Blaze leaned back against the wall, crossing his arms over his chest.

The others shrank back at Blaze's challenge, but I'd worked with him enough to realize his arrogance was mainly an act, and he was way more intelligent than he let on.

Hands on my hips, swaying with the elevator, I face him down. "No, you tell us what is happening first. What's with the alarms and everyone running everywhere? And why are you working with the Helios?"

"Didn't you hear what the Representative's son said on the vid transmission? He revealed a top-secret pact the Terans have with an alien species to pay a hefty protection fee, a tax. The Terans have been squeezing money out of us by over mining and abusing the workers of Nadun. You've only seen a hint at how bad the workers' conditions are, how dangerous the mines are. The situation here is desperate. And now the workers know why. This is going to propel them and the Workers Union into action. We don't have much time before all transportation on the moon is lockdown." Blaze's dispassionate veneer cracked. I could see the anger and fury boiling inside him. But why?

"You already knew about the tax." I guessed, but when he glanced down and away, I realized I was right. When he didn't say anything, I continued. "I know how much you care about the people here. I don't understand why you are working with the Helios."

Jeu'l broke in. "He would never do that. The UNR hates the Helios."

"I saw him speaking to them, well, her. She had something on him and made him work for the UNR." I looked at Blaze as I responded to Jeu'l. "Or, do they?"

Blaze's eyes narrowed, and he smiled. "The Helios think I am working for them. They think I was shorting the payments we make to the authorities to keep them off our back, and if Ferno found out, he would remove me from leadership."

"But Ferno knows." I guessed again.

"Ferno knows I'm shorting the payments, it was his idea. He can't be shown in a position of weakness. The Helios would suspect something. But I can. And so, I'm the leak. And I pretend they have something on me and feed them information. The right information. The trouble is they had something on someone else too."

"And now you know who that is."

Blaze's lips tightened. "Now we know. And with the rebellion starting and you gone, Flicker will think he is safe, and we can use that too. Flicker will pay for his crimes, but until then, he is going to be very useful to us."

"Any you are just going to let us go?"

"The longer you are on Teran, the better the odds the Helios will find you, so yes, I'm not only going to let you go, but

I'm also going to give you as much help as possible to leave Teran because you now know I'm a double agent." He paused and looked at the three of us. "Though, I am curious about Earth."

"How do you know about Earth?" I asked, my voice rising. This was one of many things I couldn't figure out. How did anyone here know about us when no-one on Earth knew about Nadun or any of the worlds here?

"The Helios has been trying to get back through the passage for centuries. That would give them ultimate control again."

"How?" Jada asked.

"There are secret archives that hold old scrolls. They tell about a time when five worlds were linked by passages only a keystone could open. The Helios wants to open those passages again."

"There are only three colonies and Teran." Jeu'l said.

"Unless you count Earth," I said, my voice a whisper.

Blaze nodded. I swayed with the elevator, my feet unsteady again.

"So, how do we open the passage?" I asked.

Blaze shook his head. "I have no idea. But if the Helios catch you, they will take you apart cell by cell to find out. And as soon as this rebellion takes off, the fighting will be every-where. I don't think there is a place on Nadun you will be able to hide."

33

RACE DAY

SHIM

EVERY CELL in my body was vibrating with nervous energy. It was like the first time I kissed Grace but with less certainty of the outcome. The excitement from the crowd and the tangible anticipation from the racers just pushed the energy to the next level.

Even on Earth, every race day started like this, rushing around to wait, a struggle to focus through distractions, and the pushing drive to win. But today, my focus was on finding Grace. The stunt last night—calling it a stunt was an insult to what it was, a brave act of patriotism or treason—had succeeded in one thing: everyone knew our faces.

"I swear if one more person stops you for a selfie, I will blow." Jaxon smacked away a hand that reached out for me. He cursed as we were stopped again.

I hate selfies, or whatever they call them here. But every mini-vid that went out with my face announcing we were at the race was one more reach out to Grace.

I had been diligently scanning the crowd from the moment we arrived. I was hoping to see her. We had a couple of hours until the race started, and the vehicle's migration to the start line had yet to begin, but we were running out of time.

Located a couple of miles outside of Bashita, this cracked old dome housed the ruins of what must have been a thriving suburb thirty or forty years ago. The ghost town made a spooky backdrop for this auto show.

Besides the ninety-some vehicles racing in five different divisions today, hundreds of other vehicles are on display, with proud owners showing off features. I call them vehicles because they transport people and things, but the variety was blowing my mind. There were adaptations of autonomous transports, flying platforms, tricked-out two and three-wheeled motorcycle-UTV hybrids that ran on pure solar power or hydrogen power, and insect-like pods with an exoskeleton and no wheels. And those were just the classic vehicles we had passed this far. The new technology vehicles left me speechless. It was beyond anything I had ever imagined, and in any other circumstance, I would be out exploring this nirvana.

Only the race vehicles resembled something I was familiar with. They all had wheels, and most had cage frames. And even with the filthy dome blocking most of the sun's dangerous rays and casting a yellow tinge, their chrome-like metal and shiny new paint jobs glowed.

Thousands of tourists had made the long trip to this remote dome. A large number of grey-suited Authorities were here too. The beady red eyes of their visors scanned the crowd for trouble.

Or maybe they were here for us.

The more popular race teams were being interviewed on the central stage. We were relatively unknown and unlikely to get any time on screen.

"How long does this last?" Jaxon complained.

"The race doesn't start until this afternoon." The first leg would finish in the dark and was designed to weed out the weaker teams while the racers were still close to the habitat and emergency care. Afterward, the teams would race on their own schedule with mandatory rest times. Since Jaxon and I weren't planning on finishing the race, I had yet to pay attention to all the rules and had studied the course only as a matter of curiosity.

Another person stopped me, and Jaxon huffed out a curse. "I'm gonna find some lunch." He stalked off into the crowd.

We got bumped into several times as I took the obligatory vid shots and smiled for the fan. They got distracted by another team and ran off. I hoped they remembered to post the vid. A flying platform dropped low above me, and I instinctively flinched. The crowd around me carried on. I needed a break.

I searched around to find a high perch where I could view the crowd. I finally settled on a race platform that opened up a few ways from our race vehicle as the driver preemptively moved to a position closer to the airlock.

Hours passed, and still no Grace. And Jaxon hadn't come back.

What are we doing here? I questioned myself for the thousandth time. What would we do if Grace didn't find us? Would we have to run the race?

We had the supplies, and I knew enough about the track to start, but this was supposed to be a ploy to get Grace's attention, not to get ourselves killed.

A commotion at the end of the showgrounds caught my attention. A procession of transports pulled into the dome. The crowd strained their necks to see who had arrived. I could see nothing until, slowly, the crowd parted like water. Down the center of the cleared path, in a flurry of silk and twinkling gemstone jewelry, strode my grandfather.

He did not look happy.

Neither did the crowd. There were jeers and shouted curses. A few people struggled to get to him, the grey-clothed guards pushing them back.

Like he had a homing beacon on me, the OG Shi'mmer seemed to know exactly where I was. I scramble to stand up and face him.

"Your true mission was revealed. You are a scam artist. A liar."

The fury in his face reminded me of the night he assaulted Byrn. My pulse pounded, and my cheeks flushed as I fought the urge to step back.

I tried to explain. "We didn't lie—"

"You are a thief who preys on the sentimentality of an old man who has lost his daughter and longs to be reunited with her." His face turned a dangerous shade of purple.

"I gave my life, my daughter, my blood to this moon. There are 12 Billion Terans to our 2.3 Billion Nadunese. They are stronger and more advanced. Do you think we could fight them? Compliance is where our victory lies! Allow them to be our guardians. But you, you had to ruin everything. They will crush you and your filthy little brother." The shrill sound of his voice echoed around the listening crowd.

Lips curled in disgust, and several people hissed. It felt like everyone at the show is watching this meltdown and I resisted the urge to pull away as a thousand more vid screens are turned toward us.

"Leave Jaxon out of this. He is my responsibility. My *fila*. It is my job to keep him safe. Kindle is counting on me." I pushed past my fear of the older man and stepped into his space, pushing a finger up into his face.

"What did you say?" A look of confusion passes over the Representative's features, and he stumbles back.

Grey-suited guards grabbed my arm, wrenching my finger

out of the older man's face and twisting my arms behind my back. Pain shot up my left arm, and I felt a crack. I cried out.

"Wait." With his anger gone, the older man deflates like a saggy balloon. "You called Jaxon *fila?*"

His flip-flop from anger to remorse was confusing, but I had a bigger concern as more guards headed toward us. Someone behind me slipped a restraint on my wrist. My other arm was snagged, pulled behind me, and locked to the first.

"Wait, you are Helios!" My grandfather shouts to someone behind me. "You have no jurisdiction here. Where are my guards?"

I struggled to see who was behind me, but my shoulder was clenched in a tight grip.

"You must release him. I was wrong. He is my grandson." My grandfather commands the guard, with all the regal bearing back in his voice. My mind is spinning, unable to understand his change of heart.

Grandfather put himself between me and an approaching guard. He twisted his head back to look at me and hissed, "you have to run!"

I didn't trust him. But even if I did, I couldn't move. The guard behind me steps to my side and glares at the OG Shi'mmer.

"The Authorities have put out a call for this young man's detainment and that of your son Byrn. But the Helios want this one and his brother. You would be wise to comply with this action. But then, compliance is what you are good at." The guard's mouth twisted into a sneer.

Suddenly the guard stumbled, crashing into my grandfather. They fall into another guard and collapse to a heap. I teeter beside them. A hand grabs my arm and wrenches me back and away from the pile.

Jaxon hauls me along behind him as he runs toward the stage.

"They are calling our fake names," Jaxon shouts back.

I didn't have the breath to ask what that meant as I raced beside him.

Jaxon takes the steps up to the stage in one leap. I go a little slower, knowing if I fall, I won't be able to catch myself.

"Here they are, our rabble-rousers!" The announcer jokes, and the crowd shouts and screams in response. A few throw drinks onto the stage.

Shaken by the violence in response to the joke, the announcer takes a more serious tone. "Brave of you to come to the race today! It looks like you don't need an introduction. The crowd knows you."

There is a roar from the audience. I glanced out at the crowd that had drawn like a magnet to the stage. Looking back at the glee in the announcer's eyes as she holds the linka she is using as a microphone out to me. I try to reach for it, but I can't with my arms locked behind me.

"Seriously though, what an exciting development last night. Can you tell us more about what is being done about the accusations against Representative Shi'mmer? Ah, I see he is here today." The announcer points out off-stage.

The crowd turns towards the representative and the increasing number of authorities backing him. The new people joining them are dressed differently. They look less like guards and more like riot police with thick body armor and double the weapons.

"Shim!"

I spin around at the sound of my name. My heart jumps. That voice sounds like Grace. But where is she? I'd just about convinced myself I was finally losing it when, like a mirage, I see her.

Was it a trick of that yellow light and the ever-present dust?

This girl looks different. She's dressed differently. In my mind, Grace looks like I last saw her, with brown and green hair cascading down her shoulders, probing grey eyes, and a sharp mind reading my deepest dreams. And anger. I can't forget how angry she was at me.

But this girl looks hard. All dressed in black, her hair pulled back in a severe braid. She has a cut over her eye.

Then she smiles. It was Grace!

Relief, joy, and anger flood my system. Who hurt her? I almost called out to her. But I caught myself. She was standing at the back of the stage, and I couldn't draw the authorities' or the crowd's attention to her.

"Breeze!" Jaxon gasps beside me.

"Shhh." I hiss at him to be quiet.

The host is still speaking, she asks me something, but I have no idea what she is saying or if I'm even answering. My heart starts beating again and every fiber of my being is focused on the girl at the back of the stage.

The crowd turns their attention to the large airlocks as the first few vehicles in line enter the airlock. The line moves quickly.

With the attention off of us, I race to the back of the stage and fling myself at her. Grace catches me. I forgot my arms were locked at my back, and I send us both careening into people behind her. "You are here!"

Grace laughs as she hugs me back. "Well, it looked like you were trying to get our attention."

34

THE RACE
GRACE

WHEN SHIM HURLED himself at me, I caught him instinctively, and we toppled over. My bruised body screamed in protest as his total weight landed on me.

A whimper escaped my mouth.

"You are hurt?" Shim twisted onto his side and struggled to his knees.

"It's been a hard day." I sat up carefully, self-conscious of the cameras pointing at us.

"Are you okay?" The concern in his voice soothed the panic that had been eating at me since he climbed into that stupid bucket lift deep underground.

I cupped his cheek and smiled. "I am now."

Shim gave me his lopsided smile and leaned into my palm.

"You did it! We saw you on the vid screen. How did that even happen?"

Shim pulled back from my hand and got to his feet. "Later, we have to get out of here. Helios agents are watching the presentation. They came with my grandfather. I've made a huge mistake."

As Jeu'l helped me to my feet, Breeze unwrapped herself

from Jaxon long enough to hug Shim. Jada gave both brothers a wave with a big grin.

"The Helios are still trying to control the crowd. We can get out this way," Jaxon nodded in the opposite direction Shim had been headed. "I moved our race vehicle while you were distracting Grandfather."

"You found him?" We had ducked behind a banner and skirted the back rim of the stage. I grabbed Shim's elbow as he tripped over a box and pitched forward. "Why are you hand-cuffed?"

"Later," Shim said. Regaining his balance, he jumped over a pile of cables.

As we emerged from the backstage area into the crowd, a man's voice yelled, "Stop them."

The crowd shouted down the man, a few big guys jumped in front of the uniform guards, and the crowd pushed in, blocking the Authority guards and Helios agents while strug-gling through the thick crowd towards us.

Miraculously, a path opened up in front of us. People cheered and patted Shim on the back as we passed.

"What is going on?" Breeze asked from behind me.

"I guess they are famous," I replied. Then yelling over the noise to Jada and Jeu'l in the back, "Keep up!"

As we fought through the well-wishers, an announcement commenced a countdown. The crowd surged, squeezing in on us and pushing us forward. The race was about to start.

The airlock doors opened for the next group of racers to enter the airlock. Jaxon ran through the doors, and we followed.

"This is dangerous! I hope you have a car in the race." Jeu'l's alarmed voice caused a shiver of fear to run down my spine. Did Shim know what he was doing?

The brother's stopped at a—vehicle? It looked like a bloated truck with no doors, and I didn't know what to call it. It was like a dune buggy on steroids.

The airlock doors closed behind us, and an automatic timer started the countdown for the outside doors opening.

"Who are you?" Shim asked as he tried to take the driver's seat. Jaxon shoved him into the back of the vehicle and took the seat himself.

"This is Jeu'l. He is coming with us." Jada declared.

"He helped us out so much," Breeze said.

"He saved our lives," I added.

Shim shook his head. "We thought there were just three of you. We don't have enough respirators."

Jada inhaled sharply and asked, "What will happen to him without a respirator?"

"He won't die—but he won't last long in the outside air," Jaxon said as he started the engine.

Panic crossed Jada's face. He shoved the respirator he had picked up into Jeu'l's hands. Jeu'l pushed it back with a solemn shake of his head.

They pushed back and forth as an alarm went off, a yellow light strobed the area, and the airlock doors cracked open.

"You have to get in!" Shim shouted over the noise. All the vehicles were lined up like they were exiting a ferry, and in a couple of minutes, it would be dangerous to be on the road while they moved.

Jada offered to stay with Jeu'l, but it was too late to turn back with the outside doors already opening.

Something arched through the air and landed in Shim's lap.

I jumped and turned to the ginormous quad vehicle it had come from. It was painted all black with an orange cross on the side. The huge man inside the vehicle had his respirator on, and all I could see of his features was a long beard and spiky hair.

He put his arm outside where a window would have been and pumped his fist in the air.

Jeu'l grabbed the mask from Shim's lap and pumped his fist in the air back at the driver.

We all scrambled into the vehicle as the airlock doors finished opening.

Jaxon had us moving before we were even seated. Breeze had grabbed the seat next to him. And the rest of us crammed into the back.

"Buckle up." Jaxon revved the engine.

Shim was wedged in the middle with his hands behind his back. "Can I take those off you?" I asked. I don't know if he heard me over the roar of noise.

Shim shook his head and mouthed, "No time, just belt me in." I grabbed a respirator and secured it over his head, then wrapped the harness-like mesh webbing around his hips and chest, securing the other side like he was the family vacation luggage on the roof.

The vehicle lurched forward. I snagged my respirator as it slid for the exit. Holding on with one hand, I got the respirator over my head as we shot out of the airlock.

Jaxon swung the vehicle in a sharp turn, following the other vehicles. The race hadn't started, but everyone was jockeying for a position at the start line. Jaxon did an excellent job of getting us lost among the hundreds of race vehicles. We paused at the starting line, engines revving, and waited.

"Hey," I shouted over the noise of the engines. "Does anyone know how I can get the cuffs off of Shim?"

Jeu'l shook his head. "You can't. They require a special key."

Jeu'l was squished next to Shim. Jada on his other side, hanging half out of the vehicle. While we were stopped, they rearranged themselves, and Jada ended up with his legs draped over Jeu'l and Shim and the webbed harness holding his torso inside the vehicle. I grabbed my harness and strapped in.

"Wait—are we racing?" Shim asked.

Wasn't that their plan? Did they have a plan?

"If you can get to the third checkpoint, I have people that can help us. I assume we must get back to the tunnels now that you have found each other?"

Jeu'l's response surprised everyone.

Shim scowled and turned to me. "Can we trust him?" He tilted his head towards Jeu'l.

My hands clenched on the handle over the open door. I didn't want to fight Shim on this. "Yes. He is part of our group."

"Okay, the first priority is getting away from the Helios." Shim leaned as far forward in his seat as the harness would allow, "Jaxon, I guess we are racing."

Jaxon gave a brisk nod.

Breeze had unstrapped and turned around on her seat to talk to us in the back, but now she pointed to the airlock behind us. "They're coming!"

"And we are going," Jaxon responded, adrenaline spiking in his voice. "Breeze, strap in!"

The vehicles around us took off in a roar, but Jaxon refused to move until Breeze had her harness on.

"Go, go" She screamed at him the second the latch caught.

Our vehicle surged forward with the last wave of cars. Tires spun, spitting dust and debris into the air, pinging as they hit our vehicle.

The track was gravel, and only a few vehicles could travel side-by-side. Race vehicles quickly spread out across the hard-packed ground, looking for an advantage. The land was covered in dips and ruts, potholes ranging from bucket size to swimming pool size.

Jaxon pulled ahead of the vehicles around us. Soon he was leading the pack. "Watch the curve," Shim called.

"Don't backseat drive," Jaxon shouted back. But he gripped the wheel tighter, guiding us back onto the road and taking the inside curve around a massive pile of mining trails.

Out of the corner of my eye, I saw the quad vehicle next to us swerve to avoid a crater-sized hole that could have swallowed it in one gulp. A shudder went through the quad, and it lost control.

I gripped the roll bars so tightly that sweat oozed between my fingers. Flying bits of gravel hit my face as I screamed at Jaxon. "Watch out!"

The quad swung towards us, smashing into the front wheel of our vehicle and bouncing off.

I wanted to scream at Jaxon to drive faster, but his foot was jammed to the floorboard as he threw his weight on the gas pedal.

Jaxon held us steady, letting the frame take the impact. I don't know how he did it. My hands had been itching to grab the wheel and yank it out of the way. I clenched my eyes shut, and in my mind's eye, I could see the Helios behind us, eating up the inches of space between us.

"Beezy! You okay?" My eyes popped open at Jaxon's yell. He glanced quickly over at Breeze. She was still screaming, her hands over her eyes, her body jerking like a rag doll in the harness.

I reached forward between the seats and shook her shoulder. Her scream cut off abruptly. Breeze opened her eyes and, blinking, gave a shaky nod.

We came out the other side of a sharp curve, and I could see two large hills ahead of us. The race vehicles were headed towards them, with the motorcycles pulling to the front of the group.

I tried to hold my head from bouncing around. I had a serious concern about whiplash. Shim's hands must be killing him. He grunted each time we landed but otherwise didn't complain.

"How did you enter the race?" I asked. Shim tried to respond, grunting out short explanations between bumps and swerves.

"What happened to you?" He asked.

I wasn't sure I could explain everything, so I gave him the short answer about finding Jeu'l, working with the UNR, and then seeing him on the vid.

I tried to look behind us and see if the Helios were getting closer. It was easy to spot their distinctive grey vehicles with flashing yellow LEDs along the bottom and sides. They were at the back of the racers, following the pack, but it wasn't clear if they knew where we were.

"Watch out for the rollers," Shim called out to Jaxon.

"Shut up—" Jaxon was cut off as we made a hard landing.

We slowed, and the vehicles on either side shot ahead. The one on the left hit hard, soaring up, then quickly down. We watched in horror as the nose dipped into the sand and the vehicle flipped nose over tail again and again.

"Oh no, should we stop and help?" Breeze asked.

"No." Jaxon gripped the wheel and slowed a bit more.

"There's nothing we can do, and there are support vehicles with medical staff that will catch up soon and help," Shim grunted as we went through another set of rollers.

A whirling sound passed overhead, and I craned my neck to look up. A grey shuttle with flashing yellow lights flew low over the racers. They hovered over us for a minute, then shot ahead and disappeared behind the hills.

"Do they know which vehicle we're in?" I asked.

"If that was the group chasing us, then they know what

Jaxon and I are driving. If it was the group chasing you, they know you got in with us." Shim looked queasy.

Jeu'l's voice cut through the vehicle noise. "We can't go to the pit stop."

Shim nodded. "They'll be waiting for us."

Jeu'l agreed. "My plan was to make it to one of the Union bases. We can't arrive with the Helios following us. That puts too many people at risk."

Shim turned to look at Jeu'l, grimacing as the vehicle shook. "How did you get involved in this?"

"Before I saved your friends, they saved me." Jeu'l looked out at the sand around us, then over at Jada. He seemed to make up his mind about something. "I know where we can go."

35

THE LADDER

GRACE

"WE ARE CLEAR ON THIS SIDE."

"Same here."

"Nothing above."

At our reports, Jaxon pulled the wheel, and the vehicle slid off the packed path. It was past the point of being called a road and into the soft sand.

The wheels churned a little harder but picked up speed again.

Jeu'l had brought up a map of the race and figured out the best spot for us to leave the course. We had waited until the race leaders had pulled far ahead, and the back of the pack slowed down for hazards. Eventually, the distance between vehicles increased, and when there were no vehicles around or shuttles overhead to see us, we slipped off the track and disappeared into the desert.

"Keep heading for that mountain." Jeu'l instructed as he gripped the bar on the back of the driver's seat to hold his arm steady as he studied the map.

We were all bracing against the rolling dips of the terrain as

Jaxon went way faster than he should to get us out of range before any other vehicles came into view.

"You need to zigzag Jax so they don't have a line of sight on where we are going." Shim winced as we hit the edge of a rock, and the frame bounced back hard.

"Are we still clear?" Jaxon asked, his eyes glued on the terrain as the rest of us watched for other competitors and the Helios.

At our affirmative, he made a quick turn and took a drastic nosedive. The vehicle dropped into what looked like an ancient riverbed. No water had flowed in centuries, maybe longer, but it was a smoother ride, and the ten-foot-tall banks on each side hid our vehicle from view.

"How far is it?" I asked Jeu'l.

"It's not far, but the terrain is challenging, and I've never seen it from the surface." He responded.

"My job is a little more complicated than a runner. I work directly for Ferno as a go-between for many groups. As such, I have to deliver messages to places many people do not know exist. This is one of them. It is an escape route for the people in the base I mentioned, and I use it as a shortcut when delivering messages for them."

"It's up here?"

"It is an ancient mine ventilation shaft from the time when the air was still breathable and most people lived above ground."

"How can they live below ground if all the ventilation shafts lead up here and the air isn't breathable?" Breeze asked.

"Ah, but they don't all lead to the top. There used to be great fields of Eloa in caves below the surface. It exhaled the purest oxygen, and for centuries ventilation shafts from the fields could keep whole communities healthy. People lived above and below ground. Then the Teran's developed space travel and reestablished their domain over all the colonies. They claimed they had been the original settlers, and thus all the colonies were subject to their rule. They had a massive population, advanced technology, and ruled the sky. We didn't have a choice."

Jaxon dodged a rock, and everyone readjusted their grips, then leaned back in to hear Jeu'l's story.

"So the Teran started taking more and more of our resources. They liked Eloa a lot. They over-harvested the fields and replaced them with oxygenators, claiming they were better. They demanded that we extract minerals faster to pay for all the machine's costs and maintenance. Shortcuts were taken. The atmosphere was damaged, and life above ground was dangerous, so they built us domes to live in. They wanted us to work harder and dig deeper. We rediscovered old tunnel systems that had been closed for a thousand years, but we dug too deep. It destabilized the moon."

"You talking about earthquakes?" I asked.

"Earth-quakes? The shaking? Yes. Teran's say they are not important, and they can fix the problems, but it is already too late. This world is dying. Some of the oldest cities underground have already been abandoned to cave-ins. Before long, no one will be able to survive below ground or outside the domes."

I stared outside the window at the acidified landscape. Instead of admiring the rainbow effect of mounds of mineral debris in shades of gold, turquoise, red, and pale purple as we passed, I now knew it was more evidence of the toxicity of the environment.

We bumped along the riverbed in silence for some time. Each lost in our thoughts. Eventually, the river started to snake further and further from our destination. Jaxon climbed the steep wall, each of us clinging to our seats as the vehicle seemed to define gravity in its vertical climb.

We emerged on a plane as flat and wide as ten football

fields, wrapping around the bottom of the mountain.

"Follow the base around to the right. We should be there soon. If we drive to the ventilation shaft, someone might spot the vehicle. We will have to hide it and walk the rest of the way. I'll tell you when we need to get out." Jeu'l rubbed at the top of his head, which had smashed into the ceiling with a crack at the last bump.

"We will have to walk there?" Jada asked. He was inspecting Jeu'l's head for a cut. Jeu'l shook him off with a smile.

"It's not far. We can also see about taking off Shim's restraints."

"That would be nice since I've lost feeling in my fingers, which is kinda a relief since they're all smashed to hell," Shim said. His voice was weary.

Shim hated to rely on other people.

We skirted the base of what was probably once a medium-sized mountain but, with the cut terraces climbing the side from mineral extraction and large holes tunneled deep into the sides, was considerably diminished.

The constant vehicle rocking side to side was giving me a headache, along with the bright glare of the sun. It was a relief when we turned the corner into the shade of the hill. The temperature dipped without the beat of the sun. I became even more aware of the sweat trickling down my back.

"There!" Jeu'l pointed up between the front seats and out the windshield. All I could see was rock and more rock. We edged around a big boulder that looked like the top of the mountain had broken off and pierced the ground, and a hole the size of a one-car garage became visible. It had a large rock overhang and a level floor.

Jaxon sped past the hole, then slammed on the brakes and backed into the dark space like he'd found the last parking space at a mall at Christmas.

There was a lot of screaming inside the vehicle at the sudden deceleration and direction change. Shim yelled, "Stars, dude, you could have let us check it out first!"

"I thought we were in a hurry." Jaxon shot back. He did something at the wheel, and suddenly, all the noise stopped. He slumped back in the seat, sliding his hand over his face. It came back with a smear of blood.

Breeze grabbed his chin and turned his head towards her. "You have a cut! Does it hurt?"

"Nah, must have been rock shrapnel. The blood was dripping down my face while I drove. It was driving me crazy." He patiently sat still while Breeze ripped a strip off her shirt and dabbed at the cut.

I unlatched my harness and stepped out of the vehicle into the weird, echoing silence of the cave. My legs collapsed under me.

"You okay?" Shim asked.

"Yeah, just trying to get my legs to stop trembling." I caught the dusty edge of the seat and pushed myself back up. Shim was still locked in the harness with his arms smashed between his back and the seat. I reached over to detach the belt.

"I'm sorry, Grace." Shim blurted out. His breath huffed against the side of my face.

"For what?" I asked, distracted by the stupid latch that wouldn't give way.

"For everything. I'm sorry for not talking to you. Not letting you know that you were the most important person on Earth—" He choked out a short laugh, "—the most important person in this solar system, to me. It was a mistake."

My shoulders tightened. "I'm not sure this is the time—"

Shim cut me off. "This is a perfect time. I'm not going to risk us getting split up again and you not knowing that I'm over my head, deep in my heart, crazy about you. I still have to explain why I did what I did, but I want you to know I love you. Do you believe me?"

The latch popped free, and the harness sagged. I unwrapped it from around his torso and pulled on his elbow to help him out.

Shim tried to scoot his way out and fell sideways across the seat. He didn't seem to care. He looked up at me, his head hanging out of the vehicle. "Do you believe me?"

I didn't know what to say.

"We need to move quickly." Jeu'l came around to our side of the vehicle, and in the light from the tunnel entrance, I could see him rubbing his hip. Jada was with him, and he helped me lift Shim from the vehicle and onto his feet.

Footsteps crunched through gravel as we all moved to the front of the cavern and looked out over the flat wasteland.

Jeu'l turned to Shim. "May I see if I can get you out of the cuffs?"

Shim gave a cautious nod and turned his back to the light. Jeu'l crouched down and studied the lock. "Oh, Stars. They are the new models. They lock in place. I had hoped they had used the old style, which clamps in place but can sometimes be broken apart. We can get them off when we get down into the tunnels, but I don't know how you will be able to climb down the ladder with your arms behind you."

"Well, now we are stopped, and I'm starting to get the feeling back in my arms. I can fix that." Shim flexed and widened his shoulders. Wiggling his arms, he was able to slip his arms to the sides of his body and his cuffed hands under his butt. He crouched down, wobbled, and fell against the side of the vehicle. Four pairs of hands reached out to steady him. After he muttered thanks, he stepped back through the loop of his arms.

"Nice one!" Jada exclaimed.

There was a strangled gasp from Breeze, who was staring out the front entrance. "I thought I saw something shiny in the sky."

"We have to get moving," I said

"Maybe not." Shim hesitated and gave a meaningful look at Jeu'l.

Jada glared

I tried to reassure Shim. "It's okay; we've told Jeu'l just about everything at this point. If you trust me, you trust him."

Shim hesitated, then sighed deeply and told us what he had learned about the blood stones: that they required blood to open a passage.

It made sense. Someone had always been hurt when the stones worked. "Do you think we should try it here?"

"Can't hurt."

I tugged at the necklace, struggling to unlatch it when my arms felt like jelly.

Held the necklace out to Jaxon. "Give it a try."

"All right, get ready." Jaxon swiped a thumb through the cut on his face, smearing blood all over his cheek. He grabbed the necklace with the other hand and put his bloody thumb on the stone.

We all froze, waiting.

Nothing happened.

"That would have been too easy." Jaxon handed back the necklace with the red thumbprint to me. I cringed and took it back, wiping it on my pants before putting it back on.

"Maybe we need to be in the spot where we came through the passage," Shim said.

"How are we going to find that again?" Breeze asked.

"Let's worry about that later. We must get away from the Helios and safely underground."

"Let's go." Jeu'l's impatience was evident.

We headed to the mouth of the tunnel.

"Wait," Jaxon called out. "We snuck all kinds of survival gear into our race equipment. Just in case." He pulled open the back of the vehicle and pulled out backpacks for each of us and an extra long length of rope that he settled over his shoulders. He handed Shim's bag to Jeu'l, who staggered under the weight. "Yeah, sorry, I might have overpacked Shim's bag."

Jaxon passed out beige-colored sun hats with scarfs that covered from the tips of our noses down past our necks in the back. We put on the caps, Jada pulling off the scarf, handing it to Jeu'l and then swapping bags with him.

Jaxon pulled Duchess out of his bag and adjusted her solar panels.

"What are you doing?" Shim asked.

"Just topping her off."

Shim shook his head. "Her panels are shiny and will attract attention."

I watched the brothers and waited for one of Jaxon's epic temper tantrums.

Jaxon sighed and put Duchess back in his bag. "You're right. Let's go."

Falling in behind Jeu'l we headed out.

The "short" walk took us over three hours with a lot of stopping and ducking behind rocks, if available, whenever we thought we heard something. Jaxon had found camo blankets we would huddle under if a rock wasn't nearby.

When we arrived, it was nothing more than another mound, but Jeu'l promised we were in the right place.

"Shim, do we trust this guy? He's an alien." I heard Jaxon say in a quiet whisper in Shim's ear.

"Jax, we are aliens. Grace trusts him, and I trust her." Shim whispered back.

Jeu'l cleared away the dust on one side of the mound and

revealed a small, latched door. "Okay, when I open this, an alarm will go off. It will last about the length of one of your minutes. Then it will stop. If the door is still open when it stops, an alert goes out to the Authorities. We all need to be inside on the ladder and have the door latch again by the time the alarm stops. Are you ready?"

"Wait!" Shim raised one hand, and the attached hand was raised with it. "Let's tie the rope around our waists. We will go in a line, and that way, if one person falls, everyone else—"

"—will go with them?" Jaxon injected.

"No, will have plenty of back-ups to catch them. Just for that, you go first."

"Fine, Breeze, comes after me."

"Fine. Jeu'l you go last so you can shut the door properly?"

"Yes, that is a good idea."

The brothers had even brought climbing harnesses for us, and Jeu'l used the spare. We quickly put them on and tied in.

"Ready?" Each of us nodded.

Jeu'l quickly opened the door. A loud alarm started blaring.

Jaxon disappeared quickly inside, Breeze followed much faster than I would have thought. Shim went after them awkwardly, grabbing onto the frame until he found his footing.

It was my turn.

"Just do it, Grace, don't think about it." Shim's voice came up out of the void.

I tried to ignore the alarm and drew in a shuttering breath, relieved to have Shim's steady encouragement as I plunged into the darkness. The ladder was nicer than I expected, with side rails and wide rungs. Without looking down, I grabbed on, swung my legs in, and quickly descended a couple of steps to make room for Jada, who swung in quickly behind me, followed by Jeu'l.

Jeu'l slammed the latch closed with a loud clang and locked

it. The alarm sounded for a couple more seconds, then stopped.

I was breathing heavily, the sound choppy in the darkness. The moment the light had disappeared, it hit me that I could be hundreds of feet off the ground, clinging to a slippery piece of metal.

"Everyone all right?" Shim called out. The sound echoed and kept going.

Grunts of affirmative met his question.

"This is a super secret tunnel, so know I will keep your secret as you know so many of mine. However, I caution you. These shafts are randomly monitored. So everything we say may be listened to." Jeu'l informed us.

"How tall is this shaft?" Jaxon called up to Jeu'l.

"At least ten levels, maybe taller."

Crap. I groaned.

"Grace. You will be okay. Just keep listening to my voice."

I fixed on Shim's gentle coaxing as we started to descend.

"SO, GRACE," Shim said.

"What?" I focused on the step in front of me as I stepped down. Then the next one.

"I'm going to tell you what happened," Shim said.

"When?"

He groaned. "Are you really going to make me say it?"

I thought about it for a moment. "Yep."

"Fine. My friend, Brittany and I wanted to get our parents off our backs. Logan wanted me to play football while I wanted to take a computer programming class. Brittany's parents are very conservative and she wanted to hide her girlfriend from them. So we started to fake date. It worked great. And then I met you." Shim's voice from below me trailed off.

I frowned. That wasn't the story I was expecting. It was actually kind of sad. I shifted my grip and stepped down. "And what then?"

"And then I completely screwed up by not telling you the truth and telling my parents that I was breaking up with Brittany."

"Pretend to break up. And—"

"And I messed up our relationship." He added.

I thought about it as I reached down for the next step. "But you messed up Brittany's relationship too. How awful her girl-friend must have felt."

"It was her and Britany's idea."

"Oh." I thought about it. Shim had been in a bad position. Being honest would mean telling a secret that wasn't his to tell.

"My mistake was not being honest with you. And it will never happen again. Ever. Well, I'm certain I'll screw up again at some point, but not like this if you give me another chance." Shim had paused on the steps below me.

"Why are we stopping?" Jada asked.

"Yeah, finish the story." Breeze called up.

"Do we have to talk about this now? With everyone here and maybe the Authorities listening?"

"They would not be listening, just the Union and the UNR." Jeu'l called down the ladder helpfully.

Great.

"Don't mind us," Jada added.

"Pretend we aren't here," Breeze called up from below Shim.

I wrapped my arms a little tighter around the rails and kept stepping down. It was strenuous but not too difficult. The shape of the rails allowed me to slide down to the next step without releasing my arms. But the repetition was exhausting, and the distraction was helping me not think about how high up we were.

"Fine." I wasn't going to confess that I'd all but forgiven him when I saw how upset he had been. And any pain I had felt at the betrayal was forgotten the moment I thought I had lost him. Having him back was everything. Now I had to figure out if I could trust him again.

Shim started moving again.

"Why didn't you tell me this before?" I asked, moving again.

"You didn't let me," Shim said, his voice little more than a whisper.

"No, before, when we first got together."

"Oh, then, well, I wanted to so badly. And I should have. But I had promised not to say anything. That was my mistake. The minute I met you, I should have told Brittany I couldn't do it anymore." Shim said.

I thought about that. I always did a really good job of holding at arm's length anyone that might be able to hurt me. And I was doing it again now by not telling Shim I forgave him for lying.

"You shithead!" I blurted out.

"What?" Shim stopped again.

"We are not even halfway down, and I want to hug you, and I can't."

"Really?" Shim's voice was full of hope.

Jeu'l called down. "We are just over halfway. And it is a very sad story, Shim."

"We are only halfway? I was joking!" I looked up at the glows above that highlighted Jada and Jeu'l's bodies.

"Yes," Jeu'l confirmed, not understanding it wasn't a real question. "Just keep climbing."

"Hurry up, Jaxon," Shim called down.

STARTING FROM THE BOTTOM
GRACE

A MUFFLED shout came from several yards below me.

"Jaxon, that you? Is everything okay? Can you see the bottom yet?" I paused to stretch out an arm, then curled it around the railing and stretched the others. My arms ached and my legs were trembling from the as I locked them in with each step to keep from collapsing. When Jaxon didn't respond, I resumed climbing and asked, "Shim, can you hear him?"

"No. Breeze, did you hear Jaxon's response?" Shim sounded tired, but he had double the job we did climbing down the ladder with his arms locked together.

I glanced down with my next step, the glow from Shim's headlamp pointed up at me but I was too far to see his face. The rope between us stretched tight.

"I can't see him anymore," Breeze said. Then she gave a muffled scream.

"Breeze!" Both Shim and I called out to her. No response. I moved faster, step by step.

"Shim, speed up. We need to get down and help her." As I spoke, I moved even faster. I looked down just in time to see Shim's headlamp snuff out.

Something yanked on the rope at my waist. I slipped and released one arm from the railing to grab the stair in front of my nose and keep from sliding. "Shim!"

There was no response.

"What is happening?" Jada called down to me.

"I don't know. First Jaxon stopped responding, then Breeze screamed, and now Shim is gone and someone is pulling on the rope."

"We should be almost at the bottom." Jeu'l called down, the glow from his headlamp high above me.

There was another yank on my waist. Alarming but not enough to pull me off the ladder. My adrenaline spiked again as I considered what could be at the bottom. I guess there was only one way to find out. Taking a deep breath, I started descending again.

Within minutes, arms wrapped around me from behind.

I screamed.

"*Shhhh.*" Shim whispered in my ear and pulled me off the ladder. I sagged against him as my feet found solid ground and my legs buckled.

"What—" I started to ask but I was shushed by multiple dark figures. Someone reached up and turned off my headlamp.

I panicked in the complete darkness until I heard Shim whispering, "You're safe. It's my uncle Byrn and the Union. But the Helios are close so we had to go dark to not draw their attention before everyone was down the ladder.

I breathed a deep sigh of relief and let him pull me back against his chest. I saw the glow of Jada's headlamp, heard a muffled curse and then that light went out. The same happened with Jeu'l.

Someone brushed by us and whispered, "follow me."

I plastered myself to Shim's side and hobbled along behind the faint orange glow.

It was hard to resist the temptation to turn on my linka for light.

No one spoke. Just heavy rasps of breath in the dark.

We stumbled along like that for some time. I'm sure we weren't making much progress in the dark but every so often I would hear noises from far behind us in the tunnel and it propelled me to move faster.

We made several turns and eventually, a panel lit up in front. I blink at the brightness, my eyes not having time to adjust.

A figure keyed in a card and I could now make out their features in the glow from the panel.

"Blaze?" My whisper sounded loud in the silence.

"Surprise," he said in a whisper. His sardonic tone confirmed it was who I thought it was.

"What are you doing here?" I asked.

Shim had stiffened beside me when I'd spoken. "You know this guy?"

"Yeah, he—" I was cut off.

"Really not the time for a chat." Blaze's tone was droll.

The panel light changed to green, and a section of the wall slid open to reveal the interior of an elevator.

Blaze stepped inside the brightly lit box and, with a bored voice, invited us to join him. "Oh please, take your time. I'm sure the Helios will delay in shooting me and dissecting you because you were trying to make up your mind."

My "shut up" was directed at Blaze as I pulled Shim in behind me.

Jaxon and Breeze rushed in after us, along with a strange man.

I did a double-take between the man and Shim. "He looks just like you!"

Shim gave a nod. "And still, he didn't believe we were related until a few days ago."

A shout sounded down the hall followed by the sound of weapons firing.

Jada and Jeu'l ran into the elevator with two more people who put their back to us and started firing down the hallway.

"Shut the door." The woman yelled at Blaze, who had his hand hovering over the electronic panel and immediately started pushing keys.

As the door panels started to close, the tunnel flooded with light and more weapons fired. Pings of metal sounded from the other side of the doors.

The gap between the doors disappeared with a soft swishing and I drew in an unsteady breath as the elevator started to descend.

"NEPHEWS, I'm pleased to see you safe!" Shim's look-alike exclaimed. He had a hand clamped on Jaxon's shoulder and reached over to thump his other hand on Shim's.

"How did you find us?" Shim asked with a look of confusion.

Blaze said, "I did that. I've been tracking you and watching the news about the race. I saw you in the vid feeds and when you disappeared in this area, I knew Jeu'l knew about the base and would try and make it here."

"Thank you." Jeu'l said.

"You are lucky I did. You forgot about the flushing protocol."

Jeu'l went pale. "Oh, *Stars!*"

"Caught them just in time. The Union officers monitoring

the ventilation shafts were about to do a fire flush of the vents when I convinced them you were with us."

"That is where I met Blaze." The look-alike said.

"Who are you?" I asked.

Shim turned to me, "Grace, this is my Uncle Byrn. He just blew up the vid screens with his revelations about Teran abuses and alien extortion."

"And very likely kickstarted the rebellion," Blaze added in a flat tone. "I can't believe you know someone more famous than me."

"I had an alert sent out for any news on you boys. The Union officers contacted me, and that's how I met Blaze."

With that response, Blaze gave a smile and a head nod to Byrn. "Another successful mission between the UNR and the Union."

Byrn snorted, then his lips twisted. "It's just as well we met. Now that it's been revealed I work with the Union, I won't be going undercover anymore. The Union wants me to take on a more political role."

"Ah, so you will become like your father?" Blaze laughed at the scowl Byrn gave him.

I'd heard enough of both of them to know we were safe for a moment, so I twisted in Shim's arms and faced him. His eyes widened for a fraction, then closed as I leaned in and planted a kiss on his lips.

We both sighed. Throats cleared around us and someone started humming. We ignored them.

"No more wasting time," I said as I pulled back. Shim nodded, so I continued. "My parents found out that time is too fragile to waste it keeping a distance from people you care about. I'm not going to do that anymore. And," I took a breath, "I promise to listen from now on. Not just shut you out. You are too important to me to lose."

My heart thumped nervously against my chest as I waited to hear his response.

"Yes," Shim opened his mouth to say more but was interrupted.

"We are at the first transfer spot. Prepare yourselves. I don't know what is outside this door." Blaze sounded concerned, so I knew it must be serious.

I looked back to Shim, who said, "later," and dropped a quick kiss on my lips, then let me go and moved to stand next to me.

The man and woman, whose names I still didn't know, raised their weapons as the doors slowly opened.

The other side of the door held total pandemonium. We were obviously deep in Union territory. Men in black and orange uniforms marched by. Families with bags over their shoulders packed the tunnels as they tried to evacuate. We pushed our way through the crowd, trying not to lose any of our group. I almost wished the rope was still tied around our waists instead of looping over Jada's shoulders. Someone yanked on my backpack and I spun around and looked down in the face of a small terrified child. Tears streamed down her cheeks as she asked for her mother. Fortunately, a woman ran up, pulled her into a hug, and rushed away down the hall.

"Where is everyone going?" Breeze asked.

"The UNR has space at deeper levels to take them in. This town has the most direct access to the surface, so it will be easiest for the Authorities to infiltrate. It is where most of the fighting is expected to start.

"Oh, *Stars*, this is really going to happen." Shim said.

We changed tunnels and descended stairs, then came to another elevator.

"Where are we going?" I asked as soon as the lift doors shut.

I wasn't sure if I should ask Blaze or Byrn. I didn't know who was in charge.

But Blaze was the one who answered. "We have to pick up something, and then we are going to get you back to where you opened the passage so you can go home."

WE WERE in a section of tunnels I was very familiar with. Blaze left us briefly when we reached the hall that led to the security room where Ember and I had spent so much time. He re-emerged with a bag, and we took off again, moving faster.

"Breeze!" The cute red-headed boy Breeze worked with rushed towards us.

Everyone continued down the hall but Breeze stopped and slowed down along with Jaxon had a confused look that deepened to a scowl when the boy wrapped Breeze in his arms and kissed her.

From her response, it wasn't the first time.

Jaxon growled.

Breeze pulled back with a nervous laugh and a side look at Jaxon.

"We have to go." I told her and then grabbed Jaxon's arm and dragged him towards the restricted access door Blaze was holding open.

"Who is that guy?" Jaxon said, twisting to look behind him. "She isn't staying, is she?"

"No, she isn't staying." I tried not to laugh at the bewilderment in his voice. "She just needs a bit of privacy to say goodbye."

I pushed through the door and told Blaze I would hold it. He rushed off to activate the elevator. Breeze was seconds behind us, and we rushed to catch up with the others. The doors opened as we arrived, and we piled in.

"Soar says the fighting has started in Neran." Breeze gasped as she put a hand on the wall of the carriage and caught her breath.

Byrn turned to Blaze, who nodded his head in confirmation.

"We aren't going to be able to take you the whole way. We need to get back to the command center. But I picked this up for you." Blaze pulled a small device that looked like an old video game controller out of his bag. "This is how the Helios track passages opening."

"Really? Does it happen often?" Shim eagerly leaned over the device.

"No, not often. There was one a few years ago and we know a woman came through, but the Helios grabbed her. We don't know what happened to her. With this device, you'll be able to back-track to where you came through the passage." Blaze showed an eager Shim how it worked.

"Why are you helping us?" I blurted out louder than I had planned.

Blaze shrugged like the question wasn't important to him, but I had learned enough to know that he was putting on a facade. Then he sighed. "Many reasons. You know too much about the UNR, Ferno, and myself. We don't want that info falling into the Helios' hands. And, more importantly, someday the passages are going to open and one side is going to stream through. The Authorities would like to control that narrative. The UNR would like to know that we have friends on both sides."

"And, even more importantly, you are family." Byrn rested a hand on Shim's shoulder. "And despite my father's behavior, that does mean something on Nadun."

37

THE WAY HOME

GRACE

THE LAST ELEVATOR dropped us off many levels lower than the UNR's headquarters and deep inside the moon's core.

As we stepped off, Byrn spoke up. "You'll have to make it the rest of the way alone."

I spun around to face the men and squeaked out, "You're not going with us?"

"Ah, you miss me already," Blaze said with a smirk. He reached out and patted me on the shoulder.

Byrn shook his head. "With Blaze and I with you, the Helios will be even more determined to get you. We will try to distract them as long as we can." He held an arm out to Shim, and they clasped forearms. The older man reached out to pat Shim's other shoulder. He did the same to Jaxon, who eyed the arm and then surprised us all by ignoring it and giving his uncle a quick awkward hug.

Pulling away, Jaxon stared at the ground, shuffling his feet, muttering. "Be careful."

Byrn squeezed his shoulder. "You too." Then he turned to Shim. "Please, tell my sister I—" he paused and stared up at the ceiling, then down and gave a lopsided grin, "tell Kindle I wish her a happy life."

Shim nodded.

Blaze bumped into my shoulder and turned to me with wide eyes. "Any hug for me?"

I glared at him. "You are annoying. And arrogant. And fake." Blaze's eyebrows popped, and I continued, "You pretend not to care, and yet you care more than anyone I have met on this moon. You are a true asset to your people, and I'm very glad I met you." I finished with a huff and crossed my arms.

Blaze's expression of humble surprise looked wrong, and he quickly shook it off and opened his arms wide.

"No." I glared at him until my lips smirked. I turned away while I still could.

Jeu'l's and Jada's hands were flying, and I only caught a few words they signed. Out of context, it appeared to be an apology or a promise. I wasn't sure which. When their hands stopped, Jada hugged Jeu'l, who blushed.

When Jada finally released him, Jeu'l turned and stepped towards me with a sad smile. "I also must go."

I frowned. I knew the time would come, but I'd started to think of Jeu'l as one of us. Before I could tell him, an alarm went off on the elevator. The doors began to close. Byrn lunged for the doors, pushing them back open. Blaze jumped on the elevator and studied the panel. "It's not being called. Someone is trying to override the system. They must know where we are."

Breeze and I threw ourselves at Jeu'l, hugging him between us. "Thank you, thank you. Thank you!" We spoke over each other.

Blaze grabbed Jeu'l's arm and dragged him onto the lift as he called to us. "You need to run. They are coming!"

We waved as the doors shut. At the last second, Byrn yelled through the sliver of the closing door, "Go on, RUN!"

And we did.

Hours later, as we scrambled through a caved-in side tunnel, I finally recognized where we were. The Authorities had cleared the rocks, including the giant boulder I had laid on when trying to see what was on this side of the cave-in.

How long ago was that?

"Can you believe they got that rock out?" Jaxon mused.

I shook my head. We stopped briefly to drink water from the canisters in our backpacks.

Shim frowned as he stared down at the device Blaze had given us. He had been acting as a navigator, shouting directions as we moved quickly through the tunnels. The powerful head-lamps Shim and Jaxon packed made movement so much faster than our last trip through the tunnels.

"Something is coming. It's—" he paused and stared closer at the device, "it's a lot of somethings. We have to move."

We took off again.

About an hour later, we jogged to a stop in front of a pile of irregularly shaped rocks with a rusted metal door in the middle.

"Hey, that old office."

"My phone!" Breeze raced for the door.

"No, there's no time," I yelled after her, looking behind me as if I could see the Helios in our shadow.

Jaxon followed her in.

I spotted something on the floor. I picked up a rock and unwrapped a violet-colored bracelet. I slipped it into my pocket as Breeze and Jaxon emerged from the office. Breeze held her phone above her head triumphantly.

"Come on," Shim said, his tone urgent.

WE HAD BEEN SLOWING DOWN. Our run when we left the elevators had slowed to a jog after we went through the caved-in side tunnel and a quick walk by the time we reached the old office. Now my legs were cramping from the constant movement, and without a break I wasn't sure how much further I could go.

"We're here." Shim sounded uncertain.

We all stopped and leaned against a rock wall.

Hands on my knees, I leaned forward, panting. When I could finally speak, I asked, "Here where?"

"This is where we arrived." Shim spun the Xbox-like controller around the room and seemed satisfied with whatever it said.

I straightened. Suddenly fully alert, I scanned the space. The rounded room-shaped tunnel section had clumps of dried mud and withered brown grass littering the floor. I leaned in close and shined my lamp on a pile. He was right. This was where we had arrived.

"Gimme the stone. I want to try again." Jaxon held out his hand.

I took my necklace off and handed it over to Jaxon. As Jaxon talked through his plan for getting blood, I ran my hand along a wall.

I can't believe we came through the passage here weeks ago. So much had happened in that time. So much had changed. I'd met Ember and Blaze and helped uncover a traitor. I'd overcome my stubbornness and really listened to Shim. Now we were back together. At least, I hoped we were. Shim had met his family, told me the truth about his relationship with his "girl-friend," and come to some sort of peace with his brother. Jaxon had changed. I couldn't put my finger on it, but something inside him had shifted. Breeze had emerged from Skylar's shadow and become her own person. And Jada, I hadn't known him well to begin with, but I'm so glad I did now. His strength had kept us going.

And now I finally knew what my mother, and all our parents, had gone through. Arriving alone on Earth and trying to survive. Hoping to find a way home, knowing that she was the key to opening the passage but having attempt after attempt fail. But she was the key. I was sure of it. And I think I was a key too.

"It's not working," Jaxon growled in frustration.

"We may be in the wrong spot." Jada waved an arm at the room. "This looks just like a hundred other tunnels we've passed through."

"No. This is the right spot. Keep trying. Give it more blood." Shim leaned in to look at the cut.

"It's already too much." Breeze protested, pulling the knife out of Jaxon's hand as he tried to deepen the cut on his thumb.

"I don't think it's his blood." Everyone turned to look at me. "All our parents have stones and have tried to open the passage over the years. It only opened for my mother and me. I think it has to be one of us, our DNA, like this green hair. We may be the only ones who can open the passage.

"So, you try." Jaxon held out the stone to me. I cringed away from the mess he had made. "Oh, sorry about that. Wish you'd had your big idea before I cut open my hand." He rubbed the stone on his shirt, leaving a red smear, and he held the necklace out to me.

I hesitated briefly. Could I really have DNA linked to the passage? Were my ancestors some type of guardian of this secret link between the worlds? Standing taller, I reached for the necklace and, cradling it in my palm, held my other hand out to Shim.

Shim cupped my hand and made quick work of pricking my finger. "Sorry," he muttered when I flinched.

As a drop of blood swelled the surface, a loud noise came from the tunnel behind us.

We had run out of time.

"Maybe you should hold on?" I asked and, without waiting, swiped my bloody finger down the stone.

Nothing happened. My shoulders dropped in disappointment.

Then the ground started to shake. A pin prick of bright light appeared in front of me and opened up quickly into a ring of fire. Hot air swirled through the tunnel whipping my hair into my eyes. I took my hand off the stone and pushed it back in time to see Breeze sucked into the whirling fire passage. Jaxon lunged after her.

My heart raced, and I turned to Shim, his eyes huge, "Grace," he said, the words lost in the sound of falling rock and wind.

Next to me, Jada's feet left the ground, and the passage sucked him in.

The whirlpool grabbed me, spinning me around, and I went in, back first, watching Shim follow me in.

And behind Shim, I could see a swarm of armed Authorities and Helios entering the tunnel.

"Stop!" They yelled. One fired into the passage, and another lunged for the opening.

The aperture constricted, and the passage closed behind Shim as we left the world of Nadun behind.

38

HOME
GRACE

NOTHING. And then, everything. The waves of vertigo left as quickly as they had arrived. I could still feel the memory in my cells of my body spinning and burning. I shivered as the wicked itch of a sunburn made my skin crawl.

My eyes were still tightly scrunched against the blinding glare of the passage. Something crunched beneath me. I turned my head and smelled fresh cut grass. I peeled open an eye and blinked at the bright sunlight. Long blades of grass fanned my face as a cool breeze swept over them. I breathed deep, trying to capture the hint of forest and ocean on the air and sneezed. I tried turning my head. Everything hurt like I'd fallen down a flight of stairs. My heart was still racing, but I could move, so nothing was broken.

Off in the distance, there was a shout.

Putting all my effort into moving, I managed to flip my body over. After weeks in the mines, the sun touching my body felt like a bubble bath of joy. I basked in the warmth until the shouts grew closer.

With a groan, I pushed myself up to sit and tried to assess the situation.

More groans around me alerted me to the presence of the others. I checked—we were all here. And here was a field with mud, water, grass, trees, and glorious sun. Earth, it looked like home. Was it?

"Grace!" My pulse leaped at the sound of the familiar voice.

"Dad?" I stiffly crawled to my knees, letting everything wobble around me for a moment, and then pushed to stand.

I made it just in time to be swept off my feet and enveloped in a warm, homecoming hug. "Grace, Grace, is it you?" my father was trying to squeeze the breakfast out of me while checking me over for injuries. He frowned when he got to the tape over my eyebrow and the bruises on my face.

"I'm fine. Really." I pulled back to look at him. Old, grayer, but with a big smile etched on his face. I dove in for another hug before I recognized the sounds of chaos around me and pulled back to look.

Breeze was sandwiched between her father, Arie, and her brother.

"You're smothering me!" Breeze gasped from between them. Arie backed up, but Skylar's body was shaking, and he refused to let his sister go. She rubbed a comforting hand down his back.

Jada's parents were alternating between inspecting him for damage and lecturing him, with his mother sticking close to his side and kissing his head.

Kindle had an arm wrapped around both Jaxon and Shim. Her face was streaked with tears and her red curls bounced as she sobbed. Her fist was clenched in Shim's shirt as he whispered to her. I heard the name Byrn as Kindle doubled over, dragging the brother's back down to their knees.

Arie released Breeze, leaving her in Skylar's care and went to help Kindle back to her feet.

There was an awkward moment as Arie stared down at Shim. Then pulled him into a hug. "So glad to have you back."

Shim's face broke a lopsided grin over his father's shoulder.

"What happened to your face? Where did you go? Are you okay?" my father stopped peppering me with questions long enough to call out "Arie, help, Grace is hurt!"

That grabbed everyone's attention and Shim beat Arie to my side, he asked, "Are you okay?"

"I'm fine." I squeezed my father's hand, "This happened ages ago when I was pushed down some stairs."

That didn't help.

"What? Who pushed you? Where have you been?" Dad pulled me into another hug.

When he released me, Arie cupped my chin in one hand and examined my face. "That is theraskin."

The mood of the group changed immediately as the parents gasped.

I nodded, "Yeah, it is. We've been on Nadun."

It took a while to calm everyone down enough to try and explain. But before I could start, my father tugged on my arm. "Come on. We've been camped here since you left, waiting, hoping. Come back to camp and get comfortable. I think it's going to take a while for you to explain everything."

And we did. Taking turns, we told them what we had experienced on Nadun and how we had gotten back home.

It was hours later and the fire we had started for warmth was dying down. My dad finally let go of my hand and I was able to slip away with Shim.

"Where are you going?" Kindle asked. Her tone held a note of warning.

"I'm going for a walk with Grace, my girlfriend." Shim declared.

Kindle pursed her lips, then handed him a flashlight.

"Please don't go far. I'm not sure I can let either of you boys out of sight for a while."

Shim gave her a crooked smile and kissed the side of her head when he took the flashlight.

We couldn't bear to be too far from the others either, so we parked on a rock just out of hearing range from the camp.

"What Blaze said has been bothering me."

"What part? There were so many problematic things about that guy." Shim looked a little jealous and I smirked.

"He was just my boss."

Shim hu-romped a disgruntled sound. "Did you meet someone else while on Nadun?"

I thought about Ember. "Someone was interested, but he wasn't who I was hung up on."

Shim smiled at that. "So, what was bothering you?"

"Blaze said a woman came through the passage to Nadun years ago and the Helios captured her. That was how they knew how to track the openings. But if my blood, my DNA, is needed to open the passage—Shim—could it have been my mother that came through?"

Emotion welled up in my chest. The thought of her being alive but captured by the Helios made me both sick and hopeful.

"It seems impossible. But the last few weeks have been full of impossible things. We know the Helios on Earth had her in custody when she died." Shim wrapped an arm around me as my whole body shuddered.

"Yeah, and the Federal government says she was killed. It's crazy. I'm sure I'm just getting my hopes up. This thing with the DNA opening the passage has my head all scrambled." I sunk a little deeper into Shim's hold.

"Should we tell our parents that we know how to open the passage?" Shim asked.

That did not seem like a good idea at all. Everyone would like to get a hold of that information. Right now, the stone was limited. The government had all five pieces except the one around my neck. If they knew how to open a passage, would they start treating me like a blood bank? I shivered at the idea.

"I'd rather not have the word get out that I am the only person on this planet that has the key to activate the stones." I shuddered.

Shim held me close and rocked me as we looked up at the stars. I traced the path of Orion's belt and then tilted my head up to Shim.

"So, I'm your girlfriend?" I teased.

Shim nodded. "If you will have me."

I smiled. "I will, but only if there are no more games from either of us. I have a hard time trusting people, letting them in. I'm going to work on getting better at that. But I need to know I can trust you." I twisted on the rock to face him, watching for Shim's response.

"I do not say this lightly. I know I've messed up in the past. I'm still me. I'll probably mess up again. But I've told Kindle the truth. And from now on, I'm always going to tell you the truth, even if I'm worried you'll think badly of me. I really want to be the person I know you deserve." Shim held my gaze as he made the promise. The flashlight's glow increased the intensity of his promise.

"Me too. All of that." We kissed on it, and I slid into the comfort of his arms.

It was good to be home.

THE END

(Book 3 of the Elements Series is coming soon)

THANK YOU!

Your comments and feedback are so important to me and they help other readers select a book they will enjoy. **If you enjoyed this book, please spread the word! Leave a review** on the platform where you bought it or on **Goodreads** or **Bookbub**. And thank you for telling your friends and posting on social!

To keep up to date on book releases and news, please sign up for my free newsletter serengoode.com. My (mostly) monthly emails will have bonus scenes, free books, news, and other great stuff...and no spam. SerenGoode.com/nltt.

Consider joining the Seren Goode ARC TEAM. You can sign-up at https://bit.ly/SerenGoodeARCTEAM.

I sincerely appreciate your support and would love to hear from you at SerenGoodWrites on:

Goodreads - http://bit.ly/Goodreads_SerenGoode

Bookbub - http://bit.ly/BookBub_SerenGoode

Instagram - instagram.com/serengoodewrites

TikTok - tiktok.com/@serengoodewrites

Facebook - facebook.com/SerenGoode

Pinterest - pinterest.com/SerenGoodeWrites

Cozy Mystery Books by Seren Star Goode:

Monterey Bay Mystery, Book 1 in the Amanda Warren Cozy Animal Mystery Series

Amanda Warren is looking for a second chance in the cozy coastal town of Ocean Wood, but what she finds is a psychic cat and a *purrfectly* puzzling mystery!

Out of luck and out of money, Amanda's pink dog grooming van is running on fumes when she rolls into the foggy town of Ocean Wood. Seeking a new beginning and a reunion with her twin sister, she finds her sister missing and a dead body in her house.

Amanda is determined to clear her sister's name, but all the quirky, charming neighbors of this Monterey Bay town seem to have a motive. Which one of them is a killer? With time running out, Amanda teams up with her sister's psychic, amnesiac cat to untangle this fur-midable mystery and sniff out the killer before Amanda's second chance becomes her last.

ACKNOWLEDGMENTS

It takes a lot of support to be an author and I want to thank all my family and friends that have helped me along the way. I especially want to thank Randy for always having my back, Hannah J. for editing and pep talks, and my personal cheerleader and fabulous beta reader Lori H.

ABOUT THE AUTHOR

Seren Goode was born in the Midwest with itchy feet and a dream of far-off places. She has a love of all things alien and a fascination with ritual landscape.

A jane-of-all-trades, Seren has studied communications, English, design, marketing, metalsmith, pottery, juggling, and more, and eventually ended up abroad earning a graduate degree in archeology. She started writing fiction while in middle school and thoroughly blames her family for encouraging this habit. A big fan of making her characters do their own work, Seren loves to sit back and watch them unravel a mystery or dig for the truth. When she isn't on the road, she is at home on the Central Coast of California plotting her next book, and her next trip, with her songwriter husband and puppies Clairey and Izzy.

You can follow her at serengoode.com or on:

facebook.com/SerenGoode
instagram.com/serengoodewrites
pinterest.com/SerenGoodeWrites
tiktok.com/@serengoodewrites

SERENGOODE.COM